# ALL THE BEST NIGHTS

———

## HANNA EARNEST

carina
press

**carina
press®**

Recycling programs
for this product may
not exist in your area.

ISBN-13: 978-1-335-51716-6

All the Best Nights

Carina Press
22 Adelaide St. West, 40th Floor
Toronto, Ontario M5H 4E3, Canada
www.CarinaPress.com

**Printed in U.S.A.**

This one's for me.

# ALL THE BEST NIGHTS

Wed, Mar 21, 6:03 pm

LA?

NYC : (

Sun, Jul 22, 3:47 pm

London (praying hands emoji)

Mexico City
(Taco beer guitar)

Today 1:13 pm

Chicago?

Chicago.

# Chapter One

The drumming was louder now. Three even beats tapped out by two candy-shell nails on the bar, punctuated by a one-count pause held just long enough to infuse the silence with her displeasure before the rhythm repeated.

Meeting Nelle tonight had been a mistake. A year had passed since the magic moment she'd slipped her number into Bran's pocket at the Cleffy after-party, her breath raising the hairs on his neck as she whispered into his ear, "You're it." That last image of her stood out in his memory like the bas-relief of her raised and defined shoulder blades in the open-back dress she'd worn as she walked away from him. He'd been dazzled— there was no other way to describe it—dazed by her radiance. Charmed by her audacity to go after what she wanted, her confidence to approach him even as the requisite supermodel held tight to his arm.

And he'd been an idiot to assume he could recapture that spark. He wasn't the same person he'd been a year ago. He'd cracked and broken since then. And Nelle had changed too. That night she had been green, nominated for best new artist, and now, based on the supercharged buzz surrounding her second album, her star had risen.

Nothing could touch her. Whatever might have fizzed between them that night had gone flat now. Maybe it had never really been there. Maybe he'd just been surprised, lured in by all that gold-tinged skin, by a bold display he hadn't expected from a media darling with a good-girl image like Nelle's.

Tonight he could barely focus on her. The sun had been in his eyes the whole drive into the city, glinting off the skyline as it set at his back, angry and red. He'd spent the day squinting against excess light. Everything had been too bright—the glare off the topcoat of snow covering a field of graves blinding him worse than any stage lights he'd encountered. He'd had no relief from it, his sunglasses broken and twisted in his jacket pocket. A jacket that was woefully thin against Chicago's December chill.

All that sun and no warmth.

It was a good thing he was so numb.

One, two, three, Nelle drummed again.

Bran filled the gap, setting his empty pint glass on the polished wood, the dull thud familiar, a bass note of a chord he'd heard before. They were sat on either side of a rounded corner, an arrangement that afforded room for intimacy had they been angled towards each other, but instead seemed to accentuate their opposition in the moment. They sat as disinterested strangers, each facing the man in rolled shirtsleeves busy behind the bar.

Bran leaned his elbows on the curved countertop and motioned for the bartender, not missing the man's sharp glance at the untouched cocktail in front of the woman next to him. Their server had definitely recognized her, based on the reverence with which he had placed her drink down, a two-handed approach complete with a respectfully low head bow. Nelle's face and voice had been everywhere for the last two years and even in the bar's dim light she was recognizable: amber eyes like scotch on ice under thick dark lashes and thick dark brows set in a heart-shaped face. And that hair— trademark black waves fell over her shoulders as she sat straight in the low-backed bar stool.

"Another Two Hearted," Bran said. The barkeep stalled, waiting for Nelle's reaction. Bran's own fame was apparently of little consequence to the waiter. Sure, his band, Judith From Work, had broken up. But Bran had been on the scene for years before Nelle. And he'd just come off his first solo tour, which had been deemed a critical and commercial success—if not as lucrative as his label had wanted because he'd played smaller venues. And what about hometown advantage? Shouldn't that tip the scales in his favor?

But the barkeep only had eyes for Nelle. She noticed the delay and set the man into motion with a smile. "And can we have some French fries, please, when you have a second?" she added with an aggressive pleasantry that made Bran's molars ache.

"French fries?"

"Did you want a burger?" Nelle's voice, while high in tone, had a steely weight, like it was anchored deep inside of her. Tonight it held an unmistakable edge. The clear metallic scrape of a knife against the sharpening stone.

Bran shifted in his chair. "This is a Michelin-starred restaurant. We don't need to eat at the bar—I can get us a table."

"So can I." Her cheerful yellow fingertips took up

their rhythm on the counter again. "I don't think we'll be here long enough."

He didn't doubt that assertion. There wasn't anything here for either of them, it seemed. And the longer they stayed, the more likely it was someone would notice and think the encounter more than it was.

Across the restaurant a light flashed and Bran and Nelle both swung instinctively towards it to determine the source. But the flare was just a candle flame momentarily enhanced by the curved water jug of a passing waiter.

Bran exhaled slowly. "Because we won't be able to get through a meal before the paps catch us?"

Nelle curved her hand protectively around the stem of her coupe glass, a lemon peel on a metal spear resting across the rim. "Because this isn't going how I thought it would."

Honesty saturated her voice. Genuine emotion that carried through her music, unfiltered even in recordings. And in person it just about devastated him. He'd wanted something else from this too, but he wasn't going to say it. And it wasn't her fault: he shouldn't have agreed to see her. Not today.

Bran rubbed his eyes and looked down, landing on the brimming drink in front of Nelle. She lifted the shallow bowl and Bran followed it up to her mouth as she sipped the cloudy liquid and back down, replaced soundlessly on the bar. His gaze idled on the red smudge of her lips imprinted on the glass.

Okay, so that was one reason he'd gone against his better judgment and come tonight. He hadn't been able to stop thinking about that mouth for months. Every time he heard her voice on the radio or caught a glimpse of her on some magazine cover, he'd obsess about the full-lipped curve of that smile she'd given him when the heat of her skin radiated through the lining of his pocket.

She wasn't smiling now, pulling her hands into her lap and twisting one of a half dozen rings she wore staggered above and below her knuckles like notes on sheet music. The obsidian stone disappeared once, twice, before she released it, squared her shoulders, and tried valiantly to engage him in conversation again. "Don't worry about photos."

"You don't mind?" His head tilted to the side as he considered the statement. Maybe she liked it—the attention. She was good at getting it.

"Of course I mind. But they don't know we're here. They won't bother us."

"They won't?"

"It isn't like that here. It's the Midwest. It's home. It's safe."

Home? Not really. Not anymore.

"It's like that everywhere for us. Don't tell me you're that naïve."

Nelle lifted her glass again. "I'm not. Andre and I have an arrangement."

"Who's Andre?"

Nelle motioned to the barkeep and the garnish slid into her drink with a soft clink.

"You paid him?"

"We took a photo together."

Bran laughed, the sound as hollowed out as he felt. "Oh, that'll stop him. I thought you said you weren't naïve."

A glare narrowed her eyes. "I'm not. There's nothing wrong with trusting people to help you."

She waited a beat for him to respond, giving him the chance to show some willingness, some effort on his part to salvage the conversation. But he was done here. It wasn't enough to risk the blog fodder that would be twisted out of pictures of them having dinner together.

When he didn't say anything, her lips pressed together. She'd reached her limit too. He was surprised she'd let it get this far. Nelle didn't need to sit here. She was like him. She had options, anywhere she went. Better for her to use them. And he'd have the next drink alone. Take a nap in the car. Forget the company he'd hired to ship it back to California, he'd drive it himself. The album he'd promised his label by the New Year hadn't materialized. New music just wasn't coming to him. A spontaneous road trip wouldn't put the album any further off course. Maybe he'd even be inspired. Maybe he'd find what he was looking for rolling across the great American plains. Or maybe the blazing desert sun would leave him as dry and shriveled as his current creative vision.

Nelle uncrossed her legs and inched to the front of her seat. "I really thought you'd be different."

"Yeah?" He spun his own stool to get his knees out of her way, make it easier for her to go.

"But you're just a talented dickhead."

A lot of things had been said about Bran Kelly. He'd worked his way into the spotlight by nineteen, becoming the lead singer of a world-renowned band, so people who'd been inclined to comment had had seven years to come up with some shit. But no one had ever called him a talented dickhead.

And Nelle wasn't stopping there. "If you just wanted to have a drink, flirt a little, go back to my hotel, no pressure—we could have done that. Instead you show up late in that ridiculous car, slam a beer, and call me naïve? At the very least I expected some originality from Bran Kelly—but I've heard this one. A couple versions, actually. And I don't care for a repeat."

She stretched one black ankle boot to the ground while reaching for the big leather bag hanging from a hook under the bar. Behind her, large windows framed the dark city street, his car parked across it next to an empty lot. It unnerved him that she'd seen him arrive, like a perspective in the wrong direction, a Nighthawk looking out, studying him. Headlights from a passing car cut across the room, outlining her edges in a burst of backlighting. Bran's eyes widened, taking in her flared leather miniskirt and tight black turtleneck sweater. A silhouette of black on black. Even her thick hair, loose and cascading down her back, shone with the ebony gloss of night.

Bran had wanted the day to be over and suddenly it was—of course partial credit could be given to how quickly the sun set in December, how early, but for a moment it seemed like Nelle conjured the darkness that appealed to his tired eyes. And she alone was defined in it, by it, fierce and powerful—a goddess whose blessing he craved.

And he felt it—saw again that brazen determination that had mesmerized him a year ago. A shiver rocked his shoulders as the door at his back opened, letting in a gust of winter air. He was awake. He was wired— charged by her tractor-beam stare. The words pulled up from deep inside him, the rush of creation pricking across his skin.

*She turned midnight.*

A lyric flashed in his mind.

He needed her to stay. He needed her to do that again. Another flash, another spark leaping from her to him, like static electricity jumpstarting his process.

Bran blinked. Then he was on his feet, filling the cramped space between their stools before she could.

"Wait—wait—" Bran shook his hair and settled it back into place in one involuntary movement. He scrambled to remember the reasons she was going. "I've had a long day. I'm sorry. I'll nurse the next beer."

For the first time since landing in the seat next to her he locked his eyes on hers for more than a fleeting glance. They glowed like sun caught in honey and he felt just as stuck.

"I didn't mean to be late. I was speeding. You gotta know I was—who goes the speed limit in a Ferrari, right?"

Her eyes sizzled with annoyance and he remembered her calling the car ridiculous.

Bran was so used to being the force in a room, the sun around which everyone seemed to gravitate. Normally it was his electric-blue eyes that shocked people into stunned silence. He was off balance when he was with Nelle, when it was his body that spun towards hers, his lungs that struggled under her gaze. Whatever he had that drew people in, she had it too. Only hers was fresher. Not yet faded. And it pulled something to the surface in him—something he recognized, something he'd lost.

*Queen of light.*

Another lyric. Another ray of hope breaking through his blocked mind. The hazy shape of a song formed in his periphery.

He had to make her stay.

Skewered by her gaze, Bran prepared another admission, willing to humble himself to any level, if she'd just sit back down. "Admittedly, yes, the car is a little over the top. It's the first big thing I bought." She had to understand. "You must have done something with your signing bonus?"

"I paid my parents' mortgage."

Maybe not.

He couldn't keep the desperation out of his final plea. "Please stay."

Half standing, she deliberated silently for a long, torturous minute while Bran held his breath. Finally, when his lungs had begun to ache, she settled herself back in her seat. And as relieved as he was, he had no idea why. Maybe she was curious about what had changed his attitude? Maybe she just wanted to finish her drink. It didn't matter. He had a second chance to focus on her. To catch any flashes of her brashness and hope for another burst of inspiration.

She crossed her legs and leaned as far back from him as she could. "I'm not sleeping with you now."

Bran let out a shaky laugh. "I wouldn't expect you to."

As Nelle gulped the last of her cocktail, lips puckering, it dawned on him that was all she'd been interested in. This could have been easy. Both of them intent on quick access to passion—if only he hadn't been so distracted, so stupid. That ship had sailed. But she was still here, the sour twist easing from her mouth. He could settle for a little conversation and a little hope.

He picked up the beer Andre had delivered to take a restorative gulp and caught Nelle's watchful glance. He sipped instead, to prove he could behave. The beer was cold and bitter and he held it in his mouth as she leaned forward. She took the pint from his hand, her eyes locking on his as she swigged it back, leaving him his own print of her lips on the rim as she set it down. Bran swallowed. A hidden sweetness coated his tongue. How had he not been paying his full attention to this girl?

"I'm not sleeping with you either," he told her when he recovered himself.

Unmistakable interest lit her face. "Because you've rekindled things with Francesca."

He raised his eyebrows. "Have I?"

"You haven't heard? They're saying it was backstage at the Victoria's Secret show."

"That's news to me. I haven't been in New York since October."

"*News* is a strong word for it. Same source reported my butt implants." She angled her hips to give him a glance at her backside. "Nice, right?"

And he'd been fixated on her mouth. The things he could do to an ass like that. He swallowed again. "Very natural."

"Well. It is. So." Her gilded lids glittered as she shifted her attention to the barkeep, thanking him with a smile for removing her empty glass. She stretched, the sweater pulling tight over her breasts, her sleek hair dancing over the crescent arch of her spine. Curves and shadows. This was the performer in her, aware of his attentiveness, feeding off her audience.

"I'm not with Francesca anymore. I'm not with anyone." He put his arm on the low back of her chair, thumbing the nailhead trim that lined the edge.

"But you're not sleeping with me?"

"I'm considering celibacy."

She bent towards him. "Bran Kelly. Celibate. This is a line, right? You tell a girl you're withholding your dick from the world to make her want you more? The rock-star thing not working for you anymore?"

It wasn't a line. But a solution he'd entertained earlier—when he wasn't close enough to smell the Chanel at her neck. When it felt like his only option was something drastic he'd never have considered before.

His aforementioned dick twitched at her casual shout-out and Bran tried to quiet that urge. She inspired something more valuable in him, but maybe he could turn this around and satisfy them both. He was aware of the night stretching before them, long and cold.

He had to grip the back of her seat to stop himself from sifting his fingers through the bottom inch of her hair. When Nelle coasted a hand through the waves, Bran swayed forward to inhale. Her hair swung over her shoulders, falling over the back of Bran's hand, and he had the sudden sensation that he had slipped, the stomach lurch of losing your footing.

*Black like ice, queen of light, she turned midnight.*

The line flickered through Bran's mind and he resisted the impulse to pull out his phone and type it into his notes. That would look like texting—and definitely not help his case. His fingers tensed at his side. He repeated the words in his head, trying to combat the anxiety of losing them, unaware of how the desire tethered itself to the woman sitting next to him.

Nelle pressed forward, still hunting down answers. "What is it then? A New Year's resolution—a quarter-life crisis?"

"More of a clarity thing."

"Pussy clouds the mind?"

A smile tugged at Bran's mouth. "They're wrong about you. You've got an edge."

"Because I said *pussy*?"

"Because you pursued me while I was with someone else."

Now he wished for blaring sunlight, to see for sure that her face had gone pink with a blush of his making.

Andre arrived with a second cocktail, and Nelle swiveled towards him with another practiced smile. "And we're gonna split a burger." She glanced down before meeting Bran's eyes again. "I should apologize for that."

"But?"

"I wouldn't mean it."

A soft silence settled between them, the thick snow outside muffling the sounds of the city. Her mouth curved, finally for him, and an uptick of tempo thumped in his heart.

The candle across the room winked again. Bran touched her elbow, the fabric of her sweater soft, thinner than he'd expected. "You're sure Andre has your back with the paps? I can't help thinking they'd kill for this."

She recrossed her legs, her feet tangling momentarily with his. He widened his thighs, making room for her to fit the V of her stacked knees between them. "*If* this were happening—they'd be all over us in a minute. Reporting our breakup while speculating that we're engaged—contrasting headlines over a photo of us buying groceries and holding hands—"

"That's why I have a no-hand-holding policy. Makes it too easy for them."

"And if I eat one gyro too many: bump watch."

She was right. That's exactly what they always did. Take any scrap of his life they could find to churn out stories he barely recognized as his life. Soon they'd have more than fragments to work with, soon they'd have every detail that made Bran Kelly who he was. The private stuff that made him feel like a real person.

And he didn't know how to stop it.

"Everything they can find, sold to the highest bidder." He moved his hand from her sleeve before his grip tightened. He shouldn't be talking about this. Not when he was trying to focus on Nelle, let her be the distraction from his other problems.

But she was nodding, rebalancing the metal toothpick across her glass. "Better than making things up."

His response arose from the ease of talking to someone who really understood. "Does it bother you more when they're wrong or when they're right?"

"It bothers me that I can't have any secrets." She gave up on balance and let the lemon peel splash back into her drink. "It bothers me that I don't think I can keep any."

"Then you need a tighter circle. Or a smaller one."

"Is that what you do? Keep a circle so small and tight you suffocate inside it, your secrets preserved as your body rots?"

"You're pretty dark for a pop princess."

"You're pretty chaste for a rock god."

A second line flared in his mind, warm with the possibility of what it could become, and he tried to burn it to his memory.

The French fries arrived in a paper cone with a little dish of pale aioli. The smell filled Bran's nose and his mouth watered. That numbness had kept him from registering how hungry he'd gotten.

Nelle had a crispy golden strand in her hand before Andre had managed to set the plate down. "And you know how they call you Bran and Fran? If we got married they'd call me Nelly Kelly."

Bran froze, hot fries searing his fingertips. "Would they?"

This time it wasn't a lyric rising in his mind. But an idea that only a man as blindly desperate as he currently was would consider.

She nodded with confidence. "Of course they would."

Even if he was in straits dire enough to come up with a scheme like that, Nelle certainly wouldn't accept. She was a catalyst, and he was reacting too quickly. Besides, she didn't need a last name. Why would she take his?

So Bran filled his mouth with fries and swallowed the idea with them.

## Chapter Two

"Do you have a pencil?"

"No. I've got a pen." Nelle searched through the Birkin that hung under the bar. "Inspiration deserves ink."

"Is that a saying I should know?" Blue eyes hit hers as she handed over the ballpoint and she almost forgot to let go.

"I don't like my handwriting in pencil." It always looked sloppy, like she'd lacked conviction while writing it.

Light glinted off Bran's black-and-gold watch as he scribbled across the back of the thick coaster that used to rest under his drink. He paused to hum, too low to hear, but Nelle absorbed the vibration. Fingertips brushed rhythmically on his thigh—up, down, up—silently strumming the notes he'd pair with the words. Curiosity drew her forward but he turned to slip the coaster into a pocket of the fleece-lined jean jacket that he'd slung on the back of his chair before she could read what it said.

Disappointment was the two clear notes of a cardinal call waking her in the middle of a good dream—first the high, followed by the inevitable low—and Bran Kelly had a knack for it.

He was different from how she expected him to be when he'd arrived, shrugging out of that coat and training his eyes on the bar. She had readied herself for an instant spark, undeniable interest, mutual curiosity. Prepared to feel him searching her out, pursuing her like she was the fox and he the hound. But there had been nothing flirtatious about him—there had barely been anything *present* about him. His indifference in fulfilling her expectations was an arrow through the balloon of excitement that had buoyed her here.

This was supposed to be fun, the kickoff to the Christmas present that she'd bargained for from Max and Mina, her management team: time for herself. A month off before preparing for tour. A month to do anything she wanted—mostly. Within reason. As long as she checked in. After she'd heard from Bran that afternoon, she'd even told her parents not to drive in for the show. She'd picked the night with him instead. If he made her regret *that*, he'd earn every diss-track lyric *she* penned about *him*.

She swirled a fry in aioli. "I don't think you're supposed to take those."

"I'll tip extra." He resettled his arm across her chair. "You were going to anyway, right?"

"Good Midwest boy, remember?"

"No, *I'm* the good Midwest girl. You're the morally compromised bad boy."

"I save that for hotel rooms."

Bran grinned and Nelle pressed her knees together, her fabric-clad legs between his dark grey slacks.

Bran Kelly was here now.

And that. That was the sort of uncontainable male verve that was going to get her into trouble. She should have left when he was being sullen and unbearable. When she had half a chance.

Benj had tried to warn her, brushing highlighter up Nelle's cheek. "I don't think you should go. You've liked him too long. Better to just keep liking him, than find out how much he really sucks."

"He doesn't suck."

"That's not what they say on Reddit."

"People say he's rude?"

"Oh no, sorry—people say he gives good head."

"Benjamina!"

"What? You know all the words to 'Pie in the Face.' And that is the only reason I'm making you look this good. Because you need some head. And even if he sucks, like personally, you're still gonna sleep with him."

They'd locked eyes in the mirror and Nelle hadn't been able to dispute that fact. He was *Bran Kelly.* Of course she wanted to sleep with him. He was the entire dream guy section of the vision board she'd made when she was sixteen. And everything else had come true. Why not this? Seven years later and they were on an even playing field—she wasn't an anonymous fan girl waving a sign at his concert asking him to choke her. She was Nelle now.

Benj had given her a knowing nod. "Okay, so what are we doing with this hair?"

"I've been thinking about bangs."

"Do you have clearance for that?"

"Clearance from who? It's my hair."

Benj had lifted a lock, her mouth pulled in a skeptical line. "Oh girl, no. It's not yours. It's part of your brand. It's probably insured. I'd lose my job if I did that without approval."

"Your job is being my best friend."

"I don't actually get paid for that. It's more of a public service." Benj had looked down to plug in the fattest curling iron in her arsenal, her platinum hair covering her face. "And I can't not get paid."

Nelle's stomach had twisted but she'd smiled when Benj met her eyes again. "Are beachy waves out?"

"Not if you're still wearing them."

The perks of being a trendsetter.

Bran spilled the remaining fries out of their paper cone. Imagine Benj's face when she told her how *hot* that was. Just him scattering fries across the plate. "Or," Benj might say, "you've got issues."

It was the way he wore his skin. That top layer of Bran Kelly—bold, confident. Even in a faded Repeat the 3-peat T-shirt—authentically old, with two small holes she had to ignore, lest she poke her fingers through them searching for skin—he oozed effortless style. It was probably the details, the cuffed sleeves, the suede shoes, that fancy watch. Or maybe it was his face. Being that handsome your whole life had to have an impact on a person. Imagine looking in the mirror and seeing it every day: the merest hint of a chin dimple in his box of a jaw, covered now by a rough layer of scruff. Sharp blue eyes, the kind that didn't lose color at any distance. And his hair—that signature shock of wet sand that pushed up and leaned slightly left, with one wisp separated from the rest, hanging over his forehead. A strand of hair that had its own devoted following on social media.

Nelle eyed Bran's jacket again. Hanging behind him like this was some local dive, not a place with a coat check where he'd get it back with an extra slip of paper in the pocket from some enterprising waitress. Not that Nelle was judging. She'd basically pulled the same move at the Note Awards, encouraged by a flurry of get-it-gurl gifs from Benj and four glasses of Dom. The world had become her oyster and Bran Kelly was the shell she'd wanted to crack. It had been the last thing she'd done carefree, without her dad's health scare hanging over her.

She hadn't regretted it until about ten minutes ago.

But he was rallying now. And jotting down a song idea in her presence? Yeah. That was a closer. And if it was a move, it was *way* better than that celibacy line.

What had he written on that coaster? She'd find out one day, along with the rest of the world—his voice rich and clear over some ridiculous guitar riff he made look easy as—don't think about pie.

Nelle rolled her shoulders back before reaching for her French 75, the jolt of it strong and sour on her tongue. "Are you in town for the holidays?"

Bran shook his head. "Are you?"

"Heading home tomorrow night."

"You have a place in LA?"

"No, I was thinking about it last year before... But I hardly see my parents as is. I'm heading home home. After the Jingle Jam. We released a new single off the next album—"

"I heard it. It's great."

She brushed her salty fingers on the thick napkin in her lap. "I heard you might be playing—"

"I haven't decided." He wedged three fries together

and crammed them into the near-empty aioli dish. "I've been—had a cold. Couldn't commit."

"You sound fine now."

He raised his eyebrows and tipped a measured splash of beer into his mouth. "Well. We'll see."

"It's nice to be home though, right?"

He grunted noncommittally, which only made her want to press the issue harder. But if listening to "Fly Free" on repeat for a year had taught her anything it was that Bran Kelly didn't like a corner he couldn't get out of. And knowing that, she felt like she knew *him*. Because that was the thing about his music—the words he'd written and shared and felt. A part of him was in those songs—it couldn't not be, the way he poured himself into the work—and it resonated, in her and anyone touched by the sound. She understood the urge to break him open, sort through the rubble, and keep a broken piece for herself. But she also knew what it was like to feel those millions of little hammers chipping away at you. Still, he kept opening up in his music, willing to offer himself to the clamoring crowds.

"How was tour?" she asked.

"Good."

"When did it wrap?"

"October." He'd started shutting down on her again.

Nelle recrossed her legs, the toe of her boot connecting with his shin. "So you've been free, mostly, since then?"

Bran rubbed at the spot before leveling his blue eyes on her face. She willed him to say more, to give her a reason to stay. He blinked. "I've been—when tour ended. That one was different. Lonely."

"Because of the celibacy?" She couldn't keep the tease from her voice.

He pinched the napkin in her lap, wiping his hand. A move as cheeky as when she'd taken a sip of his beer. If this was a game, they were both playing now.

"No, I hadn't come up with that yet. It was a different lonely. I'm not used to touring without Arlo and Cormac." The other members of Judith From Work. The band had split amid rumors that Bran was hard to work with. One magazine even claimed he was a pill-popping addict, prone to fits, and the band had broken up after a failed intervention. They hadn't been photographed together in over a year, which lent some credibility to the story.

Bran ate the last fry. "The backup band was top. And the audiences were unbelievable—we all really wanted to be there. But when it was over, it caught up with me, I guess. And then last week my—"

He cut off as Andre returned, sliding a white plate across the bar. Nelle waited but Bran didn't resume whatever he'd been about to say. She cut through the burger with a steak knife even though it was so tender she could have used a spoon. Juice speckled the blank china and she pulled the halves apart, picking one up and pushing the plate towards Bran.

"Thanks, I forgot lunch." His mouth closed over the burger and he released a soft moan.

Nelle bit through the eggy bun, into the meat, her tongue registering salt, fat, and something smoky-sweet. She watched him finish his half in three bites, chewing roughly. "That bacon jam, right?"

He nodded, reaching for his napkin.

"Are you working on new music?"

His arm stiffened behind her. He'd done everything one-handed since stringing it across her stool. "That's the plan. What about you?"

Nelle dipped her head to catch his eye, making sure he didn't retreat again. "Hitting the road in April."

"Arenas?"

"Stadiums."

"Big crowds."

"I can take it."

"Didn't say you couldn't." There had been a moment before, when his focus on her had flared and she'd thought he might kiss her. Her body had zinged, snapping to life. Now, his gaze dropped unmistakably to her mouth. When he met her eyes again, they'd gone electric. "Not much feels as good, does it? As fifty thousand people singing your song back to you?"

No. Not much.

Nelle swallowed. "Why'd you do small venues, for your solo tour? You could have gone bigger."

She wished she hadn't said it as soon as he shifted, taking those eyes to the wide window. She'd heard that he was at odds with his label over the decision. Why make less money than you could on a tour? On a product? Mina had told her he'd had to promise them a new album by the end of the year, three months after the tour ended. Maybe that's why he looked so tired. That timeline was insane. He must have been putting everything he had into it.

Bran didn't look at her, focused instead on tilting the water in his glass. But he didn't withdraw either. "Because it feels even better when you can *find* the voice singing your song back to you. See it in someone's face, how they connect to it. How they connect to you."

Nelle licked the last drop of grease off her thumb and folded her napkin over the empty plate, sated. At least partially. "You wanted something intimate?" She leaned over the corner of the bar to brush back that one loose curl of his, letting the satin strand slip across her knuckles. It fell right back into place. Stubborn. "You're not really going to be celibate."

"Why not?" Grazing his forehead had brought an intensity to his face that warmed Nelle's gut like she had chugged the rest of her drink.

"Your fingers are in my hair." His hand stopped midtwirl, as if he was surprised to learn she'd noticed the gentle twists and tugs behind her back. "You don't seem to be thinking about celibacy very seriously at all."

"No, I'm not," he said, completely serious. Under the bar, his free hand found the back of her knee, fingertips pressing a chord into her herringbone tights as he strummed up, down, up her spine with the other hand. "I'll start tomorrow."

The room seemed to grow hotter as the coil of attraction between them tightened. If he was winding her up, she might need to warn him that she was liable to snap.

Nelle traced his wrist, fitting her fingers around the soft skin beneath his heavy watch, her rings clicking against the hardware. She guided his hand farther up her leg, the gentle scrape of friction loud as microphone feedback to her heightened senses.

Bran licked at the corner of his mouth. His voice lowered an octave. "I think we just discussed how this can't happen."

"Because of your celibacy? You said you were starting tomorrow. Plenty of time left tonight."

His grip tightened around her leg. "Because no matter how aggressively pleasant you are to that bartender, and no matter what we tip, he isn't doing his job if he doesn't get the free publicity of a picture of us walking out of here together. Same thing anywhere we'd go."

"You don't want them to know about us?"

"I don't want to give them anything else."

A shiver rolled through her and Nelle found herself in the middle of a deep, involuntary blink. A moment of respite, having stared too long at something bright, something solar.

What Bran wanted—it just wasn't how it worked. Not for them. Even if Nelle understood the impulse, the desire to keep something for herself, it just wasn't possible. For instance, she'd agreed to a press release about her dad because Mina thought it was the best way to keep people from prying: tell them, and then request the gift of privacy.

"We traded in our right to anonymity," she told him, not fighting the resignation in her tone. "If we tried to date, someone would find out."

"Unless—" He clamped his mouth shut.

His hand stopped inching upwards but she remained trapped in his heat. Heavy-lidded and literally brought to the edge of her seat waiting for his next words.

"What?" Nelle asked him breathlessly.

"Unless we only let it happen once. A blip, too fast for them to catch on their radar."

"Get in and out. Real quick, before anyone notices?"

His mouth quirked up. "I mean. Not that quick. You'll notice. Or we could think outside the box."

"No, we definitely need to be thinking about getting inside the box." She was almost close enough to taste the bacon jam on his tongue. That errant hair of his tickled her forehead. "I'd like to have a secret."

"What if we…" He hesitated, biting his lip like he was trying to stop himself from saying it. "What if we took it further? Kept a bigger secret? That we were both willing to protect? Just to have something they'd never know about?"

Nelle put one hand on his chest, feeling the warmth of his skin through the thinned T-shirt. She angled her face in front of his and closed her eyes. "Are you proposing a murder pact?"

"No. I think—I think I'm just proposing."

Nelle jumped back, her eyes popping open like they'd been interrupted by the high-pitched screech of a record scratch. "You're what?"

"If we got married—"

"And how would that not make the news?"

Bran Kelly was unstable—she'd read that somewhere, right? This was the proof.

"My gran—she told me people used to elope to Michigan. The state allows secret marriages. Just a judge. Then they seal the file."

"Your gran?" Nelle's head spun—what was in that French 75? Gasoline? She fumbled with her phone, just to prove him wrong. Derail the crazy train. "You have to have a license. And wait three days. I'm going home tomorrow."

He took the phone out of her hand. "No—it says right here they'll waive it under some circumstances."

"You think we are those circumstances?"

"I think we can afford it. People don't often tell me no."

She tugged the phone back. "What do you think they tell me?"

"Whatever you want to hear."

She'd leaned in again and sprang back with a sky-high, nervous cackle. "You know I was lying—I was still going to sleep with you—right? I never tied my honor to waiting for marriage."

"Yes—I mean, no—I know how it sounds—"

Nelle covered Bran's fumbling mouth with her hand. Her pulse drummed a timpani roll, cresting louder and faster in her veins. Because a moment ago he'd twisted his hand in his own hair and looked so boyish and bashful and different from every public image she'd ever seen of him that it nearly floored her.

"Shut up. I'm trying to figure out how we just went from one-night stand to secret marriage."

*Bran Kelly* wanted to *marry her.*

What kind of vision board black magic was this.

They stared at each other, Bran breathing through her fingers. Nelle let her hand drop.

He rubbed his eyes. "I'm sorry. I've had a weird day. I thought that made sense. That it would feel good to know they'd missed something that big. In my head it—forget I said it. Do you want a lobster roll?"

It was a bad idea. A *terrible* idea. Anybody she told would agree. Absolutely unadvisable.

*Do you have clearance for that?*

Nelle's lacquered nails dug into her palm.

But if it was a secret, she didn't have to tell anybody. Her parents flashed in her mind. A year ago, she had sobbed over the idea that her father wouldn't walk her down the aisle. Considering it a choice not to have him there was practically therapeutic. But Max and Mina would—

Max and Mina wouldn't need to know either. And that thought was pure liberation. She'd fought hard for this time off, to spend on the things that mattered in her real life. That was what it was like being a product, having to fight for your own time.

Bran's reasoning was jaded as hell, but it made sense to her. *I don't want to give them anything else.*

Maybe it was possible—that he had found a loophole. And he was hopeless enough to suggest it. She almost felt bad for him. How would she feel after three more years of this? Worn thin like his shirt by the constant attention? At least she'd still have a safe haven, she'd still have home.

The point was: Bran Kelly wanted to marry her. Did it matter why? She wasn't delusional. This wasn't love at first sight—lust, definitely. All the lust. She'd learned to lust on Bran Kelly. But it was something, wasn't it? That Bran Kelly wanted a little piece of her too?

And this didn't feel like a bad thing. She had a sense for when the universe was telling her to push forward, when to pull back. This felt like flow. An opportunity to leap, not something that would trip her up.

"Okay."

"Lobster roll? I think that's the right choice. Lots of butter, you know, fat for brain health. Get us thinking straight."

Nelle knocked back the rest of her drink and locked her eyes on Bran's. "Not the lobster roll. The check. Let's get married."

## Chapter Three

Bran paused with one hand on the door, the other hovering low on Nelle's wool peacoat. He braced himself for the flash of lights that would put an end to this before they could go any further. "Do you have security waiting outside?"

Nelle shook her head. "Not tonight. Benj is the only one who knows I'm here. Well. Besides Andre."

Bran opened the door, relieved to discover her faith in the bartender had not been misplaced. They were alone in the night. The snow glowed in the blue-tinged shadows, and he'd have done better to brace for the cold that bit at his face. Nelle jogged diagonally across the street to where he'd parked, the red Ferrari highlighted from above by a streetlamp's triangular beam.

What were they doing?

What was he doing?

Why had she agreed?

Bran had always been impulsive, had the kind of all-or-nothing personality that left no room for middle ground. Like when he'd become obsessed with learning guitar and nearly flunked out of school. Or when he'd wanted to keep touring, writing, touring, even as the other guys were telling him they needed a break. Bran pushed. Bran had always pushed for more.

He pushed away the thought of exactly where he'd picked up that particular trait.

He couldn't see Nelle clearly in the dark car but he imagined her washed out, pale under her rosy painted cheeks. That's how she sounded when she asked to pull over in the next alley. Faint.

He had pushed. Instead of just accepting a night of sex with a pop goddess. And now *no need for a last name* Nelle was going to lean out of his sports car and vomit.

"Here?" He sidled the car up next to a dumpster.

"That works."

The seat belt clicked as she unbuckled it.

Bran leaned forward to crank the heat in anticipation of the door opening when her warm hands caught his cheeks, tugging his face towards hers. His brain stalled out as she pressed her mouth to his, freezing on the image of that lipstick print on the rim of his glass. Then he was reacting, leaning farther into her, parting her lips with his and tasting her fancy lemonade tongue. His foot eased off the brake and the car rolled forward.

The car lurched as Bran slammed his foot back down, fumbling with the clutch in between them, unwilling to break away from the sweet tang of her. But she was pulling back, her breath hitting his face in hot puffs. She nodded with her eyes closed, released him, and buckled herself back in.

They both stared straight ahead.

His hands gripped the steering wheel. "What was that?"

She sifted a hand through her hair and tossed it at

the window, exposing the skin behind her ear. Skin he wanted to press his mouth against, feel the tremble of sound from her throat on his lips.

"I had to check."

"Check what?"

"That this wasn't a waste of time. But you can kiss. And I want to kiss you more. I'm good now."

"You didn't want to agree to a one-night stand slash secret marriage if I was going to fish-mouth you?"

"Right. And you didn't. So, we're all set."

"Just based on a kiss? What if I'm bad in bed?"

She shook her head. "There was a Reddit thread about you. Consensus is you have a big dick and you know how to use it."

He'd assumed it was nerves, the way she said what she was thinking so unguardedly. But maybe it was just her. And she was completely comfortable bringing his dick up in conversation. Completely capable of bringing his dick up in general.

Bran was suddenly less comfortable, aware of the limited room in his fitted pants. "That's not at all degrading. When did you look that up?"

"It doesn't matter. I'm good—are you good?"

"Apparently, yes." He knocked the car back in Drive but didn't release the brake. "Do you need anything else? Before we go?"

"We left without dessert."

"So you want to—" *fuck in this alley* didn't sound great. Except that it sounded *so great*.

She pulled out her phone. "There's a Magnolia Bakery on State and Randolph, it's a couple blocks—here."

He pushed the phone down, the lit map glaring

through his fingers. "I don't need directions. I know how to get there."

"You grew up around here? I thought I'd heard it was outside the city."

She was full of questions, and seemed to have a knack for narrowing in on the ones he was most reluctant to answer. Still, something about her compelled him to do it, to reveal more of himself than he would normally like—maybe he was afraid she'd walk out or kick him in the shins again if he didn't.

"My gran's house was South Side. In the Ks. I spent a lot of time there."

"So why don't you tell people that?"

"Because I didn't want them to bother her." He tapped his teeth together, considering how much more to say. "When I was eighteen some people broke into my dad's house." His dad had said it was fans. Judith hadn't even been that popular yet. For the first time it crossed Bran's mind that his dad might have been lying. Bran shook his head. "She collected, she saved everything. That house is full of memories—memories to us that would be memorabilia in someone else's hands. You know what it's like—everyone thinks it's just one touch, their touch, but it's more than just them. And it's your features that are worn away."

His jaw tensed and he couldn't look over at her, where he felt her stare like a beam of light on his face.

"Bran—"

"We should go."

He eased the car back onto the road. Beside him Nelle exhaled. He hoped she wouldn't press him more on what he'd said. And she must have picked up on his desire to stop talking about it, because she turned her focus to the bag resting on her lap. She tugged a white cloth from a pack and wiped her face clean as he navigated through the busy downtown streets. He inched through a gap in the crowded crosswalk and turned onto State Street. A line of gold trumpets ran along the Marshall Field's building between two big green clocks, forming a festive arch. Red bows decorated the street posts, and fairy lights twinkled from every direction. Bran double-parked while Nelle peeled a fringe of fake lashes from her eyelids and crumpled them in the soiled wipe.

He eyed the bustling sidewalk, the bright lights. "There's a line. This isn't a good idea. We're not exactly incognito together." They were never going to get away with this. The secret would be out before he'd have a chance to revel in it.

"Just stay here. It'll be fine as long as I'm quick."

"You're gonna be mobbed. We don't have security—"

"Bran, relax. I've done this before. You just have to neutralize your distinguishing characteristics. It would be harder for you—because you have a recognizable jaw. There's no time for you to grow a beard. But I just removed my entire face. I could probably do less, really. To most people I'm completely unrecognizable without all that makeup. You've got—here."

Nelle raised the cloth to his lips, bringing with it the chemical bite of makeup remover. She leaned close, rubbing away the evidence of their kiss in the alley and he used the proximity to study her face. Scrubbed of that professionally even coverage, light freckles dusted the skin under her eyes. Her cheeks, without the contour-

ing, were fuller, rounder. Her eyes, less defined, held
no less light and gleamed back at him.

"I can still see you," he said.

Her mouth lifted up to the side. And then she was
sitting back, gathering her hair on top of her head, con-
taining those signature waves.

"Give me your coat."

Bran blinked himself out of a daze. "Why?"

"Because mine is nice. I'm a fashion icon. Style is
one of my giveaways. Do you need anything?"

"From in there? No."

When she stepped out and climbed the high curb all
he saw were the red bottoms of her shoes, the detail of
her tights. This was a mistake. He rolled the window
down, bending to call her back in. How could no one
tell that she was—

Nelle hauled the glass door open, his jacket hanging loose on her body, her hair messy. She smiled at
him. She looked normal—perfectly normal. Like she
belonged there. Nobody batted an eye when she joined
the line. Nobody even looked up from Instagram long
enough to see that the woman with the fourth-most
followers on the platform was standing in their midst.

His thumb smoothed over the glossy emblem on the
wheel as he checked the rearview mirror. A train rattled
across the street behind vertical bubble letters spelling
CHICAGO. He scanned the storefronts on either side
of the bakery.

Light sparkled in the brightest window down the
block.

*Oh.*

He reached for the blue canvas duffel behind the driver's seat.

He did need something.

# Chapter Four

Nelle spun in a slow circle next to the empty car. She hadn't been in Magnolia that long. Nobody had recognized her. There was no need for Bran to pull his chute and bail on her. Unless… She bit her lip. Unless he was completely rethinking this. Because he should be. She should be. Someone should be.

But it wasn't her. She'd read too many books that started with a carriage ride to Gretna Green. She'd spent too many nights imagining Bran Kelly had picked her out of a crowd and was singing just to her.

Was it impatience or fear, anxiety or excitement, that shook her nerves?

There—she breathed out. Bran jogged towards her on the sidewalk, a worn Sox cap pulled low over his eyes, a dark hoodie pulled up over top of that, and a scarf covering the lower half of his face.

"Where'd you go?"

"Remembered something."

"What are you wearing? You look ridiculous."

"Making myself indistinguishable—I'm neutralizing." He ducked his chin into the scarf to prove his point. And he was right, he didn't look like Bran Kelly.

He looked more like Damian going incognito in *Mean Girls*.

A smile pulled at her mouth. "You couldn't find any sunglasses? Better yet, a pair of Groucho's? I think they'd complete the ensemble."

"Hey. It worked. In and out, no problem. You ready?" He hopped off the high curb, peeled a ticket off the car's dash, and slid into the driver's seat.

Nelle frowned, climbing in the car's other side. "You parked in a bus lane."

"It's fine."

"No, it's not. There are rules." She refused to take the orange-and-white envelope he held out. "That's not my fault. I'm not paying for that."

"Just put it in my pocket, will you?"

Right. She was wearing his jacket. The fleece collar soft against her neck smelled like him, a musky male scent of woodsmoke and juniper, accentuated by the cold air.

She folded the ticket and shoved it into the jacket, the back of her hand tapping against something solid already inside. Her heart rate doubled as she palmed the coaster's curve. But she couldn't take it out and read it. Not with him sitting right there. She brushed a thumb over the writing, as if she could read the words that way—some sort of intuitional Braille.

Bran pulled across the lanes of traffic, a bus honking behind him. "What did you get?"

"Banana pudding. I got a large. In case you want to share."

"Never had it."

She popped the top off the cardboard pint and scooped a mouthful of pale yellow pudding onto a biodegradable spoon, making sure to include a bit of softened vanilla wafer. "Open up."

Bran took a left, looking away from her. "Open what?"

"Your mouth."

They stopped at a red light, the color staining his hair. He looked from her to the spoon and opened his mouth, his Irish eyes smiling.

She slid the spoon past his lips, and he licked it clean.

"Wow." He opened his mouth again and she fed him another bite. "Wow. That's really—wow."

"Three wows—you're a Cleffy-nominated lyricist?"

"Judith never got a Note nod."

Nelle almost dropped the container of pudding. "No—you—oh my god, how don't you know?"

"Know what?"

"The Note nominations are out. *Green* is up for Notable Pop Album—and 'Touch Her Back' is up for Notable Song. As of yesterday. That's you, Kelly. Who are your people that no one told you this?"

"I've been ignoring my phone. Off the map for a few days."

She waited for his reaction. He'd been nominated for a Cleffy! To be recognized at the Note Awards—dreams didn't get bigger than that. Except to win. When she'd heard her name read out last year, she'd FaceTimed her mom while jumping on the hotel bed. Bran simply inverted his lips, flattening them into a line.

"You answered my text."

Tension filled the small car as he gripped the wheel, his mouth shut tight.

Nelle had missed something. "I meant to say congratulations—"

"But you were too busy calling me a talented dick-head?"

"You are a talented dickhead. A Cleffy-nominated dickhead. Seriously, from one Cleffy-nominated artist to another, congrats. You deserve it."

"Yeah, thanks—thanks for telling me."

He kept his eyes on the road but turned his head like a baby bird.

She loaded up another bite, and, sensing an opening to make him smile, to ease the set of his face, ate it herself. He laughed and her stomach dipped.

They sped south on the highway that ran along the lake and Nelle lowered the pudding to her lap. "What if we fall in love?"

For the first time, Bran looked a little green. She'd panicked him.

"Not us. I mean. Presumably, you won't be celibate forever. And I'm young but I plan to have a family someday." She didn't have time for a boyfriend. They were too expensive—to her focus, to her reputation. But eventually she would be ready to bring someone important into her life, and they'd have to deal with it. "At some point we'll have to get divorced. So we can marry other people."

"No problem, just let me know where to sign." His gaze flicked over her. "What? You don't think it'll be that simple?"

Nelle's topknot brushed the car's low ceiling as she sat straighter. "How much are you worth?"

"I'll tell you what, we'll write a prenup when we get there."

"And where are we going? How exactly are we going to do this?"

"I need to make a call."

"Bran. This is supposed to be just between us. That's the whole point. Two people equally invested in one secret." Nelle's forehead creased and she was glad Max wasn't here to lobby for preventative Botox again.

"She's a lawyer. She couldn't say anything if she wanted to."

"A label lawyer?"

"No. Personal. My cousin. She's a county clerk. We need her to—to facilitate, get us in to see a judge. All that."

He started pressing buttons on the wheel and then the warbling treble of a phone ringing filled the car.

"Bran? I've looked it over and there's nothing we can do about the deed—"

Bran cleared his throat over the woman. "Yeah, yeah, hey, Tomi. I need you to do something else for me. Call it a favor."

A pause. "Am I your cousin right now or your lawyer?"

"My lawyer."

"Then it's not a favor. Because I'm charging you."

"Fine—whatever—but this is bigger, more time-sensitive—I did something—"

"Please tell me I am not your first call after killing a hooker because—"

"Tomi."

"—sex work is work, Bran. Hookers are people who deserve—"

"Tomi—I'm getting married. Tonight."

A longer pause. "Congratulations?"

"I need you to figure it out."

"Bran." His cousin drew out the name, stressing the vowel with a nasal pitch. "It can't be done."

"Sure it can. I just googled it. Michigan has secret marriages. I need a county clerk to waive the waiting period, a judge to seal the file. Easy peasy. You're a clerk, I know you know a judge or two—"

"Google? You're insane. I know it's been a hard week—"

Bran pushed his jaw out and cut his cousin off. "Can you do it?"

"Do you really need this?"

"Yes."

Tomi must have also recognized that hard edge in his voice, because after another long silence she relented. "I can get you a license. And waive the wait. And there is someone—Judge Jordan—he's kind of a softy and he happens to be a fan."

"What's his first name?" Excitement laced Bran's words, more excitement than he displayed hearing he'd been nominated by the Note Awards.

Tomi sighed. "Michael, okay? No relation—"

Bran laughed and Nelle bit the inside of her cheek. "This is happening—Michael Jordan is marrying me tonight, Tomi."

"You'll need witnesses."

At the mention of witnesses Nelle flared her eyes at him and Bran waved a hand, nodding that he understood. "How many?"

"Two."

"What are you and Wyn doing tonight? Wanna come to my wedding?"

"She's going to die."

"Good, then she can't tell anyone."

"She wouldn't."

"I know. That's why I invited her."

Tomi sighed again, her breath crackling through the car speakers. "I need some information from you. For the license. And why does it have to be secret?"

"I don't want the media to find out. Say something about how everyone is entitled to a bit of anonymity."

"And your blushing bride? What's her name?"

Bran looked over at Nelle, and she felt like Courtney Cox pulled onstage by Bruce Springsteen—out of the spectator role, into the spotlight. "Do you have a last name?"

In the face of such a ridiculous question, she forgot her hesitation. "Antonella Georgopoulos."

*What?* he mouthed. She ignored him, focusing on Tomi.

"And your birthday?"

"October 23rd, 1997."

Next to her, Bran was listening intently.

"Parents' names and places of birth?"

"Andreas and Maria Georgopoulos, they were both born in Patras, Greece. I wasn't, if that's important."

"It is." A keyboard clicked in the background. "What time is it?" Tomi groaned. "Bran, this is impossible— let's do it tomorrow. Take the night to think about it—"

He shook his head even though his cousin couldn't see him. "Tonight."

Another silence stretched through the connection. "I can keep Judge Jordan here until nine. Where are you?"

"Already in the car." Bran glanced at his watch. "We'll be there by eight."

Nelle pointed to the clock on the dash. "Michigan is an hour ahead."

"Fuck—okay—gotta go. Make this happen, Tomi."

"I really shouldn't—"

The line went dead. The burned-egg smell of Indiana's factories filled the car, and the seams of the tollbooth they were approaching reverberated beneath them. Bran barely paused long enough for the electronic pass to register.

"You're gonna get another ticket," Nelle worried out loud. Tickets were a sign of bad karma. A sign that you weren't vibrating at the right frequency for abundance. That you weren't in harmony. Before tonight, Nelle had never gotten one. She took care to be in tune.

"I don't think so. I'm feeling lucky. Judge *Michael Jordan.*"

He grinned, an infectious look that could spread through a crowd of fifty thousand people like wildfire. And the force of it on Nelle alone sent her head spinning. That somber Bran she'd met at the bar earlier was gone, replaced by a man of energy, a man who would not be stopped.

Nelle rolled the pudding container between her palms. "You didn't even know my name until a minute ago."

"I know it now. Plenty of people get married like this."

"Drunk people. In Vegas. Not people who have a two-hour drive to reconsider."

"It's not going to take me two hours to get to Michigan." He stepped harder on the gas as if to accelerate his point. "Are you reconsidering?"

Was she?

Bran ruffled his hair up and brushed it back into place in a practiced sweep of his hand. He took his eyes off the road and held her gaze. The lane began to curve and the car drifted out of the lines. Someone behind them honked and Bran snapped his attention back to driving.

Nelle released a shaky breath. She needed to regain control of the situation. "I just think we need to set some—some expectations."

"Like what?"

"After tonight, that's it. If we're going to do this, nobody can see us together. You're right, we've gotten lucky so far."

"Sure."

"Too many people already know we met up tonight."

"Who? Besides Tomi, the judge who has an obligation to keep it a secret, and your boy Andre?"

"Benj. And whoever Wyn is."

"Wyn is salt of the earth, kindest person I've ever met, don't worry about Wyn. Benj? Is she the one who sent you the eggplant emoji while we were looking up the statute?"

Nelle's cheeks heated and she angled the car's vents away from her as if that were the cause. "About that statute. It is handy. That your cousin is a clerk."

"That's what made me think it was possible."

"I thought you were just gonna throw money at the problem."

"I'm prepared to do that too."

That was it. All of her concerns, tossed at him in rapid fire. And he'd sent each one flying, out of reach. Momentum had reached the tipping point. They'd crossed state lines. Michael Jordan was waiting for them.

The speed of the night, the car, his answers, the rush

of the sugar, in her veins, her heart, had her giddy. Had her wanting. Dizzied from the outside in and the inside out.

Bran opened his mouth and waited. Nelle dipped the spoon into the pudding, obliging him with light dancing in her eyes.

"I mean wow." He licked the corner of his lip, leaving it wet and glistening, and she knew exactly what she was gambling for.

"You said that."

"Well, I make a living on sincere refrains."

# Chapter Five

The Berrien County Courthouse was as small-town picturesque as you could get in the daytime, a red-and-white Romanesque building surrounded by trees and grass and even a gazebo. In December, at night, shadow cloaked the charm. The only distinguishable feature was a square clock tower looming overhead, the short hand almost touching the nine.

Bran knocked the car into Park and they sat listening to the engine click.

Nelle turned to him, her seat belt catching loudly in the quiet. "Why doesn't this feel crazier?"

He knew what she meant. Ever since they'd left the city he'd felt strangely settled. Every time he'd glanced over at her on the drive, riding shotgun with her hair in a casual bun, his jacket loose on her shoulders, it had felt easy, natural. Like this was their hundredth date. Not their first. Their only.

They'd found their way into the eye of the storm—it couldn't last, but he'd enjoy it while it did.

"Madness seems like reason to the insane." His fingers grazed her hip as he unbelted her. "We need to get in there. If we're doing this."

He waited for her to open her door. After a moment, the winter night blew in.

Bran hustled behind Nelle up the cement steps. One side of the double doors opened at their approach and Tomi leaned out. Her grey pantsuit and naturally grim mouth displayed a stern disposition and Bran knew, under any other circumstances, any other week, she would have challenged this request, shut him down with that no-nonsense sensibility she'd always had, despite being a Kelly.

"Down to the wire, Bran—Wyn's stalling him but—what are you doing?"

Angling over the counter of the reception desk, Bran answered, "I need paper."

"We don't have time for this—"

"It'll just take a second."

Tomi pulled a blank sheet out of the brown folder she was holding. "Make it quick."

Nelle was already extracting a tooth-marked pen from her bun and Bran bent over the desk scratching long sloppy words on the page. "I don't want anything from Antonella Ger-go-pah—"

Perfume filled the air as she peered around his elbow. "I can help you with that."

"I got it."

"You missed an o."

"How many are there?"

"And the u."

Bran crossed out his first attempt at her name and tried again. He looked up at her for approval when he'd finished, fitting the pen into his mouth while she read his work.

*I don't want anything from Antonella Georgopoulos, except her body.*

Nelle pinned him with one of her sizzling stares. "Looks very professional."

Bran held the pen between his teeth, talking around it. "Your turn."

He bit harder as she tried to tug the pen free, adding his own set of dents to the plastic end. Nelle jabbed at his ribs and the pen popped loose as he bent and groaned. He rubbed the sore spot blooming on his stomach while Nelle narrated, ink gliding across the bottom of the paper. "Bran Kelly can keep all his shit—just let me have that d."

A grin spread across Bran's face. "I think we nailed this." He handed the paper to Tomi.

"What the fuck is this?"

"Our prenup."

Tomi pinched the corner of the paper, her arm extended. "What am I supposed to do with it?"

"You're my lawyer, put it in my file."

His cousin visibly swallowed her argument and started down the hallway instead, their steps echoing in the empty building. But she couldn't keep it in. "That's not how any of this works. You know you have a real lawyer, right? From a really fancy firm—"

"Mr. Money?"

"That can't be his name."

"But that's for the business stuff—this is personal. And you're family."

They turned the corner and reached a door flanked by two benches.

"Your personal is your business." Tomi ushered Nelle inside and blocked Bran from following. "Nelle? *Nelle.*

I've got Google too, Bran. That's who you're marrying? Is this a publicity stunt? Because I'm out on a limb here—this is my job. Can you not get her into bed any other way?"

Bran freed himself from Tomi's hold. "That's not it."

It wasn't. It was that no matter what happened with the house, he'd have something for himself. It was that even though Nelle had only been relaying the news about his Note nominations, even though that had already happened yesterday, it had seemed like she made it happen tonight. As if her magic was rubbing off on him. It was that he saw her, and heard bursts of music that didn't exist yet.

"It better not be. I told that judge you were desperately in love—that is the only reason he agreed to do this. So you'd better act like it."

"Okay, okay." Bran hooked an arm over his cousin's shoulders and pulled her into the room. "I'm sorry, Tomi. I got it. Thanks for doing this."

The courtroom had the kind of beige nondescript atmosphere that Bran associated with true crime documentaries, not the grand depictions of marble-column justice popular on television dramas. A pale room, with fluorescent lights and cheap low-pile carpet. This was where he was going to marry Nelle, the world-renowned superstar who had graced the covers of dozens of fashion magazines. It wasn't opulent, or romantic, or anything he imagined she might like. Bran frowned, unaccustomed to the sinking weight of considering that what he wanted might not be right for someone else.

But he pushed past it, faltering only once on his walk by the cramped rows of chairs, when he caught sight of a newly plastered section of wall its own wrong shade of beige. Nelle was a big girl, she'd made her decision for her own reasons. And she was fine. On the other side of a short dividing wall she was shaking hands with Wyn, who had come prepared for the occasion with a bouquet of white peonies.

"This is so thoughtful, and my favorite—I buy a shampoo just for this smell." Nelle brought the flowers to her face to inhale. Up until a moment ago, dressed head to toe in black, standing in this 1989 set-piece, she'd looked completely un-bridelike. But now, smiling gratefully at his cousin-in-law, holding a bouquet of white flowers, her eyes shining... Bran wiped his palms on his pants.

"Thank you both for your help with this," Nelle said while Bran embraced Wyn. She offered her hand to Tomi. "I'm Nelle."

"We know who you are. Don't know why you'd want to marry this—"

"Talented dickhead," Bran interrupted. "That's what she calls me."

"How sweet," Tomi deadpanned before turning back to Nelle, hand still outstretched. "I'm sure you have a whole team of people who would talk you out of this."

Nelle drew in her arm and clutched the flowers at her gut.

His cousin and future wife stared at each other, a silent standoff that made Bran's knees twitch. This would be the moment when Nelle backed out of it. Someone reasonable, someone trustworthy asking her to reconsider.

But after a pause Nelle, deploying the kindest pitch from her collection of thoughtful tones, said, "Can we get started? I don't want to keep Judge Jordan any longer than necessary."

Tomi rocked back on her heels and that was that.

Judge Jordan sat above them, behind a large podium paneled with shiny yellow wood. Tomi nodded up at him and approached the bench with her folder.

Wyn nudged Bran's shoulder and he stumbled forward to stand next to Nelle. They'd been together for a few hours now, but most of it had been sitting. He hadn't realized how much taller he was than her—a full foot apart if she took off those boots—until she looked up at him, her raised chin barely reaching his shoulder.

Bran wrapped his hand around hers, enjoying the way the hardened pads of her fingers felt on the back of his palm.

Nelle raised her eyebrows. "No hand holding?"

"The occasion seems to call for an amendment."

"Should I be concerned the man I'm about to marry lacks conviction?"

"You should be impressed by his judicious reasoning powers. I'm making an exception to ensure our success. Tomi wants us to be convincingly in love."

The smile she'd begun faltered and she faced the judge. "Right, let's hope this goes smoothly."

Judge Jordan cleared his throat and set down the pile of papers he'd been reviewing. "It looks like everything is in order." His mouth formed a serious line, but his lively eyes revealed an internal excitement.

*Bran Kelly Marries Nelle in Secret Ceremony.*

The headline flared through Bran's mind. No—no one in this room would betray their secret.

Bran stepped forward, pulling Nelle with him. "We

really appreciate you going out of your way to accommodate our...specific situation."

Slipping his glasses to the end of his nose, the judge regarded Bran. "Yes, your situation. You're interested in a sealed certificate of marriage, is that right?"

"Yes, Your Honor."

"And you understand that the union of two people is not to be taken lightly. That it requires forethought and dedication."

Bran didn't get stage fright—he loved the way his heart pounded before he stepped in front of an audience. He was eager for the attention, ready to connect, ready to sweat and move and burn. But he did that with the weight of a guitar strap anchored across his back, a monitor hooked over his ear, and his hands settling across the metal coil of wire. Now he felt too light, disarmed. Unworthy.

Judge Jordan stared down at them. "Why are you doing this?"

*It seemed like a good idea at the bar,* Bran wanted to joke. His pulse quickened and he tightened his grip on Nelle's hand. She responded with a reassuring squeeze.

Because they had an understanding.

"We're seen," Bran started, his voice quiet, "even when we don't want to be. Our lives broken down, the pieces sold without our permission, without any possibility of getting them back. Pieces of ourselves." He glanced at Nelle, those amber eyes locked on his. "We don't want to share this, we want it to stay between us."

A lengthy silence took over the room. The clock on the wall ticked. Then the robed man nodded. "I'll need you to both declare that you are lawfully free to be wed."

"I am," Bran said and Nelle echoed him.

"Now, in front of these witnesses do you profess your intent to be married?"

Bran turned to face Nelle, searching her face for doubt, for regret or fear or any sign that he had completely overwhelmed her with this plan. She stared hard back at him, lifting her chin in that way that made him want to drop his.

"I do," she said. She squeezed his hand again.

"Me too, or—I do."

"Then if there aren't any objections, you could exchange rings."

Nelle's lips parted and she looked up at the podium. "We didn't have time—"

Bran let go of her hand to fish in his pants pocket. "Got it." He pulled out a flat square of cardboard, a ring attached to the center by a loop of taut plastic.

"Where did you get that?" She studied the thin polished silver, shaped with one chevron coming to a sharp point.

"Down the block from Magnolia. I know you'd probably prefer something in a blue box?"

"No. A red one."

And he felt it again, that low pull that this was supposed to be better for her. But her eyes were dancing when she lifted them to his. Bran swallowed, overcome suddenly by the strength of his desire to slide this simple ring onto Nelle's finger. He ripped at the plastic packaging with his teeth, and a grin pulled Nelle's cheeks wide.

With a snap the band came loose. Nelle removed the ring above her knuckle and took the new one out of Bran's hand.

"Not that way." He stopped her. The metal was warm

as he turned the ring over so the point was facing the base of her finger. "Like this."

She raised her eyebrows at his correction before letting her gaze drift down to her newly adorned hand, straightening her fingers to admire the effect. She frowned. "I didn't get you one."

He shook his head. "Too obvious. It'll blend in on you—you're already wearing fifteen of them."

"They're stacking rings. You're supposed to group them." She replaced her top knuckle ring and they considered her hand again. "You're right—you can barely notice it."

It didn't seem that way to Bran. That glinting silver with its delicate dent was all he could focus on. He rubbed his thumb over it, feeling both the softness and strength of the metal between their bodies. Something tightened in his chest and he pulled her closer, placing his palm on her neck, his fingers threading into her hair, his thumb on her hot cheek.

Her face tilted up and Bran lowered his mouth, pressing a kiss to her full lips. He slipped his tongue slowly into her mouth, just for a moment, a tease, a taste—mellow sweetness lingering from their shared pudding. Nelle crushed forgotten flowers against his hip.

A dull clap interrupted them and Bran pulled back, searching dumbly for the source of the noise.

Judge Jordan tapped lightly at his gavel, a sly smile on his face. "I haven't gotten to that part yet."

Bran stared down at Nelle, her eyes still closed, dark lashes fanning across the light freckles at the top of her cheeks. He exhaled slowly. "I couldn't wait."

"If the interruption is concluded, we could finish?"

Nelle opened her eyes. "Yes, please, Your Honor."

"Do you, Antonella Georgopoulos, take Bran Kelly as your legal husband?"

"Yes."

"And do you, Bran Kelly, take Antonella Georgopoulos as your legal wife?"

"Absolutely."

"Then this institution recognizes your good-faith commitment to each other. In front of these witnesses, in accordance with the power vested in me by the State of Michigan, I declare you husband and wife. And *now* you may kiss the bride."

It was harder that time—grinning like the lunatics they were. Their teeth clinked together twice before they managed to keep their mouths shut, straining to seal their lips tight long enough to kiss.

## Chapter Six

Nelle needed to stop looking at the ring. Stop checking to confirm it was really there, on her finger, placed by Bran Kelly himself. She had just married Bran Kelly. Bran Kelly was her husband.

And she couldn't tell anyone.

Since she'd been a teenager, she'd known Bran Kelly's voice was a force. And tonight he'd proved just how captivating he could be, how hypnotizing. He had pulled off some gift of gab, Blarney Stone, leprechaun trick—not that she could fully blame him. She hadn't needed much convincing.

There was a flurry of signatures as Tomi and Judge Jordan took over the paperwork.

Wyn smiled at them and held up her phone. "Do you want a picture?"

"No!" Bran and Nelle responded to the offer simultaneously.

No. They were agreed. This was just for them. Private, like nothing else in their lives. And she didn't need a picture to remember it. How could she forget any of this? The soft yellow walls would glow in her memory, along with the scent of peonies released into the air by bruised petals. No picture could capture the heat of Bran's hand on her cheek before he kissed her.

Bran Kelly, her husband, he could kiss.

She'd surprised him back in Chicago, in the car when she'd pressed her lips to his, and he'd still reacted like a pro, jumping in and matching her rhythm, her beat. But when he'd taken the lead and kissed her—it had been all style, soul, spark.

She would never forget that.

And she had the ring.

A wedding ring.

Real metal cuffed around her finger.

Judge Jordan climbed down from his podium. That was it. They'd done it.

Since the bar, everything had happened in a dark blur. But as Tomi handed Bran the folder, the room seemed brighter and reality sharpened into focus. Nelle blinked herself awake, jarred out of her stupor by Tomi's words.

"The record here is sealed. This is your copy. Take it home. Do not lose it."

Record. Sealed. Copy.

That was a legal document. A legally binding document. She hadn't signed anything in years without a team of lawyers clearing it first, checking over her shoulder, dedicated faces reflecting up at her from mirrored tabletops. And that prenup—her breath felt shallow. That prenup. How vulnerable had she made herself? What could Bran take her for if this went south?

Bran's eyebrows pulled together. "I can't keep this in my house. Someone could break in and find it."

"Break in? You live in the hills."

"It happens all the time."

"Put it in a safe."

"That's the first place they'd look."

Tomi sighed, leading them to the door. "You'll just have to risk it. Someone breaking in to your house to find this paper is the least dicey part of what you're doing here and you know that."

Dicey. That's what this had been. That's what this was. A gamble. A risk. She hadn't had the nerve to get unauthorized *bangs* earlier, how could she do this just to bang Bran Kelly? A sudden wave of nausea rushed through Nelle. What if someone found out? Her managers, her publicist, the label, her parents. She had risked their financial security too.

It wasn't just the money at stake. What if Bran was just using her for publicity? Some stunt to bolster his bad boy image—and ruin hers. No one would talk about her album after this. They'd look at her and see him. Maybe he'd arranged this whole thing to play her, convinced her to go along with it just to splash it in the tabloids himself. Big news to set the scene before *his* new album dropped. An old story trending again. There could be a swarm of photographers outside waiting for them. He could have tipped them off himself.

Nelle spun the ring, pinching it between the fingers on either side.

The universe was usually on her side—but that hadn't stopped her dad from getting sick. That had felt like a warning, for her to keep her priorities in check. A reminder of why she worked so hard and where her energy should be. Through that lens, marrying Bran Kelly was selfish, jeopardizing the reputation she'd built her career on.

Nelle™ was witty but kind, stylish in a natural way,

and profitably sexy. She was chic and casual and cool. Levelheaded and charming. Never foolish. It wasn't part of her brand.

Now she had leapt without fully vetting where she might land.

The harsh rectangular overhead light shut off and Nelle stopped in the middle of the hall. The cameras outside would find her, blind her, she was sure of it. She couldn't go forward. And she couldn't go back.

Staring down at the ring on her finger, vertigo swelled behind her eyes. Was it the dark hall or panic that prevented her from seeing the point clearly? She could feel it still, of course. Metal digging into her skin as her fingers squeezed tighter together.

Bran dropped back from the others. "You okay?" His pale eyes flicked back and forth between hers. "You probably—I'm sorry if—this wasn't—"

He cut himself off, looking away from her.

Was that guilt she heard in his words?

*We don't want to share this, we want it to stay between us.* That's what he'd told the judge. And yeah, he was a masterful performer, but not because he manipulated a crowd. Because he opened up to them.

Nelle wet her lips and he followed the movement automatically. He stepped closer to her, his head bending over hers, his scent catching in her lungs.

She wanted to trust him. Trust that she hadn't gotten him wrong. That he wasn't some devil. Some liar. But there could be photographers outside. She had to know.

"Let's go," she said, the words as unsteady as her steps past him.

She had to know if they were really in this together.

If his proposed secret had been part of a game, or the prize itself.

She didn't take his hand as they left the building. Instead she pulled herself in, wishing she hadn't left his coat in the car, wishing she hadn't left all semblance of sense at the bar. She ducked her head down in preparation for the onslaught, wanting to watch her step when the strobe of camera flashes interrupted her vision, when it would be revealed that they'd been discovered—or she'd been set up.

But outside the night was still, black. The red Ferrari and a blue Prius the only cars in the lot.

Nelle's breath clouded the air as she released a hot sigh of relief. It felt like something. That he hadn't played her. That she hadn't been *that* wrong, that foolish. That maybe she'd get what she wanted out of this: a secret that felt good to keep. She had said yes, and the universe hadn't let her down.

For better or worse—for the time being—Bran Kelly was her husband.

"Thank you again for the flowers," Nelle recovered herself enough to say to Wyn.

Tomi pulled Bran in for a hug. "I liked seeing so much of you this week."

Bran nodded into her shoulder. "Me too."

"And I'll call you, about the—"

"Yeah, thanks." Bran stepped back. "For everything. I owe you."

Tomi almost smiled. "Yeah, I'll send you the bill."

He raised his hand in salute and opened the door for Nelle. She sank into the seat and pulled his jacket over her lap. They hadn't been gone long but the car had cooled in their absence. They had raced away from

the city, lights blazing behind them. But as they made
their way back, Bran drove with a contemplative air.
The Ferrari winding through country roads was as out
of place as his silence.

That changed when they reached the highway. Nelle
grasped for the door hold as Bran pressed the pedal
into the floor, the engine roaring its appreciation loud
and clear.

"Hey, Ferris Bueller, slow down. We're making a
clean getaway, the last thing we need is to be pulled
over together right now."

The blinker clicked as Bran passed between a truck
and a minivan. "It'll take another two hours to get
back."

"Yeah, so?"

A simmering determination set in his eyes as he
looked at her. "So what hotel are you staying at?"

Nelle's body clenched at the intensity of his question.
She'd been so preoccupied with the reality of their marriage, the possibility that he'd betrayed her, she'd forgotten the other half of their agreement. Bran's rush to get
back proved he hadn't. "The Waldorf. You?"

"I'm not checked in anywhere."

She glanced at the duffel bag behind his seat, where
he'd tucked the brown envelope into a flat side pocket.
"Where were you planning to sleep tonight?"

"I'm not planning on sleeping anywhere tonight. And
neither should you."

The car accelerated and so did Nelle's heartbeat, cir-
culating the heat that burned her chest to every inch
of her body. His energy was contagious, his urgency
became hers. But they had to be smart about this. She

put her hand on his leg, feeling the tendon of tightened muscle that urged the car forward.

"Bran. We've got time. We have all night. But not if we get caught."

Under her hand his leg relaxed and he eased off the gas. He breathed out next to her, slowing the vehicle down to the speed limit. She lifted her hand and he grabbed for it, bringing it back to his leg. His thumb brushed over her angled ring. "It's going to be a long drive. Tell me something interesting. Tell me about Iowa."

Even if it had been day, and there had been something to see out the window besides black trees blending into black night, Nelle wouldn't have been able to pull her attention from Bran. The whole world was the two of them alone in the car, talking in the dark. "Iowa's not interesting."

"I think hometowns deserve a bit of loyalty."

"That's what I like about Iowa, thank you very much. It's predictable. Exactly as I left it. I can't wait to get back."

"Kind of early for Christmas?"

"I'll be traveling most of next year on tour, so I'm taking some time off first. And I want the full holiday experience. Cutting down the tree, stringing lights, not just showing up for twelve hours to open presents."

"Can you have it? Now that you're Nelle?"

"Of course. It's a small town, they all know me already. Nobody bothers me there. It's home."

Bran cleared his throat. "We played a show in Des Moines, pretty sure. And then I convinced the guys to pilgrimage with me up to the Field of Dreams—you know where—"

"Dyersville. I know. Never been."

"You gotta go. It's incredible. Except—and this is a business idea worth millions, so don't steal it—they need to be selling hot dogs at that place. Or corn at least. All those stalks, green and swaying in the breeze. Imagine them roasted, unshucked, *buttered*—but I never wanted a hot dog more in my life. I would have paid top dollar for one. And not a fancy food truck hot dog with duck fat or whatever Cormac would put on it—but char-grilled by someone's kitschy-apron-wearing relative, you know?"

That was one of the things people loved about Bran Kelly—the way he used detail to draw a moment, an emotion. Nelle could see it immediately. She could see home. "Some little girls setting up a PBR stand and selling packets of ketchup—"

He shook his head, that one loose strand shaking side to side with the force. "You don't put ketchup on a hot dog. Hot dogs need mustard. Best-case scenario: pickle, peppers, tomato, onion, celery s—"

"You're describing a salad. Not a hot dog."

He looked over at her, incredulous. "You've never had a Chicago-style hot dog?"

"*That's* the line you should be using to get girls in bed."

His tongue touched the corner of his mouth as he played along. "It'll change your life."

Nelle's fingers pressed into his leg. "Big talk."

"Big—dammit!" Gravel from the road's shoulder clattered against the car's undercarriage with the rapid percussion of a snare drum. Bran swerved back across the white lines.

"You need to watch the road!"

"It's hard."

"Is it?"

He laughed. "With you distracting me." His hand left hers to turn on the radio, spinning the tuner until it picked up a signal from a local station. Familiar notes filled the car and Bran groaned, twisting the dial again.

"Hey! That's one of my favorite songs."

"You're kidding."

"Go back."

"You're really going to make me listen to my own band?"

"I am. I love 'Fly Free.' I used to—" Nelle clamped her mouth shut. Why was she about to tell Bran Kelly that?

*"Words fly off the page,"* Bran sang on the radio, while he sat in resigned silence next to her.

Nelle tried to listen. But she couldn't stay quiet. She knew the song too well. The lyrics on her tongue forced themselves out and she harmonized with the voice coming through the car's speakers.

*"Birds free from the cage, a flutter plenty heard, pen my own twenty-third."*

She'd always wondered what it meant, and she turned to ask Bran, seize her chance to find out. He had gone stiff next to her, a pained expression on his face. She'd been a guest judge on an episode of *Supermarket Star* and knew firsthand how excruciating it was to have to bear witness to someone butchering your music.

The song ended and Nelle's face flushed. She took her hand off his lap under the guise of adjusting his jacket. The air in the car had become stuffy, unbearably heavy. She tried to joke through the embarrassment. "This must be some classic rock/oldies station."

To her relief, Bran eased his tense grip on the wheel. "I'd be offended if you hadn't just implied the lasting, timeless quality of my music."

"My songs are still *current* hits," she replied, hoping another tease would dispel the rest of the awkwardness she'd created.

He checked his watch, despite the glowing time on the dash in front of them. "Tell you what. J99 is about to count down their top requests—their nine at nine—and I bet you a million dollars 'Touch Her Back' ranks higher than 'Under Water.'"

"I'm playing their Jingle Jam tomorrow night. I'll destroy you."

Bran stretched his hand across her body for her to shake. "Willing to wager on it?"

Nelle slipped her palm into his, their matching calluses scraping together. She had no doubts about winning. He might be feeling lucky, but the universe had her back. "Double or nothing I'm number one on the countdown."

His solid grip squeezed her knuckles together. "Deal."

Bran let go to change the station. The DJ's exaggerated persona blared out at them and Nelle winced. "Hey, hey, hey—we got that nine at nine starting right now with your girl—"

"Nelle," Bran finished.

"No way am I *ninth*."

"—Miss Charma with 'Drop It Down.'"

The DJ ticked off the songs, playing each one after announcing its position. Nelle bopped along with them all, confident from the get.

"Time for the number number number, two two two,

most requested song of the week. You know this one—
one of the hottest singers out there, and I do mean hot,
it's Santinooooo!"

Bran scoffed. "Is he the guy with the face tattoos?
That guy's number two?"

"You have to admit this song is catchy."

"It's synthetic." He sat up straighter, smiling as he
told her, "Let's turn this off. Forget the whole thing, I
don't want to have to take your money—"

The song ended and Nelle pumped the volume up
as the DJ returned.

"No surprise here, folks, that the number one slot
goes to an artist you can catch tomorrow night at the
Jingle Jam if you're lucky enough to have tickets—
listen all day tomorrow for the final giveaways—" Bran
beat a drum roll on the wheel "—but now it's 'Under
Water' by Nelle!"

Nelle raised her hands in triumph as her song blasted
from the speakers. She couldn't wait to play this one
live—see the thrum of it capture her fans, let it wash
over her too. She was so proud of the album she'd written, inspired by the last few years, the mix of amazing
and heart-wrenching things that had happened to her.
She'd written in hospital rooms with her dad and flown
to NYC and London to get in the studio with some of
the best producers in the business. This album repre-
sented every kind of triumph she could think of, especially over loss and uncertainty. But this song told the
story of what it felt like to go through it.

She tapped in to the music, the intentionally overwhelming sound expanding behind her vocals. There
in the car, she let herself be transported to a vivid future where an entire crowd of people were connected

together through her words. She didn't notice Bran singing next to her until the song was almost over. She
stared openmouthed. It was almost as inconceivable
as the rest of the night, that he'd know her lyrics, that
she'd get to hear him sing them.

Bran's shoulders rocked along to the staccato hook.
He took his hands off the wheel to clap as her voice
faded out.

Nelle shut the radio off. "You owe me two million
dollars."

Bran stopped clapping to guide the car through a
curve in the road. "It wasn't a fair contest—"

"You came up with it!"

"But my stuff has a different sound, J99 doesn't cater
to indie folk—"

"'Touch Her Back' is not a folk song."

"And 'Under Water' is not a pop song."

"What's wrong with pop songs?" She bristled at the
words. "It's like anything made primarily for young
women has to be downgraded—that's ingrained nonsense. That's misogyny."

"Hey, I don't care what they call my music or who
listens to it—as long as someone is listening to it. But
before production, your song was something else." He
sang again, unaccompanied, and Nelle's eyes drifted
shut to better memorize the sound of it. "*Ebb and flow,
e-e-ebb get low.* You work with Charlie, right?"

Nelle's eyes popped open. "You know Charlie?"
Charlie was Nelle's writing partner, they always col-
laborated together, it was one of Nelle's favorite parts
of the whole process, bringing something to Charlie and
discovering what they could pull out of it.

"Charlie's great," Bran agreed. "They really know

their stuff. But what did you write, before that get-low hook? What was the original lyric?"

"That was the original lyric."

He paused, his mouth pulling wide and flat. "Oh."

Her shoulders curved forward defensively. "What?"

"Nothing."

"Clearly not nothing."

"I just—did you come up with it or Charlie?"

"What does it matter?"

"That's what it's like working with other people, you know? You lose control."

"I like working with Charlie, the songs are stronger when we collaborate. We were both happy with it." The December air seeped through the car's steel frame.

"But if you were writing it yourself, do you think you would have dug deeper?"

"I *did* write it myself."

There had been a discussion. She had wanted to linger on the line, wasn't sure it conveyed precisely the feeling she'd been struggling with, but she trusted Charlie. She trusted herself. The song was a hit. Even if it wasn't up to Bran Kelly's standards. *Dug deeper.* "Dug deeper?" she repeated, the words dry like ash in her mouth. "Like 'Touch Her Back' is deep?" Nelle monotoned the lyrics, *"I wanna touch her back. Bend it low, lick it wet. I wanna touch her back. Every part of it, because she started it."*

He raised a finger. "That song was inspired by the most *base* and *consuming* of desires. And the rest of 'Under Water' was too, I can tell."

She shouldn't ask. Because she didn't want to know. "But."

"But you didn't get personal. In that hook. It might have been better—"

"Better? It was good enough to beat you."

"Yeah, on the J99 nine at nine." He finally looked at her and his smile fell, like he'd just realized she'd taken offense to what he'd said.

Bran Kelly was amazing at articulating a feeling, sharing it, making it universal. And he'd just told her she'd fallen short trying to do the same. Nelle shivered and let Bran's jacket drop to the floor in front of her.

"You're such a dickhead."

## Chapter Seven

Bran had been coasting. Now he released the gas to roll his ankle, his muscles cramping behind his shin.

Were they fighting? It felt like they were fighting. He wasn't a relationship genius, but he knew what it meant when a woman folded her arms, angled her knees away from you, and glared aggressively out a window seeing nothing.

He'd been trying to compliment her. "Under Water" was good. Really good. That's what he was trying to say. That she had something. All he'd wanted to do was offer a little advice about taking on collaborators, how they tried to push their own ideas on your music. He'd meant it as a heads-up, a warning, from someone who'd been vigilant, gotten through it without intervention.

He replaced his foot on the pedal. Warning Nelle, though, when he thought about it, wasn't entirely necessary—not once tonight had she revealed herself as someone easily pushed around.

Buzzing sounded from the wheel well across from him. Nelle bent forward and pulled a vibrating phone out of her bag.

She had to have a team. There had to be people wondering where Nelle was.

"You can answer. I'll be quiet."

She silenced the device, holding it facedown in her lap. "It's just my mom. She wants to know if I want her to make baklava or galaktoboureko."

"Gala-what?"

"Milk cake. It's my favorite."

This felt like stuff he should be writing down. Her favorite flowers, her favorite foods, her favorite songs— *his* song—when she had been singing it earlier, he'd barely been able to move. Hearing her next to him had been exhilarating and—

No. He didn't need to remember her birthday or her parents' names or her favorite anything. He had to remember that he only had tonight to get what he wanted from her. They were going their separate ways in the morning. It wasn't like he had to prepare for a celebrity *Newlywed Show*. That was the opposite of the point.

"So tell her. What you want."

"It doesn't matter—she's gonna make both no matter what I say."

He tried to catch her eye but she'd turned back to the window again, those yellow nails drumming against the hard case of her phone.

Bran shifted in his seat; he was ready to be out of this car. Ready to spend the energy that had been collecting in his body for hours now. His foot ached and he let up the gas momentarily to spin his ankle again, bend his knee. Everything was starting to feel tight and he should have been relieved when the city lights came back into view, but that easy camaraderie they'd established on the drive was gone.

Bran needed it back.

He found Nelle's hand in her lap, turned her phone

over, and clicked the screen on to display the photo he'd caught a glimpse of earlier. "Are those your parents?" Nelle stood between a dark-haired couple, both of them kissing her cheeks as she grinned with her eyes shut.

"Yeah."

"They couldn't make it in for the show tomorrow?"

She laughed, one syllable, to herself, not sounding particularly amused. "Mmm-hmm."

"They look nice. You're close to them?"

She nodded.

He'd gone from a one-word answer, to nonverbal humming, to silent agreement. The next stop on that path was her ignoring him completely.

"Nelle. Hey. I'm sorry." He squeezed her knee. "I don't know when to shut up sometimes. People scream my name. It's an occupational hazard."

She wiggled the ring on her finger. Was she going to take it off?

"That's a very male privilege: the right to talk without thinking."

Bran exhaled slowly. Conversing with Nelle was like feeling his way along a tightrope. Blind across a never-ending drop. Like being back in school where he'd never done the required reading. But at least she was talking now, even if he didn't know what she meant. "How's that?"

Nelle shrugged and they passed under a series of streetlamps, light to dark, light to dark. He'd almost forgotten the question when she said, "It's always been your world, right?"

He put his hand back on the wheel. Well, it looked like they'd be going their separate ways sooner than he'd thought. And he'd just have to deal with his *energy* himself. Certainly wouldn't be the first time. He consoled himself with what he was taking from this night: the seed of a song buried in his jacket pocket and the knowledge that they had done something that would set off a media frenzy—and that no one would ever know.

He'd have one memory secure again, when the rest were released into the wind. That was enough. Even if he'd been looking forward to the rest of the evening, locking himself in a hotel room with a woman who revved his dick like a sports car engine. Sharing this secret with Nelle was better than nothing.

"Okay, so I'll just drop you at the hotel then—"

"You can drop me down the block and I'll walk."

"I'm not going to—"

"We can't pull into the drive and go in together."

Bran whipped his head to look at her. "We're still going in together?"

"What? Bran, have you completely forgotten what's happening here? We were never going in together. I'll go up first. You check in and then come to my room instead." She gave him the number and looked hard at him, waiting for him to get on board.

"You still want to—"

"I've got the rest of my life to think about what an asshole you are. I'm not going to waste time doing it tonight."

No, Nelle didn't get pushed.

The Ferrari sped over the river that divided Chicago north and south and Bran felt the internalized sensation that he had crossed sides, to the other team's half. He curved off Lake Shore Drive's exit ramp and pulled over a block away from her hotel in the heart of the Gold Coast. The sidewalk was lit but mostly empty, the temperature dropping low enough to keep people off the streets. "I can't leave you here."

"It's a nice enough neighborhood, Bran. That ATM dispenses cupcakes." She leaned forward to shrug on her peacoat, hooked the bag handles over her elbow, and climbed out of the car. Bran swore, throwing the car into Park and jumping out after her.

"Ne—" She turned, her eyes wide with warning before he finished shouting her name. Right. He had to get a hold of himself before he gave them up.

"Take the car." A shiver racked his body as a harsh wind swept down the street. She must be freezing in those thin tights. "I'll walk. You drive."

Nelle considered the car behind him and stepped off the curb. "Okay."

He followed her back to the driver's side door, reaching in to grab his jacket and his duffel bag. On the sidewalk he layered on his sweatshirt, while she adjusted the seat and tilted the mirror with those mustard-tipped fingers. The engine growled, and he caught her smiling as she swung the car into Drive.

Something stirred low in Bran's gut at the sight of it. He needed to get to that hotel room.

It wasn't just the December chill that set him walking briskly down the block. His hand ached, clutching the bag, exposed to the winter air, and he chugged along like a steam engine, his breath a white fog in his wake.

Bran turned into the Waldorf's entrance, a Parisian-inspired motor court strung with even lines of round bulbs. The building's interior windows were capped by purple awnings and as Bran passed the brightly lit branches of the towering green Christmas tree that covered the fountain at the courtyard's center, black-jacketed valets surrounded the red Ferrari.

Bran slowed, pretending to admire his own car, hoping to stagger his and Nelle's arrivals, give her time to clear the lobby.

One of the valets whistled. "A woman that gorgeous in a car like this? I'll never get the image out of my head."

What began as a frisson of pride gained power from the cold and Bran shuddered—he'd spent too long in LA, had lost his conditioning for a Chicago winter. He hadn't even packed a real coat. Not that he'd been thinking straight when he'd packed.

A gust of warm air hit his face as he entered the hotel, and he waited for his muscles to relax their chill-induced tension. Passing under a silver starburst, he strode to the desk in the glittering black-and-white lobby.

He gave the name Kinsella, paid cash, and pulled his Sox hat as low as he could. The precautions weren't enough. The concierge handed him an envelope with the key card to his room and ten extra digits penned inside.

Part of the reason this whole night had happened—had worked—was that no one knew he was in Chicago. He hadn't seen anyone but family and clergy until today. Now a bartender knew, and so did a concierge. It was only a matter of time before someone Snapchatted him walking down the street. All he needed was a few more hours of anonymity to spend with Nelle.

Ignoring the number on his key, Bran hit the elevator button for Nelle's floor. He bounced on his heels as if to propel the rising motion. The carpet muffled his quick steps as he wound through the hall to her room, and he barely remembered to stop, pull his phone out, and keep his head down, waiting for a laughing couple to stumble past him. The coast finally clear, Bran approached Nelle's door and raised his knuckle to knock. His whole body felt stretched, a too-tight guitar string in need of tuning.

*What if she didn't answer?*

His shoulders shook as a leftover shiver reverberated through him.

The door swung open while he was still gathering his courage and Nelle stood in front of him, lower than the last time he'd seen her, having removed her boots and the bun that added two inches to her height.

"Hurry up and get in here!" She fisted the sweatshirt under his jacket and tugged him into the room.

Bran fumbled forward, catching his free hand on the wall before he crushed her into it. Their bodies pulled close, almost touching, barely apart. He lowered his nose, inhaling the scent of peonies in her dark hair.

"You're trembling." She whispered the words, even though there was no one there to overhear them.

Fifty thousand people didn't set his nerves shaking like this one woman did. It wasn't the cold, or the fear of getting caught that had him wound like this. It was Nelle. The possibility of her becoming real.

It would have been enough, to share the secret.

But he wanted more. And now was the time to get it.

# Chapter Eight

Nelle ducked under Bran's arm. "There's a fireplace, come on."

Two low, patterned armchairs faced each other in the sitting area in front of the large evenly made bed. The bed that Nelle ignored, kneeling to click on the chair-flanked fireplace.

The bed. And the fireplace.

*Heating things up*, Benj would no doubt comment when Nelle relayed the night's events.

Except. She couldn't tell Benj, could she? A secret's value decreased with every person who knew it. She was already dying to tell somebody. Would she be able to hold it back?

Bran shook out of his coat and dropped it on the floor next to his bag before claiming one of the chairs, sinking into it, and letting his knees fall wide. Nelle sat opposite him, bending forward, her elbows on her top knee, her arms and legs crossed. They regarded each other from a distance, the room silent besides the *whoosh* of gas flame under the mantel's wide molding.

She was going to have to tell Benj. Not about the secret marriage and all the private little moments in the car. But she had to share with her best friend the way Bran Kelly looked sitting across from her, out-smoldering the actual fire in the room. If she didn't, she might not be able to remember if it was real, or some new fantasy born out of years of distant pining.

"I'm still cold." Bran raised his arms, grasping the hoodie behind his neck and pulling it off. If he was so cold, he should probably stop losing layers, but Nelle wasn't going to say so. Opposite him she was growing hotter by the second, sweltering under the sweater that rose to her throat. She gulped in air. Taking off clothes seemed like a really, really good idea. Best idea all night.

He shook a hand through his rumpled hair and pushed it back into place. His mouth quirked up and he cocked his head to the side. "Come here."

Big. Dick. Energy. Eggplant-emoji energy.

That's what he had. That's what she'd tell Benj. *Bran Kelly can get it.*

Slowly she unfolded her body and stood. Reaching behind her, Nelle unzipped the leather skirt that flared around her hips and shifted it to the ground. She stepped out of the garment, pulling her sweater up and over her head.

Bran leaned forward to meet her as she stepped between his legs, her curvy silhouette on display before him. His hands went first to her wide hips, before sliding to the round ass she'd been accused of enhancing. He squeezed her roughly and she dug her fingers into his hair, tugging his head back. A guttural sound of appreciation rumbled from his throat and Nelle climbed onto his lap, eager for more, wanting to devour that sound and any other he might produce under her hands.

Her short waist was bare between navel-high tights

and a black bra, and Bran's cold hands sent a shiver through her body as he trailed them over the exposed skin. Icy knuckles brushed the underside of her breasts and Nelle gasped, her nipples pulling tight at the touch, the sensation exaggerated by the temperature. She arched forward and Bran slipped his hands under the wire of her bra, warming himself on her sensitive skin.

All at once Nelle felt the room narrowing to the chair they shared. Her body overtly aware of every little motion: the soft slip of her hair on her back, the hard lines of Bran's lap beneath her—strong thighs pulling apart to allow the rock-solid thickness of his dick to press up against her.

Bran's hands were roaming again as he pressed his cool lips to her jaw, humming a quiet breath into her ear and raising goose bumps along her shoulder. Nelle's eyes drifted shut, her arms wrapping around his neck. His hair, still smelling of winter night, tickled her chin.

And then he was pulling back, his hands running along her arms as he leaned away from her.

Nelle sat upright, straddling his hips, her head hot and dizzy, her center aching with anticipation.

Starting with the pinky of her right palm, Bran twisted off her rings, easing them over her knuckles one by one. He collected them in a pile on the table next to the chair, stopping when the angled wedding band was the only one left. Her chest rose and fell heavily as he cupped her left hand to his cheek, turning his head to kiss the palm side of the ring he'd given her.

"Why like that?" she asked, thinking back to the moment he'd put it on her finger. "Why did you want me to wear it with the angle at the bottom?"

He threaded their hands together, pulling her forward

so her chest flattened against his T-shirt. "You know what a claddagh ring is?"

She nodded, her nose grazing his. "Angel gave Buffy one on her birthday. Before they had absolutely unethical sex because he was a villain with or without a soul."

His full-bellied laugh bounced her up. "Right, so you know the heart points down—"

"When you have someone." Nelle sat up, planting her hands on his chest for balance. "It means I have you?"

Bran's blue eyes seemed to deepen. "You can have me." He paused before amending, "For the night."

Well. If they only had one night to do this, she was going to make the most of it.

Nelle bore down, grinding against his hard dick. Bran opened his mouth to groan and Nelle's lips met it, capturing the sound as her tongue rushed against his. She wanted to feel his skin against hers, soft and warm. She wanted to lick the dip of his clavicle, follow the raised veins that disappeared under his cuffed sleeves and bite at the hollow bend. Nelle pulled at his shirt, but it was tucked tightly into his pants. Craving contact, she fingered the hole she'd noticed earlier.

Bran broke away to chide her. "You're gonna rip it."

"It's already ripped."

"It's vintage."

"Take it off then, if you're so worried about it."

The room shifted as he stood. He gripped her bottom firmly as he carried her to the bed, setting her down gently, one leg at a time. Bran unbuttoned his pants, pulling his shirt loose and over his head, revealing pale skin and a triangle of dark hair between his unsculpted pecs. While his abdomen was flat, it was undefined compared to his arms, curved and hardened by muscles that were in demand every time he picked up a guitar. Nelle didn't doubt the strength, the endurance, Bran was capable of—touring was a marathon, hours of cardio every night. He owned his confidence, and she felt it like a DJ's mix, the way he would last, blending track to track, an endless build that crested in that one perfect moment when the beat dropped.

Bran lowered to his knees, pressing his mouth against the layers of nylon and satin that covered her slit. He breathed in her heat and tongued the fabric until it was saturated from both sides.

"Bran—" She gasped his name and pulled at his hair and he pressed harder against her. Nelle's knees buckled and she fell back on the bed. Bran took the opportunity to peel the tights from her legs, taking the satin underwear with them.

Reddit had not oversold his talented tongue. When Bran reapplied himself to the wet throb between her legs, the barriers stripped away, she learned the power of his mouth unfiltered. She moaned and writhed and was completely incoherent by the time he released her, pushing her knees wide and sucking at her clit until she broke. Waves of satisfaction spiked from the spot, amplifying outward.

Oh *god* she'd needed that. Something just for her. Something worth the sacrifice.

Bran's weight pressed her to the mattress and she lapped grateful, sloppy kisses on his neck, his jaw, his lips. He shifted their positions so she was on top of him again, helping her out of her bra as they kissed lazily.

Nelle sat to sweep her tangled hair back and looked down at him. Her brows furrowed and she pushed his shoulder, rising up on her knees and rolling him over between her legs. Her palms swept over his back. "Where are your tattoos?"

"What tattoos?" He groaned into the mattress as she massaged a knot of tension pushing against her fingertips.

"Guitars, women, tattoos—you missed a rock star stereotype."

"I'm not a rock star, I'm a singer-slash-songwriter now. Haven't you heard my solo stuff? Rolling Stone called *Green* a tonic and tenable folk album."

"You memorize your reviews."

"Insecure artist, remember?" He twisted onto his back and she fell forward. "I'm very flawed. But no tattoos. I've got commitment issues."

"You just married me."

"You could have done better." He kissed her neck. "I haven't come up with anything I want permanently on my body. Except maybe you." He pulled her hips down on his, her bare opening catching against the unhooked button flap above his zipper, shooting pleasure up her spine.

Nelle fought to keep her mind on the conversation. "There has to be something—the chorus of 'Fly Free'?" She'd considered that herself once before chickening out.

"My own lyrics? You really do think I'm a dickhead."

"Something about your gran then?"

"You're suggesting a tattoo for my grandmother would make me more rock and roll?"

He rubbed against her and her mind fogged with lust. "Do you ever stop talking?"

"You keep asking me questions." The sly tease in his smile was almost enough to undo her again.

This was temporary. She had to stop wasting what little time they had with words. They had talked enough.

"Good point. Let's just fuck."

Bran's eyes burned into her before he urged her off of him and rose from the bed. He wrestled a condom out of his taut pants and shoved them to the ground, removing his underwear and socks in the process.

He stood, framed by the fireplace, his dick straight and hard, straining towards her. Another win for the internet, proving it wasn't all fake news.

Bran handled the foil wrapper and knelt on the bed.

"Come here," he said again.

Nelle didn't hesitate before climbing over him. Bran held her hips as he eased her onto his dick. She gripped his shoulders, stuttering, "Ah, ah, ah," as he sank deeper inside of her. She took him to the hilt, his hands applying light force to her sides to make sure he'd filled her completely. Her breath hitched as he found the back of her.

"Okay?" Bran asked looking up from their connection to find her eyes.

"Very okay—ah!"

He lifted his hips in a thrust and her eyes closed. Wrapping one arm secure about her waist and snaking the other up her back, he held her to him, his grip at the base of her neck, gentle but firm. They moved together slowly, her knees drawing tight to his toes and his knees pushing her feet wide. She sank even lower onto him, breathless from the fit, the stretch of accommodating his substantial cock.

Her breasts grazed his chest as she rose and fell. His hips held all the rock and roll she needed. They kissed periodically, coming together in whispers of appreciation, but their mutual concentration was on the heat building between them, winding them up. She was right about his endurance, the momentum of pleasure lasting and lasting.

Nelle's back was hot, slick with sweat, and that one famous strand of hair that hooked over Bran's forehead had darkened and stuck to his face. His eyes locked on to hers as her exhausted pussy finally tensed. Her muscles clenched around him and his mouth opened as though her grip pained him.

The force of her second Bran Kelly orgasm nearly tore her in half. Like the throbbing bass of a festival amp, pulsing through every inch of her body, overwhelming her from the inside out.

Her legs and feet cramped and she could do nothing but continue to ride him as he finished, gripping her neck and gasping her name.

*Antonella.*

*Nella.*

*Nelle.*

## Chapter Nine

Bran rested his eyes, but he didn't sleep. He lay on his back, left arm hooked under his head, Nelle in the nook of his other shoulder. He strummed his right hand over her back, where it dipped in a low curve, the points of her spine reminding him of the even nailhead trim he'd thumbed earlier in the evening.

It was always a gamble, staying after sex. Sure, sometimes it meant *more* sex, but sometimes it meant nonstop talking, requests for tickets, confessions of feelings they couldn't possibly have because they didn't know him, just his cock. Bran never knew what a woman might want from him after. And Nelle was no different.

The longer the comfortable silence lasted, the less comfortable it felt to Bran.

"No sleeping," he reminded her with a nudge.

She sighed across his chest. "I'm performing tomorrow."

"And I'm performing tonight."

"I forgot, this is Bran Kelly: One Night Only. Should I be clapping?"

"Only if you enjoyed it."

"Clearly, I enjoyed it."

He knew that. He had felt it—how she had contracted

around him, wrapping and squeezing as tight as a boa constrictor. And just as dangerous, because his first rational thought after spilling into the condom was that he needed to feel it again. And again. But they only had tonight. That was the deal. Their secret was worthless if they got caught.

"Bran?" Nelle's fingertips circled through the coarse hair of his chest. "Did something happen to you today?"

"Yeah, I got married." He clasped his hands together around her.

She turned to look at him, her chin at his collarbone, and he resisted the urge to squirm under her scrutiny. "I mean before. Why were you off the grid? How did you not know about the Cleffy nod?"

He loosened his hands with the intention to reach up and shake his hair, but Nelle's fingers were already sifting through it. She was ahead of him. There was no point in trying to keep this from her.

"My gran's funeral was this morning. I was trying to tie up some loose ends when you texted."

His hands broke apart as she sat up, pushing hard against his ribs. "Bran. Why didn't you tell me that?"

"It didn't come up."

"Yes, it did." She ticked off the times on her fingers. "Your gran told you about secret marriages, you lived with your gran in the K streets—"

It was actually terrifying to realize that she had *really* listened to him. He made a mental note to try not to say dumb things around her. Things he'd regret and be unable to take back because Kellys were notoriously shit at admitting they were wrong.

"Okay—I didn't want to talk about it." He tried to lie still, look relaxed, but feeling tightened his gut, winding him up into a sitting position. "I really wanted to not talk about it."

Her hand slipped to his thigh but a second later she clutched it back. "I can't believe I took advantage of someone grieving for their—"

"You did not take advantage of me. If anything, it was me using you for a distraction—which I did not." Not for that. Bran lifted Nelle's hand to his mouth, gliding the smooth curves of her glossed nails across his lips. "Look. I loved my gran—she practically raised me. She was my biggest fan and I'm going to miss her—but she was ready to go."

"What was she like?" A wince or something like it passed over her face. "I never met my grandmothers."

That honesty in her voice—Bran couldn't resist it, his walls bent to serve her. "You wanna know about Faye Kelly?" Nelle nodded, squeezed his hand, and the details stuttered out of him. Things nobody mentioned at the funeral. Things that made her *his* gran. "She loved coffee." The house always smelled like it. In the winter the kitchen windows would fog over with the steam from the kettle. "She had a little French press. Brewed two cups a day. Morning, and night—the evening one she 'watered down' with whiskey." *For my health*, she'd say with a shrug, then raise the glass, winking as she added, *Sláinte!*

"She liked clear mugs. I got in the habit of buying her a set every year for her birthday because she'd carry them with her and lose track of them." She'd leave one on a neighbor's porch or—more likely—put it on the roof of the car as she was loading in her purse and coat, forget about it, and come home to smashed glass in the driveway. "I got her a travel mug one year. She hated it." Gran's voice floated through his head, thinned from age but spiked with conviction: *It keeps coffee too hot! Undrinkable, Bran—only thing it's useful for is leaving some on the counter so I have a hot cup when I get home.*

"She liked things her way," he said after a moment, savoring the memory. Nelle's eyes had gone a little watery and she squeezed his hand again. Bran cleared his throat and tried to change gears. "She liked you."

"Me?" The misty look cleared from her face, replaced by surprise.

"That first single, 'Say Yes.' That was her jam."

"Your gran liked a club beat?" Nelle lowered her chin skeptically.

"Oh yeah, Faye Kelly could get down. Lots of knees and hands." He was gratified by Nelle's laugh. "I didn't waste my time with her. I don't want to waste my time with you either."

"It's a waste—telling me about yourself?"

"It's a waste for you to worry about me. I'm fine."

"Oh sure. You're a big boy who can take care of himself?"

"You know I'm a big—"

She laughed again before glaring at him and he touched one of her yellow nails to his tongue, half expecting to taste fancy lemonade like he had when they'd kissed in the car.

That's what they should be doing. Not talking about how he'd had a hard week. How it was only going to get worse.

Nelle looked thoughtful again. "It must have been comforting to be with family today, to remember her together."

Comforting. Not exactly. Not with his father, standing at the pulpit, appropriating Gran's words, "Mom always said: *We Kellys may fight, but we always unite.*"

Bran exhaled, letting Nelle's hand go. "I'm gonna shower, you rest up for the encore."

Nelle pulled his face to hers. "I'm sorry. For your loss."

He nodded, his throat tight. But the shower eased his tension. The water rained down on him and he turned his face into it, feeling the spray against his eyelids, his cheeks, a quiet sting that lessened the longer he endured it.

After roughing a towel over his hair, Bran pulled on a plush white robe and returned to the bedroom, expecting to find Nelle where he'd left her. The blanket and sheets were in respectable shambles, but the bed was empty.

Bran opened his mouth to call her name and snapped it shut. Her voice reached him from the door, just on the other side of the wall. He leaned into it, listening.

"Was there anything else you needed?" That voice was familiar, sweet as pastel sugar coating dark licorice.

"This is it—thank you so much," Nelle responded sincerely. "I know it's late and cold and—"

"Of course, the hotel is happy to be of service."

Bran waited to hear the door close before stepping into the sitting area. "Who was that?"

"I got snacks."

The white T-shirt that landed at the top of her thighs was his. When she tried to breeze past him, he caught her around the middle. "Are you not the snack?"

"You need fuel. You've made promises."

"So what did we get? That's not room service—"

Her shoulder pulled up as he nuzzled into her neck. "Chicago-style hot dogs."

Her face reddened the tiniest bit when she said it, as if she was embarrassed, having been caught in some sentimentality. But honestly a Chicago-style hot dog after sex was just about the hottest, most romantic thing anyone had ever done for him.

The yellow-striped paper bag rustled as she released it into his grabbing hand. "I would have gone myself, but I think we used up our luck—"

He paused, his hand halfway in the bag. That's what she felt bad about? Who was this girl? "You used your fame to make some poor bellhop go out and get us hot dogs. For shame. The worst abuse of power I've ever heard. Did you demand that the desk lady deliver them up here, personally?"

She snatched the bag back. "No. There was another guest on the ninth floor she was on her way to check on, actually. So I'm not the only one—what?"

"Ninth floor?" He laughed. "It was the desk attendant with the blue eye shadow?"

Nelle nodded and he grinned.

"Yeah, me, she's going to check on me."

"What would—oh. Right."

Her eyes darted to the ground and her shoulders stiffened, making the whole thing a lot less amusing.

Bran pushed his hands into the robe's pockets. "I didn't invite her. She slipped me her number with my key."

"And you didn't mention it?"

"It wasn't worth noting."

"People do it all the time?" Her eyes pinned him to the spot, daring him to remind her: present company included. The intense set of her mouth loosened into a frown. "So she's going to your room. But you aren't there?"

"Would you prefer I were?"

"I mean, she's going to wonder where you are."

"She's not going to wonder anything. She's going to knock and when I don't answer she'll think I'm drunk and passed out and she'll leave."

Nelle paced, and Bran worried about the delicate steamed buns as her grip crushed the air out of the hot dog bag. "Unless she uses her key card to let herself in."

He'd tell her that was insane, but it had happened before.

Bran let his jaw drop open. "You're right! Help me with this window—I'll climb up the balconies back into my room—" He was wrestling with the slatted shutters when she tugged on his arm.

"Stop, okay—I get it. I'm being over the top and you're competitive."

Bran widened his legs, bringing his eyes down to her level. He set his hands on her hips. "There is nothing to worry about here. The only thing we have to do is get me out of the room without anyone seeing. That's it. And it wouldn't be the first time I snuck out of—forget that anecdote, pretend I said something reassuring. I'll leave unseen. Until then, we're in the room. Let's not bring them in here. Keep them out there." He nodded to the door. "They don't belong in the room. That's the whole point. The room is nice. The room has been the best part."

Nelle worried her bottom lip and bent her ankle. "I'm in your shirt—if she—"

"I was wearing layers—she didn't see it."

"But your jacket, and the bag—" She gestured help-lessly to his duffel on the floor next to the chair.

"She couldn't have seen them from the door. Okay? Nelle, we've got this." He brushed her hair back and tilted her head up. "I got you."

That generic hotel silence rang in his ears and Nelle shivered.

She put her hands over his on her cheeks, seeming to forget the bag of hot dogs.

He inhaled and closed his eyes. "Those smell amaz-ing."

"We should eat them. Before they get cold."

"You're cold."

"This shirt is thin."

Very thin, her nipples showing dark through the fabric like it wasn't even there. Bran swallowed and dropped his hands to his sides. Food first.

Settling herself on the rug next to the fire Nelle opened the bag and offered him a hot dog wrapped in see-through paper. He peeled it back to reveal a mildly smashed dog, the mustard and relish running together, but the tomato and peppers were still tucked safely into the bun. Bran waited for Nelle to take the first bite. She angled her head, searching for the right entry point. Then she closed her eyes and went for it, crunching through the pickle, onions falling sideways. Forgetting the chair, he lowered himself next to her instead, wait-ing for her to open her eyes.

Her face flushed when she caught him staring. "Is it the phallic nature of the hot dog or are you one of those guys who gets off on a girl wearing your clothes?"

"Take it off and we'll see."

"Bet you'd like that." She took another bite. "I'll try not to spill on it, if that's the problem."

"You're a gesture person."

"What does that mean?"

Bran took a bite and chewed to avoid the question, but her patience outmatched him. His face heated as she watched him. Or maybe it was just the hot peppers. "You like to do things for people."

"Yeah, I do." She lifted her hand, hesitated, and then wiped mustard off his cheek.

They ate side by side, their backs warmed by the fire, the bed staring back at them across the room.

Nelle cleaned herself with a paper napkin, balled it up, and replaced it in the bag. She looked at his duffel again, probably still wondering if the desk lady had seen it. He almost choked in surprise when she asked, "You're traveling without a guitar?"

Bran coughed and swallowed. "Short trip, didn't need it," he lied. God, she noticed everything. Even what was missing. A few months ago he'd have forgone clothes and traveled only with the guitar if he'd had to. It was vastly more important cargo to a musician, a songwriter. But there had been no point in lugging it with him. Not when he hadn't played it in weeks, when the music refused to flow from his fingers.

He finished the hot dog and lay down, resting his head on her inner thigh, not meeting her eyes.

"You're having trouble writing, though, right? Hence the mind clearing?" Her fingers played in his hair, untangling the wet strands.

Bran didn't answer, busy lifting the edge of his shirt and rubbing his nose over the soft skin between her legs. Grasping the back of her thigh, he bridged her leg, opening her silky pink insides to his curious tongue. He'd deal with that tomorrow, tonight he'd deal with her.

After a minute under his mouth, Nelle tensed and squirmed. "The hot peppers—"

He pulled back. "Should I stop?"

Her hand in his hair urged him back against her. "No fucking way."

The room was dark, the fire glowed yellow, they had more night left. He helped her strip out of his shirt and she untied his robe. Their kiss tasted of salt and spice. Reaching sideways to drag his jacket closer, Bran freed another condom from the button-flap chest pocket. And then he was inside of her again, thrusting over her, the flames lighting his back. Tangled hands above their heads, in her hair, in his. He kept a slow, languid pace as she writhed under him, building the heat even as his muscles burned from the exertion.

Later she'd prove to him there was a reason he'd been obsessed with her mouth for the better part of a year. Knowing that he had been right about it wasn't going to make it any easier to walk away.

The room was nice. He wasn't leaving it until he had to.

## Chapter Ten

"Make it stop."

Nelle flailed for a pillow, curling around it and burying her face in the soft fluff. Her hair hurt where it had been flattened to the bed and her eyes felt coarse like sour candy as she squeezed them tighter to block out the light. The bed shook as Bran fumbled towards the sound, a phone rattling against something as it rang and rang and rang.

"It's just Aya. Again."

Nelle tested the name with her groggy tongue. "Aya." Hoping he didn't note the hint of possessiveness in her tone, she continued, "Do you need to tell *her* about the celibacy?"

Bran fell back into the bed and she bounced, loosening her hold on the pillow long enough for him to grab it away from her. "Aya is my team. Manager, agent, publicist—"

"Those are all different jobs." Nelle unfurled, pulling at a triangle of sheet that had tornadoed between her feet.

"Not for Aya. Now I know that she's hounding me to congratulate me on my Note nominations—"

"I cannot with the complaints in that sentence."

She squinted into sky blue eyes. Bran drew up one cheek to smile at her, a perfectly lopsided look that twisted her stomach more than it should have for some- one who had seen the most unseemly emotions take res- idence on his features last night. He tugged at the sheet, revealing one of her breasts to the sunlight streaking in through the blinds and covering it with his mouth in- stead. He was shameless, insatiable, and he had to go.

"Bran Kelly, they've turned on the house lights, time to unplug and move on to the—ah!—next town."

"This is the last stop on my farewell tour, let me play a little longer." He nipped at her tightly budded peak and she bucked her hips in response, her sore muscles screaming at her to just stop moving.

"What time is it?"

He rolled over her, his torso pressing her into the mattress as he reached for his watch on the nightstand.

"There's a phone right next to you," she said with the air that hadn't been crushed from her lungs.

"I like watches. It's almost noon. What time do you have to be at the jam?"

"I think I have sound check at one? I have to get mov- ing. And you should have been out of here hours ago. Bran, are you listening to me?"

He wasn't. His mouth had moved to her neck, suck- ing on the skin just below her earlobe. She put her hand on his shoulder, with the intent of pushing him away, but it slipped up, her fingers digging into the soft mess of his hair and urging him closer. She arched under him and Bran groaned, grinding into her, the evidence of his interest hard and demanding.

"You're not human," she moaned.

"Think of it like my last night on earth—"

"It isn't night anymore. It's midday. And I don't know how you're going to get out of here—"

He was inching the sheet lower. "I'm much more concerned about getting back in there."

Nelle released his hair and pushed at his chest, her fingers curling into the dip of his collarbone. She stared up at him, mesmerized by the reality of him in the daylight. His hair had dried wavy and wild, looking like a beach after a storm, and she had a sudden thrill that this was what Bran Kelly looked like unfinished, behind closed doors. Then there was the smell of her shampoo coming off of him—she breathed in peonies and felt her chest contract. Impossible wetness warmed her aching, exhausted center and Bran must have caught the melting conviction in her eyes because he grinned again and swept the sheet out of the way.

"Antonella!" The rattling phone had nothing on the *bang bang bang* of Benj pounding on the hotel room door. "You better be in there naked and not murdered!"

Bran glanced in the direction of the sound with a frown. "There wasn't anything on Reddit about me murdering someone, was there? People keep bringing it up like it's a thing. It's not a thing."

Nelle reached up to stroke the bristle of stubble on his cheeks. "You're a bit of a Salinger lately, what do you expect?"

"Salinger was workin—" He shook his head, changing his argument. "Salinger didn't kill people."

His arm trapped her waist as she scooted to the end of the bed. "Get off—"

"I was trying to."

Nelle had to close her eyes, it was the only way to be sure that smile didn't get to her. She could still feel it, pressed into her shoulder blade, along with his knuckles tripping over each knob of her spine. She lunged blindly forward as the knocking continued, opening her eyes only when she reached the safety of the little closet off the bathroom. A foolish glance back at the bed revealed Bran had rolled to his back, crossed his legs at the ankles, and locked his hands behind his head. His dick stood tall, beckoning her back to the rumpled sheets. Naked and washed in sun, he was every inch the sex god he claimed to be—he proved to be—and her resolve to get him out of the bed faltered.

"An-to-nel-la!" Benj was going to break the damn door down.

"Get dressed," Nelle hissed, shrugging into her bra. She called in the direction of the door, "Hold on, Benj!"

"So you're alive, then?" came the retort from her best friend. "Just your phone is dead? Do you know what time it is?"

"Just. Hold on! One minute!"

Nelle stumbled around the closet, finding a pair of leggings and an oversized cable-knit sweater. She turned to scold Bran again as she yanked the sweater over her head and slammed into his chest.

That frantic panic eased out of her as he stood over her, blocking the light from the other room.

"We got this," Bran said quietly, freeing her hair from the sweater's neck. "I got you."

"Why are you so calm?"

"Eggplant emoji. She already knew. Just let her in. I'll get out of here and we'll…"

They would nothing. This was the end of it. That's what they'd agreed. One night. And a morning, that was bonus. The real victory was the secret, if they could keep it. She should be glad. And she would be, as soon as he was gone, and she was sure no one had seen. That worry had to be the reason her stomach tightened, twisted like the sheets behind him.

Bran kissed the side of her head. "Let her in." But he didn't pull away. He breathed her in again, a tingle spreading across her scalp. "You smell amazing."

"I smell like sex. My hair smells like sex."

"You should have showered with me." His voice dropped low, a growly whisper that revealed his own regret about the missed opportunity.

Nelle realized that they were swaying, inertia growing between them as their bodies pushed closer. Her head went fuzzy, her eyelids weighed down by his gravity.

"ANTO*NELLA*!"

Bran stepped back and Nelle blinked.

Then she was in motion, swinging around the wall dividing the bed area from the door's short entryway, fingertips dragging across textured wallpaper. Nelle ushered Benj in through the narrowest gap she could and shut the door with a swift click, her hand flat against the surface. Her eyes widened, her heart beating double time at the one ring on otherwise bare fingers. Snatching back her hand, she stretched the sleeve over it and turned to face her best friend.

Benj, wearing almost the exact same outfit as her, was scanning the room, clocking the robe laid like a bearskin rug by the fireplace, the man's jacket crumpled next to it, and—Benj stepped forward to peer at the bed—the sheets pulled almost completely off the mattress that said enough.

Slipping behind her friend, Nelle made for the chairs

by the fire. She managed to shove a few decoy rings over her fingers before Benj completed a full-circle turn to find her.

Eyes glittering with triumph, Benj whispered, "He's still here."

*I know*, Nelle mouthed. She stooped to collect a condom wrapper and another condom wrapper. Bran had a knack for making contraception appear out of every garment of clothing he owned. She wasn't complaining, but she couldn't leave them littering the floor like this for the cleaning staff to find. She bundled them together and thrust them into the empty hot dog bag.

Holding the bag close to her chest she stopped in front of Benj. "I need you to help me get him out of here without anyone seeing."

"You need to tell me what happened in this room last night."

"Please, Benj—scope out the hallway, hold the elevator. Text me when it's clear and I'll send him out."

Benj held up her hand, only her pinky extended. "If I do this, you will tell me every depravity you and Bran Kelly engaged in."

Twisting her pinky around Benj's, Nelle nodded, desperation tightening her throat.

"Like I lived it." Benj shook the knot of their fingers and was gone just as Bran came through the bathroom wearing a dark red flannel buttoned to the top and carrying his bag. Pancakes, Nelle thought immediately. They should be eating pancakes and there should be melted butter and sticky syrup. Those blue eyes hit her again and Nelle looked away, collecting the rest of the trash and excavating through her discarded clothing to find her phone.

Bran hitched up his jeans and sat to fit his feet into the suede oxfords he'd worn the night before. He was head to toe touchable—soft but durable. Nelle sat opposite him, pulling his jacket onto her lap. She smoothed the denim, her hand finding the pocket gap and sliding inside. It was her last chance to read the coaster—but her fingers closed over a pair of sunglasses instead, mangled, she saw, when she brought them out. Wrong pocket.

He sat back and sighed as she twisted the bent sunglasses back into shape. "I know I was confident last night, but I'm trying to figure out how we're going to do this now."

The phone in her lap buzzed. "That's Benj. She's holding the elevator and the hall is empty."

"Oh." He opened his mouth and closed it. "You got me, I guess."

She flicked her eyes to the door behind him. The end game. "You should—"

"Right." Bran stood, patting his back pockets, gathering his things. He pulled the Sox hat over his hair and accepted the sunglasses, sliding them over those blue eyes, closing himself off. "You fixed them."

"They weren't broken." She gave him his jacket too, all the final pieces of himself to take on his way. Her hands were empty. And Bran was going.

"Your car key!"

Bran paused, his hand on the door's metal latch. "Keep it. Have your accomplice park my ridiculous ride somewhere near the venue and I'll pick it up later."

"You don't have to do that—the valet guys won't remember—"

His mouth quirked up. "The gorgeous woman in the

gorgeous car? Yeah. They will. And—" he shifted his grip on the bag "—I was thinking of coming anyway. I want to see you perform."

"Yeah?"

"Yeah. I mean, I know we can't...talk while we're there. But. I'd like to watch—if that's okay?"

"That's okay."

"Okay."

Her phone buzzed again and she held it up for him to see. Bomb, clock, explosion.

"Time's up," he said.

She nodded.

And he left.

"Bran Kelly rocked your fucking world."

Benj wasn't wrong. But she needed to keep her voice down. Nelle swiveled in the makeup chair, making sure the door to the hall was closed. Otherwise, anyone walking through the concert's backstage could overhear them.

Completing her spin, Nelle covered her yawn with the back of her hand and sank lower in the chair. The bulbs surrounding the mirror were too bright and she careened away from them.

Benj's reflection watched her. "How was your nap? Are you going to be able to do this tonight?"

"Just patch me up and get me out there, Coach."

Concealer, highlighter, gloss—Nelle would be fine. Once she got onstage, instinct would kick in. She could already feel it, the energy starting to swell in the arena. Her personal favorite drug.

Benj produced a small fruit from her bag. "Open an orange."

"I'm not hungry."

"First of all, you don't eat a clementine to feel full any more than you would take a shot of mimosa to get drunk. It barely qualifies as food. Second, I didn't tell you to eat it. I told you to open it. You wouldn't believe what an orange signifies—creativity, enthusiasm, success, sexuality, *freedom*. And the smell reduces stress. Get those essential oils in the air. I'd buy you a spray from Goop, but it's more cost-effective to get a bag of Cuties from Costco."

"Should I return the jade yoni egg I got you for Christmas, and just get you a mini avocado instead?"

Benj put the orange on the counter next to the open eyeshadow palette. "Bran fucking Kelly," she muttered, getting to work on Nelle's tired hair.

Bran fucking Kelly, indeed.

Benj froze, her hands on either side of Nelle's head. "Did he—"

"No. Not in my hair."

"I'll find out if you're lying when I try to get a comb through here."

"I told you everything that happened."

Nelle's head snapped back as Benj teased the top of her hair. "You told me the bare minimum—and then clammed up, claiming you needed vocal rest."

"I'm performing tonight—" Nelle winced as Benj twisted her hair into a voluminous, crown-high ponytail.

"Oh like that mattered to you when you were shrieking Bran Kelly's name and deep throating his—"

A burst of sound signaled the door opening and Benj cut off, her lips flattening.

One of the event coordinators entered the dressing

room. She was blessedly distracted, with an earpiece connected by a wire to a radio chirping on her hip as she reviewed the phone in her hand. "Nelle? We're doing bonus content for YouTube, can you come sit in the lounge for an interview segment?"

"Let me check." Nelle pulled up the group chat that included her publicist and managers, and sent a text. That was the condition of her solo trip to Chicago. That she wouldn't do anything without approval. Nelle touched the point of her wedding band. As long as it stayed a secret, she didn't have anything to worry about—and that twinge of guilt? It didn't compare to the flood of warmth she rode seeing the ring on her finger.

Her phone buzzed with a response from Mina. "Yeah, that's fine," she told the coordinator.

A half hour later, wearing a tight long-sleeved navy shirt under a red-and-navy-checked pinafore, Nelle sat on a black leather sectional holding a microphone in her lap.

"Just one more minute," a production assistant assured her, and Nelle smiled.

"No problem."

She recrossed her legs and leaned back. It was hard to make anything out beyond the burning set lights, and she had the distinct feeling that she was on display for the rest of the people in the room who got to exist in shadowy anonymity. She should be used to the feeling, but today it set her on edge, so different from the intimate night she'd spent in the quiet hotel room with Bran.

Bran.

Her eyes narrowed at movement between the tripods, a familiar silhouette passing between them. Someone tall, someone who moved with the confidence that eyes would find him. Someone who brought a hand up to mess and smooth his hair in one languid motion.

And then she was standing, leaving the microphone on the couch.

"I need some water," she told the PA, stepping over the cables taped to the floor.

Her vision dimmed on the other side of the lights but she found the shape of him over by a folding table set with compartmentalized containers of dry vegetables and carafes of too-hot coffee.

Bran "I got you" Kelly. He looked cool as hell, yet seeing him inspired nothing but heat. Especially that memory of the flames at her back, the spicy tingle his tongue spread through her. He'd found time to brush his hair straight, the one rogue curl curving over his forehead. She grabbed a cup and poured hot water into it to keep her hands occupied. Her phone buzzed in her pocket but she ignored it, reaching into the other one to remove his car key.

"I don't know if you remember, but we met at the Note Awards last year." She put the key down next to a plate of oversized cookies. Her gaze followed his hand as he reclaimed it.

"Yeah, I remember. Nice to see you again."

She scanned a plastic dish filled with tea bags, flicking them back one at a time, like perusing records. "Are you performing tonight? I didn't know you were in town."

"No, just wanted to stop by, see the show."

The humor lacing his voice pulled her eyes to his and then to the last bag of organic peppermint tea pinched between his fingers. She took it.

Their eyes held and she forgot how tea bags worked,

submerging the whole paper envelope in her cup. Laughter flickered across his face but he frowned a moment later, pulling his phone from his pocket. "Aya—"

His manager's voice was loud enough for Nelle to make out clearly. "Where have you been, Kelly?"

"Busy." He raised his eyebrows at Nelle and she fought her blush, making it worse.

"That's great. Did you decide about—"

His voice cooled. "Not yet."

"Okay. Well. Then let's talk about your other financial concerns: like what the fuck is this Cartier charge, Kelly? Another watch?"

Bran disappeared into the hall and a PA called Nelle to the set. "Nelle, Santino, we're ready for you."

Nelle settled on the couch again, placing her "tea" by her feet. Santino, another established indie-rocker who'd failed to beat her on the countdown last night, sat next to her, his arm over the back of the couch. They ran in the same circles so his smile was easy as he looked her over.

"What up, Nelle—where you been? I haven't seen you in a minute." Santino's tan skin glowed under the set lights, the powdery residue of concealer under his brown eyes. What looked like a flame tattoo swirled over one of his brows.

"Studio, European press, photo shoots. A few festivals," she answered distractedly, her mind snaking out of the room, following Bran Kelly down the arena's tunneled halls. How was it Nelle still wasn't satisfied— after the size of her helping last night, how could she still want more Bran Kelly?

"You coming to LA soon?" Santino let his knee bounce against her leg.

A man with snowflakes etched into his fade lowered himself on the other side of the couch, his hand out. "Hey, sorry to keep you waiting. Chris Kidd, DJ CK."

His voice was familiar, even without the megaphone affect he'd used on the radio last night.

Nelle shifted forward and shook his hand. "You do the nine at nine, right?"

"I do—did you catch it last night?"

"Nine at what?" Santino extended his hand to Chris next, closing the inch of space that separated him from Nelle.

"Nine at nine—'Under Water' was number one last night."

Chris laughed. "'Under Water' is number one every night. That song won't quit."

The PA appeared again, nodding at Chris. He turned on his radio voice and the cameras started rolling. It was a short interview, the DJ asking both of them about their holiday plans, their favorite Christmas songs, who would win in a snowball fight. Nelle didn't see the last question coming and it brought a hot panic to her face.

Chris turned to her with a wink. "We hear you've been enjoying the local flavors."

"What?"

"Insiders report you had a special delivery to your room last night."

That flush of panic turned quickly to simmering frustration. This was exactly what she and Bran had talked about. How nothing, not even the most mundane details of their lives, were off-limits to the press. Nelle forced herself to answer. "The Chicago-style hot dog is a game changer."

Chris laughed again and threw to the camera, reminding watchers to subscribe to the J99 channel for more behind the scenes at the Jingle Jam. Nelle was up almost before he finished. In the hall, she lowered her head over her phone as she walked. Her thumbs flashed over the keyboard before she realized that her publicist had texted. Just before she'd sat down. That buzz in her pocket when she'd been talking to Bran. She included a link to the blog article, but the headline was enough. Nelle didn't bother clicking it.

Back in the dressing room Benj handed her the orange without a word and Nelle broke through the mottled wax skin with her thumbnail, taking a deep breath of the citrus that filled the air. There was nothing she could do about it. And no one had mentioned Bran. So this was just one more speculation she would endure. Nelle sipped a fresh tea, warmed her voice, and focused on the show. By the time the event coordinator returned for her, the energy of the crowd crackled in her veins like a Geiger counter.

Being onstage was a radioactive feeling, hot and intoxicating, lighting her up from the inside. Her focus narrowed with every step that brought her closer to it. Her heart pounded to the beat of Santino's last song as she paced in the wings for her turn. Someone handed her a guitar and she leaned over it, pick between her teeth, to check the tuning.

When she took the stage, everything else fell away. It was like skydiving—the crowd's screaming an indistinguishable roar in her ears. Adrenaline sharpened her mind—and for a moment there was a heart-stopping fear of plummeting. She clutched the guitar, strummed the first notes of "Under Water," and it was like pulling the cord on her parachute. All she had to do now was let herself drift back to earth, enjoying the view.

With one chorus left, Nelle stopped singing, confident the energized crowd would belt the lyrics back to her.

"Your turn!" she shouted, stepping away from the microphone stand. The audience surged after her, screaming at the top of their lungs, *"Under water, sinking farther, cheeks salt wet, can't get over it!"*

Nelle whooped, playing the last notes even as the cheers drowned them out. She lingered on the stage, not ready to step out of the blaring lights. Her heart pounding, she wanted to keep soaring, keep the rush of wind in her ears.

"Can I do one more?" she asked into the mic, before the wild feeling left her. She looked to the side for some jam hand to give her the go-ahead. The audience hollered and the event coordinator held up her hand signaling Nelle could have five more minutes. Nelle grinned. "I'm gonna do another." Her hands were already plucking out the melody, one of the first songs she had ever learned, one she practiced on the long drives to perform on little state fair stages, gazing out the window at Iowa's green hills.

"This song's been stuck in my head since I landed. It's by a local band. Feel free to sing along if you know it."

Of course they did. "Crash" had been Judith From Work's biggest single.

Nelle's backup band caught the beat and the crowd was with her from the first verse. Her eyes shut as she sang.

*"It's cracking and it's breaking,*
*The ground beneath us shaking,*
*I'm giving and you're taking,*
*We're gonna smash,*
*You wanna clash?*
*So watch me crash."*

And then somehow the crowd was screaming louder. A wave of excitement pressed them forward, overflowing in her direction. Only the railings of balconies, the rows of abandoned, temporary chairs barely held them back. Nelle was lost in the music, the way the notes transported her through time, back to her little bedroom, under the glow of fairy lights twisted around her bedframe, this song playing through her earbuds—the memory so strong she could almost hear the original recording over her cover.

No, she *did* hear the original.

Another guitar joined hers, practiced fingers taking over the chords as naturally as hearts beat. Nelle opened her eyes as the smell of Bran Kelly filled the air. He leaned towards the microphone, inches from her face, the raw rasp of his voice loud and clear, but all she heard were the echoes of her name from his mouth, heavy in her ear. Chills rolled through Nelle's body as he finished the second verse and she launched automatically back into the chorus again, Bran singing with her, their voices tangling as easily as their bodies had last night, fitting together seamlessly.

She was singing "Crash." Onstage. With Bran Kelly.

And he was smiling that one-sided grin at her, and even though they were in a room with thousands of people holding their cameras high, that smile was just for her. He lunged back for a quick riff on the guitar and then forward again to share the microphone with her, close enough that his most famous lock of hair brushed her forehead.

It was a dream. It had to be, she'd wake up when they finished the song, open mouths drawing out the last line—

*So watch me crash.*

It wasn't until the confetti cannon blurred her vision, the crowd cheering loud enough to shake the arena's foundation, that Nelle felt the sweat she'd earned onstage turn cold. She and Bran left the lights behind. She fumbled to unplug her guitar and ignored the people clapping Bran on the back, moving on as soon as she had freed herself. *She* remembered their deal: one night, and then as much distance as they could put between them. That deal, that secret—keeping it mattered, at least to her.

But he caught up with her in the hall, pulling her into an empty room.

"What the fuck was that?" She shrugged him off, and they stared at each other, breathing heavy, twin guitars slung across their backs.

"You were playing my song—I just—I wanted to sing with you."

"That's great, Bran. Did you forget that we're trying not to be seen together?"

He twisted his hair up and forgot to bring it back down. "I'm sorry—I got—"

"Do you even want this to be a secret? Or are you trying to play me?"

"How can you ask me that?"

"You just made a huge scene, how can I not?"

"You were singing *my* song to a sea of iPhones. That isn't a scene? That doesn't link us?"

She gripped the strap at her chest. She couldn't explain why she'd decided to do that. "Your concierge already told some blogger I had hot dogs delivered to my room last night, Bran."

"But they don't know about us—"

She laughed. "No, the spin on that one is disproving my ever-so-flattering plastic surgery rumors by implicating my binge eating as the reason my ass is so 'thicc.'"

Bran's jaw tensed. "Neither of us want this in the press—we're on the same team—"

"No, we aren't. We can't be. Because if this gets out, you'll be the hero who fucked a pop star, and I'll be the slutty punchline. I'll be the cliché."

"That's not fair."

Nelle had to get out of this room before someone saw them together. It had finally hit her, how much more at stake she had than Bran. She glanced into the hallway and then back at him. Her chest heaved up and down, the guitar on her back tapped against her hamstring as she let herself sink into those clear blue eyes one last time.

She stepped backwards into the hall, shaking her head. "Of course it's not fair—but you know how this works. And you just gave them a lead."

The last image she'd have of him would be the rush of emotion in his eyes, the one step he took to follow her, and the way his fists clenched as he held himself back.

Bran FUCKING Kelly

Wed, Mar 21, 6:03 pm

LA?

NYC : (

Sat, Jul 14, 3:47 pm

London (praying hands emoji)

Mexico City
(Taco beer guitar)

Fri, Dec 7, 1:13 pm

Chicago?

Chicago.
[...]

Wed, Mar 21, 6:03 pm

LA?

NYC : (

Sat, Jul 14, 3:47 pm

London (praying hands emoji)

Mexico City
(Taco beer guitar)

Fri, Dec 7, 1:13 pm

Chicago?

Chicago.

## Chapter Eleven

"We should have gone." Cormac stretched his leg onto the upholstered ottoman that served as Bran's coffee table. A U-shaped sectional fit around the tufted square, and an oversized TV loomed above them between two doorways, one leading upstairs, the other to the front hall that separated this side of the house from the kitchen.

"Where?" Arlo closed the book in his lap, one finger holding his place. "The funeral? B said no."

"Not that. Yes, that. But not that."

"It was small," Bran broke in. "Just Tomi, me, a few of Gran's friends from the block."

"And your dad," Arlo said. "We should have been there."

Bran's bandmates each took a corner of the couch while he sat between them. He imagined them at his sides at the funeral, when his dad had ripped the sunglasses from his face. Arlo's voice would have been low and steady at his shoulder, urging him to walk away as he stood frozen, his fists deep in his pockets. And Cormac. Cormac would have reacted, as Bran never could when it came to his dad. A celebrity brawl would definitely have made the news. "You had finals. And C was working."

"We would have come." Arlo paused, like he was considering how to phrase his next thought. "Was he... okay?"

Bran stuffed his hands into the pockets of a zipper hoodie, merch from the band's first tour that would do reasonably well on eBay, even if the buyer didn't know he'd worn it. "I didn't want a media circus. And we agreed not to be seen together." He retrieved the coaster he'd slipped into the pocket earlier and ran his thumb along the edge. It was one of two souvenirs from Chicago, and he couldn't very well carry the other around in his pocket.

"I'm not talking about that, anyway." Cormac gestured to the soccer match on the screen. "We should have gone *to the game*. What are we doing getting up at the crack of dawn to watch it here like chumps?"

Arlo eyed the coaster in Bran's palm. Bran shoved it back in the pocket and shrugged out of the hoodie, his back hot.

After a moment his friend's attention shifted, answering their ex-drummer with a nod at his packed bag waiting by the den steps. "I'm flying back to Boston tonight. I couldn't have gone."

Bran's leg swayed as Cormac knocked it. "What's your excuse?"

"The album. I'm writing."

Cormac leveled his eyes on Bran. "B."

"What?"

*"B."*

"What."

"You are not writing. You've just been strumming that one lonely refrain over and over again."

Bran's brow furrowed. "Which one?"

Arlo's eyes were on his book again as he said, "The one that sounds like drowning in paint."

A laugh escaped Cormac. "Exactly. You are stuck. Inspiration has left the building. We should be in Spain—maybe a little flamenco in the sheets would—"

Bran's arms tightened as his hands balled. Might as well tell them. They knew everything else about him. Well, almost everything. "I couldn't have done that either."

"Why not?"

"I'm celibate."

"Yeah, we can celebrate in—"

*"Celibate."*

He didn't know which one of them to look at, feeling both their stares on either side of his face, so Bran kept his focus on the game. Like he hadn't just admitted something completely absurd.

"Like a New Year's resolution?" Arlo asked, and the echo of Nelle saying the same thing had Bran sinking lower in his seat.

He had to not think about Nelle. For one thing, Nelle-related urges were not good for celibacy. For another, his stomach did this weird backwards roll thing whenever he imagined her contacting him again. It would only be for one reason, and it was only a matter of time, before she called for the paperwork. Before she called it off.

From the couch's corner, Cormac broadcast his incredulity. "Like. No sex? What the hell for, man?"

"I thought it would clear my head."

"You gave up sex because you have writer's block? *This* is why we can't be seen together."

Arlo scratched at his beard. "I thought that was just our mutual discouragement of an overzealous media?"

Cormac shook his head. "It's because I'm embarrassed by both of you. I can't be associated with this kind of decision making. You're *reading* during El Clasico. And this guy—it's shameful. You know what it is? It's bad for business. Don't come to my restaurant. I mean it."

Bran exchanged smirks with Arlo. When the band had broken up, they'd agreed not to make appearances together, preferring to keep their relationships private. Rumors of course kicked up in the press, but the three of them knew the truth. That feeling that Bran got whenever the press ran something dumb about his rift with Arlo, a man who slept on his couch whenever he was in town, was part of what inspired the deal he'd made with Nelle. He liked the way it felt, to hold the truth close, warm himself on it, knowing it was safe.

For a month he'd gotten to do the same with that secret night in Chicago. It had been a month since he'd jeopardized the pact that she'd call to dissolve any day now. A month since he'd been impulsive, been reckless—but she'd been playing his song. The one he wrote fueled by the strongest teenage sensations, the feelings you never get over—first love, first heartbreak. And she knew it by heart. He had heard it in her voice, in the way her fingers owned the notes, that song had meant something to her. Bran had managed to mean something to her, before he'd even known her—and what was he supposed to do with that?

He must have been thinking her name too loudly

as they watched the game, because Cormac wondered aloud, "Are you just lying low because of the Nelle thing?"

Bran swallowed. "There is no Nelle thing."

"Sure there was—you interrupted her set and she didn't appreciate you taking the chance to shine so bright at the expense of her moment."

"That's not what—"

*"Says a source close to the starlet,"* Cormac mimicked. "Why are you letting this bother you so much? Aya can get anything—ask her for Nelle's number. Text her. Say you didn't mean to offend. If she knew you, she'd know the only thing you overthink is how long to fade an outro—"

"I'm not saying anything. It's whatever. One story. That's it."

Bran's pocket buzzed and he stretched his leg straight to slide his phone out.

Security Steve: You order food?

Bran typed back: probably one of the guys. It's fine. He dropped the phone into his lap. "Can you ask next time you get food delivered to my house—I'd have gone in. I need a snack."

Cormac had brought chicken and waffles ("the ultimate Sunday breakfast"), but they'd finished that before kickoff.

"I didn't order anything." Arlo directed a questioning look at Cormac. "C?"

The drummer shook his head, his eyes glued to the screen again. "I would have too though—there is nothing remotely edible in that fridge of yours. You don't even have ice."

"Machine's acting weird," Bran said defensively.

The television glowed green as the camera panned wide to follow a player breaking away from the others. He headed towards the stark white net at the opposite end of the field, and Cormac and Arlo leaned into the game.

Bran's lap vibrated. He almost dropped the phone, seeing the contact initials in the text preview. He fumbled his thumb across the screen twice before it slid open.

Above him, the action neared goal. Casillas rushed Messi but the only star that mattered to Bran was Nelle. The shot went wide and Arlo groaned, deflating in his seat.

"Shanked it!" Cormac dropped his head back.

NK: LA?

Bran leapt to his feet, one fist held high.

Cormac looked at him sideways. "You know good guys wear stripes, right?"

"What? Oh. Yeah, of course." Bran sat, hunching over his phone.

LA! he replied. And regretted the exclamation point immediately. What was he excited about, anyway? If she wanted to talk, it would be about divorce. He had just been surprised—that's all his reaction was. She surprised him.

NK: Can we meet?

He sighed and wished he could pretend he hadn't seen. But there was no point in delaying the inevitable. Sure—when?

A knock sounded at the door.

NK: Now

And Bran was moving, up and out of the den, around the corner to the hall.

She *always* surprised him.

Caught in momentum, it didn't matter why she was here, he just cared that she was. He just wanted to see her. But he slowed as he approached the big grey door. Stopped to press his palm against the smooth surface. Whatever excitement he'd felt in the den condensed, heavy and cold in his chest. It was over. She was here to end it.

He took a breath and heaved the door inward.

And there was Nelle, standing next to a large Steam-Line suitcase wearing a printed shirtdress and brown ankle boots. Her hair was pulled up high on her head, and she pushed tortoise-shell sunglasses into the mess, revealing the freckles across her nose and glowing amber eyes. "Hi."

Bran had only rushed from the den, but he felt like he'd been the one dodging defenders down the field's left flank. He gripped the door and the frame, his breathing rough and uneven. "It's upstairs."

"What is?"

"The—um—you know." Bran took a breath through his nose. His knees nearly buckled as he caught the scent of her on the breeze. The soft, familiar smell of flowers. And hints of something else, something bright, something spicy. He closed his eyes to finish the sentence. "The form, the certificate. Of marriage." When he opened them, her lips were pressed together and she was staring down the stairs at a Subaru waiting for her in the driveway. "That's why you're here, right?"

She swung her gaze back to him and he felt exactly how he had the last time he saw her: like the weight of her disappointment was crushing his chest.

"No. That's not why I'm here."

"Then why—"

The glasses tangled in her hair as she tried to put them back on. "I start tour rehearsals Tuesday morning in Washington."

Bran barely knew how to respond—he'd gotten it wrong so many times. "How was your break? How was home?"

That seemed like a safe enough question but her eyes narrowed.

"Are you gloating?"

"What? No, I'm—I have no idea what I'm doing, honestly."

"You didn't see the pictures?"

"Of us?" He leaned into the jamb for support.

"No, Bran." She huffed out a sigh. "Of me. At Mass? With my parents on Christmas Eve? The paps didn't need to infiltrate my town, because someone I knew was happy enough to snap a pic on their phone of what was actually a sacred moment for my family." She pulled up the photo to show him. The image was dim, a candle in her hand reflecting light in her eyes, and a wet streak on her cheek. Her parents stood next to her, her mother leaning into her father, her face buried in his shoulder, his raised up. Nelle bent her foot at the ankle. "Did you know my dad was sick?"

"I think maybe I heard something—he's okay now?"

"He's okay now. But he was sick last Christmas. And I was working up until the last minute, because they didn't tell me. I found out and we thought—we thought that might have been his last one and I had missed most of it. So, this year was—this was joy that was just for us." Her voice wavered. "Why does it have to be like this? Why aren't there boundaries? Why isn't family off-limits? It isn't *right*. My parents are uncomfortable attending services now. That's how my mom got through Dad's recovery. I hate that someone took that from them, and I can't do anything about it."

If the door had been any less sturdy, Bran's grip could have crushed it. He understood perfectly. At the bar, he'd been drawn in realizing they spoke a language of shared experience. Now, Nelle's fluency in it made his blood hot. *Who was it?* he wanted to demand. He'd make sure they didn't do it again. But it'd be someone else next time, and the time after that. The only way to beat the house was to never start playing—and she was already mid-game, cards in hand. "I'm sorry that happened to you. People are scavengers."

She swiped a finger under her glasses. "I'm sure they needed the money." Of course she'd defend the person who'd sold a chunk of her. Bran had never been that charitable. "Anyway. You told me so."

He stood a little straighter. Not because he liked being right about something that hurt her. But he recognized the returned force in her tone, and it pulled something tight inside him. Did she doubt his confidence? That he'd keep what they shared to himself?

"Why are you here, Nelle?" His pulse was so loud in his ears, he'd be lucky to hear her answer.

She pushed the glasses up again, her eyes wet but focused. "I want to keep this secret. Our secret. I want to have something they can't touch."

She wanted to tell him she was still in. That was better than divorce. She could probably have texted it, instead of risking someone seeing her here. Not that he was worried about that. His house was up in the hills, a small building on a big lot, acres of trees surrounded by a Very Expensive Fence. He'd even installed reflectors on either side of the door, in the event that someone got past Security Steve and attempted any flash photography.

She seemed to be waiting for him to say something.

Bran wet his bottom lip. "Okay." Of course he was still down.

"Wow, *okay.*"

She grabbed the handle of the suitcase and started for the flight of steps that would take her back down to the Subaru idling in the driveway. It was Benj, Bran was sure, the person she would trust to help her deliver her message. He was also sure he hadn't said the right thing. The suitcase clunked against the top step as she moved down a level.

The suitcase. That she had lugged up all these steps.

Benj wasn't waiting for Nelle. She was making sure Nelle got in.

"Wait, wait—" The doormat scratched Bran's bare feet as he went after her. He caught her wrist, fingertips over her racing pulse. "You want to keep our secret? Or have something?"

Three thin necklaces were layered on her neck. A

bird, an arrow, and a geode pendant hung at varying lengths and he dropped his gaze to the stacked rings she always wore. There, glinting on the ring finger of her left hand was the wedding band. Right where he'd left it.

*It means I have you?* she'd asked, looking down at him, her weight pressing comfortably into his lap.

"You want to have a secret or you want to have me?" Two options. Two competing desires.

"Both." Nelle answered with the air of someone who wasn't accustomed to having to choose. She'd have her milk cake and eat baklava too.

He shook his head. "We agreed both wouldn't work. It's more likely someone will find out the more we try both."

"It's more likely someone will find out if we stay out here on your porch."

Nelle wanted to stay. Bran could hardly believe it. She was upset, and she'd come to him. He didn't want to make more of that than he should. She'd known he'd get it. She'd come to get him.

Now they'd both reneged on the deal, they'd both put the secret at risk. That wasn't a habit they could get into. And if *she* became a habit, Bran didn't think he'd have the willpower to break it.

"Just for the night?" he confirmed.

"I have thirty-six hours."

He let go of her and spun an outer dial on the watch at his wrist, marking the time. She stepped back on the landing, her gaze sweeping to the door behind him. He moved aside and she started past him. Towards his home. His room upstairs. His house where—

Bran caught her wrist again. "You can't come in."

"Why not? It's my house."

That outrageous, possessive rebuttal should have stiffened his resolve to keep her out, but it stiffened something else instead. He lost focus on the reason and blinked before remembering. "The guys are here. The game is on."

"The guys?"

"Cormac, Arlo. We used to be in a band."

"I thought you—" She bit her lip. His gaze fixed on her mouth. That set of plump pink lips that he had never gotten to kiss goodbye. And now she was here. On his stoop. Her heartbeat twitching in his hold.

One night, they'd said.

One night.

It should have been enough.

But it wasn't. For either of them.

"Fuck it." Bran tugged her to him, sliding one hand up her neck, the other across her lower back. Her mouth met his in a hungry kiss. She fisted the T-shirt at his sides, pulling him even closer—he didn't care if she ripped it this time. He had missed this. He had missed her. She was a song he couldn't get out of his head, one he played on repeat and wasn't sick of yet.

His forehead rocked against hers. "You need to come inside."

She nodded and he hated the way the motion took her mouth an inch farther from his. Quickly, he claimed her lips again.

"We're gonna— Okay—" Bran pulled back, dazed, trying to force the blood back to his brain. "You'll sneak up the back stairs and I'll get rid of Cormac and Arlo."

Nelle reached for the suitcase but he already had the handle. He wrapped his other arm around her waist and hauled them through the door.

"I can walk," she said, trying to twist out of his grasp.

"Basic marriage rules: I have to carry you over the threshold." Bran grunted through the effort. "I'm being romantic."

"You're crushing my ribs."

He set her down and kissed her again, backing her into the wall. Flattened hands against the surface forced him back, and it was work ignoring the way her eyes had gone dark, the way her lips had transformed so quickly to lush and swollen. He opened the door to a closet and maneuvered the suitcase out of sight. "We'll leave this here. You don't need it."

"I do actually—it has all my clothes and—"

Bran pulled her in for another kiss, sweeping his hot tongue against hers. "You don't need clothes." They staggered through the open kitchen opposite the hall from the den, and he nodded to a set of steps. "Get upstairs."

"Get rid of them." She countered his command with her own.

This was insane. This was absolutely insane and made no sense. The skirt of her dress floated around her thighs as she climbed, and he caught a glimpse of lace. Bran didn't need any more reason than that.

He crossed the hall, padded down the steps into the den, and stood lamely next to the TV, staring at his friends.

"Who was at the door?" Cormac sat forward again, his elbows on his knees, his eyes following the movement of the game. "Is there food?"

"Special delivery."

"Of what?"

*Nothing*, Bran tried to say. He couldn't get the word out. "Something I needed."

"A blow-up doll?"

Bran's gaze lit on a pencil resting on the tray on the coffee table. "Something to sign."

Cormac turned his head towards the door. "Aya's here?"

"No, a courier."

"Aya trusts you to sign something without her?"

Bran's face went hot as he botched the excuse.

Arlo tapped his book. "You gonna sit?"

"No. I've got…a…headache. I'm gonna go…lie down."

His former bandmates exchanged glances, Cormac voicing their shared confusion. "It's El Clasico. You want to nap. During the last fifteen of El Clasico."

"You guys don't mind—Barcelona's up. You can go—"

"Go where? By the time we get anywhere the game will be over."

Nelle was upstairs.

Nelle was *upstairs*.

*Nelle* was upstairs.

He didn't have time for this. He didn't care what they did, as long as he got upstairs too. Soon.

Bran passed in front of the screen, standing in the arch that opened to the other staircase. "So then. Just close the door. When you leave. And get A to the airport, will you?"

Cormac went slack jawed. "You're seriously going to nap."

Bran nodded. "Yep. Okay. Bye."

He took the floating steps off the den two at a time.

A glass-walled hall connected straight across to the kitchen stairs, leading past the open music lounge to the door of his bedroom. Slightly ajar. Bran all but broke out into a run getting to it. He burst into the room, expecting to find Nelle sinking into his extra-stuffed duvet, ready and waiting for him. A quick scan of his empty bed kicked up an embarrassing panic that he'd hallucinated the whole thing—it made more sense than the events of the last ten minutes.

"Nelle?"

"In here."

Bran followed the sound of her voice to the walk-in closet, pausing before he entered. A second chance to not be such a desperate mess in her presence. He took his time, an eight-count of deep breaths, forcing himself to calm down, and then turned the corner.

And there she was, holding half of a pair of leather Chelsea boots, the other resting on a near-empty wall designed to display shoes. The four walls of his closet were covered in storage built-ins meant for all manner of clothing and accessories, but mostly displaying the rich dark wood of the building material.

"You need more clothes. Your closet is so sad." The three suits—coal black, deep navy, and heather grey—swayed on their hangers as she walked by, hand outstretched. She circled the island of dresser drawers where he kept a limited wardrobe consisting mostly of cotton shirts and denim. "Is Marie Kondo your stylist?"

"I don't have a stylist." He leaned a shoulder into the doorway. "I don't need a lot."

She finished her lap and replaced the boot, gesturing to the open safe in the corner where his collection of watches were secured in their slots, spinning like astronauts preparing for space, the door, again, slightly ajar. "And yet, so many watches. Why are they rotating?"

"To keep them wound up." He took two halting steps into the room. "That was locked. I know that was locked."

She shrugged, but a self-satisfied smile gave her away. "I was looking for something."

"Our marriage certificate is in the firebox."

"And your Cartier watch?"

"I don't have one."

"Aya made you take it back?"

"How did you open the safe, Nelle?"

Nelle lifted her eyebrows. "Two-two-three-seven-one."

The sensation that this was a dream hit him again. "*How* did you know that?"

She sang and he had to brace himself on the island between them. *"Taste your cherry, your French silk, your coconut cream. It's constant, girl you got me primed."*

"I'm familiar with the lyrics, I did write them."

"It's a play on *pi*, right? 223 over 71? I have no idea why you're obsessed with those numbers. But you are. They show up in everything. 'Second Best,' 'Burn Out,' that acoustic cover of 'Right Now.'"

"Those are some deep cuts." The counter was warm, sticky under his palms and he worried about the telling imprint he'd leave on the glossy surface if he lifted his hands.

"Two. Twenty-three. Seventy-one. It's all over the artwork too." She unhooked his black-and-gold Blancpain from its spot and slipped it over her wrist, concealing the clockwork visible underneath. "Your first album cover was a train with 7-1-K on the side."

"We used to hang out at a train yard, 71st and Kostner."

"That first tour, there's not a single picture where one of you isn't wearing a Michael Jordan jersey—"

"What do you expect from three Chicago kids." He rounded the island, his eyes sparking with discovery, recognizing the curiosity in her movements. Would it be cocky to call it reverence? Not if that was what it was, he decided.

"I know—the *second* city." She held up two fingers, the watch sliding halfway to her elbow, and met his eyes. But she must have seen that he'd found footing in the conversation, that he was the one taking over the pursuit, because she tightened her bun in a defensive maneuver. "It's not like you hid it."

"I can't believe it. I married a *stan*. I mean, I knew you appreciated the music, figured you were a Worker, but—tell me you've written a Wattpad story about me."

Light feet moved her just out of reach and they stood on either side of the island's corner. "I haven't."

"But you've read them—the dirty ones, right?" He had. Or he'd heard them. Drunk and amused, he'd listened to Cormac, drunker and more amused, perform a dramatic reading of what some fan imagined would happen on a tour bus.

"I can't believe she wants us each to take a turn," Arlo had said.

Cormac had grinned, scrolling ahead. "She doesn't."

"Of course I read the dirty ones." Nelle blushed but didn't look away.

That thought, of Nelle alone in her bed, reading

about him, touching herself—an urgent masculine need warmed his groin, one exacerbated by the long weeks he'd spent without relief. She smiled then, both of them realizing he'd lost his chance for the upper hand.

"What are we doing here, Nelle?"

She fingered the button between her breasts and the fabric parted. Did he need more of an explanation than that?

"How's the celibacy?" she countered.

"Fine."

The color seemed to have jumped from her to him, a scarlet heat that warmed his cheekbones.

Her smile rose. "Fine? You look a little tense."

Another button opened and she let the dress gape, revealing lace and skin.

"I'll admit that at this moment, it seems likely I might come just looking at you naked."

Nelle stopped toying with the button at her navel to blink at him. "Then I should definitely not get naked." But as she said it, she shifted the lace under her dress down to the ground and stepped out of it. She perched herself on the shelf beneath his jackets.

"Are they gone?" she asked thickly.

With a groan Bran remembered his bandmates downstairs. "They refuse. Until the game's over. Less than ten minutes." Ten minutes. He'd waited over a month—he hadn't even been expecting her to show up here. How could waiting ten minutes seem so daunting? They'd waited hours that first night. Driving, talking, singing. Necessary buildup to an absolutely unforgettable night of release. "Plus stoppage. It's been a clean game. A minute. Two tops. We can wait."

But he wasn't waiting. Nelle was here. Now. What

mattered more than that? He was pressing forward, filling the space between her parted knees, loving the way they opened to welcome him closer.

Nelle rolled her forehead against his, her eyes down, focused on where she played with the tie of his joggers. The material stretched, revealing the obviousness of his arousal. "Or we can be very, very quiet."

"Yeah, that's a better idea." Bran grabbed his shirt at the shoulders and pulled it over his head and the next moments were a flurry of tugs and pushes. His hands on her neck, her breasts, her hips. Her mouth pressed into his collarbone, nipped his ear, gasped his name as they bent forward and back, trying to get closer together. His cock rubbed against the perfect place between her legs, and even through the layers of fabric Bran felt a shock of pleasure.

Bran's nose grazed over her dark hair—white flowers filled his lungs and he remembered the way her body had moved against his in the hotel. How had he accepted he'd never do that again?

He scrunched the fabric at her sides, pulling it up to reveal her thighs spreading on the ledge. And then he wasn't thinking about anything. He was jamming his hands into the pockets of the jackets hanging next to them, one hand in the grey and one in the navy, his groin pressed securely to hers. She bit at his shoulder as he tugged a condom out of the grey suit, the soft lining coming out of the pocket with it.

Nelle muffled a laugh into his neck. "You keep those everywhere."

"They come in handy."

"In case Bran Kelly wants to fuck the shit out of

someone in his walk-in closet—I do feel like I read this one."

She lifted her eyes to his as she joked but he went still. He'd been surprised by her, confused by her, but suddenly he was scared that she was just like everyone else. Wanting a piece of Bran Kelly, to make the character in her mind real.

He didn't want to stop. But he had to understand. "Last time I saw you, you were pissed at me."

"Yeah. I was." She teased the curls on his chest. "You went back on what we said."

"And what are you doing now?"

She dropped her gaze like she had something to hide, and his stomach fell with it. But then she was looking up at him again with an answer he didn't expect. "Getting what I want."

He wasn't sure if that confirmed his suspicions about her motives or not, but he'd figure it out later, because a woman like this saying a thing like that was too much to resist. He drafted a silent prayer that Arlo and Cormac had cleared out and let it go.

He needed to be inside of Nelle, knocking against the wood panels. He needed her cries loud in his ear, both of them forgetting how they got here, who might be listening, or what it would mean later. He needed heat, rhythm, the rush of pleasure replacing any reason they might have to stop.

## Chapter Twelve

When Bran tugged his dick free, letting it bob over the waistband of his sweats, Nelle knew they were on the same page about one thing at least: that they needed to fuck. On the immediate.

He ripped the foil packet with his teeth. She pushed her hands under the elastic at his back and gripped his butt, urging him into her with one hard thrust. She was ready for him, slick with lust, but her body still strained against the size of the intrusion. Her hold tightened, keeping him fully submerged while she adjusted around him.

Bran hooked his hands under her knees and managed to push farther into her. So deep it felt like falling and having the wind knocked out of her. There was no room for air—her body didn't need it like she needed Bran, and, right now, she was willing to make room for him any way she could.

Her nails dug into his skin for a second, two, as he stood still, just filling her. She eased her grip on him, smoothing her palms over his curves, feeling the tense muscles clenching beneath them as he pulled back and thrust into her again. The rhythm steadied, quickened, steadied.

Bran caught her mouth with his, his tongue searing hers with heat and desire. The heels of her boots clunked loudly against the wood drawer fronts under her. Ten minutes had to have passed since they'd started fooling around. She mentally mapped the house, picturing the closet above the hallway between the den and kitchen. What if Arlo and Cormac were still watching the game? Wondering if Bran was hammering something? What he'd decided to nail to the wall? She didn't have long to worry about it. This was going to be fast. The build of it rising higher and higher, threatening to overflow already. That was the thing about sex with Bran: he had some extra sense, some way of knowing just what she needed from him. He was a mind reader—a body reader. She didn't have to say anything, but Bran found the words in her drawn brows, her angled hips. That first night together, he'd used that knowledge to make her last, tease her. Now he wasn't playing. Hands tilted her back, opening her up and ensuring that his base rubbed down on her pelvis, steel on bone, harder and harder.

She let go and braced her palms behind her, head falling back into the shadowy corner of the shelf. Bran shifted, rolling his hips side to side, connecting her swollen clit to the circuit with a satisfying click. He leveraged himself up and pushed deeper still inside of her, hitting her clit again and again. The pressure above her center crested for a glorious heart-stopping moment and then broke, scattering pleasure through her body as her heart pounded forcefully.

Bran's mouth dropped open as she closed around him. "Nella—Jesus!" He shuddered and she leaned forward, grasping her hands together behind his sweaty back, holding him close as he came inside her. His shoulders sagged and he hung over her, one hand against the wall behind her head. "Fuck."

"Jesus fuck?" she repeated back, her amusement apparent even through her breathless words. "More creative than three wows, I guess."

"It's hard to be eloquent with your tight-as-hell pussy wringing my cock out."

Her aforementioned pussy clenched around him and he gripped her hip.

"You don't want eloquence anyway. You like the dirty stuff." He skimmed up her side to brush the loose hair off her forehead. His blue irises were electric in the dark cabinet.

"You don't know that," she said against his mouth.

He cupped her cheek as he kissed her. "Yes, I do." He grazed his nose against hers. "I should…untangle us." His eyes dropped between them, where his dark curls were still flush against her.

She frowned when they separated, feeling empty where she had been full. While Bran disposed of the condom, she brought her knees back together, her hips aching from the width they'd achieved.

That was…exactly what she came for. She'd missed the way it felt to be with him, how it shut out the rest of the world. Like a snow globe, the two of them at its glitter-storm center. The cocooning power of a hot kiss on a cold night.

Bran understood her. Knew what she needed before she did. Like this secret. When Nelle burned with fury at the unexpected violation of her family holiday, her mother's anxious disbelief, her father's quiet anger, it was knowing she had something else tucked safely away that eased the pressure of rage. That distracted from the guilt. When the value of privacy skyrocketed, the secret she kept grew more worthwhile by the minute.

She hadn't been able to save that moment with her family, but she had a whole night of dark, scandalous moments—an entire chapter of her life that no one knew about, that no one could touch. She fixated on Bran until he was the only thing she could think about. The balm to a bad burn. And then she'd told everyone she wanted a relaxing break with Benj before rehearsals started Tuesday, imagined the relief her absence would bring her parents, and carved a day out of her life where no one would look for her.

It wasn't running away if she had somewhere to go.

"What if he doesn't want me to stay?" she'd asked Benj, filling the cup holder with scraps of orange peel.

"It does concern me that he doesn't know you are coming," Benj had said practically, idling in Bran's drive. "But you're showing up to demand sex. And you're you. He'd be a fucking idiot to turn you away. And if he does—"

"Then you and I spend the night in Ojai."

"I don't see any lights on."

Benj had grabbed for the gearshift and Nelle reached out to cover her hand. "Is this stupid? This is stupid."

Her friend had let go of the stick to hold Nelle's palm. "No. It is not stupid to want something and it is not stupid to try to get it. And you're not the kind of person who has to get real and move on. You're the kind of person who wills her dreams into reality. Who deserves them. So get out of my car and do it."

She'd certainly done it.

Nelle lowered her feet back to the ground, but her legs were unsteady. She leaned against the cabinet.

Bran reappeared from the bedroom as she was buttoning her dress. He stooped on his way over to her to grab the lace hip huggers she'd discarded. The graceful recovery of her underwear activated a dark heat under her cheeks. Still, Nelle lifted her chin to meet Bran's smirk.

He dangled the lace from his finger, setting it swaying side to side. "Prisoner exchange."

"I don't have anything of yours."

She followed his gaze to her left hand. His thumb brushed over the angled ring at the base of her second finger. He wanted it back?

"My watch," he clarified and she exhaled. With her underwear hanging from his wrist, he unfastened the band at hers.

Nelle held her hand out to complete the trade and Bran unlooped the lace from his arm. And scrunched it into his pocket. "You're not gonna need those for a while."

Nelle's heart, which had struggled to find a rhythm, beat steadily in her veins. Bran was smiling, she was smiling—they understood each other so easily sometimes.

"I like this one," Bran said, turning the watch between his fingers, "because if you flip it over, you can see what's going on inside." He handed her the watch so she could see the gears through the little glass window underneath the face. She didn't see his face when he asked, "What's going on here, Nelle?"

Nelle offered the watch back to him, lifting her eyes

and her brows. "Why don't you flip me over and find out?"

"Give me a minute. I'm still recovering from your arrival." Bran stepped away to replace the watch in the safe, setting it spinning. *Keeping it wound*—she knew the feeling.

"You're not the only one who likes to make a surprise entrance," she said to his back.

"About that. The press said I embarrassed you—"

She crossed the closet, her dress soft against her skin, her thighs sticking slightly—reminders with each step that her underwear was in his pocket. "The press said what I told them to say. I thought you knew that was me. I planted that one. Nudged the story away from us being friends."

"Because we can't be friends." He slotted two fingers between the buttons of her dress, his knuckles brushing the soft pillow of her breast.

"They'd say it was more."

"They'd be right." His breath raised her scalp. "I'm sorry. I should have texted to tell you. I messed up in Chicago. I wasn't thinking. You were singing and—"

"And I called to you like a siren?" Nelle boosted herself onto her tiptoes to kiss his neck.

Bran rounded a palm over her butt. "We can't really do this, if we don't want them to know," he whispered, his voice like gravel in her ear, his grip tightening.

"I won't let them take this from me." Her lids grew heavy as she inhaled the sweat on his skin, her nose at that lovely dip of bone at his clavicle. And something else too—citrus, from her own fingers, transferred to him.

"We're playing with fire." He found his way beneath

her dress, unclasping her bra and snaking the straps out from under her short sleeves.

"You don't think it's hot?" The dress felt like little more than a silk slip with nothing underneath it and Bran's hands prodding her out of the closet, towards his bed.

He stopped in the doorway, leaving her untethered, spinning to find him. He'd gone back in to ransack the other jackets, a drawer of pants, tossing each condom he discovered onto a messy pile on the island, with a few guitar picks scattered in for good measure.

He left a cabinet open and moved to the next but her gaze snagged on the familiar jean jacket that hung from its fleece collar on the back of the door. The image of Bran scribbling on that coaster at the bar, capturing a spark, filled her mind.

Was it still there?

Nelle sank her hand into the pocket to find out— she would say she was helping, if he asked. Her fingers closed around the contents. She frowned at what she'd found.

"Bran."

He had lowered himself out of sight behind the island.

*"Bran."*

"Yeah, what?" Hands braced on the wood, his gaze landed on the plastic baggie of three white pills that sat in her outstretched palm.

"What's this?"

She expected the question to still him, but he dropped down again, focused on his search. "Vitamins."

"Vitamins?"

"I can show you the bottle if you want."

Bran stood, counting the loot he'd uncovered, like a kid sorting Halloween candy. "Eight," he told her, a promise that had her insides clenching and her knees weakening. He leveled his gaze on hers, blue eyes glacial in color and just as bracing. Nelle felt the air leave her body in a rush.

She walked backwards as Bran collected the condoms and stalked after her. The bed surprised her and she fell into the down. He loomed over her, catching her face in his hands.

"You're mine for the next thirty-six hours?"

Nelle could only nod. Then Bran lowered his mouth to hers and she knew they were done talking.

## Chapter Thirteen

Bran liked any sex. He did. He really did. And he'd done it all—every variety of position, partner(s), and place. But there was something to be said for the basics, a woman flat on her back beneath him, her hips cradling his. Dark hair loose and wild between his forearms. Her mouth and neck there to kiss and taste as he ground into her again and again. Or maybe it was Nelle, her curved body cushioning his, willing to be had for as long as he could have her. Heavy lids slanting over amber irises, watching him with such intensity. Consuming him.

The way she looked at him. He was addicted to how it made him feel—like an actual rock god. Even though it was her, making him that hard, giving him that power. It was her he needed to worship, for as long as she'd let him.

Torn foil shrapnel poked uncomfortably at his side and his stomach rumbled. Stretching a sleepy arm out, Bran groped through the empty sheets. No Nelle. He sat up, rubbing his eyes. The bathroom door was open, the light off. Dusty yellow sunlight filtered in through the long rectangular transom windows that lined the wall of his bedroom.

They'd fucked all of yesterday, into the afternoon. He hadn't even noticed the sun fading until he'd rolled off her, blinking in the shadowy room. And he'd only had a few minutes to breathe deep and wonder about the lack of light before she had climbed on top of him and his world became the black of her pupils, growing darker and darker as she rocked above him.

He counted his condom supply. Down to three. That would last another few hours. What time was she leaving again? 8 p.m.? He made a mental note to get more.

If she was still here.

She had to be still here.

He needed her to still be here.

But Nelle's dress wasn't crumpled on the floor. He tugged his sweatpants on, tripping as he rushed to walk before his second ankle was through the fabric.

Standing on the glass-walled landing he stopped to listen, breathing a sigh of relief when a metallic clang sounded from the kitchen. He took the stairs to his right, arriving in time to see Nelle click the gas range on, lowering the heat to melt butter in a pan. One of his favorite shirts—a baseball tee from high school with his name on the back—grazed the top of her thighs. His dick lifted, sensitive skin rubbing against the inside of his sweats.

It was effortless, the way she affected him.

Nelle noticed him standing on the last step. "Hi." She looked down to whisk eggs in a bowl. "You slept hard."

Everything was hard around her. "I was worn out."

"I figured. Are you hungry?"

"Famished. But I don't—I don't have food?" He opened the fridge, taking in red, yellow, green in the vegetable drawer, his beer pushed to the side to make room for a pack of tortillas, a container of hummus, pico de gallo, some Greek yogurt, two pints of raspberries, and a giant bag of tiny oranges.

"I know. You didn't even have olive oil."

She nodded to the center of the concrete island where a bottle gleamed like an emerald in the morning light. It had friends too: a pepper grinder and a green-and-white box of sea salt.

"Don't tell my mother I forgot the cinnamon. Absolute sacrilege."

Cinnamon, that was the spicy scent he'd caught on her yesterday. So she'd smelled like home.

"You went out?"

The pan sizzled as she added the eggs. "I used your Postmates account. On your phone. You have like a million messages, by the way."

"I need a new passcode."

"You really do."

She pushed the cooked folds into the center of the pan and tilted it so the raw egg covered the ceramic coating again. The oven pinged. "Can you get that?"

"Do I have oven mitts?"

Nelle laughed, taking the eggs off the heat. "In the drawer under the knife block. I'm surprised you have such nice knives. And pans. The only thing in your fridge is beer."

"There's vodka in the freezer."

"A veritable pyramid of health. No wonder you rely on vitamins."

Bran slid a baking sheet of toasted tortillas onto the counter. Cheese bubbled from the center of each, spilling over some edges. He loved the way she danced around him, grabbing the salsa from the fridge, a spoon from the drawer. His hands found the cement ledge, gripping it to keep from interrupting her. He backed into the counter as she piled scrambled eggs on the tortillas and topped each with a spoonful of saucy tomatoes. He wanted to touch her just a hair less than he wanted to watch her make him breakfast. Of course, part of it was how sexy she looked in his shirt. But there was something else, something he hadn't realized he'd wanted, in the way she took care, ensuring each taco was dotted equally with diced avocado. Something in her kindness.

He felt light-headed, and attributed the sensation to exertion combined with deep sleep and hunger.

"You can turn off the oven," she told him.

"I don't think I can."

Her eyebrows raised in pointed disbelief and mild annoyance.

He lifted a shoulder. "I've never used any of this stuff." He wanted to now. Suddenly he envisioned a lot of uses for this island, versions of bending her over it being the most prevalent and distracting.

Nelle pressed a thumb against the spotless oven controls, leaving a greasy print. Then she sidestepped, stretching up on her toes to reach two plates. His shirt pulled up to reveal the peachy curves of her ass and Bran released the counter, wrapping his arm around her waist to pull her tight against him. He nuzzled into her neck and she pushed back, determined to stay focused on the food.

"After breakfast."

Reluctantly he let her pass, and was rewarded with the plate of scrambled egg tacos she pressed into his hands. He leaned against the island as she hoisted herself onto the counter next to the stove. She crossed her legs and he crossed his ankles. They didn't talk as they ate. Just stared across the yard that separated them.

"I'm done with breakfast," he said, setting his empty plate to the side. "It was delicious."

She finished chewing and held out her dish. "Then you can clean up. Basic marriage rules. We're doing things traditionally, after all."

Bran exhaled, holding her gaze. He brought the plates to the sink. A little bowl was sitting next to the soap, filled with Nelle's rings. He sifted a finger through it and smiled to himself that she had kept the wedding band on despite removing the others. Maybe because it was less expensive, and she didn't worry about it getting damaged. But still. Something about it completed the domestic fantasy he was forming around them.

Mrs. Kelly piled the dirty dishes on one side of the sink and laid a clean cloth on the other for the dishes to dry on. Mrs. Kelly removed some vegetables from the fridge. Mrs. Kelly pressed her mouth to his shoulder blade as she passed them under the flow of water, her hands running suggestively up and down the green length of the cucumber.

Bran stiffened, sudsy water squeezing out of the sponge and through his gripped fist.

But she was already gone, back to the island. She was as efficient at scrambling eggs as she was at scrambling his senses. He tracked her as she stationed herself in front of the chopping block on the counter.

"I found two more condoms when I was looking for a dish towel. Wasn't sure you had any more jackets to pillage."

"What time do you leave?"

"Benj is coming to get me at eight."

"Five condoms, twelve hours. We'll make it work."
He grinned. He liked making Mrs. Kelly flush.

"Why don't you just keep a box in your bedside table
like a normal person?"

"Because I don't need them *here*, I need them when
I am out."

She stood a little straighter, biting in the smile that
pulled her cheeks. "Because you don't bring women
home?"

"That's right." He cocked his head to the side, considering her. "You're looking a bit smug."

She shrugged and looked down. "One of them had
a note with a phone number. So we should be sure to
thank Jane for that round."

"Where'd you put it?"

She used the knife to motion across the counter to a
stack of slate hand towels. With water dripping down
his wrists, Bran found the condoms nestled on the top
of the stack. His phone was next to it. He pocketed that
with the foil pack that was his normal brand and tossed
the one he didn't recognize into the trash under the sink.

"Bran. I'm not mad. I don't mind."

"You mind getting pregnant? You didn't feel the pin-
pricks? I only use condoms I buy."

Nelle didn't have anything to say to that. Nelle. Not
Mrs. Kelly. They could play house while the clock
ticked—they weren't getting any more serious than that.

He turned back to the dishes. Behind him the knife
sounded steadily on the wooden chopping block.

"Cormac outfitted this kitchen?"

Curiosity coated her question. It reminded him of
how she'd prowled through his closet the day before.
She was digging into his life, but Cormac seemed like

a safer topic than how often someone tried to trick him into using a sabotaged prophylactic. "He's into food. Trying to get a restaurant up and running. He'll just about fall over to open that fridge and see vegetables."

"And he'll see them? Because he comes here? I mean, he was here yesterday."

"You thought we weren't friends anymore? Because of what some magazine reported?" A quick glance over his shoulder confirmed her reddening face.

"The band broke up."

"The family didn't."

"Bran Kelly, I'm not even chopping onions and that brought a tear to my eye."

The dishes clean and lined up to dry on the towel, Bran turned to watch her chopping peppers into dippable spears.

"So you're pretty domestic, huh?"

"I made eggs."

"And you're chopping stuff."

"For store-bought hummus."

He bracketed her body with his arms, standing behind her. "Crudités," he whispered across her skin, smiling as she tensed against him.

He liked crowding her, he liked that she let him take up all the space around her. He was so used to people coming on to him, forcing him to retreat. He liked being in control of the advance.

"You keep all your relationships out of the press?" she asked.

"The ones that matter."

"Someone could easily take a picture of their cars coming in and out of here."

"No one bothers because it's a better story that there's a rift between us."

"So what really happened?"

"They wanted to do other things."

"And you?"

"There's nothing else for me. Music is it." He rested his chin on her shoulder. "I forced them into it anyway. And they went with it because I refused to spend my time any other way." He paused. The memories were thick as the shag carpet in his gran's basement where they practiced. "We weren't even that good, you know? We just had chemistry. Arlo's always had soul, direction. He's the quiet one, the steady one—which is the perfect disposition for a bassist. And Cormac. He could bang the hell out of those drums when he got riled up—which was always back then."

She stopped chopping and they swayed together to some silent song. "And then?"

"We got better. We picked up steam. Then we exploded. After a few years they were done. Arlo always wanted to go to school. He can afford as much institutional learning as he wants now. And I think that rage in Cormac burned out, or leveled off anyway."

"They didn't need it like you did." She turned in his arms to look him in the eye.

That goddamn understanding in her words, the feeling of being known, had his mouth crashing into hers. She opened up to him, threading her fingers into his hair, tugging at the back of his neck. He could smell raw peppers on her skin. Bran groaned and crushed her into the counter with his hips. Then, thinking better of it, he lifted her onto the cement ledge.

He'd had breakfast, he'd cleaned up, now he was going to devour her. Here in his kitchen.

They didn't hear the front door open. Nor the click of stilettos on Bran's polished floor. They did hear the cough, professional and cutting. Bran broke away from Nelle to see Aya, one hand on her hip, the other holding a cellphone that might as well be glued there. A silk blouse was tucked smartly into her wide black pants, and her kicked-out hip meant business.

"What's up?" he asked. Of course she hadn't knocked. She had a key, she ran his life. From Aya there were no secrets. Except Nelle's.

"Wellness check." Aya's sharp gaze shifted between the back of Nelle's head and his face. "Cormac said you were acting squirrelly. You haven't answered your phone in a day. And your card showed a Postmates charge at 7 a.m."

"So?"

Nelle slipped off the counter, which only brought her closer to him as he refused to pull back farther.

"So a 7 a.m. alcohol delivery concerns me."

"It was groceries."

"What are you going to do with groceries?"

"Not me." Bran nudged Nelle's side so she'd turn around. "Aya, Nelle, Nelle, Aya."

This wasn't an introduction he had planned to make, but there was no getting around it. Maybe they'd get along—the two women that kept his world and his head spinning.

Nelle lifted a palm to wave. "Nice to meet you."

Aya narrowed her eyes at Bran. "Can I talk to you in the hall for a second."

It wasn't a question. And now when Nelle tensed, it wasn't because of him.

Bran sighed. So much for that kitchen fantasy—Aya's presence meant one thing: it was time to get real.

## Chapter Fourteen

When she'd arrived yesterday, Nelle hadn't had time to think about it, but that morning when she'd slipped out of bed to explore, her first thought was that Bran's house was a lot like Bran. Hard to get to. Remote. But the curb appeal, chef's kiss. Modern, confident, long and sturdy with great lines. It was purposefully separate. It had levels. Out front, a garage sloped down on one side, a set of steps rose up on the other. And inside: a house divided, compartmentalized. The first floor had two big rooms: a den and an open kitchen with a dining area. Upstairs was dominated by his large master. At the top of the stairs from the den was an open space dedicated to music, as indicated by the guitars on one wall, and the gallery of awards on the other.

In the rest of the rooms, Bran's décor moved away from music. Over and over she encountered paintings of water and sky, waves and clouds. She'd expected at least one framed Springsteen poster but all she found were horizons stretching blue across wide oceans and lakes.

On the front wall, all the windows started above her head, letting in light while revealing nothing of the inside. But upstairs, in the back of the house, glass walls opened to a yard with a manicured patio surrounding a pool. The area was wrapped in a tall planked fence, edged with trees. A little hidden Eden. Open and surprising.

The size of the house also surprised her. It was small. So small that when Bran and Aya moved into the den, she could still hear them from the kitchen.

She considered going upstairs. At the very least, she could outfit herself with some pants as they weren't alone in the house anymore. Instead she perched on the last stool at the island, closest to the hall, tugging Bran's shirt to her knees.

Nelle was going to listen, because they were going to talk about her.

Aya spoke first, her voice low and powerful like undertow. "This is the holdup? You can't afford to be distracted right now."

"I can afford plenty—"

"She better be here to inspire you—and I mean inspire more than your dick. Because you promised the studio a big album. Fast. And you haven't delivered. They were going to fast-track a stadium tour. Now you're going to have to wait until next summer."

"So what?"

"So that's a long time before you bring in any money."

"I have an extensive back catalog."

Aya sighed and Nelle got the feeling they'd had this argument before. She hugged her torso. They'd stopped talking about her, which lessened her claim to the conversation. Still, she stayed put.

"Which your fans already have. To reach new audiences you need to be making appearances." Aya shifted her approach, her tone becoming gentler, more persuasive than forceful. "Like the Jingle Jam. That was good for business."

Nelle sat straighter. Now they were getting to it, and she shouldn't have been surprised that Bran's people— person—had the same reaction as her own. Almost a year ago, with the rush of approaching Bran glowing hot on her cheeks, Max had tracked her steps back to their table at the Cleffy after-party. "We can make that work," he'd said. "It would sell." Like that was the reason for any decision she made. Like there was nothing worth keeping to herself.

Would Bran be drawn out? Under Aya's coaxing? She held her breath waiting for his response.

"I told you to forget about that."

"Bran—"

A cloud moved over the sun, the house growing as dark as Bran's voice. "It doesn't exist outside this house. I'm handling it."

"You don't handle anything. That's why you pay me three salaries."

"Nelle isn't business."

Nelle could almost feel the house shudder as Bran dug his heels in. Her body did shudder, a deep shiver that rocked her shoulders. Goose bumps rose on her arms when he spoke her name with such vehemence. Protecting what they had. Bran got it. They'd written the rules together—she let her guard down, her shoulders relaxing, knowing she could trust him.

Aya huffed out another exasperated breath. "I need something from you, Bran. I need you on red carpets, doing interviews—performing *anywhere*."

"They're gonna ask me about new music."

"And you'll tell them it is coming."

"I'll be at the Note Awards. I won't skip the carpet."

"That's a given. I need more."

Nelle imagined the single nod, the half shrug he offered Aya as he said, "Fine. Book some stuff."

"Interviews? Festivals?" Aya asked.

"Whatever," Bran agreed. "And you forget what you saw in the kitchen."

"Done."

How many conversations had Nelle had with her team like this? None. She was never obstinate. They were professionals she hired to help her. They were on her side. She trusted them to consider what was right for her. And they did. The only time she'd pushed was to get that time off for Christmas before tour prep. And because they knew she didn't ask for much, and she made clear she wouldn't compromise on it, they'd all tried to make it work.

She expected some of the tension between Aya and Bran to recede after they came to an agreement, but a silence stretched taut as a wire.

No, not a silence. Aya was whispering.

Nelle climbed off the stool, wincing as it scraped against the floor. She all but tiptoed to the kitchen doorway and hid behind the wall.

"He wants money."

Bran swore. He'd be roughing his hair and settling it back. "I need more time."

"You need to make a decision. He's getting impatient. Or, just let me pay a little now and we'll *buy* you more time."

He sounded pained when he replied. "Okay."

"Okay."

The sun streamed back in through the windows,

glancing off the polished floor, bathing the kitchen in bright yellow light and warmth. But Nelle had gone cold, like she'd plunged into a mountain stream, the icy water knocking her lungs flat.

Bran needed money.

Bran wasn't protecting their privacy or their secret or her.

Bran was trying to keep them married for as long as he could, running up the tab, so when the time came for divorce, he could wring more out of her.

The signs were all there.

The small house? It wasn't a choice. He didn't shirk opulence because he "didn't need a lot." He couldn't afford it.

The empty closet? She imagined Aya selling Bran's old Tom Ford suits on eBay. That pinstriped number from last year's Note Awards probably fetched a real nice sum at auction. She wished her number had gone forgotten in its pocket to the new owner. Happenstance saving her from this debacle of her making.

The fucking watches. He'd part with them last, living off them while he ratcheted up the days they'd been married, ensuring a bigger payoff.

And she'd kept it from her team—the people who would have stopped her from making such a huge mistake. She and Bran weren't the same, they didn't understand each other. That's just how hustlers made you feel when they were telling you what you wanted to hear. Nelle tugged at the shirt's hem again. She'd exposed herself to an impoverished con man.

Nelle was dizzy on regret when Aya clicked back into the hall, heading for the front door. She stopped just after the kitchen, to look back at Nelle leaning heavily against the opening.

Aya considered her, dark eyes round and alert. "Mina Hassan, right? In Max Field's office? She knows you're here?"

Nelle pushed off the wall. "Are you threatening me?"

"Just trying to get a handle on the situation."

"There is no situation."

Not anymore. Nelle was already forming the plan in her mind: she had to tell Mina. And Mina would assemble her publicist, her lawyer, maybe someone from the label if they needed it? There was that clause in her contract about image representation. Was eloping with a rock star a breach of her legal obligation to be a good role model? Mina would know what to do. That's what managers were for. To have your back.

Nelle stared at Aya. This woman, in her flowy pants and shirt, both loose and fitted, she was who Bran trusted. She was the one who took care of his problems. Knew his secrets.

"Careful," Aya said, as if reading her mind. "He's…" She trailed off and Nelle filled in the rest: a liar, a predator, a hack. "He's figuring some things out."

Yeah. Figuring out how he can use people.

When Aya had gone, Nelle stared across the hall. She had two options: storming upstairs to grab her dress from where she'd hung it in the bathroom, shoving her feet into her boots, and walking, epitomizing an anthem. Or telling Bran Kelly off.

Nelle froze on the second step down to the den, unable to bring herself closer to him.

Bran had sunk into the grey sofa, his elbows on his knees and his head down. "Sorry, I needed a minute."

He rubbed his eyes and looked up at her. "And don't worry about Aya. She won't—"

"How much?" Nelle interrupted.

His head angled. "How much what?"

"How much do you owe? How much do you want from me? I can tell you right now, you're not going to get it. We're going to fight—"

"What are you talking about?" Bran stood and she held one finger up to stop him.

"I heard you."

"You eavesdropped." He crossed his arms. Like *he* had been wronged.

"You're out of money. Spent it all on Rolexes and Ferraris and there's no more coming in? So you used me—how much do you owe? Tell me, Bran."

"I'm not using you—cash flow isn't an issue for me."

"Sure—that's why Aya is so worried about your purchases?"

"Because she's nosy. And I—"

"I can't believe this. God—what *wasn't* a line? The celibacy, the *secrets*. The longer we're married, the better your claim, is that it?"

"I didn't use any lines—you're the one with the line."

"Me?"

"*You're it.* Literally asking me to chase you. Tagged me in. You got me. I was game."

Her face flushed at the memory. How embarrassing—that he was right. That she'd all but thrown herself at him. Made it so easy for him. "And what are you playing at now? How much do you want from me?"

His head shook. "You started it. You showed up here. You came after *me.* You're the one prying into my business. Which incidentally, has nothing to do with you."

Her accusing finger curled back into her fist as her hand dropped. "And what is that business, Bran? Who are you paying off? If you don't have cash-flow problems, why wouldn't you just pay for whatever it is—is it drugs? *Vitamins?*"

"Really, Nelle."

"Yes. Really."

"Are you here to do this thing or justify why we shouldn't? Self-sabotage isn't very on-brand for you."

"Fuck you."

Her bag was in the hall closet. She wasn't going to spend another minute in this house. The smooth floor allowed her to pivot on the ball of her foot, turning away from him in one graceful spin.

"It's my dad."

She stopped. His voice tore over the words, like he was resisting saying them. But she couldn't trust his voice—she believed it too easily. She had to face him and read the truth in his eyes.

Bran stood in the den, his legs askance, frozen mid-step. "He's the one with debts. Gambling, mostly. He can't help himself—used to make bets in the Little League stands about whether I'd choke at bat. But at least he was there, right?" His laugh lacked weight. "When my gran died, he got her house. And he's threatening to sell it—sell it with everything inside. Every sketchbook, journal, picture of mine that she kept. You think someone stealing that moment at church was a violation? My father is extorting me—using my whole life as leverage."

If it was a performance to keep her here, he shouldn't just be getting a Note Award. There was Oscar-worthy pain etched on his face. Real pain. It wasn't an act.

"Bran, I—"

"I'm not using you for money. You want to see my bank accounts?" He set his hands on his hips. "I'm surprised you didn't check when you had my phone—you already know the code."

She lowered down a step into the room. "Why don't you just pay him and be done?"

"Why should I? Why should I have to buy my own life from him? He's my *father*. We're family." Bran's mouth flattened as he went silent.

The thick carpet cushioned her feet as she met him in the middle of the room.

"I'm sorry," Nelle said softly. She meant it. She put her hand on his chest. Her thumb dipped in his collarbone as she slipped it up to knead the tight muscles at his shoulder. "I'm sorry," she said again. Two apologies. For two reasons. For what was happening to him, and for her assumption.

"You can't keep thinking I'm fucking with you, Nelle."

"I know."

"We're in the same boat here. And you're rocking it."

"I forgot that was your job."

A half smile flickered on his face and her guilt eased. She took a deep breath in. Bran's skin gave off a familiar scent—warm and salty. Like August air. Stubborn and reluctant to break. She wanted him to crack another smile. "We never fought like this before we were married."

He toyed with the hem of her shirt. His shirt. KELLY it said. And she felt the weight of the letters across her shoulders. He was trying to hold himself together and she kept pulling him apart.

Nelle edged forward and Bran moved instinctively back. His knees caught on the couch and he landed where he'd sat when she came in. He'd looked defeated then—having made the concession to let Aya buy more time from his father. His head was up now, his attention on her.

"I know a trick for stress," she told him. His legs widened to make room for her. The smile dropped from his face when she turned and disappeared into the kitchen, returning with a clementine, cold from the fridge.

"What are you gonna do with that?" Bran's brows pulled together skeptically.

"You're gonna open it, release the oils into the air." Nelle played it cool as Bran rolled the clementine in his palm. "Benj swears it's the best way to relax."

He huffed out a laugh. "Yeah, sure, let's give that a try."

He'd just broken through the peel with his thumb and pressed the fruit to his nose when she lowered herself between his legs. His jaw opened slowly, wordlessly.

They were inching back to where they'd been, rewinding to the moment before Aya had interrupted them. Skipping back on an album to play a favorite track.

"And what are you going to do down there, Nelle?" The obvious slant of his mouth told her he'd caught on to her game.

"Plan B, in case the clementine doesn't do it for you."

His eyes burned the inner blue of a flame as her palms ghosted over his knees and up to the waistband of his grey sweats.

"Is that working?" She flicked her eyes to the fist at

his side, orange rind peeking through the circle of his thumb and forefinger.

Bran could only shake his head, eyes riveted on her face.

She fit her fingers under the band and pulled it taut, maneuvering the eager cock from inside. "Plan B then?"

A groan rumbled through Bran as Nelle fit her mouth over him. Warm and salty. She took her time memorizing the taste. Memorizing the sounds of his pleasure. Memorizing the feel of Bran Kelly. Finding out what *he* needed.

And when he came, squeezing his balled hand so tight the clementine within burst, she tried to ignore the thought that she was just like everyone else: that the more she had of him, the more she wanted.

## Chapter Fifteen

The den was in disarray, couch cushions strewn about the room like a tornado had come through. And it had. Nelle was a solid Midwestern twister, blowing through his life, his home. Touching down unexpectedly, making Bran wish he'd had time to shutter the windows closed.

But even if he had, would it have helped? It was impossible to keep her out. She'd rattle the glass in its frames until it broke—which was why he'd just given up and let her in.

She'd been here a day. And had the complete run of the place. He hadn't planned on telling her anything about the situation with his father. But she'd thought he was playing her. His chest rose and fell as he drew and released a quick breath. She'd thought him capable of that. She'd been convinced of it. The jagged look she'd cut him with still smarted.

He'd had to tell her about his dad, had to reveal more to Nelle than he'd ever intended. He had to trust she'd keep it to herself.

She would. He knew she would. They wanted the same things from each other: sex and secrets. He fit an ampersand between the two words, and an image materialized in his mind, twin s's on an album cover, black and blue and inky like midnight. Like it hurt. That was the other reason he needed her close. Because she made the future of his music clearer.

Bran Kelly: *sex&secrets*, that was an album his label would wait for.

He was looking up. Lying on his back on the middle section of the couch. Wood beams striped the ceiling, swirled knots intensified by the stain he'd chosen, and sun blazed through the high window. Nelle was nestled in the crook of his arm. She'd fished his phone from his discarded pants to stream Carly Simon's *Greatest Hits Live* through his built-in speakers. Her fingertips tapped his chest one by one, punctuating the lyrics with a light press the length of each syllable. She rolled thumb to pinky through the infamous accusation and lifted her head.

"Imagine being vain enough to think a song is about you and being wrong."

"It's pretty detailed. Whoever it's for would know."

"Whoever it's *about*. Not for. I agree he'd know, but there would still be people presuming to be the subject. That's the level of ego that concerns me."

Bran shifted to his side and Nelle turned to mirror him, letting her palm rest on his coarse cheek. They shared a long flat pillow from the armrest at the other end of the couch. He wasn't sure how it had migrated all the way to that corner, but he had a rough idea it had something to do with the slow doggy-style thrust and crawl that had taken them across the sectional.

He brushed his knuckles across her skin, lazily strumming her back, rephrasing her words as a question. "Whoever it's about, not for?"

"You tell someone when a song is for them. You have to say."

Bran stopped his hand. "But the specifics—she makes it clear. She wants him to know."

"Of course she does. That's where the power is. When it's not a gift, it's a move. To make someone hear a song and realize it's about them. If you never tell them, it's for yourself."

His fingers closed on her wrist and he raised her hand off his face. Bran rolled over Nelle, freeing his arm from under her and planting his feet on the carpet.

"Now I'm cold," Nelle whined, snuggling into the plush spot he'd left.

"I have to get dressed." Bran sorted through the couch debris.

"Why?" Nelle sat, her long hair falling over one shoulder, skimming her back. It didn't smell like peonies anymore. It smelled like that orange she'd given him. He'd pushed his juice-covered fingers through her waves and pulled her face to his, tasting himself on her tongue. Then he'd spread her out on the upholstered coffee table and returned the favor.

Bran's brain stalled, trying to remember the question. "Aya's reported back to Cormac by now." Nelle blinked, her mouth dropping open, and he hurried to explain. "She'll have told him everything is fine and there's nothing to worry about." He pulled on his pants, his shirt. "He's probably on his way."

She scanned down his body, the full outfit he'd pulled together from their two discarded components. "And I'm going to be naked when he gets here?"

"You're going to be out of sight when he gets here."

She stood, stretching her arms above her head,

her nipples growing hard as she left the warmth of the couch. "Where am I going to hide? You have four rooms."

Bran reached out to stroke her breast. He gave it a gentle tug, pulling her into him, her bare form curving against him. "In the shower." He breathed in the citrus on her neck. He'd never be able to peel an orange again without getting hard. "You're sticky."

They rocked to the song, slow dancing as his palms cupped her ass.

"Alone?" she whispered before her teeth sank into his earlobe.

There were such better things they could be doing than worrying about intruders. Maybe he was wrong about Cormac. Maybe he didn't have to waste any more of their precious final hours dealing with his meddling bandmate—

The unmistakable bass of Cormac's pimped-out Crown Vic shook the room around them.

Unfortunately, Cormac was as predictable as a click track. With the timing to match.

"Shower," Bran said, but Nelle was already rushing from the room. His palm clapped against her ass as he sent her up the stairs. The slap rang out, clear and sharp, music to his ears. *That ass.*

He trailed up the stairs after her before remembering the car parking in his driveway. The front door clanged shut like a cymbal crash announcing Cormac's entrance. Like Aya, he had a key. Unlike Aya he was not stealth. After a minute of obvious prowling on the first floor, footsteps beat a rhythm up the stairs and Cormac emerged from the steps off the kitchen.

"Hey, buddy."

"Why the visit, C?"

An innocent shrug did little to counterbalance the devilish grin on Cormac's face. "Just dropping off some leftovers from recipe testing. So you don't starve. Took a year off my life opening your fridge to find honest-to-goodness ingredients."

"Aya told you not to worry about me."

"Aya told me what you pay her to tell me. You think I don't know the difference?" He glanced at the door to Bran's room and then back to Bran to repeat the proof. "There's food in your fridge."

"I was hungry."

"Just you?"

Bran suddenly doubted whether Cormac had the decency not to burst into the shower searching for Nelle. He needed to get his friend out of his house. "I'm fine, as you can see, so why don't we make plans for you to come back tomorrow—"

"You're busy now?"

"You know I'm trying to write."

"Oh yeah, suddenly you're working away on that album?"

"Don't you have a restaurant you were supposed to open six months ago?"

"You can't rush perfection. Or a liquor license apparently."

Nelle chose that moment to turn the shower on, and for the first and only time in his life, Bran cursed the oversized rain faucet that pounded out water in a torrential downpour. Loud enough to be heard clearly through two sets of doors.

Cormac charged down the hall, giving Bran just enough time to tuck in his elbows, protecting his organs from the battering of jabs landing at his sides. "You lying sack of shit!" The insults rang out, full of glee.

Bran ducked into the opening to the music nook and fell into a brown leather Eames, spinning defensively away from Cormac. Giving up the chase, the drummer slanted himself across the green chaise opposite Bran, like he was goddamn Rose DeWitt Bukater. Admittedly he looked just as good. Cormac was comfortable anywhere, unencumbered by the artistic angst that plagued Bran. Since the band had broken up, he'd taken to working out, another outlet for his immeasurable stores of energy, and his hulking frame dwarfed the lounger. His eyes gleamed with interest. "There's food in your fridge. And someone in your shower. I knew you weren't celibate. Why aren't you in there with her? Him? Her?"

Bran let his knees fall wide in the chair. "Because I knew you'd bust in on us."

"And you're the only one busting a nu—"

"Why are you like this?"

Cormac laughed, his head tipping back. "I'm intrigued. You're taking my advice for once."

"How's that?"

"Didn't I tell you yesterday? Beat this writer's block thing. Bang it out. Get those juices flowing. Let it rest and then cut into the meat—"

"I think that metaphor got away from you."

"It was never my department."

Behind Cormac, the evidence of that statement was set in frames: records that had been certified gold, platinum, double platinum. A shelf with shining awards in various shapes and materials, silver rocket ships stamped with a cable logo and glass stars from the Besties, with one iconic combination missing.

Bran sighed, trying to release how badly he wanted that damn gold clef. He relaxed his grip on the chair's arm rails. "Will you get out of here now? Before she—"

"She! Why can't I stay and talk to Shower Girl? She's in there because she's dirty, huh?"

"We're keeping it private."

"Aya knows."

"Aya knows everything."

Cormac's smile softened and then he frowned. "It's not Francesca again, is it? The rhyming was really too much. And you gotta know she just wants the hottest date for the big dance."

Bran laughed, forgetting himself for a moment. "Shower Girl doesn't need me for a prime seat at the Note Awards."

Cormac sat up. "She's industry?"

In the silence, the rain-head stopped thundering. Bran stood. "Thanks for coming by, don't come back because I'm barricading the door."

The drummer's body went limp. Bran tugged at his meaty arm. "Cormac, get up."

"I want to meet her."

"Not happening."

A struggle ensued as Cormac let his body drag them both to the floor. Bran fell back, huffing out a curse, and rolling sideways to inspect a rug burn at his elbow. Cormac reclined against the chaise. "You're so weak."

"I'm not weak. You're an ox."

"Thank you."

"It wasn't a compliment."

Cormac laughed and heaved himself off the ground, biceps bulging with the effort. He offered Bran a hand, but Bran pushed up on his own. With Bran on his feet,

Cormac started to leave, pausing before he reached the hall. He turned in the opening and stretched his arms wide across the arch.

"You clammed up on us yesterday."

"Like I said: *it's private.*" Vitally private. *Secret.* Something they had to protect, or lose.

With a narrow look, Cormac corrected him. "I meant before your guest arrived. What happened at the funeral? Your old man wasn't 'okay,' was he?"

"What makes you think that?"

"I've met the son of a—" He stopped himself. "No offense meant to your gran. I don't know how he managed to get so mean, with a mother like that."

"I asked her once," Bran admitted, not meeting Cormac's eye. "She said he always took his coffee black." Bitterness became a habit. A craving. Bran had seen it in his father's scheming eyes at the funeral.

"I tried getting into the house this morning, tried to pick up some of my old things," he'd said as they stood on the church steps, collars up against the wind. "Did Gran change the locks?"

"About the house," his father had replied, without answering the question, "it was real nice of you to send Mom those checks each month."

Bran's shoulders had risen, like he'd anticipated the blow.

"Maybe we keep that going for a bit."

"I don't think she has many expenses now."

His father had snatched the glasses off his face in a blinding flash. Bran had squinted in the sun, cold wind stinging the scrapes on his nose.

"You think that's funny?"

"No, sir," Bran had said automatically, hating how

his father produced that child's role in him. But he'd rehearsed it too many times. The performance had become too natural. He had seized up, listening to his father with his eyes down, memorizing the pattern of the salt on the steps.

"That's my mother you're disrespecting," his father had continued in a low snarl. "And while you've sent *checks*, I've been here, I've put my own money *and* time into taking care of her. And now I've got to get the house fixed up and ready to sell. New kitchen, new windows, stuff you should have done for her while she was still here, but it's too late now."

Bran's gaze had shot up and his father had raised his fist in response, crushing the glasses inside and holding one finger up as a warning. "She could have paid for it herself if she'd sold some of the junk you left behind. So could I, come to think of it." Like he hadn't already thought of it. Like he hadn't changed the locks, to make sure Bran was a step behind. Bran had fumed, his elbows tucking in as he held himself together, held his mouth shut, the way he'd learned, repeating to himself Gran's advice, *When he's like that, Bran, don't give him anything else.* Don't feed the fire. Wait for it to burn out.

His father had noticed Tomi then, walking up the path from the parking lot to join them. He'd clapped a hand on Bran's shoulder. He'd squeezed. "But I know you'll do the right thing by your pop. Keep sending those checks and when I've got it all worked out, we'll talk about what you earned from inside."

Cormac sighed, loud enough to break Bran out of the memory. "You're not gonna tell me, huh?" His gaze lifted to the far wall, where Bran's collection of guitars rested on hooks for easy access. He tapped a thoughtful rhythm on the frame. "You ever think that's the real problem? You're keeping too much to yourself? How can you write if you won't let anything go?"

Bran waited until Cormac was halfway down the stairs. "Ask Aya."

"She already told me," Cormac called back. "I wanted to hear it from you."

Bran didn't respond as his friend finally departed. He stood in the center of the room, listening for the front door to open and close.

Then he and Nelle were alone again, their secret safe. He sank into the chair, kicking his feet up on a matching stool. Running one hand over his face, he tried to shake out the tight feeling in his chest—a heartstring, overtuned. He rubbed at his collar.

The final cheers of the album Nelle had put on faded into silence. He was starting to get used to it when she peeked into the room. He managed a smile. "All clear."

"I thought so, I didn't hear anything," she said, but her attention was on the walls. She walked slowly through the space, her hand grazing the frames, as she'd done in his closet. Her hair was still wet, seeping into the grey T-shirt she wore. Another one of his that he'd always picture on her.

Nelle stopped at a shelf of awards. Deft fingers began shifting them each an inch to the side, rearranging them so there was a space in the middle. She looked over her shoulder at him, her eyelashes still thickly spiked from the shower. "You need an open spot, for that Cleffy."

He brushed at his shoulder and raised his eyebrows. "I'm nominated for two."

She picked up a rocket ship and moved it to the back row, clearing a second space.

"You're that confident I'll win?"

"I am, but you should be too." She put her hands on her hips, scrunching the fabric of the shirt. It rose just high enough to tease the bottom curves of her ass. She glanced back. "Close your eyes."

"I really don't want to."

"You have to visualize it, Bran."

Nelle swung around and he lost the view anyway. Sighing, Bran closed his eyes. Because she said so and because he'd do anything to make sure those Cleffies came home with him. When the band's last album had been snubbed, and Judith dissolved shortly after, he'd thought it was over—that he'd never be good enough, especially on his own. It was a message he'd heard often enough.

But Bran wasn't listening to his dad anymore, he was listening to Nelle. She moved purposefully through the room and he pivoted the chair to follow the sound.

"Okay. It's your night. They are *your* Cleffies. You win them both. You're leaving with everything you want." Fingers sank into his hair, nails scratching his scalp, and he chased after them. "Cultivate a mindset of abundance. Say yes. And manifest that shit."

Bran laughed, opening his eyes to the bright room. "Is that another Benjism?"

Nelle stood, stroking his hair, the wall of guitars behind her. "That's all me."

All Nelle. He couldn't think of anything better.

"You just bend the universe to your will?"

"I think the universe hears you, if you make yourself clear, if you let yourself trust. It's a conversation: the universe sends signs, and if you say yes, if you believe, you receive. Positivity, patience, no fear. Then the universe does what it can, and you do the rest—like any partnership."

"And that works for you? You didn't win last year."

"I had my heart set on something bigger. The universe responds to intention. To desire." She leveled him with a look—did she mean him? "Notable New Artist wasn't my category. When I know I earned it, when I'm not competing against the other beginners, when I'm in it with the greats, that's the win I'm taking."

"You're talking about 'Under Water.'"

"I know." She twirled and ran a hand along the wing of a black-paneled Rickenbacker. She held up fingers layered with dust. "You want to talk about it?"

He shrugged. "I'm thinking of pitching a Springsteen cover album."

"I knew you liked Springsteen!"

"Oh, could you tell from my beating heart?" He grasped her hips, tugging her onto his lap. His hands moved under the shirt, drawing a shiver out of her as he plucked at her nipples. "How are we going to do this?"

Her eyes closed and her voice grew husky. "Here is fine."

"I meant—*us*, this. Having something. And keeping it secret. Both." The impossible. They'd have to choose—wouldn't they?

Nelle blinked, sighed, linked her fingers together at the back of his neck. "Well. We take it one night at a time. That's all I have. My schedule is booked—I won't be in town again until the Note Awards."

"You're performing?"

"That's right. And next year, universe providing, I'll be giving my own uplifting Notable Song speech."

"You already know what you're going to say?"

"Don't you?"

"Not even a little bit." Bran rested his palms on her thighs.

"You should work on it. Make sure you use your platform to matter." She stared into his eyes, thoughts spinning behind them. "This year you'll be busy celebrating after the show, so let's plan on me sneaking out of the hotel the night before. I'll stay here and head back early in the morning, before the glam squad is scheduled to show up at my room."

"And at the awards? What do we do?"

"Nothing." Her eyes narrowed as his thumb stroked higher. "Nothing like that. We don't speak. We don't look at each other. Nothing. It doesn't exist outside this house."

"So I'll divert my gaze and pretend I didn't spend the last twelve hours making you moan my name? You think that will work?"

"There's no story if we don't give them one. And…" She trailed off, lifting her hips as he ran a knuckle through her crease. She was wet and warm, but he pulled his hand back, wondering what she had been about to say.

"And?"

"And. We can always give them a better story. Like I did before. Make it public knowledge that we can't stand each other."

Bran pushed a hand into his hair, sliding it up and back, breaking Nelle's hold on his neck. "I don't like involving the media."

She sat back as much as she could on his lap. "It's not involving them. It's using them, the same way they use us to get what they want. If they don't have to abide by common decency, neither do we. We'll beat them at their game. And gloat in private. You said you did the same thing with Cormac and Arlo. It's a better story that there's a rift between you."

"I didn't give that story to anyone. I just haven't said it's not true."

"Because it benefits you."

"It's not the same."

"How?"

"You're talking about setting the house on fire with us inside."

"It's easier to hide when the smoke is thick."

"Also easier to choke, stifle, and die."

"It's a backup plan. We'll only need it if you—"

"Me?"

"Yeah, Bran, you're the one who can't keep his head down."

"I can too."

Nelle ducked her chin and ground down against his lap, where his dick had begun tenting his pants.

He gripped her hips and held her there, sitting up to bring his mouth to hers. "Is that a problem now?"

She rocked in his lap, her hands sliding up his arms and tightening on his shoulders. "The problem is how much I like that." Her head dropped back and she rolled her hips harder as she spoke. "I married you not knowing how much I liked that. But I like the first part too—" She broke off to gasp, then swallowed hard and continued, "The original plan to have something that was just ours. Burning the whole thing down is the last resort. Don't you want to keep doing this? Without anyone calling a hashtag meeting?" Her brow furrowed. "Don't you want both? Me, and a secret?"

His chest twisted, his brain fogged. She was a tornado, lifting him up, setting him down dizzy. Making it easy because he didn't have a choice.

"One night at a time," he agreed, before carrying her down the hall and tossing her onto the bed. She wanted both: sex and secrets blurred together into one. He wanted her, and the only way to have her was to agree. If the universe didn't dare deny her, what chance did Bran Kelly have?

Bran Fucking Kelly

Today 12:17 am

LA?

yeah but

it's too late

# Chapter Sixteen

Nelle bobbed forward as her driver, Albi, tapped the brake. The sea of black SUVs and one lone Tesla was as LA as the sun beating down from its peak. Even with the AC on full blast, the combination of tinted windows and hot metal made her feel like she was driving in an oven. And for the second year in a row, she'd made the wrong fabric choice. Last year she'd shivered down the red carpet in thin blue silk with a low, low back and a temp to match. Now she was sweating in a swath of green velvet, at odds with more than the weather, and running up regrets.

The first, of course, was choosing the dress for its hue, ignoring its breathability. The deep emerald was a subtle nod to a man she could not back outright. Her team had helped pick it out weeks ago. "Green looks good on you," Benj had said, and Mina had agreed, missing the wink. "Gem tones," she'd said with a decisive nod.

Nelle had spent the morning in processing, packaged into her picture-perfect public persona. Because on days like this she wasn't so much a person as she was a product. She had yawned through the preparations, cementing her second regret: staying up, knowing she had an early call, waiting to see what time the aforementioned man would remember that they had plans. She should have just gone to sleep. In the month since she'd barged into his house, Bran Kelly had apparently forgotten she existed. He hadn't texted, he hadn't called—he hadn't so much as sent a *New York Times* link to an article that might interest her.

He'd just let her go. Out of sight, out of mind.

She didn't expect daily check-ins. She was too busy for that anyway, crawling into bed exhausted, her mind crammed with blocking and transitions. But when she married a man known for his ability to string a line together, and then they agreed to see what might happen, was the occasional exceptionally worded sext out of the question? Bran had said he wasn't writing, she just hadn't thought that applied to typing more than two letters as a late-night booty call.

Nelle recrossed her ankles, kicking at the stupid thick dress as it tangled in her physics-defying gold platform wedges. Today was not the day to have a bad attitude. It didn't go with her outfit. But she'd brought one anyway. She was used to being hot and bothered about Bran, just not like this. And despite the traffic jam, she felt herself hurtling forward on a collision course towards him.

There was no way she wouldn't see him. That was what audiences loved about award shows: all their faves overlapping in one place. She didn't want to overlap—well, she had last night—but today she was committed to running parallel, keeping their storylines separate. It was going to be a big night for them both, on their own merits.

If Albi could get her there.

Nelle closed her eyes, leaning into the fan's airflow.

"Are we concerned that even if we're in time for the red carpet, my face will melt off?"

Mina answered without looking up from her phone. "Yes."

"No," Benj countered, hanging over the back seat. "Your face is under your face. And it's perfect. Besides." Nelle's best friend surveyed the half ponytail and loose curls she'd arranged. "Your hair could resist a hurricane. And if you hadn't stayed up so late, I wouldn't have had to pack on so much concealer—"

"You were up late?" Mina asked, her head still down. A potential problem was worth a bit of her attention. "Why?"

Nelle tried and failed to cross her arms over the wide couture bow at her bust. She shrugged her bare shoulders instead. "I was writing. You know. Making music—that's kind of the point of this."

It wasn't an outright lie. Nelle had composed a number of strongly worded text messages she hadn't sent. And the last few had the kind of underlying rhythm she recognized as lyrical. She'd screen-grabbed them to come back to when she had time.

Mina didn't waste any energy debating whether the Note Awards red carpet was more or less a part of Nelle's job than writing music. "We're supposed to be seated by 4 p.m. There won't be time for touch-ups. Just try not to sweat too much."

Nelle tongued her teeth. "Yeah, no problem. Just like I'll try not to need air or sustenance."

"You had breakfast."

"Egg whites aren't food. And typically people eat more than once a day. I told you I wanted to stop for a milkshake."

Mina finally looked up. "It's the Note Awards, Nelle. People will be scrutinizing every frame looking for something snarky they can say to help them go viral. Do you want that to be at your expense? Again?" Her manager sighed when Nelle didn't answer. "I got you a juice."

Nelle glanced at the plastic cup of liquid spinach in the holder between them. The paper straw had gone wet and gummy, closing off the hole. Mina produced a pair of emergency scissors from the bag of supplies she always carried and snipped a fresh opening.

"Here we go!" Albi called back to them as the car swerved into the next lane.

Behind her, Benj lifted Nelle's hair from her neck, offering a cool reprieve.

Nelle took a long sip of the juice. It tasted better than it looked, with a kick of ginger and lemon. Much better for her than a milkshake, considering she was singing tonight and didn't need to coat her throat with dairy.

Everyone in the car was here to support her and she was acting like a brat.

"Thanks, guys," she said to rework her mood into an attitude of gratitude.

Mina bobbed her chin and took over directing Albi.

Her friend waited a beat and whispered, "You could have texted him."

"But it's always me, Benj." She wanted Bran to come after her.

Nelle spun the angled ring on her finger as the car lurched forward once more and stopped. She tried desperately not to let the movement remind her of her first kiss with Bran, but she could still remember the moment he reacted to her, how hungrily he'd kissed her back, forgetting to shift the car into Park.

"Ready?" Mina waited with the silver door handle half sprung for Nelle to respond.

When she got out of the car, Nelle knew she wouldn't have time to worry about Bran Kelly, last night, or being tired or hungry or hot or any of it. These kinds of events were like rapids—the night would have its own course. All she could do was push off into the current and hang on for the ride.

Nelle nodded. "So ready."

Stepping out of the car was like stepping into a fever dream. The noise hit her like a wall. Next was the blast of heat, but Nelle had played Midwestern state fairs in August, so she squared her shoulders and dove in.

The red carpet under her feet seemed to pulse through her body, turning her on and charging her up. She raised a hand to wave as someone straightened the hem of the gown behind her. They would make her look as good as they could, and she would do the rest. She would be Nelle.

Heading downstream, interactions hit her like flashes of light: a hug from a fan there, a promise to come to India soon, a smile and a thank-you, spinning from one moment to the next.

The crowd, the glitz, the sun. Glinting light glanced off phone screens, lenses, glasses, up, down, and all around her.

Nelle twirled out of a selfie and into an embrace from fellow bop-maker Miss Charma. There was just enough time to compliment her fresh look before Mina steered Nelle the other way. "*Music Now!* wants an interview."

"Kara Robins?" Nelle asked, taking a swig of water Benj offered.

Mina shook her head. "Maternity leave. It's Nick Stone. Don't make a face, it's part of the job."

As long as Stone was with *Music Now!* Nelle couldn't avoid him. They had him set up on a platform to the far side of the carpet. Nelle wobbled up a rickety set of steps, wishing for a handrail. The production team had apparently spent as much time on Nick Stone's ensemble—a neon suit with stark stitching that had an inside-out look, like it was taken off the tailor's dummy unfinished—as the stairs leading up to him.

She kept her focus on her feet until she reached the top. In the monitors, an inflexible smile on Stone's un-lined face revealed teeth so white they were almost blue. "And now we're being joined by the beautiful Nelle!" He didn't turn to greet her. His priority was keeping his face on the air.

Nelle breezed forward, coming into frame. The pro-duction footage showed a square outline over her body, uncomfortably reminiscent of a sniper narrowing in on a target.

"Hi!" she said as brightly as she could.

"Big night! Biggest night in music!"

Nelle nodded. "It sure is."

"So let's get down to the important stuff."

"Please." She couldn't wait to talk about what she had planned for "Under Water" tonight.

Nick cocked his head, loading his question in the chamber. "Do you have a date tonight?"

Nelle watched her smile dim in the monitors, and she charged it back up again, pretending the highlighter on her cheeks was iridescent war paint. This. This was exactly why she had to keep Bran Kelly a secret. People like Nick Stone cared more about who she was with than why she was here.

"My parents couldn't make it," Nelle said, purposefully misinterpreting the question.

She didn't add that they were camera shy after what had happened at Christmas. That when she'd asked if they wanted to come out and see her perform, her mother had gone uncharacteristically subdued. "Your father's not up for it, I think, Nella."

"Is everything okay?" Nelle had immediately jumped to the worst-case scenario. "Is Papa—"

"He's fine. Everything is fine. We're more comfortable at home."

Nelle didn't add that because it was private. Her father had never wanted a press release about his illness. Her mother had never consented to having her vulnerability monetized. Now they were pulling back, watching her from a safe distance. If she had pushed it, they would have come. But how could she blame them for trying to reclaim some sense of privacy—wasn't that exactly what she was doing, practicing discretion with Bran? To show her love, her support, she had to respect their decision, their healing.

So she walked the red carpet alone.

Stone forged ahead with another frivolous question. "Who are you wearing?"

Nelle kept her smile in place. This was the script, even if her opinion was that it desperately needed a rewrite. And she'd picked a designer she was proud to plug. "Very excited to be in Shonda James."

"Absolutely stunning, of course."

"She's amazing, especially the work she's doing in her community—"

"Tell me how the heat's treating you in that fabric. Are you looking forward to changing out of it for your performance?"

"I'm looking forward to the performance," Nelle said, taking any opening she could. Stone held the microphone tight to his chest even when she was talking. She leaned closer to him, keeping her sentences short in case he cut her off again. "We're getting ready for tour. Working so hard. Very excited. Can't wait to see everybody, to dance together and sing with you guys. And tonight's really special because we get to give people a glimpse of what we're putting together for them."

She smiled at the camera, glad to have gotten her whole message out. And she'd done her part for the conversation, helped lead him into the real important stuff—like stats about the tour running April through September, over three continents, with fifty sold-out shows—but that wasn't what Nick Stone thought the people at home wanted to hear.

"What do you eat in preparation for something like that?"

Nelle blinked. "Food?"

That earned her a laugh and a wink. Then his glassy eyes were staring at the camera just off her shoulder again. "All that dancing must be great for your metabolism."

Nelle caught her breath and held it until the response she wanted to blurt become secondary to the air she needed to exhale. By the time she was ready to respond without calling Stone an asshole, the tide was changing. Producers motioned for Stone to toss her back to the carpet, and then everyone was shifting, making room for the next catch. In a matter of seconds Nelle found herself facing the stairs again. Her forehead was hot as she started down them. Under the layers of Benj's makeup, she was sure her face was red. Not from the unrelenting sun, but from inner frustration, that she hadn't put her words together fast enough to tell off a man in an ugly suit who had tried to reduce her accomplishments to the shape of her body.

Nelle took a rushed step down the narrow set of ledges, forgetting to gather her dress to the side in her haste. Her shoe twisted in the slit. On one foot, the other caught in the folds of her dress, Nelle felt the world lurch sideways. She was going to fall, tumble straight off the edge of the steps. Her arms flailed, finding nothing to hold—

And a hand clasped her elbow.

Instinctively she grasped at the suit sleeve that pressed against her forearm. Steadying herself, she looked up. Blue eyes met hers. And the air left her lungs, knocked out of her like she'd landed on the carpet below after all.

Bran Kelly had caught her. He shared the space in a wine-colored suit cut to fit his body like it was made for him—which of course it was. He was here to win not one Cleffy, but two. The whole night was custom-designed for him. Her mouth went dry—Bran Kelly looking like a tall glass of red made her thirsty.

"I got you," Bran said as his calloused palm scraped down to her wrist, shooting fireworks through the rest of her body.

So much for parallel lines. Arm to arm, they literally overlapped, the sun serving as a spotlight.

Nelle sucked in air, trying to ignore the way his eyes flickered to the top of her dress, her breasts testing the hem of the strapless gown. She blew it out through the ring of her mouth, performing a friendly "phew" for anyone watching. Her voice low, she told him, "This is not what we talked about."

His mouth pulled in a casual smile, one for show, that didn't match the intensity of his gaze or the heat of his skin on hers. "Neither was last night."

He tilted her arm, surreptitiously checking that the ring he'd given her was nestled among the others she wore. It was a gesture that would go unnoticed by the millions of people watching, but it set her cheeks on fire nonetheless with its audacity.

She tugged her hand back and his slid lower, linking them palm to palm. The watch glaring up from his wrist left spots in her vision. "Just help me down and then you can get back in line for the oral surgery that is talking to Nick Stone."

Bran eased them away from the top. "Seemed like a pretty standard interview from down here."

She fought the instinct that told her to stay close to him, his palm frustratingly familiar, his shadow providing momentary relief from the sun. With her feet on solid ground, she was able to roll her eyes without risking loss of balance. Nelle broke her hand from his, letting it float just off her shoulder as she turned. "If only I had time to explain misogyny to you again."

Mina fell in step just behind Nelle as she swept down the carpet. "What a dickhead."

"Bran Kelly?"

"Nick Stone."

Nelle's mistake fizzled in the air between them. As

much as it appealed to her, she could not come undone around Bran Kelly.

Mina's mouth pulled to one side. "Bran Kelly is—"

"A Cleffy-nominated dickhead. Different variety."

Nelle pitched into the final step and repeat before her manager could raise an official red flag. Tonight was not the night to let him get under her skin. Whatever unfinished business they had, she'd handle it later. She was here for her.

# Chapter Seventeen

The Staples Center was split into three stages, and Bran sat front and center. Nelle had been seated a few rows back, on the aisle. He'd seen her on his way in. It had taken more effort than he'd expected to walk by her without making contact. He'd wanted to stop, dip his head, press a kiss to her bare shoulder blade. Lips to skin. He'd wanted to drop next to her chair and ask, kneeling at her feet, why she had changed her mind about seeing him last night.

*It's too late.*

That was the only explanation Nelle had offered when she hadn't come over as planned. He had done everything her way, no contact, no nothing—with the exception of stepping in to make sure she didn't become a fixture on someone's list of top-ten red carpet stumbles. And she hadn't even thanked him. She'd said: "If only I had time to explain misogyny to you again."

The message was clear: time was up.

But why?

He closed his eyes.

Bran had a good ear. A remarkable ear. People loved working with him because he could hear when something was off, pick up on the wrong note or the wrong chord without a moment wasted. Even three rows back, he heard what was wrong immediately: Santino's voice, chatting up his wife. His wife who he wasn't allowed to look at or speak to. His wife who changed her mind like she changed shoes, never wearing the same pair twice—no wonder he couldn't keep up with what she was thinking.

His hand fisted as Nelle's voice filtered through the crowd. "Contraband! You like pineapple?"

Santino spoke with slow, relaxed words. "I like not having a blue tongue on television."

Bran's eyes snapped open. He wasn't allowed to look at Nelle, but some dude with face tattoos could tell her about his tongue.

The wildest image rose in his mind, fueled by jealousy and pent-up sexual frustration—because it was pure fantasy. He imagined Nelle next to him, instead of Aya. And unlike Aya, whose elbows were tucked in tight, Nelle's arm would rest casually across the molded shoulders of his suit, her fingers skimming under his collar for everyone to see—

Bran shifted in his seat. This was insane.

There was no balance to this arrangement. Nelle called all the shots. She said when it was on, when it was off. She invaded his home, made it impossible for him to be in any room without remembering the way his name in her voice echoed off that set of walls. She was inescapable. She'd left imprints on every surface and walked out the door without a mark on her.

And now she was done with him?

He stretched his leg straight to slide the flat phone from his pocket, pulling up their text chain before he could stop himself.

We need to talk

I want to know what's going on

I shouldn't have tried outside

With Stone and the carpet

There were too many phones under one roof and it took forever for the messages to send. Bran held the phone low, willing them to go through. Then he reread them and realized how desperate he sounded. Before he could figure out how to stop them, the service icon flushed full bars. And a call popped up on the screen.

He stared at the caller ID, letting the phone shake in his hand. When it stopped buzzing he shoved the device at Aya. She read the missed call log with a frown. "He called my office last week, asking for his money—"

"*His* money?"

"He made threats, Bran. Told me he'd have to start selling stuff to cover the cost of the house."

"What cost? The mortgage has been paid off for years and we sent him enough in January to cover the property tax ten times over."

"If you won't pay monthly, he wants a big payout. He said—" A voicemail notification shuddered the phone again and she brought it to her ear. She held his gaze as she listened.

When Aya failed to conceal the anger in her eyes, Bran's teeth ground together. "What did he say?"

"Nothing."

"He didn't wish me luck?" He couldn't imagine his father bringing up his big night now. A Cleffy only mattered to his dad when he hadn't had one, because the man dealt in deficits, in negatives.

She looked down at his phone and her frown deepened.

"Aya."

Her eyes met his again. "He said he hopes you win."

Bran started nodding. That was unexpected, that was—

"If you win," Aya went on, "the value of his inventory increases. So."

The words hit him like a punch to the gut and he lurched forward in his seat before remembering where he was. He tried to play it off like he was just adjusting his position, shifting up to get comfortable. He tried to play it off like it didn't matter. Like his father hadn't just tainted the wins Bran so desperately wanted.

Fuck that. No. He wasn't going to give his father that power.

Bran pointed to his phone. "Can I get that back?"

Aya stacked it under her own in her lap. "I don't think so."

"I'm waiting for a message."

"She says 'you won't get it.'"

Bran sucked his front teeth. The nerve—of both these women—for sidelining him on his own affairs.

"And 'Stone is just a symptom.'"

What did Stone have to do with her not coming over? "I need to respond." He had to find out what that meant.

"No. You need to sit there and enjoy this. It's the Note Awards, Bran. Nothing else matters."

Bran looked sideways at her. Aya arched a single thin brow, daring him to argue. He didn't. Not just because he knew he'd lose. Last week Arlo had worried about

Bran being alone for the show. "Do we need to be doing this anymore? Keeping our distance? What's the point if it means we can't support each other?" he'd asked. When Bran insisted again that Arlo not miss classes to fly in, the bass player had laid his concerns out. "What if you start wishing you could have taken her?" And for a moment panic had gripped his chest, only for regret and guilt to tighten the sensation. Arlo hadn't been talking about Nelle, he'd been talking about Gran.

He'd worried Bran would feel lonely on the biggest night of his career.

Here, now, at the Note Awards with Aya at his side, looking out for him, Bran didn't feel alone. Bran reached for Aya's hand in her lap and squeezed.

She blinked a few times and then got back to business. "I thought you handled the carpet well. Especially Stone asking you about new music."

Bran let go of her hand to smooth a wrinkle on his thigh. "Did you hear him ask Nelle anything inappropriate?"

"No."

That's what he thought. She'd looked gorgeous, talked about her performance, and smiled—god that smile, and that bow on her dress like she needed to be unwrapped—

"Is that what you don't get? She has to explain it to you that he asked you about your work, and her about her dress?"

The lights didn't dim as the show began but brightened, so the cameras could catch all the action onstage and off. To Bran it felt like a giant lightbulb turning on above his head. He tuned out of the real world, thinking about Nelle and what Aya had said.

Had Stone treated Bran like an artist and Nelle like a tapestry? Objectively it hadn't been the best interview experience. He'd been annoyed by some of Stone's inane questions too. But what he could shrug off with cultivated indifference, Nelle had to smile through. It wasn't fair, she'd said. It was his world. A man's world. She didn't have time to explain misogyny to him because she was busy dealing with it.

Aya flipped her phone over and light winked off a ring she wore. Bran flashed immediately to Nelle's wedding ring, glinting in the sun. She'd told him in Chicago the risk was hers, and yet she was the one walking around with the evidence on her finger.

If she was done with him, why was she still wearing it?

Aya poked his side. "You want to pay attention to this one."

Bran fumbled for the present, trying to break out of the knot of thoughts in his mind. A new set of presenters had taken the stage. The category at bat was Notable Pop Album, and Bran's album—his solo effort—was being announced as a nominee.

Bran pressed his feet flat to the floor in their black boots. Energy coursed through him but he wouldn't let a shaky leg reveal how much he was anticipating this moment.

If he lost, he had to keep his face neutral.

If he lost, he still had another shot.

If he lost—Nelle didn't think he would lose.

"Bran Kelly, *Green*," said the announcer with a wide smile.

And then Bran was standing. Hugging Aya. Her eyes were shining when she released him, sending him on his way. His ears buzzed. Mirrored black stairs reflected the lights above him—like walking in the night sky—so dreamy they almost made him doubt this was real. When someone pressed a gold clef into his hand, his finger curled around the base. The metal was surprisingly warm, like he'd already been holding it for some time. Like it was already his.

He felt a rush of pride and disbelief and something he couldn't name that felt like the best parts of fame: that he was worthy, that he'd done something people cared about. That he'd earned his place.

A sea of faces looked expectantly up at him. He should have listened to Nelle's advice about having a speech prepared. She'd been so sure of him. As sure as she was about herself. Bran envied that confidence—he needed signs. Proof that people continued to care. Like that ring on her finger.

She was still wearing it.

Bran shook his head, trying to focus on what to say. Possibilities rattled inside his brain. *I wish my gran could be here tonight,* he could tell them, if he was in the mood to bare his soul to millions of strangers. *Fuck you, Dad,* he might add, if he really wanted to get into it. He tried to push the thought that his father would be happy with this outcome as far down as he could, but it kept rising to the surface as he stood there.

His heart picked up speed and his feet shifted as everyone waited for him to say *something.*

*Get it together, Bran.*

He fixed his gaze on Aya's calm face and his mind quieted.

What mattered most in this moment?

"I put a lot of energy into trying not to be recognized," he started. He paused for scattered laughter. "But this is truly a privilege." The word hooked another memory of Nelle, calling it up. With the ring, she'd given him a sign: she might be mad but she wasn't done. He'd send her a message back, prove to her that he did get it. He looked up, clarity producing confidence. "Outside someone asked if I was disappointed not to have gotten one of these when I was in a rock band. There's a perception that pop music is for young girls, and the implication that I should be disappointed in that audience really bothered me. It is a privilege to make music liked by such a discerning, smart, powerful group and I hope to make more music that meets their high standards—thank you."

The stadium burst into applause. And even though he wasn't supposed to, he looked right, to the third row, only to see Nelle's seat was taken by a filler, a live television extra who turned beet red under his gaze. He gripped the Cleffy close. Nelle had wrapped herself up in the win like one of his shirts—she'd told him about the nomination, she'd told him to be ready to win. The Cleffy and Nelle were linked. She wasn't even here and she'd always be part of this moment for him. He'd always feel like she had made this happen.

The urge to track her down drove him forward. And this time he was setting the terms: as long as that ring was on her finger, she was his for the taking.

## Chapter Eighteen

The chair's metal armrest dug into Nelle's side as she bent around Benj to see the screen mounted in the corner of the dressing room.

"By all means, if the Joker is the look you're going for, keep doing what you're doing."

"I don't want to miss it," Nelle said.

"You want to see him lose because he stood you up?"

He had stood her up. He'd also sent a pair of texts right before the ceremony started that had surprised her.

Bran Fucking Kelly: I want to know what's going on

Bran Fucking Kelly: With Stone and the carpet

She'd written back that he wouldn't get it because it was too complicated to explain over text and he hadn't tried again. But he had reached out. It wasn't nothing.

Nelle let Benj lift her chin, but couldn't hold her mouth still. "He's not going to lose."

After scanning Nelle's face, Benj stepped back, out of the way. She started a final warning, "But no more—"

Grinning, Nelle dropped one of the last two gummy bears Santino had given her into her mouth.

Benj pursed her lips. "You suck that—no chewing. Mina will blame me if it's stuck in your teeth on camera."

"Exactly why Santino only brings the clear ones." Tucking the candy into her cheek, Nelle turned her attention back to the TV. A split screen drew her to the edge of the seat. In a little rectangle, bottom right, was Bran. He looked perfect, relaxing back in his seat. Calm and still and focused.

And then his name was called. And Nelle realized what else he was: unpresumptuous. Bran's head bowed, hiding his raw emotion. But when his eyes lifted, the rest of his face composed, Nelle could still see the disbelief. He hadn't expected to win.

She brought fisted hands to her face—and Benj leapt forward to pry them off.

"Do you want to smudge?"

Nelle shushed her friend, twisting her hands free. Bran climbed the stairs, gripped the award, and paused. With each breath he took, the red suit jacket gaped open and shut.

"Ready?" Mina popped her head into the room. "You're on after the next break."

Nelle put one foot on the ground, but couldn't complete the descent from the chair. She shouldn't care so much. He'd won. That was what she wanted to see. But she couldn't look away. That was Bran—*her* Bran. Onstage. Living a dream. Their dream.

"Nelle. Let's move," Mina spoke over Bran. The audience laughed.

"One second!" Nelle snapped, her eyes glued to the screen. She felt Benj's hands in her hair.

"Let me make sure this doesn't come loose," Benj said to Mina.

*Thank you*, Nelle mouthed.

It was finally quiet enough in the room for Bran's voice to be clear, but she wasn't sure she was hearing him right. Even Mina turned towards the screen, her eyes narrowing, like she didn't trust the source. Nelle had expected Bran to win. She didn't think he'd try to take on the patriarchy in his acceptance speech.

He left the stage and them in stunned silence.

"What was that?" Benj said, her hands resting on Nelle's shoulders, hair forgotten.

"That was Aya Cooke," Mina added in a mutter, "God, she's good." She looked over her shoulder at Nelle half sitting on the chair, and clapped them back into action. "Okay, let's go. That's us in eleven minutes."

Nelle let herself be guided through the crowded backstage, following behind Mina with her mind on the performance. She'd rehearsed, she'd warmed up, and now she was visualizing her triumph one more time. They stopped near a water fountain to let a marching band go past. Her palm felt hot and—sticky? She unclenched her fist and discovered the final gummy bear.

Mina stepped closer. "What's in your hand?"

"Nothing," Nelle answered, shoving the candy into her mouth before her manager could take it.

"You have ten minutes to disappear that."

Nelle started to say it didn't take ten minutes to eat a gummy bear, but a sudden intake of breath cut her off.

Bran Kelly, fresh off his Note Awards win, was surging down the hall towards them, and her body pulled in oxygen like it was preparing to dive. His eyes held a wild look that sent a shock down her spine. He moved through the crowd as more force than person, an unstoppable wave rushing forward to meet her. And secrets be damned, he would meet her—in this packed hall, filled with eyes and cameras and phones—she knew it as soon as his gaze washed over her. She couldn't even be mad about it because she prepared to let him: her self-control and Bran Kelly looking at her like that didn't exist long in the same space.

Nelle stepped behind Mina for protection, but her manager moved to check on the dancers waiting ahead of them. Nelle rocked on her heels, seeking somewhere else to hide.

There was an opening next to the water fountain, a sign for restrooms fixed to the wall.

"Cover me," Nelle whispered to Benj before ducking through the gap. She took two quick lefts in pursuit of safety. From Bran and from herself. From the urge to throw herself into his arms and congratulate him without a care for who saw. From the urge to overlap and give up everything they'd gained.

The corridor came up short, dead-ending with a door to a maintenance room. Footsteps followed her and she spun, ready to tell Mina she was fine—

Bran Kelly turned the corner. Long, confident strides brought him closer and he didn't stop. All that power crashed against her, forcing her flat against the wall. His hands raised to her hair and she caught his wrists, pulling them down to his sides.

Her head rolled on the wall, straining away from him as he brought his mouth down towards hers. "You can't—"

His lips pressed hot against her neck. He murmured against her skin. "It's my night—I can do anything."

Her grip tightened on his wrists. "I'm onstage in nine minutes."

If he got her lipstick on him, someone would color match it and compare it to everyone there—that was how the internet worked. There was probably an algorithm.

He groaned, grinding his hips into her, pinning her to the wall as his forehead leaned against it. Nelle closed her eyes, counting the pounding beats of her heart. A full eight-count passed before she felt Bran take a deep breath and ease off of her. She released his wrists and he brought one hand up to the wall next to her head. His eyes skimmed down her body, and she was suddenly extremely aware of the expanses of her skin exposed by a low-cut sequin bodysuit smoothing under black-and-gold houndstooth shorts.

Bran trailed a knuckle from her neck to just above her navel. "You still don't have time to talk?"

She shook her head with her lips parted and he nodded.

"Then come home tonight. We'll talk there."

Sensation fogged Nelle's mind as he dragged his knuckle back up. "What?"

"Come home with me."

"I can't—"

"It's my night. They are my Cleffies. I'm leaving with everything I want." His eyes gleamed as he repeated her words back to her. "I want you."

"People will be watching you. We can't leave together."

"We won't. You'll go first and I'll follow after." He

traced the curved side of her breast with one finger. Her nipples puckered against the tape that covered them. "I'm ending tonight satisfied. Deep inside of you."

A dangerous smile pulled at one side of his face because he was well aware what that kind of talk did to her. Nelle swallowed. "That doesn't make you sound very celibate."

"Maybe I'm not celibate. Maybe I've forsaken everyone but my wife."

Nelle's pulse kicked up. It was a tease. She knew that. But still. To hear Bran Kelly say he'd forsaken all others for her—to have him openly call her his wife—her body responded everywhere. A shiver of pleasure ran across her shoulders and swept down her spine, urging her hips into him.

He reciprocated the pressure below her waist, his dick hard between them. "You wanted to come over last night, didn't you? And you want to come tonight. We can make that happen. I can update my manifestation."

Her breath was heavy and sweet between them. "Winning two Cleffies isn't enough for you?"

Bran closed his eyes. "I'm adding you in." He gripped her hips. "There I am. And there you are. And I'm doing things to you I've never done before."

"That's not possible."

His palms slipped over the curves of her butt, squeezing her cheeks, pulling them apart. Nelle's eyes widened with understanding. They hadn't done that. She hadn't considered that.

Bran had. Bran was. Right then. And the look of rapture on his face made her wonder—should she be considering it too?

No. Because she wasn't considering *any* of this.

Bran's blue eyes opened slowly, like he didn't want to leave the place he'd created in his mind. He found the chevron ring on her hand and stroked it with the pad of his finger. "The way I see it, as long as this is on, so are we."

"We can't—"

"Are you willing to gamble?"

"Not when I'm still waiting on two million dollars from our last wager."

"Let's figure out a sign. Let's say: if I win again, you're coming home with me. The universe will have spoken."

"I can't," she said, but the repetition only weakened her conviction. A refrain repeated too many times, losing all meaning.

"But you want to. And you get what you want." Half a smile graced his face, the one that she thought about most—the one that made Bran look like he had a secret. "Maybe if the visual was clearer—" He leaned in.

She put her hands on his chest, stopping him from landing the kiss.

"Just a taste?" he whispered.

He was going to win. That's what she'd been telling them both. It's what she knew in her heart. Why fight it? Nelle wasn't one to argue with what the universe put in her path.

Nelle felt Bran's erection throb as her tongue swirled against her cheek. She brought the last gummy bear forward, holding it between her teeth, her red lips parted around it.

Bran angled his head, careful not to touch his lips to hers. He bit into the sweet, drawing it into his mouth.

Nelle stared at him as he pulled back. There were a

hundred things she should be focusing on before going onstage to perform, but she couldn't pull a single one to the surface of her mind.

Everything was Bran. Could she bet on his success for another night together? It was impossible. They'd never get away with it. Or maybe they would? Against the odds they were alone now, weren't they? There were no cameras here, no people, no one to stop her from—

"Nelle?" Mina's voice traveled down the hall and Nelle froze.

## Chapter Nineteen

Nelle's palms were hot through his coat. She'd slipped them under the lapels like she couldn't help getting just a little bit closer to him. The gummy bear he'd taken from her teeth had lost definition, worn smooth by her mouth. He bit into it. The tang of pineapple coated his tongue as she stared up at him with wide amber eyes. Had she felt the air stutter out of his lungs?

Bran felt drunk, buzzing with adrenaline from his win and intoxicated by the sight of Nelle in thigh-high boots and little else, looking like she hadn't come to play. Fuck the awards, he wanted to take her home—he wanted to take her now. But he had to win another Cleffy first.

A voice he didn't recognize interrupted his thoughts. "Nelle?"

Panic set the intensity in Nelle's eyes and a primal urge to help her spurred Bran into action. He tugged her off the wall, sending her back the way they'd come. She disappeared around the corner and he heard her collide with someone just out of sight.

"Is this another Barcelona?"

"No." Nelle dropped the one-word sentence like a mic and he imagined her eyes glowing hot and fierce

as she said it. "I'm fine. I was taking a moment for myself. To get focused."

"And are you?"

"Absolutely."

Focused? Bran fell against the wall as the two pairs
of footsteps faded away. How could she be focused right
now? He could barely remember his name. He looked
down at the extremely noticeable bulge in his pants, the
cause of his limited brain function.

Bran racked his mind, trying to think of something
unsexy to shut down the launch process, something that
was the opposite of Nelle. *No Nelle.* He couldn't think
of anything worse. It wasn't a particularly advanced
thought, but it worked: missing Nelle's performance
because he was contemplating jacking off in a maintenance room was not sexy.

Nelle's friend Benj had ushered him into the corridor
saying, "Bathroom's to the right." Now Bran found it,
staying long enough to wet his hands and grab a paper
towel, which he made a display of tossing into a black
bin next to the water fountain when he returned to the
main hall. In case anyone wondered where he'd been.

Nelle and her team were gone.

He found an assistant producer to get him back to his
section just as the commercial break started. Aya looked
up when he jostled the seat next to her. She studied his
face. "Tell me you didn't try to see her back there."

"How did you—"

"You look like you do when you come offstage after
a long set."

"Hot and wired?"

"Bran. The two of you are already a meme."

She held a phone low in her lap. Someone had made a

gif out of their moment on the red carpet. Bran squinted down at a loop of himself staring hungrily at Nelle as she rolled her eyes and walked away. Aya scrolled and the picture became a still, a screen grab with white block letters over his chest reading, "Milk that's organic and grass-fed but not local."

"I don't get it," Bran said.

Aya let out an exasperated breath and kept scrolling. He read the text over his body out loud. "'A free UberX but the cooler is full of off-brand La Croix.' 'Artisanal candles but the glass jar isn't recycled'? What does that even mean?"

In each one Nelle was walking away, one hand above her shoulder like she'd tossed a match and didn't care to see what exploded. The word NOPE slanted across the green bow of her dress.

"It means: You're not perfect enough. And she's in a discerning, self-respecting mood."

"That's not so bad."

"It is if you don't want it to exist outside of your house. It is if you won't let me get involved—"

"I won't."

Around them people were settling back into their seats and Aya clicked the screen black. "Your speech was good. It'll probably offset this nonsense. Arlo asked me how I came up with it and I won't tell you how hard it was for me not to take credit. But you can't be seen anywhere near her again tonight. I don't want your name in the same paragraph of copy."

Bran folded his hands over his stomach and leaned back. Aya should have known better than to tell him not to do something. *You can't*—the words heated his blood so it seared through his skin, but in his mind it was

Nelle's voice saying them. The scent of her hair thick in his nose, the sequins of her top winking up at him.

*You can't* was a challenge. He was going to get close to Nelle again. Tonight. He was going to win and she'd come home with him. And if he didn't, there was the after-party. There were dark corners. He could admit that not getting caught was part of the draw. That he liked living on the edge. Aya had seen it on his face—sneaking around with Nelle affected him like the roar of a crowd. Like live drums that *boom-boomed* in veins like heartbeats. Hips that moved to the music like sex.

Like rock and roll.

"Kelly, are you listening to me? If I see one more picture of you two together, I'm stepping in."

Spotlights roamed overhead and someone coaxed the crowd into applause. On the farthest stage, an actor—one of the brothers from those cop movies, Jackson or Milo Fox, he couldn't tell which—was making an announcement Bran ignored until the last word: *Nelle.*

"You don't want to do that to her."

The arena went dark.

He used the momentary hush to ask Aya, "Do what to her?"

"Make her night about you."

A single beam of gold light snapped on, and the audience erupted into genuine cheers. High above them, at the top of stage steps leading nowhere—nowhere but to her—stood Nelle, a silhouette of confident curves and backlighting.

Someone whistled long and loud, the shrill ringing in Bran's ears, and Nelle waited, absorbing it all, second by second.

*Her night.*

Half an hour ago, he'd congratulated himself on his ability to see things from her perspective, never thinking of it as anything but *his* night.

Nelle was performing at the Note Awards. And minutes before she was about to go on, he'd been trying to distract her, to make her focus on him. Because he'd needed an antidote to his father's poison, a reason to win that would block out any thoughts of how it would benefit the old leech.

Bran's stomach dropped out. What if she'd needed that time to prepare, what if because of him Nelle missed a step or a note? He had a sudden image of her tripping down the stairs, without him to catch her, and it felt like he was spinning, falling uncontrollably.

But then Nelle started to sing, and Bran's face grew hot in the dark. Because she was a pro, her unaccompanied voice clear and strong as she walked gracefully down the stairs. Each step she took sent shockwaves of light across the black screens, a goddess spreading her power through a dark sky.

She was the queen of light and he embarrassed himself imagining he'd affected her ability to spark.

Nelle finished the first verse of "Under Water" and paused at the bottom of the stairs. All at once the music kicked on, the lights blazed, and she was flanked by a V of backup dancers.

Bran hid a grin behind his fist as Nelle took over the stage. The lights flashed and the bass shook and Nelle commanded it all, glittering from head to toe, performing perfection.

The song rose with the bridge and she sang, *"Devotion's an ocean, unstable in motion, I want to make it freeze—"*

The music broke off, the lights cut out. In the dark, the audience was suspended in a state of rapture. This was why Bran loved live music. The crowd on the hook, captivated by a performance that transformed a song into something new. Nelle was incredible at it.

Switching back to a cappella, lit by a semicircle of dancers kneeling with candles, Nelle set them free.

*"Ebb and flow,"* she sang, her face lit by the flickering light.

And for the first time Bran understood it. He heard the heartbreak in her voice. It was a line about the inevitable, the things she couldn't control. He braced himself for the next part—the part he had told her hadn't dug deep enough. *Get low* wasn't a dance-floor cop-out, it was tragedy, her acceptance of being pulled under.

Nelle's voice rang through the darkness, loud and clean and powerful. *"Ta-ta-ta, take me home."*

The dancers blew out the candles and it seemed as if the entire arena took a sharp breath before bursting into raw applause. The room lurched around Bran as people rose from their seats. But he couldn't move. Because on live. National. Television. Nelle had trolled the hell out of him.

*Take me home* was a challenge.

She was that bold. She was that fearless.

She was indescribably sensational and provocative and inspiring.

And he wished he could be backstage, part of her inner circle when the throngs of people cleared. When the dressing room door closed and the tight embraces began, the fiercest whispers of triumph, the *I knew you woulds.*

But Aya was right. He couldn't be seen with her.

Not to protect their secret, but to protect her night. He wouldn't risk a headline like Prom King and Meme overshadowing the success of her performance. Tonight Nelle had proved herself iconic. And he'd keep his distance to ensure nothing detracted from that.

He'd need to get to her after. Alone. At home. All he had to do was win.

# Chapter Twenty

"You killed it. You absolutely murdered everyone in that room, and at home, and the people who are planning to wake up tomorrow and watch highlights on their phones before breakfast—they never will."

Nelle held the emerald bow to her chest, listening to Benj with her mouth open. "Yeah, it doesn't sound like a good thing when you say it like that."

"Well. They're dead. They're all dead. Zombies, walking around, because you snatched their souls from their bodies." Benj raised her eyebrows, waiting for Nelle's reply.

"I came for them."

Benj grinned, pulling the zipper up Nelle's side. "They should have known to run."

Nelle smoothed her hands down her torso. "I may need to disappear later."

"Where to?"

It was Nelle's turn to raise her eyebrows.

"How are you going to get there?"

"I'm bringing Albi into the circle of trust. Would you stay in my hotel room and tell people I'm with you?"

Benj tapped the excess powder off a brush. "I'd have

to order a lot of room service. I mean a lot. For anyone to believe you were there."

Wrapping her arms around her friend, Nelle said, "You're the most perfect person I've ever met."

"I'm sure I've seen a picture of you with Dolly Parton."

"I said what I said."

Mina was waiting outside the dressing room when Nelle emerged in the velvet gown, after taking a very loud, very enthusiastic call from her parents. They weren't here but they were happy, and she was grateful for that. "Let's get you back to your seat for the last few awards. Give them a chance to cut to you."

"Have they done Notable Song?" Nelle asked, ignoring Benj's sudden coughing fit beside her.

"Not yet." Mina stared at her for a moment and Nelle held her breath until her manager reached out and picked lint off the top of her dress. "You didn't rehearse that lyric change."

"I wanted it to be a surprise," Nelle lied. She hadn't planned to do it until she'd been standing onstage in the dark, waiting for the lights to kick on, wanting Bran to know he had better make the universe heel.

It was a little reckless. But what wasn't reckless about being Bran Kelly's secret wife?

Besides, no one would know what she really meant but him. And she felt mighty, like the impact of her steps still sent ripples of light in every direction, even offstage. Making her way back to the audience, Nelle absorbed all the extra glances that came her way.

Santino pretended to faint when she reclaimed the seat next to him. He righted himself, and cupped a hand around her ear. "I'm hosting an after-party, sponsored by my buddy's tequila company. It's the one to be at."

"Sounds like a time," Nelle said.

If Bran won, the attention on them both wouldn't make it easy to get away later. People would be looking for her. But they'd be looking for her less if they were blind drunk on free tequila. And there was no way Bran would be at Santino's party—he'd head for the hotel scene where big-name record companies set up champagne towers. If they were doing this, she had to consider things like that.

The rest of it was out of her hands.

By the time the three final awards of the night arrived, Nelle was antsy, too edgy from her performance to sit still. Three rows ahead, Bran sat up straighter in his chair as his name was read among the nominees for Notable Song.

Was she really going to let the name in that envelope decide whether she risked being caught in order to fuck Bran Kelly tonight? Nelle drew her ankles together, the tendons of her calves pulling tight. She would let the envelope decide. Only because she knew what was in it.

Nelle bit her lip to keep from mouthing along with the announcer, *"Touch Her Back,"* Bran Kelly.

In front of her, Bran turned his head, revealing his profile, and she choked in anticipation of him turning towards her, but instead he landed a kiss on Aya's cheek and rose.

*That should be me.* The thought emerged from her gut, unbidden but true. She would have held his face in her hands and kissed him back. If she'd been closer, he would have climbed that stage with his hair in complete disarray, raked by her fingers. Smudges from her painted lips visible on his cheeks for the world to see. She would have forgotten it all in the rising swell of her heart—the pride in this moment, this man being recognized so deservedly. And relief—the proof that their plans were supported by cosmic powers.

She should have tried to divert her gaze, stopped staring at him so openly. But the Bran Kelly that turned towards that audience, Cleffy in hand, was at one hundred. He was pure, solid-gold confidence. He was an eclipse. They'd all be blind but who could look away?

"Wow," Bran said. His cheek twitched with a private memory and Nelle swayed forward. "I should be able to do better than *wow. Thank you.*" He looked up, taking his gaze to the top seats, to the fans, talking to them. "Thank you so much. Tonight just keeps getting better." He adjusted his grip on the award. "A year ago I thought I'd finished an album. And then I came here, to the Note Awards, to this room filled with all your talent. Guess I took a pocketful home because I spent that night writing one last song—the whole thing poured out in a couple of hours. And then the album wasn't just done. It was complete. And a year later I get to share this moment with you. You inspired me. You made this possible." Bran paused and Nelle willed him to look at her. Slowly, his eyes slid down the rows of his peers and stopped at Nelle, holding her gaze as he finished. "This one's for you."

The music kicked up and Bran broke their eye contact to exit stage left. A tribute started playing and Nelle sank back into the shadows, her heart racing along with her thoughts.

He was teasing her again, saying he'd won for her, that he'd done it to get her home tonight. But Bran Kelly loved a double meaning. And images swirled behind her eyes, flashes of last year's show: the scooped back of her dress, the pocketful of her phone number Bran had taken home. And the lyric that called her out: *Because she started it.*

Suddenly Nelle became hyperaware of everything around her, her vision sharp and her mind clear. She had been sure of so many things tonight, and now she had one more to add to her list.

Bran Kelly had written "Touch Her Back" about Nelle.

## Chapter Twenty-One

When Bran left the house that afternoon, he couldn't have imagined a more perfect way to return. Stumbling out of the hired car, he hadn't had to wonder if Nelle had followed through on their deal. Light beamed through the slitted front windows like lens flares in an action movie.

He took the stairs two at a time until he slammed sideways into the cement banister. Then he adjusted his pace, to make sure he got into the house in one piece. Sauntering through the hall, he reached the opening to the kitchen and stopped, needing time to adjust to the ambush of sensation his brain was trying to process.

Van Morrison blared through his house speakers— Van Morrison, a musician who knew what it was like to have a performance crisis. Bran put a hand to the wall in solidarity.

And for stability.

In front of the stove, Nelle was shaking her hips, her dark curls damp, the ripped neck of one of his oldest shirts slipping off one shoulder.

Something smelled incredible. At first she was too busy stirring it and singing along to the song to notice him staring. But then she turned and screamed. Her hand flew to her mouth. "Jesus! I thought you were a burglar!"

"Not a burglar," he told her, taking a step into the room.

The light blue tee was worn so thin he could see straight through the peeling slogan (I Survived the Chicago Blizzard of '67). He'd never buy a new shirt again. He was hypnotized by the deep breaths she took, the dark points of her nipples through the soft fabric. He only raised his eyes when she cut off his view, folding her arms over herself. Her freckles were back. He hadn't realized how much he missed seeing them all day. But they'd always been there, constellations that didn't come out until daylight had faded.

He fumbled for a pen on the buffet, and then the receipt next to it. After scribbling something inane about daytime stars, Bran crumpled the paper. Now wasn't the time. He was in no frame of mind for lyrical genius. The last song he'd written had been easy and perfect—the proof of it earning him this night. He shifted his focus back to Nelle, moving into the kitchen half of the room.

"You showered. And you're cooking. How long have you been here?"

"Since eleven." She pointed a wooden spoon at him, red sauce spattering on the cement island. "You kept me waiting."

"I texted you."

"No, you didn't. For a month you didn't."

"I thought that was what you wanted. But I texted tonight. I said midnight." He groped for the phone in his pocket but the icons on his home screen were too blurry to be of use.

"I didn't get it. Came home to a dark house. My

driver almost wouldn't leave me here because he said places this remote are easy targets. Especially on big nights like this—when everyone's out late at parties."

"The only valuable things I own are in the watch safe." He paused to think. "And my guitar case."

She had found a deep baking dish and was layering food into it.

"What are you making?"

"A very rustic moussaka." She reached for a third pan and poured a thick white sauce over the other layers. Unlike the last time she'd cooked in his kitchen, everything she did seemed a little slow, and a lot sloppy. "I found some interesting things in your fridge." A tasting spoon disappeared into her mouth and came out clean. "Milk, presumably for your stash of cereal, leftover mashed potatoes and tomato soup. And a wild bag of groceries."

Her eyes hit him and Bran staggered through his next step, hanging on to the edge of the island for balance.

"Bran Kelly, you shopped. You shopped in preparation for my arrival." She started making her way over to him, talking like she was thinking out loud. "I thought you forgot I was coming. I thought you didn't care."

She trusted the universe, she trusted a bartender, but she was determined to think the worst of him.

Nelle moved closer before he could respond. "But then I look in your fridge and—" she made a *poof* motion with her hand "—ground beef."

"You like cheeseburgers."

Nearer now. "An eggplant?"

Sentences weren't forming in his brain. "For hummus. Crudités?"

"That's not how eggplant works."

Bran swallowed. He was hot under his jacket and the low-hanging pendant lights glaring off the polished surfaces.

She inched closer to him and her signature spice overwhelmed him—the one that smelled like home. "There was ground cinnamon in your fridge, Bran. I want to know why."

"Is that not where it goes?"

Her head tilted back as she laughed and he caught her jaw between his hands. She exhaled a startled breath, the whites of her eyes showing.

"Sorry." He gentled his touch to stroke her throat, her skin smooth like satin. "I'm a little drunk. This interrogation doesn't seem fair."

"What's not fair? I'm a little drunk too." She drew up on her tiptoes to nuzzle her nose against his. "Did you mean what you said?"

Her near-naked body rolled against his suit-clad one and he pulled out of his jacket, one arm at a time to keep hold of her, thrusting his fingers into the hair at the base of her neck when he was finished, keeping her face to his. "Remind me what I said."

"You said a lot. That things made for girls matter, because girls matter." Her lips brushed against his. "Did you say it just to get into my pants?"

She wasn't wearing any pants. Bran closed his eyes, knowing his answer had to make sense. "I said it to show you that I'm listening. I hear you. What you say matters to me."

Under his fingertips, a sharp sigh tangled in her throat. "And the other speech? You meant you wrote this year's Notable Song about me?"

Hearing her say it was too much. Bran was done answering questions, done waiting, done doing anything that wasn't kissing Nelle. Her mouth opened to him the instant his lips pressed against hers. Her tongue crashed against his in searing, rapid passes.

She pulled back, spinning in his arms, the shirt twisting about her hips under his hands. Raising up to reveal her bare butt. Nelle leaned into the counter and Bran fit himself behind her. "And in between—you said you'd do things to me you'd never done before."

"I meant that." He thickened at the idea, at her bending forward and pressing herself back. "If you want me to. If you like that."

She looked back at him, her eyes a little glazed, her mouth a little parted. Nelle, not quite together, not knowing her own mind, wasn't something he was used to. "I don't know if I like that. I haven't—I've never done that. Doesn't it hurt?"

"It's tight. Um. We'd go slow. It might."

Nelle turned again, and he pressed the solid length of his dick into the seam of her butt, testing the position through his clothes. Her back arched. "But then it feels good?"

He barely got the promise out. "So fucking good."

She lowered herself to her elbows on the counter and shook her head. "It's so dirty."

"It's not, it's—"

Nelle laughed. She pushed herself back up on one palm and gestured to the mess of pots she'd abandoned on the other side of the island. "No, I mean, it's so dirty."

*The dishes?* How was she thinking about the dishes?

Bran groaned. He finally had Nelle bent over this island. She was pinned between his legs, a little drunk, and asking about getting a dick in her ass. And if she was distracted by the dirty pans it meant she wasn't sure. She wasn't ready. Bottom line: she wasn't comfortable.

He eased back, strengthened his resolve, and pried his hands off the edge of the counter. Stiff steps took him around the island, but he made it.

"What are you doing?" Nelle asked, her bottom lip pushing out in a pout.

Bran grabbed two of the pots, turning to the sink. The rush of water echoed inside the metal as Bran braced himself on the ledge.

Behind him was Nelle. Ass up. Pouting.

He locked his knees and focused on the filling pans, then rolled his shoulders back and turned to collect the rest. Her breasts pillowed against the cement and she held her chin up with the heels of her palms.

Bran smiled through the throb of need. "It's basic marriage rules. You cook, I clean."

# Chapter Twenty-Two

Nelle had felt loose. Loose like dancing without choreography. Loose like everything just came naturally and she didn't have to think about anything she was doing. She just had to do it.

Nelle *had* felt loose.

And now she felt tight, the kind of tight that made her aware of all the places inside her that had been left unfulfilled.

Bran had been pushed up against her, his heat at her back contrasting with the cold cement that seeped through her shirt. Bran had been talking, about how good it would feel to fit himself inside her. Bran had been making a good case. And then she'd opened her mouth about the dishes and now he was over there, doing them instead.

He lifted the casserole dish of moussaka she'd prepped while waiting for him to come home. His brows raised in a question.

She waved a hand at the fridge. "We can bake it tomorrow."

Tomorrow. That was when they should be doing this domestic shit. Tonight should be for celebrating. For getting loose and staying that way. They only had one night at a time.

With a wet sponge, Bran wiped down the counter, concentric circles growing wider with each swipe.

He had been the one who'd said it. He'd come up with the idea of doing something new. Something they'd never done before. Something had stopped him. She hadn't said no.

His shirtsleeves were rolled and when he stretched for a final pass, slipping his hand between her elbows, she grabbed his arm.

She hadn't said yes either.

Thumbing the ridged vein that pushed out of his forearm, she asked, "You done?"

"I was just—"

Her grip tightened until he dropped the sponge. "You were giving me a moment to reconsider." His eyes tracked her tongue as she wet her bottom lip. Bran paid attention to her. She'd been so wrong. He hadn't forgotten about her last night. He hadn't texted because she'd said no contact. He'd been doing what she'd asked. He'd stocked his fridge. As surprised as she was to find ground cinnamon in there—because what? why?—it made it easy to trust that the things he did were for her. "I've considered. Now come back over here and tell me how we do this."

There were moments when she looked into Bran's eyes and saw awe. She recognized it from when fans got close and called her their idol, when producers who weren't expecting her to have any talent couldn't hide their astonishment that she did. Sometimes Bran looked at her and it felt like an honor, to get to amaze him. It felt like power.

But then his face changed, the look of admiration swept aside by tenacious lust that curled his mouth and glowed from his eyes. And that look, that look felt like power too—his power over her. She let go of his arm and he tossed the sponge into the sink. As he rounded the island, Nelle melted into it. Her mouth opened in a breathless pant as his hands skimmed up her sides. He clasped his fingers around her neck, drawing her up and against him.

"We do this slow," he whispered into her ear, sending shivers down her curved spine. She relished the feel of his hips behind her, the hard cement in front of her. There was nowhere to go and nowhere else she wanted to be.

He breathed her in, the gentle cuff at her throat, his palm across her stomach, holding her there, trapped. The seconds passed and his chest rose up and down at her back. But he didn't move. *Slow.* This was really fucking slow. Nelle squirmed, unable to keep still as wet heat pooled between her legs.

And finally the hand on her stomach began to lower.

"I wasn't sure if you only liked talking about it." He reached the hem of the shirt she'd borrowed and slid his hand underneath. Curled fingers strummed along her slick opening and she moaned. Bran pressed his lips to her shoulder with a curse. "You really liked talking about it, huh?"

She could only nod as he sank two fingers right into her.

He leaned them forward, pressing her back down to the counter with his weight. Inside her, spinning fingers made her dizzy and she dropped her forehead to the cool cement.

Bran straightened, releasing her neck and gliding his fingers out of her, setting both hands on her hips. "That's about where we were." She looked back to see him take stock of the position. The strength of his arousal powered through his pants, and he pushed it into her, nodding his head and biting his lip.

Nelle faced forward, searching for something to hold and only finding the polished expanse of clean counter. This is how they had been before he'd pulled away, leaving her disoriented and—

The pressure behind her eased again and Nelle released a frustrated cry. *Not again.* She hadn't said anything! She turned to tell Bran as much, only to see he'd sunk to his knees. Eyes sparking with mischief, he bunched the shirt at her waist, baring her rounded butt.

"Now what?" she asked.

"Now we stop talking about it."

An openmouthed kiss to one cheek that ended in the scrape of his teeth had her head falling back to the counter.

She was exposed, on display as she'd never been before. Just for Bran. And that thought kept her flat and open. Bran understood her, Bran didn't get off on vulnerability. He got off on wanting big things. And however salacious this was, she wanted it, too—she wanted him to give it to her.

The first touch of his tongue to the seam between her cheeks was jarring. The skin was so sensitive, and Nelle was so unused to being caressed there, she could barely process the pleasure. But as Bran licked and sucked and pressed into the tight opening, the sensation registered with a flood of desire. Her pussy clenched and she rocked her hips.

Fluent in body language, Bran understood and slotted his fingers back inside of her. She rode his hand as waves so intense she had to grip her elbows above her head washed over her—through her. Every muscle in her body tightened, her hamstrings burned, and the tendons in her feet ached from stretching up on her toes. But then Bran sucked harder, pressed deeper into her and the first wave broke. Nelle sobbed out a startled gasp, the counter smooth against her lips. Coming as Bran Kelly in his disheveled Note Awards suit kissed her ass was The Most. She pulsed on every level as gratification crashed over her. The tightness ebbed, leaving her loose and delighted.

She couldn't move, couldn't speak, and lay splayed across the island, waiting for whatever came next. She didn't question it.

Bran grasped her hips again, standing behind her. "Don't move."

She almost laughed, as if that were an option. But as he stepped back, awareness threatened to pull her taut again. "Where are you going?"

"I think there's some lube in my bathroom upstairs— I'm manifesting some lube into the bathroom upstairs because there has to be some lube in the bathroom upstairs."

She needed him to stay, to anchor her here. Just like this. Pushing up on her elbows she lurched across the surface, dragging the bottle of olive oil with her as she rocked back into him. "Can we use this?"

Just from handing him the glass, a residue of grease coated her fingers.

His voice was low, disbelieving. "You want me to—"

"I want you to. I want you inside of me, now, everywhere, anywhere, wherever, and however you want. Because I know you're good for it. Okay, Kelly? Is that clear enough for you?"

The metal cap bounced off the counter. The first trickle of oil felt cool, but it warmed quickly as Bran rubbed it into her overheated skin. She whimpered as he set into her, pushing some digit slowly, so slowly, past the muscle that didn't want to give.

She willed herself to relax and he groaned as the entry eased open, allowing him access. He spun a few circles, loosening her up, and she twitched and bucked in response.

"It's going to be tighter when I—"

"I can take it."

He'd learned not to doubt her and so next thing she felt was a rushing release as his thumb or finger or whatever it had been pulled out of her. Her body clenched, as if trying to stop him from going had become a biological effort.

She panted into the counter, her hot breath warming her cheeks and tasting of tequila. Her eyes closed. Time seemed to jump and stall. Her heart hammered loose and wild. She felt as if she might fall, even as her body lay flat on the counter. She focused on the music. A tangle of piano keys grounded her, providing sequence and stability. The notes spun up and down—or was that last run a zipper? Her fingers pressed a chord into the cement as Bran pressed into her.

It *was* tight. But he went slow. And she took it. She wanted it that way. Feeling as though there was no way they couldn't be together.

Soon nothing existed but her little gasps, his little pushes. The music flowed around them, filled with rhythm and deep soul. Until Nelle was filled deeper than she'd ever been before and Bran was coming, interrupting the beat and stressing her name.

## Chapter Twenty-Three

Bran hadn't meant to take such a long shower, but he'd stood under the stream as time slipped down the drain with the water. It warmed him, flowed off him, and it was all he could do to remain standing. To not sink down the wet tiles and contemplate life from the bottom of the fogged stall.

He was—

He was without words. Tonight had been——

He was coming down.

He needed a pause. A prolonged hold. Just until he could get his mind to catch up with the night his body had had. The day. The full day. From the red carpet to the show—he'd won *two* Cleffies!—and the blur of the after-party, shaking hands with interested producers and Aya telling him to nod and smile and enjoy it. He hadn't been able to avoid the label guys wondering what was next.

Everyone wanted to know about new music, but he wanted Nelle. Nelle waiting for him at home. Nelle spread on the kitchen island like his personal dessert buffet.

Tonight had been full. And yet he already saw the dull promise of emptiness on the horizon. Beyond today, beyond this night, what was there? Tonight had been full, but it was already draining away, and Bran wasn't sure he'd ever be able to fill it back up.

His lungs pulled in the spray and he coughed. Panic seized his body and he reminded himself he couldn't drown in a shower. He turned off the water anyway. His skin prickled in the cold.

Roughing a towel through his hair, he tried to shake the thoughts away. The bottle of L-theanine he found behind the mirror rattled as he forced it open. He took one, bending his mouth to the faucet to swallow. The vitamins were probably little more than placebos, but they helped sometimes. He had tried prescription meds to ease the pressure, the anxiety that sometimes overwhelmed him, but they dulled his urge to write when he took them. Not that he was writing anyway.

He folded the towel around his waist. The night wasn't technically over. Nelle was still here, staying for the length of time they'd determined they could get away with. Any more would put too much strain on their secret, threaten its security. Like all the nights with Nelle, he had to put off his existential music-making crisis until she was gone. He could deal with his father's threats after that.

Bran tripped on his way out of the bathroom. It wasn't the transition from slate tile to the soft carpet that got him, it was the sight of Nelle on his bed. One leg folded under her, the other connecting to the floor with a pointed toe, she sat with a guitar tucked into her lap.

Not just a guitar. An acoustic Taylor made before he was born. One he favored for songwriting, one he traveled with, so it didn't live on a set of pegs in the music room. He kept it close by, under his bed, in its case, ready to accompany him wherever he went. It was an instrument with miles on it. Years. It had experience, as seen by the hairline cracks in the lacquer. But the sound was whole, the tone reliable. Perfect for working out what you were going to say.

He hadn't touched it in a month. Not since his attempts to pull something together from that spark of a song he'd thought up at the bar in Chicago had gone nowhere.

Bran held his breath, his lungs painfully full. She hadn't noticed him, and he wouldn't interrupt. Not when it was clear that she had something to get out.

Nelle had her phone propped on a pillow in front of her. Using long, simple chords, she sang towards it.

*"You pocket a secret, we said that we'd keep it.*
*Your watch on my wrist, the time that we fit.*
*Tick tock, how long we've got, before the clock*
*stops."*

Nelle frowned and played the last part again, trying out something else. *"Tick tock, count the seconds, the mess that always threatens."*

She played it twice more without words. On the third time she sang, *"Tick tock, watch and see, it's gonna be you and me."*

"That's it," Bran said. "That's the line."

Nelle looked up, her eyes taking a second longer than usual to focus on him. She stopped playing, picked up the phone, and said, "So, yeah, that's what I've got. It's muddled by tequila and I don't want to tell you what else." She blushed and Bran swayed forward. "Not ready yet for the studio but I wanted to keep you in the loop. N3, Chaz, we're doing it."

An uncomfortable twist burned in his chest. "Are you on the phone?"

"Voice memo. I couldn't find a pen."

*Inspiration deserves ink.*

It had been him doing this last year. Sitting here. With that guitar. On this night. Writing a Cleffy-winning song. He shouldn't begrudge her the moment.

"Just let me send it to Charlie." After a moment, Nelle dropped the phone. She tilted her head looking at him. "What's that face? You still don't approve of my collaborative process?" She hiked the guitar closer to her body. Her breasts pushed up over the curved wood. She wasn't wearing the shirt anymore. It had been stained by olive oil—not to mention he'd come in her so hard, twisting the shirt at her hip, he'd ripped another hole in the worn cotton.

That's what he should be focusing on. Nelle naked, in his bed. Not that she was sitting there sending song ideas to someone else. He should definitely not be this readable.

But the twinge of jealousy had spiked. He walked forward and kicked the guitar case closed. "Whatever works for you."

It was hard not to feel it. He was stuck and she was in motion. He'd been entertaining the idea of resting on his laurels. Nelle would have used them for tinder. She had just released a new album, was going on a giant tour, and she was already working on her third? When did she have time for that? When would she have time for him? When would he get more lyrics out of her?

It was the most childish of thoughts. Selfish and unkind. True and false. He wanted two opposing things at once. He didn't want to be her problem. But she felt like his solution.

Bran sat at the edge of the mattress, next to the bedside table, and lifted his own phone from the charging pad, needing to get lost in some other feeling. But the stream of notifications only reminded him that people were waiting for him to do something else, make something new.

He cleared the screen with aggressive thumb swipes, stopping only when he got to the thread with Cormac and Arlo. He scrolled through the messages, his shoulders rising at the congratulations, stiffening at the complaints. We should have been there. Arlo challenged the status quo of their relationship. But Bran relaxed as he skimmed along. Arlo had sent the dates for his spring break, asking if either of them were interested in New York City. He'd heard great things about a new Broadway show. Cormac had suggested Cabo. Arlo insisted on New York, it was his break, he was going to museums. Cormac countered with a picture of bikini-clad women. Arlo sent a naked one—headless and carved from marble.

Bran laughed out loud.

He had won his Cleffies, and his friends were proud of him, but they also held a place in the world where he could still just be Bran. The same guy they had always known. They didn't care what he was doing next in his career, they just wanted to know if he was down for spring break.

"Something funny?"

Nelle's mouth had flattened, her thumb hooked into the rim of the guitar's hollow. On the other side of the pale wood, in the dark space, he'd been a kid when he'd Sharpied the numbers, 2-23-71. He hadn't wanted to ink them on his skin, displayed for the world. Nelle knew how to find them anyway.

"Yeah," he said, taking care to look her in the eye, to be straight with her before he did something more stupid than snapping at her and moping. It wasn't her that had him on the verge of a shame spiral. "Arlo and Cormac arguing about 'hot and tropical' or 'cool and topical' for spring break. C says he's not taking time away from the restaurant to have to check his coat at the Guggenheim."

He angled the phone at her, showing off the juxta-position of images they'd sent.

Nelle raised her eyebrows. "Battle of the busts." She thumbed the inside of the guitar, so intuitive, finding everything he'd ever hidden. How could one woman be so impossibly clever? "I'll be in New York one of those weekends."

Bran bit his bottom lip and released it. "MSG?"

"Two nights. And some interviews and stuff that week before."

"So I'll vote NYC."

"Bran. I can't see you. It's New York. It's impossible."

"We only need one night."

"The press only need one picture."

"We won't get caught." He put the phone down and smoothed his hair back. "Can you go your whole tour without seeing me? Because I gotta tell you, I think that might kill me."

She wiggled her fingers, thinking it through. "*If* you

can figure out a way to get into my hotel without a single person seeing you—"

Bran fixed his eyes on the guitar case he'd knocked into the middle of the room and he smiled. "I'll figure it out." He felt better. Maybe the L-theanine had kicked in, or maybe it was knowing he'd be able to see her while she was gone. He rested against the headboard. "Come here."

She climbed over to him. A slight wince when she sat down lifted his dick under the towel wrapped over his lap.

Nelle had other plans, bringing the guitar with her, shoving it into his hands. He took hold automatically, drawing it close, his fingers testing the tension of the strings. His hands moved on instinct and Nelle frowned.

"What?" Bran asked.

"This affair has been clandestine from the start, and now is the first time I've ever felt like your mistress." She glared at the guitar. "That's what belongs in your arms." She clapped her hands to her thighs, sitting up on her heels. "Play something. You know you want to."

He did. He really did want to.

Fingertips pressed into the frets, strings finding the grooves in callouses he'd have the rest of his life, even if he never wrote another song. What came out wasn't his own music, even if it felt like a part of him. He played the slower version he'd fallen in love with.

"What's that?" Nelle asked.

"'Bird Song.'" Bran hummed a little. "Grateful Dead, the one about Janis Joplin."

"You'd rather play a song about Janis Joplin than a song by Janis Joplin?"

He shook his head, wet strands of his hair falling

across his forehead. He stopped playing to push them up. Nelle was looking at him like she knew something else was coming. So he didn't bother holding it back.

"February 23rd, 1971."

Bran took up the song again while she put it together. "Two, twenty three, seventy one."

He nodded. "The Grateful Dead played 'Bird Song' at the Capital Theater. They did six shows that week. *Six*." He'd stumbled on the February 23rd recording while pirating music. "And each one was different. Had a different energy. Had a different feeling. That version killed me. Made me want to be able to do that. Transform a song, bring it to life in whatever way I wanted depending on how I was feeling."

He knew she understood. He'd seen her do the same thing with "Under Water" a few hours ago. She'd played live albums over his speakers every chance she got. Nelle got it, she got him.

But her brow furrowed. "Why aren't you writing, Bran?"

He shrugged.

"You love music. You love to perform." Nelle moved her hand to his knee. "I think that's the only time you don't mind asking for support. When you're with an audience, you open up. You let your guard down."

She was asking him to do it now. For her.

"Why aren't you writing?"

He looked up to drink in the whiskey of her eyes, to absorb a bit of her courage. "Nothing's coming."

"So? Go get it."

"It's not that easy. I can get…" He searched the ceiling for a word. "Overwhelmed."

"And you think I don't? Have you listened to 'Under Water'?"

"That's why I listen to 'Under Water.'"

He started the first few notes of the song. Nelle clamped her palm around the guitar's neck, dampening the sound.

"No. I want to hear BK2," she said.

"There is no BK2."

"There has to be something. People like us always have something we need to get out. If we try to keep it in, we explode." Her mouth shut too quickly, holding something back.

Now he pressed for answers. "What happened in Barcelona?"

She nodded, like she'd been waiting for that question. "Nothing happened." Bran opened his mouth to call bullshit, but Nelle was still explaining. "What *almost* happened in Barcelona was me quitting. Confessing to Mina that I couldn't do this, I didn't have it in me."

"But you know that's not true."

"Obviously. I was upset about my dad. Unaligned. And I thought I could fix it, if I gave something up. If I rebalanced the excesses of prosperity in my life."

"Is that how the universe works?"

"That's how desperate people think. Don't tell me you haven't considered heading down to Georgia and bargaining with the devil to get a song out of it."

He rubbed a knuckle into his eye. She was so close to being right. He had traded his soul for the possibility of a song. But not to the devil, to her. He'd tried to get a song out of her infectious light only to realize he was losing himself to her instead.

"How the universe works is you have to trust, to love more than you're afraid. Fear blocks flow," she said.

"And what am I afraid of?"

Nelle waited for Bran to fill in the blanks. What was he afraid of? *No Nelle.* It was the second time he'd had the thought today. He reached for her hand, weaving their fingers together, backwards so their palms didn't touch, only their knuckles, with gaps of space between. That's how it had to be. It wasn't their secret he needed anymore. He needed this. The secret allowed him to have Nelle, one night at a time. The silence pressed at him. He had to say something that was on his mind, without giving away too much. "Maybe creativity isn't a renewable resource. Maybe you get what you get and when it's done, so are you."

Nelle wrinkled her nose. "Or maybe I can help." And then she was rearranging them, fitting between him and the guitar. Her back warm against his chest and her hair falling soft on his shoulder. Her slender fingers curved around the string board. She nodded to the body.

"You pick."

"How will that work?" He tried strumming as she pressed chords into the guitar's neck. It sounded like someone's first time holding an instrument, not like two accomplished musicians working together.

Bran laughed, lifting Nelle and the guitar. His hand dropped away and she pulled it back.

"Play with me. Just sing something. Whatever you're thinking."

Bran let his hand rest on the Taylor's familiar face. Then he rolled his wrist and swiped his fingers up and down over the strings. Their timing was better, sound recognizable as a tune vibrating from the instrument.

"I want you to stay," he said quietly, but with a hint of rhythm.

She sang back, her voice lively, teasing a duet out of him. *"To fill your fridge with crudités?"*

"So you can't?"

*"I've got plans."*

"How long for?"

*"Six whole months on a sold-out tour."*

He kissed her cheek. "You deserve it, by the way."

"Thank you."

He moved her hands on the neck of the guitar. "Chord change for the chorus." This time, he sang instead of speaking. *"I think tonight was the best night of my life."*

*"Was it winning Cleffies, or the anal with your secret wife?"*

Bran dropped his hand from the strings. "You're too good at this."

"I know, it's probably making you feel worse." She rolled over, flattening herself under the guitar, the smooth wood at her back, her chest flush with his. "That part about the best night of your life was nice."

"It was trite."

"It doesn't have to be." She was going to ask again about BK2, he could tell by the way her lips pursed. He adjusted his eyes up to the ceiling and waited. She rested her head on his chest and said nothing.

*Best night of his life.* And now it was over. The best was behind him. That's exactly the feeling he was trying to wash away in the shower. And Nelle had brought it right out into the open and left him with it.

He could grasp both ends of the guitar with her like that, and he did, surprising himself by playing the scrap of song Arlo called "drowning in paint." He used to do a thing when he was learning the guitar, where he'd play something six times, six different ways. In case he ever played six nights at the Capital Theater. It was how he used to write a song, when he was a kid, he'd play with it first. He'd try to find room in the melody for possibilities, explore the nuances, make sure he picked the best one. Because only the best songs would earn him an audience, keep him onstage.

He was tempted to try it now. Play the line again and again until it sounded just right. But he didn't. He didn't want to work at it, like he'd had to as a kid. He wanted it to just come. He was an award-winning performer now. He hated still feeling like he was that kid, unable to escape the dark shadow his father cast over his life.

He played "Bird Song" again instead.

Nelle listened with her head on his chest. Her eyes closed and her breath evened. Bran put the guitar in the bed next to them and turned off the lights with his phone. His hands threaded behind her back and he took in the scent of her hair. She may have thought the guitar belonged in his arms, but he was happier to wrap them around her. It was easier than holding on to something that felt like it was tugging away from him.

Transcript of *Tonight with Tony*:

Tony: You've been in New York all week, getting ready for two sold-out shows at Madison Square Garden this weekend. [Audience cheering] Bran Kelly has also been spotted around the city this week.

Nelle: Oh, yeah?

Tony: You know there's speculation about a feud between the two of you. First he interrupted your Jingle Jam tribute, and then he didn't clap for that Note Awards performance that brought down the house. And of course there's the meme.

Nelle: I use the gif regularly.

Tony: [laughing] But have you heard about the fan conspiracy theories?

Nelle: That we hate each other?

Tony: That you *love* each other. The *Clever and Cleavage* podcast tweeted the "real" reason he's in town at the same time you are.

Nelle: Oh, I did see this. They said he's here for my concert. I can't blame him, it's going to be a great show.

Tony: They said you guys got married—

Nelle: Over the weekend, right? [laughter] Sorry to disappoint.

Tony: So he's not your—

Nelle: Husband of four days? Also untrue.

Tony: I didn't think so. Sounded like a pretty far-fetched scheme. But the feud between the two of you? Is there truth in that? You were overheard calling him a Cleffy-nominated dickhead.

Nelle: And I need to amend that—he's a Cleffy-winning dickhead.

## Chapter Twenty-Four

Bran had arrived in a box.

A big black tour trunk with stenciled white letters. Nelle had thought it must be costumes, mistakenly sent to her hotel room instead of the venue. Then Bran had texted her a cardboard box emoji.

An aesthetician had hold of one of her hands, painting constellations on her fingernails, and Nelle had to wait and thumb a one-handed response telling him, "dob't die." She'd eventually gotten him out of the box and into her, and had been panting, pinned to the wall when Mina knocked in her sharp "time is of the essence" way. Bran had been shoved into the bathroom next and Nelle had gone about her schedule, which included shooting a segment for *Tonight with Tony*. A segment that had just aired.

The hotel couch was shallow, yet Bran had managed to tip back into it, taking himself away from her. His arms were folded, and his eyes remained locked on the screen where commercials played soundlessly.

Nelle turned sideways to look at him. "You're mad."

"I'm not mad."

She slipped a bare leg out from her robe and under the matching one he wore, her calf on his thigh. When

Bran didn't untwist his arms and take hold of her foot
she kicked at his leg.

He let go of his elbows. "What?"

"You're mad."

"I'm not mad." But he tugged his hair forward and
didn't push it back.

Nelle rested a bent arm on the back of the couch and
threaded her fingers together. "What did you want me
to say? I thought my makeup was going to melt off, I
was so flustered." Her neck had been hot, her hair unbearably heavy.

"You really want them to think we have beef."

"I don't want them to know we had a cheeseburger
and decided to elope. I thought we both did. That's the
point of this secret, right? To keep it to ourselves." She
didn't want to doubt his motives—not again—but his
reaction to her subterfuge made her stomach spin. "Unless you don't care if they find out—"

"If I didn't care, would I have shipped myself across
town crammed into a goddamn tour trunk, Nelle?" Bran
stood, pacing to the bed and turning back to the sitting
area. He flattened his hair and nudged the trunk with
his toe. "A dick in a box," he muttered.

Of course, with that kind of stunt, she couldn't doubt
his commitment to keeping their secret. What she really wanted to know was if he'd felt the shift from being
together to have a secret, to keeping the secret to be together? Like she had.

Even when they were apart, they didn't act separate. Since February, Bran had been texting her. He'd
send a photo of his feet up on the ottoman in his den, a
blurry baseball diamond on the TV in the background.
Or he'd snap a picture of the wallpaper samples Cor-

mac was considering for the single-user bathrooms at the restaurant. Bran Kelly's official Instagram had been stagnate since his tour ended when Aya (she assumed) had stopped posting professional shots from each show. But Nelle had access to a private feed—push notifications *On*—and her phone was vibrating with the kind of stuff his fans would die for. Everyday moments that proved Bran was more than a rock star, that he was a guy you could know, someone you could fall in love with close up.

She was getting used to her backstage access to Bran Kelly. At one point she'd resigned herself to knowing she would have to give it up, but the thought seemed impossible now. Against all the odds, despite all the paps that crowded her every move, they hadn't been caught. Wasn't that the universe's way of giving its blessing? Wasn't this working better than they'd ever expected? Couldn't they try to make it last…and last?

Nelle wasn't ready to open that box. The box filled with questions she couldn't answer, like: Is teenage infatuation a healthy place to start a relationship? Can you fall for someone you've only spent four nights with? When is the right time to tell your husband you might actually love him?

Nobody was ready for that conversation.

She lowered her head to her folded hands on the back of the couch. The angled ring dug into her chin and she spun the V to the underside of her finger. "I don't know what else to do. With the exception of the Note Awards, we've been completely off grid. There are still rumors just because we're in the same giant city. Maybe we can only see each other in LA—"

"You won't be back in LA until the fall. And Aya

booked Super Saturday. We'll both be in London in May."

"Maybe we should avoid each other—"

"No. If I have a chance to see you, I'm taking it."

Her stomach twisted again, not with doubt, but from the truth in his words. He would see her. He had to see her. And she loved hearing the conviction, the need in his voice, even if he was talking to the wall.

"But…" He faced her way, looking past her, his hands gripping his hips. "You're performing."

She lifted her head. "Excuse me?"

Bran nodded to the TV where Nelle danced, the lyrics of her new single, "Cosmic Order," scrolling in black-and-white captions. *"Leo rising, enterprising, uncompromising—she does it for herself!"* On tour, her fans were going absolutely feral over that line. They'd scream it and jump as flames erupted behind her. It was one of her favorite moments every night.

"That one must kill," Bran said.

"Yeah. It does."

He leaned a shoulder into the arch separating the two rooms of her suite. "If I wanted to sneak into your show—"

"That's out of the question."

His jaw bobbed like he was chewing something tough.

On the glass table, her phone began to buzz, interrupting the silence with demanding vibrations.

"My parents are calling."

"Something wrong?"

"No—they call after everything. Your dad didn't call after the Note Awards?"

"He did. Asking for money. Said, 'You used to give it to Mom, why not me? What's the difference?'"

"What is the difference?"

"When Gran broke glasses it was an accident."

Her heart throbbed. "You didn't pay him."

"No."

Nelle resisted the urge to shake her head as she sighed. Bran's problem was that he had solutions, and he just didn't like them. The night he'd won the Cleffies, he'd had a moment like this. He'd kicked a guitar case and sat with his back to her, his shoulders up and covered in goose bumps. But he'd shaken it off quickly enough, invited her in on a joke with his friends. He'd opened up to her.

Nelle's hand tightened around the shaking phone. It felt risky bringing a bigger part of her identity into the tiny bubble they'd formed around themselves—like maybe there wouldn't be enough room, and the bubble would pop. But she wasn't in the habit of making herself small.

"My mom wants to take credit, and my father uses any opportunity he can to lament my piano playing."

"You didn't play the piano."

"Exactly." Nelle held a finger to her lips and answered the call, putting it on speaker.

"Antonella?" her mother's voice demanded.

"Hi, Mama."

"What time is it? Why aren't you asleep? You have a show tomorrow."

"Why are you calling if you think I should be asleep?"

"A mother can't call her daughter she just saw on television?"

"You can always call me, Mama."

"Oh! Well, thank you for the permission."

Nelle rolled her eyes only because her mother couldn't see.

The woman paused and for a second Nelle worried she *had* seen somehow, but her mother had only been gathering breath to launch into her thoughts on the segment. "Well, you sang beautifully—of course—and you looked wonderful. Was that blue or black?"

"Navy." Nelle had offered, again, to fly them out. Her mother could have seen *in person* the color of her dress. But they still weren't ready. It felt like they might never be. She'd started to worry she'd never see their faces cheering her on again. That was fear. So she let it go.

Her mother hummed her approval. "We can wear dark colors, unlike your cousin Alex—I told you about his interview? I thought he was too pale for television but he's going to be a correspondent for the morning show. I told his mother to get him sunscreen so he doesn't burn under those lights. You looked flushed yourself when Tony asked about those rumors."

Bran had been standing still, but now his head lifted and Nelle regretted putting the phone on speaker. She tried to change the subject. "You were right last week, I need a haircut—"

"Married, Nella. If only. Then I'd be one step closer to being a grandmother."

If her mother could see her now, she'd see another flush as Nelle avoided Bran's gaze.

"I'm nowhere close to having a baby."

"Not without a husband. Hold on, your father wants to say something."

"Antonella?" Her father's voice this time.

Nelle let out a sigh of relief. "Hi, Papa."

"Twelve years. I paid for twelve years of piano lessons, Nella. Not that anyone would know."

Nelle made hesitant eye contact with Bran, now that her mother wasn't talking about real marriages and babies. She raised triumphant eyebrows and his cheek ticked. "You paid for dance lessons too."

"You didn't need dance lessons. You take after me." Her mother must have protested because her father's voice faded to address his wife. "Yes, me!" Then he was back to explain, "We move with music. It's natural for a Georgopoulos. You had to work at the piano, you should be so proud. Overcoming your mother's meat hands. Ow!"

Her mother took the phone back. "Your father has to go to bed. And so do you. But you play the piano for him soon. We'll call you tomorrow."

"Okay, love you guys."

Her mother never hung up, just put her phone down and assumed Nelle would do it. Sometimes Nelle stayed on the line, listening to her parents go about life at home. But she didn't today. Because Bran Kelly was standing across from her looking like he was going to burst.

"Let me see them."

"My parents?" She held up the lock screen of her phone.

"No, the 'meat hands' you inherited from your mother."

Nelle dropped the phone into the cushions and held her hands up for inspection. "He exaggerates because he's got the most exquisitely dainty fingers in the family. Surgeon hands. And he said the moment I was born he knew I'd never follow in those footsteps. But he was thankful I already had my mother's hair."

Bran put his hand in the robe pocket and frowned. He felt around like he was searching for something and then shook his head. "And they call you Nella."

She blinked. That wasn't something she'd noticed, let alone the part she expected him to latch on to.

"Yeah. They do. Most of the time. Everybody did until this year. Now I'm Nelle even to people I grew up with. People that should know me better." She paused to look him over. "You call me Nella sometimes too."

"Do I?"

"When you come."

The corners of his mouth pulled down thoughtfully and he pushed off the wall. "Think you can prove that?"

He stopped behind the couch and she reached forward to undo the tie at his waist. She pushed the sides back to reveal his willing dick. Her hands on his hips, she pressed a kiss to his pelvis and whispered, "You were mad."

"I wasn't mad." He caught the back of her head when she pulled back. "I was mad." She licked down, caressing the soft, loose skin of his balls with her tongue. A reward for honesty. "But not at you. I'm mad there's no other way for us to do this and have it be ours. Except to lie. To bring the press into it."

"It's still ours. I wasn't bringing them into it. I was keeping them out of it. And I didn't lie. I said I didn't marry you this week." She didn't add that she had liked doing it. That it felt like her own taunt, her chance to twist the truth to fit the story she wanted told.

"And you called me a dickhead."

"I always call you that." A bead of lust had accumulated on the tip of his dick and she licked it off.

Bran hissed. "It's different when it's on television. Why can't we just say nothing?"

Nelle stopped to look up at him. "Doing nothing doesn't work." Sometimes it felt like she had read a few pages ahead of him and she had to help him catch up. She nuzzled his hip. His skin was warm and soft. He always smelled so good, fresh and woodsy and another underlying scent that was more abstract. She inhaled possibility, attraction, heat. Spotlights. Her eyes closed. "I like it this way. I thought you did too?"

"I do. I like this."

"So if I say I won't see you in London unless we also stage a screaming match backstage…"

"Is that necessary?"

"Or I could have dinner with Santino somewhere flashy. Take the lens off us?"

His hand tightened in her hair, maybe from jealousy, or maybe because she'd sucked his dick down to the base.

"No," Bran huffed out, his eyes closing and his mouth hanging open. "I'll fight you. And then we'll make up."

Nelle knew she wasn't playing fair, but Bran wasn't thinking straight. He was too busy avoiding the things that caused him discomfort. He could pay his dad, and have the house. He could work it out and write a damn song already. He could accept that they had to do something to protect themselves. The solutions weren't easy, but they were simple enough.

This was the way to keep them together. And it bought her more time to work out her own answers, the complicated ones. Even if she admitted that Bran was a man she might love, they couldn't risk going public. Not when it was her reputation on the line. What was considered on-brand behavior for a rock star was the kind of salacious gossip that would eclipse her accomplishments. Being with Bran—really with Bran Kelly—was too much fantasy for the universe to deliver. She had to get him on the same page while she figured out where she wanted the story to take them. While she found a way to produce her happily ever after.

NK

Today 11:13 am

London?

almost
(sparkle hearts sent with echo)

# Chapter Twenty-Five

Bran yawned and someone offered him "a cuppa" for the thousandth time since landing. He didn't need tea, he needed something he could drown in. Wasn't London gin a thing? But Aya nodded and the production assistant hurried out of the room.

The plan had been to sleep on the flight over, only that was when Aya had broken the news. Now the no sleep and jetlag made London feel like Vegas. Too bright when it was supposed to be the middle of the night. Designed to take you for all you had. Bran rubbed his eyes, glad Aya had set up a radio interview and not a TV appearance because he was sure he looked like shit.

He felt like shit. And he deserved it. He'd waited too long, made a shit decision, and now his past was forfeit.

His dad had sold the house. And everything in it.

This albatross that had been weighing him down for months was gone. Replaced by a black hole. The dark gravity of an unknown outcome that would pull him in whether he liked it or not. He was powerless now. He'd had a chance to take control of the situation and he'd been too stubborn to do it. Too weak to break from the old pattern. He'd practiced too often how not to react to his father and reverted to a teenaged version of himself, waiting his old man's anger out, shutting down, until he could get up to his room, unclench his fists, work his fingers over the chords, and let it all out. Only he hadn't done that either. Now his life was in someone else's hands.

Why had he thought a few small payments would be enough to appease his dad? Fucking stupid. Nothing was enough. Kellys pushed.

He fucking knew that.

*Fucking idiot.*

*Fuck.*

Bran's fist connected with the wall and Aya was on her feet.

"I shouldn't have told you."

Bran shook his wrist. That was more stupid. He could have broken a finger and he had to play tomorrow. And he had to produce…something soon. Aya had also said the label wanted to meet with him when he was back in LA. She was full of good news. He flexed his fingers. The knuckle of his pinky was bruised but that was fine. "It's not your fault."

"Of course it isn't. I told you to pay him."

"Remind me to listen to you next time."

"Why didn't you?"

Bran shook out his hand, his pinky aching. "I didn't think he'd go through with it."

Every holiday, every gathering, every family toast Gran had made—his dad had heard it too: *We Kellys may fight but we always unite.* At the end of the day, he hadn't expected his father to sell him out. It wasn't what family was supposed to do. He'd never thought it would get this far. He'd expected something to stop him. Or someone.

*Gran.*

The thought was sudden, a sucker punch he hadn't seen coming. He'd expected Gran to broker the fragile peace between him and his father, like she had all his life. But she was gone, and she'd taken that supposed Kelly loyalty with her.

The PA returned and Aya thanked him for the tea, handing the cup out to Bran. "We'll get you something stronger later."

He shook his head. "I've got something lined up later."

An eyebrow shot into Aya's forehead. "Oh, you do? Funny the person who makes your schedule doesn't know about it."

"She doesn't approve."

Hot tea sloshed over his hand when Aya shoved his shoulder. "You're not going to see her."

"I am," Bran snapped. Aya blinked at the force of his reaction and some of the heat left his chest. "I am. I have to." Everything was shitty. And the last time everything had been this shitty, he'd let his eyes adjust to the dark and seen Nelle. Really seen Nelle. And she'd fixed everything. Nelle had made him forget the rest. He had to see her again soon. These weeks between nights with her were killing him, making him impatient and irritable.

"That's what you need?"

He nodded. "And I need it to stay a secret."

A secret. That might have been how this had all started, but Bran had to admit it had escalated. When Nelle had suggested a public affair with another man—if he hadn't been otherwise engaged—the wall wouldn't have stopped Bran's fist. He'd have struck straight through. That was too far, too much to protect the game they were playing. Bran let out a frustrated breath.

It wasn't the secret he had to protect anymore. It was his ability to see Nelle, according to her terms. And her terms… How long could they keep this up? What would they have to do? Realistically, what was the longevity on an arrangement like this? Could he handle pretending to date other people and meeting up five times a year when their schedules overlapped unsuspiciously? At least they'd always have Cleffy night.

It wasn't enough. And even his place at the Note Awards was contingent on him staying industry relevant. On his ability to work.

Aya snapped to get his attention. She set a hand on her hip. "How did you see her in New York?"

"How did you know—"

"Arlo said you disappeared for a day. Her MSG show was that week. It doesn't take a podcaster to figure out what happened."

Bran took a gulp of the hot tea. "I had myself delivered in a tour trunk."

He hoped that sounded more rock star than desperate, but the soft shake of Aya's chin told him it hadn't. "It's worse than I thought."

What was worse than him liking Nelle and pursuing Nelle and secretly marrying Nelle so he could fuck her in a hotel room every other month? That he also needed her, to talk to and laugh with and to feel understood. What was worse than falling without a parachute?

"It's as bad as it can be," he agreed.

Something like pity flared in Aya's eyes, and then she sighed and asked him where Nelle was staying. She walked behind him, her eyes on the phone screen, as he was ushered into the studio. With Aya perched in the shadows against a padded wall, working on a solution to get him to Nelle tonight, Bran felt better.

Oversized headphones pushed his ears into his head, the tops heating uncomfortably under the pressure. But he could do this. Nelle was waiting and he was even excited for the concert tomorrow. The crowd would be huge and the sun might come out. Nelle wanted to exchange words backstage, and he'd agreed. She thought that was the best way to keep them safe. He had to keep them safe. Soon he wouldn't have any secrets left but her.

"One last question." Peppa from GBR1 looked at him around a mesh microphone protector. "You're headed up to Super Saturday. Lots of big acts this year."

Bran leaned forward. "Yeah, yeah, it should be an amazing show." He felt Aya's eyes on the back of his head. She'd told him not to say amazing—said it made him sound like a clichéd American. Whatever. The dark booth was warm and he was getting sleepier by the minute, one foot-in-mouth moment was fine. "What's the question?" Fuck. Now he sounded like a rude American.

Peppa tilted her head. If she had been going to softball him, she wasn't now. She was going to ask about new music. Aya had rehearsed with him what to say about that too. *It's coming.* Grin. Show excitement, show promise. No specifics. *It's coming.* She'd made him repeat it, like a mantra, like a warning.

*It's coming.* Bran took a sip of water.

"We English love a spot of tea, so can you comment on the rumors swirling that you don't get along with one of the headliners—what do you really think of Nelle?"

Water caught in his throat at her name and Bran coughed.

He wanted to turn and look at Aya, but she hadn't prepped him for this one.

Nelle had.

The professional truth was he thought she was talented—more talented than him. She deserved to be recognized in every way he had. And she would be—because she was driven, determined, unstoppable. There was a spark that lit her up inside and she wasn't ever going to let it burn out.

What did he really think of Antonella Georgopoulos? He thought he might be in love with her.

That wasn't what Peppa had asked. The question was: What did Bran Kelly really think of Nelle? Bran Kelly wasn't supposed to know Nelle, not like that. Not if he wanted to keep their secret, to keep her. Bran Kelly wasn't supposed to be fantasizing about dark curls caressing his skin like a blanket of silk, soft and light and the antithesis of the weight that threatened to crush him.

The room had gone extra quiet, his answer taking longer than it should.

He tried to shoot a hand back and forth across his head, knocking the band of the headphones and fumbling them back over his ears. "She's—" amazing.

*No.*

"I—" love her.

*Fuck.*

"It's…"

His thumb found the edge of the coaster in the pocket of his leather coat. The thick board that had once been solid had softened, fraying into individual layers. Bran pictured Nelle in that moment she'd turned to go at the bar in Chicago. The black waves of her hair catching the gleam of the streetlights outside. "Hair," he choked out, just wanting the interview to end. "It's a lot of hair, but the girl's got a killer voice."

That was it. The interview ended. Relief flooded Bran as he freed himself from the too-tight headphones and left them on the desk. That was the last obstacle between him and Nelle. He checked his watch. She'd have landed. Now he just had to get to her.

His phone buzzed in the pocket of his fitted jeans, Nelle calling to say she was on the way to the hotel. But he couldn't answer it here, in the hallway of a media outlet. He had to be smarter than that. The buzzing stopped. And started again. Bran caught Aya's eye and nodded towards the elevators. She gave him the "one second" finger and motioned to a PA waiting to take a photo with him.

He posed and smiled, the vibrations in his pants pulsing constantly.

Nelle couldn't wait.

Neither could he.

Bran plunged down the hall and took the elevator to the building's lobby. He was out on the street, the air smelling of damp stone, when he finally answered her call.

"Hey, okay, so I haven't quite worked out how to get to you but Aya is—"

"What the fuck, Kelly."

Bran stopped cold, the familiar sharpened-knife quality of her voice sending a chill down his spine. "What what fuck?"

"Hair. I'm a lot of hair?"

"And a killer voice."

"But hair first."

Bran rubbed the back of his neck. "I don't know, Nelle. They caught me off guard. You don't want me telling the truth—"

"We. We don't want that. We agreed."

"Right. We agreed to stage a feud. That's what you want to do tomorrow, right? So what's the problem?"

"The problem is you belittling my career. My work."

His mouth dropped open. "You called me a dickhead on late-night television, how is that different?"

"I called you a Cleffy-winning dickhead. You called me a *girl*. You reduced me to *hair*."

Bran looked around, seeing nothing but an unfamiliar blur of grey. He was sick of this game and now she was mad at him for playing along? "Well, I'm sorry I'm not as good at faking this as you are. It's not me."

"But it's me? I'm fake?"

"I didn't say that."

"But you did. You did on a fucking radio show."

"A radio show that has nothing to do with us. Not really." Months ago—*months* ago—he'd gotten an inside tip, a heads-up that this would happen. When saving-the-day Benj had stared him down as the elevator door slid into motion, he'd expected a don't-fuck-with-my-girl threat. Instead he'd gotten a different warning through the closing gap: *You should know, she won't compromise.* Nelle's best friend had told him that. And he should have listened. "Why does it have to be your way or nothing—why can't you compromise?"

Her sigh in his ear coincided with a gust of wet wind, and Bran braced himself against the coming storm. "This was your premise, Bran, I'm just executing it because you can't. Or you won't. You won't do anything. You won't even be Bran Kelly the talented fucking musician. You're too busy acting like some mercurial suffering artist who won't just pick up the guitar and work it out."

That hit landed and Bran pushed back. "Is that it? You need me to be Bran Kelly so you can have a rock star to chase you?"

"That's not—"

"To satisfy *your* ego? I can't be the perfect version of me you've cultivated in your head. He doesn't exist." Bran's hand fisted. "I mean, what am I supposed to do? You're twisting me up—my hands are tied. I can't give everyone what they want. My dad sold the house, Nelle."

He was expecting her to understand, like she had so many times before, but her voice came through the line flat and uninterested. "Oh yeah? That sounds hard. Really hard, Bran. And when things are hard you can't be expected to do anything about them, huh? If it isn't easy, you give up. Because you're scared shitless to try."

"That's not fair."

"Fair? Really? Has it been *unfair* for you growing up a handsome, famous man in America? My father was a surgeon in Greece and he left it behind to be a shop clerk because my mother wanted to raise me somewhere I'd have more opportunities than she did. They sacrificed and I strived and you tried to tear that down."

Bran's mouth opened wordlessly. He was unequipped for this conversation. Her parents had taught her to achieve, while he'd learned to look out for himself. The problem was that they spent too much time apart—because of *her* rules. If he could just see her—he bent at the waist. He was so tired and so angry and the nerves holding him together were raw and worn thin. When he came back up one of them snapped.

"If I'm so terrible, why don't you ask your universe to intervene on my behalf—make your little wishes and have it all come true—"

"I *work* for this success!"

"—fix me up just the way you want—"

"That's not my job!"

"You should be happy, Nelle. You've been so determined to find the worst in me and here it is. I must have planned this. I must be playing you. That's what you've always wanted to think. And you're right. I was using you. I thought you'd inspire me. And then I could write this damn album and—" Bran cut himself off, breathing heavily into the phone. She'd stopped interrupting. He should apologize, but his back teeth ground together in frustration and he couldn't get the words out.

Nelle had gone so silent he thought she'd hung up, but then she spoke, slow and calm to make sure he heard. "Listen up: I'm not your muse, Bran. I'm not here for *your* benefit. And I can't fix you. You have to work on yourself."

He squeezed his eyes shut. "You're making me look like the asshole here."

"Oh, baby, you're doing that on your own."

She hung up and his scalp burned from the grip of his hand at the top of his head. He let go and his hair stayed clumped together, wet from the fine rain that had started to fall. His throat was tight and his ear ached where he'd smashed the phone to it.

He made his way over to Aya, waiting under a black umbrella next to a town car. The long lens of a paparazzi camera on the hood of a sedan across the street caught his eye. Great, so there'd be photos of "Bran Kelly distraught on phone." They'd probably run next to a photo of Francesca with a story about how desperate he was to get back together with her.

Bran Kelly. Distraught. Desperate. Looking like shit.

He slumped into the car's seat and Aya closed the door behind him. He'd lived up to the real family legacy: a Kelly pushing for more until there was nothing left.

Bran Kelly. Chip off the old block. Deserved what he got.

## Chapter Twenty-Six

"Cut it off."

"You know I can't do that."

"Then I'll do it myself." Nelle grabbed for the trimming shears, tugging them from their black fabric strap and upending the travel case Benj had spread on the narrow dressing room counter. There was a quick scuffle as Benj tried to stop her but Nelle twisted away in triumph. With the scissors raised and a fistful of hair, she met her friend's eyes in the mirror and stopped.

Embarrassment fizzed in her gut. Every time she thought about the things she'd been planning to tell Bran, it was like she'd washed back a mouthful of Pop Rocks with soda. She couldn't be still with all the unwanted emotion bubbling inside her. She had to do something.

Benj held her phone up, thumb hovering over a blue call button. "Put the scissors down."

"Or what? You're gonna call Mina?" Mina would be back any minute anyway. She'd seen a GBR1 producer in the hall and gone to hammer out the details for Nelle's interview the next day.

Steady-handed Benj shook her head. "No, I'm going to call your mother, Antonella."

"You wouldn't. You hate talking on the phone."

"If it meant stopping you from giving yourself bored sophomore bangs, I would answer unknown spam."

Benjamina Wasik didn't bluff. She was steadfast and loyal and for a friend, she would lean all the way in. She would follow through. Nelle normally appreciated that initiative, that resourcefulness, but not right now—not when her friend *would* push that button.

Nelle imagined the call, her mother's sharp greeting, "Benjamina? Is something wrong?" And if she heard her mother's voice now, she'd lunge for the phone and confess *everything was wrong.* She'd been so selfish, thinking a cheap secret was worth what her parents had given up. Her father's health should never have been public knowledge. They had lost that family moment in church because she was there. The universe had given her so much and taken her parents' anonymity, their sanctuary, their faith in their community. Why did they have to pay that price? How could she have ever thought the value of a few nights with Bran Kelly was anything compared to what her parents had paid up for her?

"I'm over it. I'm just so over it." Nelle's elbow lowered slightly. "And it's my hair."

Benj took a step closer. "Then I will do it. But we're not going to have it look like some idiot boy got under your skin. We have to do this smart. I'll help you. *If* you put down my fucking scissors."

Metal clattered against the counter as Nelle let the scissors fall from her hand. Her body vibrated with coiled tension. She had to face Bran in half an hour, when his set ended and hers began. He'd had all day to say something to her and he'd done nothing. She wasn't like that. She made moves. "It's not just him. I'm tired of it. Last night it tangled in my bridge pins during 'Cosmic Order.'"

"I get it." Benj collected her shears.

The standoff was over, but her friend was still holding the phone. "Shouldn't you put that down too?"

"No, we need to get a bafter." Benj sighed when Nelle drew her eyebrows together in confusion. "A before and after? Ready? Smile through your eyes, please. There you go. Then we'll take one when we're done and you're gonna post them both with the hashtag hairforcare. I have a friend trying to raise awareness and money for kids whose parents can't afford health care— you're also gonna need to make a donation so you don't look cheap."

"And because I care." Nelle forced out a prolonged breath.

"Right. Do you want to bring Mina into the loop now or—"

"When we're done. She'll get on board when she has no choice." Once in the chair, Nelle's knees still trembled. She pressed them tight together. Noise from the hallway filtered through the thin door. "Can you hurry up?"

"Oh, I'm sorry, I thought we wanted this to look like a fashion decision, not like you got too close to a fan blade." Benj shook out a cape and it settled over Nelle with a soft flutter. She closed her eyes and waited for the sound of the first snip. Her heart was in her throat when the weight of Benj's hands landed on her shoulders, a firm comfort.

"I'm all out of clementines."

"I think this is bigger than clementines. And oranges.

And grapefruit." She adlibbed a quick hook, *"Citrus can't fix this."*

Benj remained serious. "He's an idiot."

Craning her neck, Nelle looked over her shoulder to agree. "He is."

"But you were going to stage a fight with him today anyway. Is it possible he's an idiot who was trying to help?"

"Yeah." Nelle twisted the ring on her finger under the cape. Bran knew the stakes. He knew what would happen. And still he'd been careless. How many times did she have to explain it? Once should have been enough. If he cared, once would have been enough. If she was worth it to him, she wouldn't have to keep explaining why. He would have heard her. The performer in her knew: what he couldn't hear, he couldn't correct. She'd fallen for his hoax after all—she'd believed that he wanted to listen. "But he said worse stuff when I called him on it." With squared shoulders, she faced the mirror again. "So fuck that."

Bran was an idiot. But so was she. She was the idiot who'd been living in a fantasy. Who'd let a couple nights in a six-month span sustain a dream that they were building something real.

"What stuff?"

Nelle shifted. She just wanted Benj to start already. "Like, that I have to get my way. I want to be chased. Life's not fair to *him* and I can't compromise—" Benj sucked in a breath and Nelle twisted back again to look at her. "What?"

With a sharp drop of her chin, Benj exhaled. "I told him that. In Chicago. He is an idiot. Because he did not understand what I meant."

"And what did you mean?" Did her best friend think she was selfish too?

Tucking back a loose curl that framed Nelle's face Benj said tenderly, "That you won't compromise yourself. That you've worked too hard. I wanted him to understand what you had on the line. To value it."

Nelle bit into her cheek and turned back to the mirror, blinking the blur from her eyes. Why had she let herself imagine a future with someone who didn't understand what mattered to her? Who didn't value her vulnerability? Or her purpose?

Benj shook out her hair. "I'm making sure that when he sees you with this haircut, he's gonna know what he—"

"No. I don't care what he thinks. I just want it off." Nelle pulled the ring off her finger and held it in her fist.

"Okay. Here we go."

Benj swiveled Nelle towards the door so she had a clear view of her manager's soundless, openmouthed shock when Mina walked in. She staggered against the door, shutting it tight, as if she could solve this problem before anyone came in and found out.

"Why?" Mina fixed her attention on the mess of shorn hair at Nelle's feet. "Why right now?"

"Because…" The truth stuck in her throat. Because she'd exposed herself, and she'd misplaced her trust, and she hated it.

Benj unclipped the cape. With nowhere else to hide it, Nelle pushed the ring back onto her finger as her friend removed the cover and distanced herself from the crime. "Because I wanted to. Benj stepped in when I threatened to do it myself. How does it look?" She spun towards the mirror and tried to find herself, instead of Mina's deep frown.

Benj had given her a lob. Her wavy hair made it look slightly disheveled, choppy, but in a way she immediately recognized as cool. As enviable. Her eyes shifted back to Mina's as her manager drew the same conclusion. This was a look Nelle could rock. It was a look her fans would try to attain. It felt light and fresh but beyond what it did for her personally, it was good for business. Nelle posed for Benj and let her explain to Mina about #hairforcare. The mention of a hashtag galvanized Mina and she'd soon drafted the post on Nelle's phone.

"Your mom texted," she relayed while Nelle warmed up. "Wants to know what show they can come to next."

Relief flooded Nelle's body. She raised her face, a soundless *thank you* passing her lips. She'd released her fear months ago, and the universe was responding now, right when she needed a sign that she had her priorities straight. That real love was understanding, that real love was support. "Any one they want—can you handle it?"

Mina nodded. "Of course. And I'm going to wait on posting the photo until after the set. Better impact for us to debut the look onstage."

*Impact.* That's what Nelle wanted to have. But hers was an audience of one. Benj was right, she cared about Bran's reaction. What they shared now was so much more than a secret. Maybe they would exchange words. Maybe they would fight. And maybe they'd even make up.

But as she watched him finishing his set from the stage wings, the words she planned to say slipped away.

She watched Bran Kelly perform. She watched him

tussle his hair—*he* was hair! She watched his mouth pull in a slow, lopsided smile as he told the sea of people in the field in front of him that they'd see him soon with something new. That was rich. She'd seen him scribble lines, and she'd seen him discard them. She'd never found that coaster. No doubt he'd thrown it away when it didn't immediately flourish into a completed song. He'd had an idea but couldn't follow through. Despite what he'd told that crowd, Bran Kelly wasn't making new music. They'd fall for his act, like she had. All of it for show. The worst part was seeing how easily he could pretend as long as it was to his benefit. Now she knew: doing what was best to keep them together didn't make the cut.

He could perform for an audience, but not for her. That crowd was what he needed, and she got that. She got it because if she weren't going onstage in the next fifteen minutes, if she didn't have that hit lined up, she wouldn't have cut her hair, she'd be tearing it out.

An orange sunset blazed in his mirrored sunglasses as he unplugged and turned her way. He'd thought they were broken and she'd fixed them. And now he expected her to fix everything for him. She was glad he had them on when he passed her coming off the stage. Glad she could focus on herself in their reflection, look herself in the eye instead of meeting icy blue that might have pierced through her resolve.

It didn't matter what Bran thought of her new look. It didn't matter what she had thought they could be, what she had wanted to say to him, the things she had done for him. He had tried to reduce her to a spark when she was a star, burning endlessly.

Nelle lifted her chin and Bran paused, expectant,

waiting for her to start the fight they'd discussed. She stood silent. He unhitched his overear monitor and hesitated. The need to react crackled through her like feedback. But she held. She waited to see what he'd do if she didn't make the first move. And when he couldn't say a word, she looked past him.

In ten minutes the crew would have the stage turned over to her. She'd have the spotlight, a backing track, and the crowd. Her parents would be at her next show. Mina and Benj were always at her back. She'd have everything she needed. Especially that moment when her voice dropped out and the fans carried her words forward, lifting them up and giving them a life of their own. When she sang "Under Water" tonight and seventy thousand people chorused the new hook back to her—*take me home*—she'd think of Bran Kelly as *her* muse. Someone she used for a good line. The arc of N3 formed in her mind, a love story that curved up one side and sloped down the other. She looked past him. To a year from now, when the crowd would still be there, and Bran Kelly would be an echo on their lips, words she'd write about a burnout, a man who was so afraid of failing, he just gave up.

NK

Sat, May 25, 10:53 pm

I thought we weren't going to let them get to us
Read 10:55 pm

## Chapter Twenty-Seven

Nelle had made herself clear. When she hadn't started a scene at Super Saturday Bran had known it was because she didn't need to. She had nothing to protect. They were over. But it was the next day, when she went on GBR1's *Cover Corner*, that she twisted the knife to make sure he felt it.

Bran was watching it again. He was probably solely responsible for half the views on the damn thing. But he couldn't stop himself. It was important that he remember just how much she wanted him to hurt. Because there was no doubt that performance was about him.

Nelle sat at a piano (that part was for her father). Her short hair was just as jarring as it had been when he came offstage at Super Saturday. Curls that had felt like his salvation were gone, and with them the soft promise of night. A statement he understood intrinsically. The camera panned over Nelle's fingers and Bran braced for another blow, a mallet to a hollow drum. Only the drum was his heart, because the angled ring he'd grown used to seeing on her left hand, the one hidden in plain sight for months, was gone too. He was undoubtedly the only person in the world who noticed. He was definitely the only one who understood.

Nelle sang along as she played "Piece of My Heart." Her rich voice was packed with confident emotion, pained but daring, as she made the well-worn song her own. Like one of his shirts. He remembered her indignant accusation: *You'd rather play a song about Janis Joplin than by her?* Technically, this was Erma Franklin, but he got the message.

And if he hadn't, there was the direct mention. The callout. When Peppa joined Nelle to thank her and asked if she had a response to Bran's own comments. "Anything you want to say to Bran Kelly?"

Bran pulled the phone closer to his face to watch Nelle lift one coy shoulder and destroy him. "I'll say what we're all thinking: Where's that new music?"

"Ouch," Cormac deadpanned as Bran rolled onto his back on the teak patio. He crushed his eyes closed against the harsh sun and rested stinging palms on his heaving chest.

"Get up."

"That fucking hurt."

"You're soft, everything is going to hurt." Cormac stopped rearranging the Hula-Hoops Bran had scattered when he tripped to kick his foot. "Get up."

Water splashed on his face and Bran lurched up, his abs aching. "Hey!"

But it was Arlo, heaving himself out of the pool and offering a hand to pull him to his feet. Bran ignored it, examining his throbbing knee before meeting Cormac's eyes. "Can you get me some ice?"

"Your freezer fixed?"

Arlo laughed, pulling a Hula-Hoop out of formation. "You haven't heard it?"

Cormac reached for the hoop and missed. "Heard it? It's an ice maker."

"It's loud now." Spinning the hoop around his middle, Arlo rotated his hips in small circles. "Really fucking loud."

Cormac set his hands on his hips. "Why are you so good at that?"

"Rhythm, C."

"Yeah, I know rhythm. Give it back, Bran's running my course again."

Bran moved into the shade, collapsing on the couch of the outdoor lounge and putting his feet up on the low wall of the firepit. "Bran's taking a break."

"I'm trying to help you, B." The drummer frowned. "This is mental. Tell yourself it's easy—stop thinking about the rest of it and push."

"I'm not thinking about anything, I'm just tired."

"You're thinking about something. Is it Aya's wheeling and dealing or the cinnamon next to your bed?"

Bran's foot slipped off the ledge as he strained upwards. "What were you doing in my room?" Sun glinted off Cormac's wrist. "Is that my Patek Philippe?"

Cormac bobbed his head with a knowing nod. "Okay, that narrows it down. What happened with Shower Girl that she's not here making you moussaka anymore and you're jerking off alone while huffing ground spices?"

"I am not—"

"This is part of it, right?" Cormac produced the worn coaster from his pocket and Bran lunged for it, with no regard for the pilfered, wildly expensive watch on his friend's wrist. They wrestled for a minute, knocking two cushions off the couch before Bran managed to liberate the coaster from Cormac's grasp.

"You can dig deep for that, huh?" Cormac propped himself up on the firepit wall.

Bran rolled to his back on the teak floor. Again. "Fuck off. And stay out of my room."

Aya's trademark cough, sharp and clear, drew their attention to the French doors off the kitchen where she stood. A man in a suit looked over her shoulder. "I need to borrow Bran for a minute."

His knee throbbing, Bran rose to his feet and followed her into the cool house. He slammed the coaster down on the counter. It had bent in the scuffle, one side of the circle rising up from the surface. Fucking Cormac. Bran nodded to the suit. "What's Mr. Money doing here?"

"It's Moony," said the lawyer.

Aya put down her phone and Bran took a step back, hitting the exposed side of the deep porcelain sink.

"I had a meeting with the label today."

"I thought that was next week." He hooked his thumbs over the wide glossy edge behind him. So this was serious.

"We moved it up. Decided it was better for me to handle it myself." That's what she was doing now. Handling everything herself, without his input.

"And?"

"And I told them they'd have an album by the end of the year and a tour next summer."

"What—"

"*And.* They asked that I have Mr. Moony come remind you what happens if they decide you're in breach of contract. Which you are. But I convinced them the music is coming and you're acting in good faith to provide it."

That wasn't true and she knew it. Bran frowned.

Moony started to speak and Bran cut him off. "No, I got it. You don't need to explain." He roughed a hand across his head. "Is that it?"

"No," Moony said. "I thought it might be a good idea to discuss the Nelle issue."

Bran glanced at Aya, whose mouth opened and closed. She hadn't known about that part. "There is no Nelle issue."

"Mr. Kelly, it could easily become a libel suit—depending on how far the girl wants to take it."

"Woman," Bran corrected, rubbing at his side.

"As your legal counsel I need to explain the risks of what it looks like if the two of you keep exchanging barbs, and you say something over the line."

"I won't. I won't say anything about her."

"If she wants—"

"She doesn't want anything from me." He held Moony's stare. "You can go. Have the rest of the hour on me."

"The label pays me."

"Even better."

When the sound of loafers had faded into the hall, Bran met Aya's eyes. "What do we do in six months when I need more time?"

"You won't need more time because you're going to write an album."

"Aya—"

"No, Bran. It's enough."

Cormac poked his head into the house, his attention on Aya, as usual. "You okay?"

"I'm fine. I'm working. Apparently I'm the only one." She picked up her phone and pointed it at Cor-

mac. "I invested in a restaurant that still hasn't opened."
She turned it on Bran. "And you've been moping for a
month. You wanted me to buy time with your dad and
that backfired. We tried to—" She stopped herself.

"We tried what?" Bran said, leaning into the island.

Cormac answered. "We tried buying it for you. But
your old man's a piece of work. He didn't want *my*
money or Arlo's. He wanted you to bend or face the
consequences. Said he was going to find a motivated
buyer."

"Motivated to make money off my pain?"

"That was poetic, write that down."

There was a sudden crash from inside the freezer,
like ice cracking directly off a glacier and falling into
a frozen sea. Bran flinched, Cormac jumped, and Arlo
yelled through the open door, "I told you it was loud!"

Bran ignored the incredulous look from Cormac.
The ice machine wasn't his biggest problem at the mo-
ment. "I'm not writing, Aya. I can't make that deadline.
You can't just—"

"No, Bran. You can't. You can't just stop. I'm going
to keep doing my job and making plans for you, and if
you don't want to embarrass yourself—" she motioned
to the deck, cluttered with Cormac's weights and resistance bands "—you're going to get to work."

Bran gripped the counter. She was betting on his
vanity. And that might have worked for the advertis-
ing campaign she'd signed him up for, but it couldn't
override his writing block.

Arlo pushed past Cormac to grab a Guinness from
the fridge and Aya continued. "I know you're heart-
broken—"

"I'm not—"

"You told me to remind you to listen to me. And I say: write some sad songs and move on."

"It's not that easy."

Beer fizzled as Arlo popped the top off a bottle using his fist and the countertop. "She didn't say it was easy—she said you had to do it."

"Okay, summer lovin', I don't need this shit from you too. Or you can check out of Hotel Kelly."

"Easy," Cormac warned.

*Easy, easy, easy.*

Fuck. It was so hard. It was so hard to try and not know if he could do it again. Writing alone and touring alone and being alone—

Bran looked around the room at the three people who were staring back at him. People who had been there for him and were still there for him and had tried to help him even when he hadn't asked for it. Maybe that's what all this meant.

His palms grew warmer, like he was getting close to some hidden key. "Okay. Let's get the band back together—"

Cormac groaned and Arlo shook his head, mouth secured to his upturned bottle.

Aya pinched the bridge of her nose. "That's not the answer."

Bran held out his hands. "Why not?"

"Kelly," Cormac said, "you can drag me back on tour again when I'm fifty, thrice divorced, and strapped for cash, until then, I will happily collect my royalty checks from the comfort of home while you caravan across the globe singing your gypsy heart out."

"Don't say that." Arlo set down the beer and hooked

his hands together over the hoop he wore across his bare chest. "The Traveler community has been—"

The hoop rattled as Cormac took hold and yanked him back. "And obviously A has school, where they don't mind him being absolutely insufferably woke."

"They encourage it," Arlo clarified.

Bran looked them over again and his three friends— his *real* family—no longer looked like the Avengers assembling to help. The set of their faces juxtaposed with the soft concern in their eyes looked a whole lot like an intervention—if you ignored the half-naked man wearing a Hula-Hoop and holding a Guinness.

"Your dad—"

But Bran cut Aya off. "Who?"

"The man formerly known as your father—"

"Better, but we don't have to talk about him. Ever."

"What if he—"

"He won't. I took care of it."

Cormac scrunched up his face. "You offed your pop?"

Bran threw up his hands. "What is the deal with people assuming I'm out here on a murder spree? I didn't 'off' him. I ended our association."

"You did?" Aya looked unconvinced.

"He called. I answered. I finished it."

It had been a few days after he'd gotten back from London. And he'd figured he was already scraped up, why not cut all the way to the bone? But he'd stared at the caller ID so long that when he picked up to silence on the other end, he'd thought he'd missed the call.

Then his dad's whiskey-soaked voice had scratched out his name. "Bran?"

"Yeah."

"You know I had to—"

"No. You didn't."

"You wouldn't—"

"No. I wouldn't."

Something crashed on his father's end of the line. "You gonna keep interrupting me or let me talk?"

Bran's grip on the phone intensified. "I'm gonna let you listen. I'm done. I'm done with you. You made your profit, you got what you wanted from me. Now cross me off your list. I'm not someone you know anymore. We're through."

"Oh, we're through?"

The familiar heckling tone made Bran's throat dry. He sucked in air through his mouth like he was running for home. If he kept talking, there could be no reconciliation—he'd have to give up hope for a cathartic spirit-dad game of catch. He paused, pulse pounding. He didn't have the hope to waste.

"Bye, Pat," he'd said and ended the call.

From across the island, Aya watched him carefully. "I know the house was a blow."

Bran gripped the counter. "I don't care about the house, okay? The house is gone. It's gone and I can't get it back."

"What can you get back, B?" Arlo cocked his head to the side and Bran was surprised he didn't stroke his beard.

"Back off, Freud."

Cormac maneuvered to the fridge for his own beer. "Yeah, tell the doctor what hurts."

"My knee." Bran shifted his feet, as if to shake off the weight of their combined gazes. Three against one. It wasn't fair.

*Fair? Really?* He couldn't forget the hot anger in Nelle's voice.

"What isn't gone?" Arlo said, interrupting Bran's thoughts. He sighed when Bran refused to answer. "You want our help? Let's say it on the count of three. Come on, everybody, to assist our favorite lead singer on his journey to enlightenment. One, two, three—"

Aya was checking her phone again but didn't miss a beat. "The money."

Cormac swallowed in time to say, "The beer."

Bran guessed a second late. "The music?"

Arlo shook his head. "The girl."

"The girl is gone." Bran stuck out a hand, palm down. "Trust that I'm certain there."

"How do you know?"

"I gave her a ring—"

"Bran," Aya and Cormac said in unison, their tones expressing varying degrees of disbelief and concern.

"Like an engagement ring?" Arlo asked, his eyebrows high.

"No. It wasn't an engagement ring. It was…" A wedding ring. "It was simple. Silver with like a—" Bran drew a V in the air. "It doesn't matter. She stopped wearing it. And I don't need you all in my house and in my business and in my fridge. I need space and time—and my watch back, Cormac, seriously."

Aya's phone buzzed in her hand. She glanced at it and then at Bran. "You've had time. And space. Now you've got a deadline. And I need to get back to the office. Get to work, call me if you need help booking a studio." She headed for the door, glancing back to confirm with Arlo, "Drinks this week?"

He nodded. "Saturday." When she was gone he

looked sideways at Cormac. "Do I need to put you on this meeting docket? You okay financially? Why is Aya investing in your place?"

"So I have a reason to stop by her office every week," Cormac countered. "She talk about me when you two meet up?"

"I can only handle one of your love lives at a time, and B is mid-surgery, so can we—" Arlo gestured at Bran and Cormac nodded. "Tell us about the girl, Kelly."

Bran's heart pulsed faster at the thought of Nelle. *The* girl. Singular. The *woman*. The only one that mattered. "Why?"

"In the last year, when have you been closest to writing—what have you wanted to write about?"

Bran held the heels of his hands to his eyes. He lowered his face into the counter so the answer echoed back up at him. "Her."

Arlo picked up the coaster, bending it back the opposite way, and laid it flat. He spun the circle so the words Bran had scribbled were right side up. "So start with this. What does it mean—get specific."

Cormac nodded. "With details."

"Not sexual details." Arlo glared at Cormac.

The drummer wiped beer from his lip. "To hell with that."

Arlo pressed on. "*She turned midnight.* That must mean something. She signals change, she has power—she's special?"

"Yeah, she's special." Bran's sweaty forehead stuck to the polished surface. "She's a genuine one-in-a-billion superstar."

Cormac clapped his hands together. "Look at you

go! That's a neat metaphor. You could get a chorus out of that, right?"

"And I fucked it up." Bran moaned into the counter. He couldn't hold it in anymore. "I fucked it up," he repeated, punctuating each word. "Being with someone like that—someone so fucking sure of herself—it was like her light pushed through my cracks, you know? She's so smart and has so many levels, I could barely keep up." He lifted his head, his hair sticking up. "It was supposed to be one night but that one night was all banana pudding and midnight hot dogs—"

"Are those euphemisms?" Cormac whispered to Arlo as Bran spiraled on, spilling everything out.

"And then we decided to keep it going and, god— after the Note Awards, Van Morrison was playing and the olive oil was gleaming and I was in so deep, right there—"

"In deep literally, right?"

Arlo silenced Cormac with a look so Bran could continue, as if he could stop now that he'd opened the floodgates.

"—but also *figuratively* because it's not even the sex part. I can't stop thinking about the way she had me. She was always calling me out and making me crazy. Making me—" He stopped.

"Making you what?" Arlo asked.

Bran's head connected with the counter again, his voice muffled by arms folded over his head. "Making me fall for her."

Arlo raised a toast. "There it is."

Cormac held up a hand. "Yeah, I'm gonna need you to back up to the kitchen-themed sexy Mad Libs—"

"I love Nelle." Bran let the last of it go. He couldn't

keep it secret anymore. Not that there was anything left to protect between them.

Shock opened Arlo's features. "Nelle? Nelle Nelle?"

"Nelle. Nelle. Nelle," Bran chanted, falling to a squat behind the island, even as his glutes burned. "She didn't want anyone to know." He sank lower, landing back against the stove. How could he blame her? Who would want to be associated with a soon-to-be-has-been mess like him? He hadn't been good enough for her. He hadn't—he hadn't tried. Hope sputtered to life in his bent abdomen.

Just like with Gran's house, he hadn't tried anything with his dad. He'd frozen up, stood silent, refused to break away from the pattern. He hadn't fed the fire, but he hadn't attempted to put it out either. He'd hoped his dad would Kelly up—they were family. With real family, he thought, looking at Arlo and Cormac, each offering a hand to pull him to his feet, you didn't have to hope they'd be there for you. They just would be.

He resisted a moment, two. He was supposed to do it on his own. But if he pushed their hands away, he'd be on the floor for another hour, feeling sorry for himself, feeling heavy. How much was he expected to carry on his own?

Cormac had asked him: *How can you write if you won't let anything go?*

Arlo had challenged: *What's the point if we can't support each other?*

And Nelle, she wanted him to fix himself, but she'd also been the one to tell him: *There's nothing wrong with trusting people to help you.*

Bran let his friends pull him up and when he'd found

his balance, he shook out his hair, smoothed it back, and took a deep breath. "Now what?"

Arlo shrugged. "Now you write it down. And if it doesn't come—"

Bran knew the answer, felt it warming him, different from the hot prickle of his sore body: softer, golden— like amber eyes glowing in the dark. *Fear blocks flow.* The fear of failure that stopped him before he started. The fear of trying to write a hit and not being able to do it again. The fear of *no Nelle.* Without trying he'd succeeded in living the failure, and it blew. It was time to tell fear to fuck off.

He yanked the junk drawer open, searching for a pen. "Then I'll go get it."

@BKgreen71k tweeted: got tickets to the jingle jam but it won't be as good as last year. anyone else feel like they wish whatever was going on with @theBranKelly and @nelle23 would end so we could have more magic like that performance? like, dude, get us the collab we deserve.

@theBranKelly tweeted: I tried. Been left on read since I wished her a happy birthday.

@nelle23 tweeted: Read 2:23 pm.

@werkerB tweeted: anyone know if the girl who posted this is okay?

@BKgreen71k tweeted: she's not. this is her ghost.

## Chapter Twenty-Eight

Nelle had spent six months dancing onstage in four-inch thigh-high boots, but she tripped on her way into the restaurant in her oxfords wedges like it was her first time out of flats.

Bran Kelly was sitting at the bar. His back was to the room, but she'd know that head of coiffed hair anywhere. His fingers traced the rim of a half-empty old fashioned and she stood frozen in the aisle, following the circles and growing dizzy.

"You good?" Santino pulled away from their group and bent his head to catch her eye, drawing her gaze from Bran.

Nelle nodded, not trusting her voice. It was just her husband who she hadn't seen in four months. Who hadn't tried to contact her except to say happy birthday and then comment that he'd done so on some random tweet so her mentions had exploded.

Santino held out his arm and ushered her towards one of the big curved booths at the back of the room. She passed behind Bran, a row of busy tables between them, and swore his shoulders rose under his dark cardigan. Hackles up sensing danger. Sensing her. Or at least, sensing the way a wave of whispers followed her across the room. It was LA after all, everyone thought they knew something about Bran Kelly and Nelle, and now here they were in the same room together. She almost turned around and left, but that would have caused a scene. And Bran Kelly wasn't going to get a scene from her.

Nelle scooted across the dark red leather, into the middle of the booth. The rest of the restaurant had a brassy glow, but the booths were up on a platform where the low ceiling provided a shadowy privacy.

Across the restaurant, over a flickering candle in a red warbled glass, Bran dragged out a long sip. Of course he was here. Bran Kelly belonged in rooms like this—dark, sexy places that looked like ads for luxury watches and expensive scotch. A shiver went through her as she remembered what it was like to be up close to Bran at a bar like this. When the smell of winter wafted off him in tantalizing ripples like fog off dry ice. When it was her sitting next to him not—Nelle squinted through the wavy air above the candle—Arlo?

That afternoon, when Santino had invited them to Cormac's buzzy new steakhouse, she'd only agreed to come after dismissing the possibility that Bran would be here. He'd told her they made a point of keeping their friendship out of the public eye.

He'd told her a lot of things. Her mistake had been believing him.

And now she'd walked into a goddamn band reunion.

Arlo nudged Bran's side and Bran shook his head. She knew what that meant. He wasn't leaving.

Well, she wasn't either.

Nelle addressed the heavy menu, flipping it from side to side without reading any of the words. A waiter in a black button-down came by and she ordered a burger, hoping they had one.

"Great choice," the waiter said with a smile. "And to drink?"

Water would be another great choice, given her already shaky equilibrium.

"Tequila, white, a double, lots of ice and lime." Nelle exhaled. "Please."

"I'll have the same." Santino handed over his menu. "Has anyone heard it?"

"Nobody," said Santino's cousin Bri. She was an influencer, so when she said nobody, she meant nobody because she knew everybody.

"Heard what?" Nelle asked, jumping into the conversation to distract herself from Bran fishing the cherry out of his drink.

Santino slung his arm over the back of the booth. "Kelly's got a new single. He's closing the Besties."

Bri's friend, Lana, sighed. "I wish I could go. It's barely an awards show. It's a televised party. Like a concert with speeches."

Nelle folded her arms on the table. So she'd be seeing him tomorrow too.

"You didn't know?" Santino asked. "It was all over my feed this weekend."

"I'm taking a social media break," Nelle said. It seemed necessary when, instead of ignoring the random comment Bran had made about her online, she responded and got the exchange screen-grabbed by @Celebpetty. She didn't need that attention. The Note noms would be announced in a month. That was her focus. Not the unbelievable fact that she'd have been married to Bran for an entire year without anyone finding out.

The waiter gestured to the curtains on a pole above them. "Should I?"

"No!" Lana said.

Benj tucked her chin back and shot Nelle a look that asked, *You okay with this?* There were two people too many between them, so Nelle responded with a slight shrug.

She couldn't avoid it any longer. If it wasn't today it'd be tomorrow. When Bran was singing his new single for the entire country.

There had been a time when part of Nelle's Bran Kelly fantasy included the moment he finally finished a new song. And the first thing the Bran Kelly in her head did was send it to her. Wanting her to be the first one to hear it. It hadn't happened that way.

Nelle sipped the tequila, feeling it bloom warm and alive in her stomach. It was at that moment Bran turned halfway in his chair and looked directly at her. The tequila detonated. Dizzy heat threatened to consume her as she held his gaze.

Despite the circumstances—because of the circumstances—they needed to talk. They needed to clear the air before their staring competition transformed into audible static, lightning heat that consumed the room with a deafening smash. Holding Bran's gaze, she finished her tequila then pushed at Santino's side to get out of the booth. She excused herself, and started for the bathroom. She didn't watch to see if Bran stood, but she knew he was following her from the tingle that spun up her spine.

The room was dim. The sink and toilet and floor a

shiny obsidian. Three mirrors reflected a black-and-green jungle print wallpaper that covered every inch of wall. It was like stepping into a different world, disconnected from the one outside in the restaurant. Like space: with no up or down to orient herself. Nelle turned just as Bran entered. The door closed behind him with a heavy click, cutting off the sound from the other side with it.

She stepped forward to flip the metal lock, expecting him to move back, but he stayed put. Suddenly they were alone, and inches apart. That hadn't been part of her plan.

His breath wafted warm over her left shoulder. He lowered his chin and she braced her hands on his hips to keep herself from tangling them into his hair. But her hands slipped up, under his shirt and—

She tried to shove him back against the mirrored door but he was too solid.

"What have you been doing?" she asked, pulling up his shirt to reveal freshly toned abs and Adonis lines that dove into his jeans where she shouldn't follow.

He glanced down at the defined stomach she was admiring with eyes and hands, like he didn't know what had caught her attention. "Aya roped me into an underwear campaign. I let Cormac take over my fitness. So I don't embarrass myself."

"You won't."

She let herself explore, intoxicated by his proximity and the fact that Bran Kelly had made himself hotter. When her palms slid to his back, she switched to fingertips dancing over the grooves of muscles at his shoulders. She scraped down his spine with her fingernails and Bran vibrated with a telling groan. His hand pushed into her hair, cradled her head and he pulled her close to inhale. "I missed you."

"You didn't call."

"I was waiting. Until I'd done what you wanted."

"This is for me?" She traced the trenches of his pelvis and his grip on her head tightened.

"I fixed myself."

Nelle fixed her eyes on his chest. The neck of his cardigan came down in a V. With her chin down, the first tiny grey button landed directly in her eye line. She stared at the X of thread keeping it stitched in place because if she looked up, her mouth would find his.

Bran thumbed her elbow, locking them together. "Last year I was in a rough place. Coming off tour, I was beat, but I missed it. Missed having something to keep me busy, keep me from having time to deal with my shit. You know that feeling like: Without those people singing with you every night, what's left? I was coming down, and I kept getting lower when my gran died, and my dad blackmailed me. What was left, you know? And even the Cleffies felt like more weight that could sink me. It felt like this shadow had covered everything, this endless dusk, and then…" He pressed his lips to her forehead.

"'She Turned Midnight'?"

He tilted her head up so their eyes met. "You heard the song?"

Had she heard the song? The one nobody had heard?

She had *felt* the song. She had *tasted* the song. She had *lived* the song.

She had pressed fingers to her earbuds as Bran's voice pumped through the little wires, holding him there as he sang about her.

*Easy, easy, easy to run*
*Easier said than done*
*She told me it could be fun*
*Hard to pretend she wasn't the one.*

*Twist of lemon looking bitter*
*Said she wasn't gonna sit there*
*Drinking sour eating salt*
*Knew by then it was my fault*
*Fucking up something brand-new*
*Showed up cold but she came through*
*Broke the ice, that queen of light*
*She turned midnight*
*On all the best nights of my life*
*She turned midnight*

Nelle pulled back, breaking away. "Don't be mad, Charlie sent it to me. You used my producer, we go way back—"

"I asked Charlie to send it." Bran prowled after her.

Nelle's palms met the edge of the black counter, her fingers curling around it. "Because it's about me?"

He hooked his hands over the counter on the outside of hers, leaning down and dragging his nose across hers. "You came out of the darkness."

The kiss happened slowly. Her chin tipped up, his tilted down. Their lips touched in one glancing pass, and then another. Nelle opened her mouth to take in his breath and closed it before their tongues could meet. Kisses so light she could still pretend they hadn't happened.

This couldn't be happening. It might feel like they had stepped through a portal to a place where time didn't exist, where the pain they caused each other was as far away as the people in the buzzing restaurant—but everything was waiting for them outside that door. They couldn't ignore—

"I owe you an apology." Bran's tongue brushed his lower lip and the next time she skated the bow of hers over it, the skin caught, stretching the connection longer.

"You do," she agreed, her hands shifting their grip to cover his.

"I got mad. I lashed out. None of it should have been directed at you. I'm sorry."

"Your dad's house—"

"Doesn't matter." And then he stopped waiting and brought his body flush against hers. Nelle gasped at the contact and Bran kissed her. Really kissed her, mingling the sweet cherry on his tongue with the tang of lime on hers. Nelle forgot the rest—forgot her reasons, her plans, her reservations. She forgot how it felt to be apart while she was on tour, forgot how hard it had been this last month, staying at home with her parents in a childhood room where the Bran Kelly she imagined existed simultaneously with the one she'd known.

This was the fantasy Bran Kelly brought to life. The one consumed by her, the one who used his words and said just the right thing, sang just the right thing. And he was still the real Bran Kelly, unguarded and confident. The one she'd spent the last few weeks polishing her songs about, getting ready to head into the studio for N3.

He was the Bran Kelly she wanted to love.

He was her Bran Kelly, for the last time.

Nelle bit his bottom lip and thrust her hands into his

hair, pulling hard. Bran groaned in response. At her back, his hand fisted in the vintage polka-dot dress. The skirt twisted up, exposing her lace-covered bottom. Bran skimmed his other hand over her butt, driving his thumb under the lace. Nelle nodded into his mouth and helped him shimmy the panties over her hips and down her legs. As she perched on the counter, he looped the garment around his wrist twice for safekeeping.

She'd shoved a hand halfway into the pocket of his cardigan before he stepped out of reach. He stood back, regarding her, his chest rising as he took three deep breaths.

Nelle opened her legs, drawing her knees wide. "Come here."

Bran pulled a condom from his back pocket. Slowly he came forward. This might be a random bathroom hookup, but he wasn't going to rush it. He undid his pants, slid his hands up her thighs, and kissed her, so deeply her whole body tilted back. Nelle slipped forward, and Bran used the momentum to guide her onto him, full and hard and the fit she'd been aching for for months.

Nelle went limp with pleasure, but Bran's arms wrapped around her back, securing her to him. He might not have wanted to rush, but their desire was so close to the surface, it wouldn't be long before they both broke.

He snaked one hand up her spine to hold the back of her neck and Nelle whimpered, giving over the last ounce of her resistance and letting him take her weight—he could so easily, his body more powerful than it had been months ago when he'd heaved her over the threshold at his house. She let him take complete control too. He knew what he was doing and she trusted him to do it. Long strokes, easy rhythm, all building to a crescendo that would crash through her like storm waves over stone breakers.

Nelle clasped her hands to his shoulders and pulled herself up. Her mouth on his mouth, an orgasm pulsed through her, her body tightening like a string brought back in tune.

With one final thrust Bran pumped heat into her. Nelle held him close, still floating on the ripples of pleasure that rolled through them both. He pressed a kiss to her throat and sighed and something stung the corner of her eye. She forced the tension out of her fingers and smoothed his sweater, adding a gentle push so he'd get the idea and remove himself. He did. Bran had always been good with body language.

He disposed of the condom in a gleaming black trash can before returning to her and bending to her feet. Nelle's brow furrowed until he unwound her underwear from his wrist.

They were done. It was time to get back to—to whatever it was they were supposed to be. Nelle brought a hand to her temple. What was she doing? She had to get out of here. She had to say what she needed to say before Bran did anything else to confuse her.

But she opened her mouth a moment too late, giving Bran the advantage. He started speaking from below her, where he knelt, threading her underwear back up her legs.

"I figured me out. I felt out of control, so I shut down. But I never had control, I only had fear. That I'd be alone. And I'd have nothing for myself. It took me a long time to admit that, but I'm admitting it now.

And you." His fingers pressed into her calves. "You like the game best when you're winning. And if you want to keep playing with me, you have to know you might lose."

"I called Tomi." Her voice sounded far away, but she felt it crack on his cousin's name. The outer-space quality of the room gave her nowhere stable to look, and she felt like she was spinning, detached, drifting away from…everything. Out in the universe alone.

"You what?"

"I'm—I'm planning to file. After the Note noms. She thinks she can do it quietly—" She broke off to give him a chance to respond. His jaw had gone slack. He hadn't moved from the ground at her feet. "This can't surprise you. We haven't spoken in months."

"Then why now? Why'd you wait? If it's been over. You took off your ring in May."

"And you never put on a ring, Bran. You were never on the line the way I was. I waited because I didn't want Tomi to get in trouble." And because it had required effort, working up her courage, convincing herself that her career was strong enough to weather a scandal if Tomi couldn't get it done without revealing the truth. "She went out on a limb for us with Judge Jordan. And a five-month marriage doesn't look very—"

He stood up, stepped back. "Who cares how it looks! You heard the song, right—"

"And it's a good song—it's a great song." She hopped off the counter, pulling her underwear all the way up and scrambling to rebuild a line of defense. "But it's about a moment that happened almost a year ago. From this distance, a talented writer like you—who doesn't embellish? Play things up? Once you have that hook, that after-the-fact catchy phrase, you blur the truth to fit it. You know, if you really want, we could talk about how *funny* it is that you don't want anyone profiting from the private details of your life—except when it comes to your own ability to sell out."

"That's not what I did. That song—"

"I don't care, Bran. I've got a hundred more about you." Nelle fisted her hands, regretting her quick tongue and trying to control herself. They were writers, their words were their weapons.

She had to stop thinking about Bran as a secret and start thinking about him as a mistake. She had to get out of this room and hope no one was waiting outside to take a photo—Good Iowa Girl Caught Fucking in Steakhouse Bathroom—it was too easy a headline.

A sharp knock sounded through the door. A familiar *rat-ta-ta-ta-tat* Nelle's fuzzy mind couldn't place but a rhythm that made Bran sigh and reach for the handle. Cormac's wide shoulders wedged into the opening. He regarded Bran with a measured glance and held his hand out for Nelle.

"I give tours of the kitchen, did you know? Kind of a secret operation, had to clear this hall to sneak you back there, but people who can make moussaka out of the nonsense in his fridge make the list."

He was offering an out and Nelle nodded gratefully, putting her palm against his. The drummer's fingers closed over the back of her hand.

Bran stepped into her path. "We're not done—"

"Yes, we are," she said, looking him directly in the eye.

With a hand on his shoulder, Cormac eased Bran

out of the way. "You are, unless you want everyone out there to know. And everyone they know to know."

The palm guiding her was heavier than Bran's as Cormac pulled her through the hall into a swinging door for servers. Nelle blinked in the new space. Cormac steered her through an assault of white light, glimmering chrome, heat and motion and a clatter of sounds. The "tour" lasted only a few seconds before they came through another swinging door off the side of the dining room, right at the bottom of a small set of stairs leading up to the booths.

"Sorry I've kept you from your table so long," Cormac said, loudly, purposefully, leading her up the steps. Nelle wanted to sink down next to Benj but her friend was at the end of the seat, and neither of the other girls picked up her motion to scooch. Santino moved in, clearing a spot for Nelle on the opposite end.

Cormac glanced at the half-eaten artichoke dip on the table. "I hope the backstage peek was worth a cold appetizer. I'll send another up."

Nelle wanted to tell him not to bother, that she wouldn't be able to eat a bite of anything, no matter how hot and delicious it looked. But they had a show to put on. Her heart hammered in her chest as she nodded.

"Thank you, you're very thoughtful. I appreciate it."

Cormac smiled easily, pulling the booth's curtains as he left. Nelle hadn't been able to see whether Bran had returned to the bar or left the restaurant or—but that was probably Cormac's point. She didn't need to know what Bran was doing. To get out of this restaurant without making the news, she needed to sit here, behind thick muslin drapes, pretending Bran Kelly didn't exist.

The new dip arrived with their entrees and the others

started eating with a chorus of praise. Under the table, Nelle tried typing out a message to Benj. The curtain flashed open and closed before she pressed Send.

Arlo and Bran stood in the small space inside the fabric.

"We were on our way out," Arlo said, his words laden with warning and directed at Bran, "but Bran just couldn't help himself. Insisted on saying hello."

Now the other girls caught the idea to scooch inward, calling for the newcomers to sit.

"Just for a minute, we wouldn't want to ruin your dinner, would we, B?" Arlo lowered himself next to Benj and Bran waited for Nelle to make room for him next to her. Slowly she moved away from the booth's end, and he claimed the space, the scent of rye stronger on his breath than it had been in the bathroom answering her question on whether he had made it back to the bar.

"I got you another," Santino said, motioning to a fresh glass of tequila. Apparently, he thought she'd need it to get through Bran's arrival.

"I've had enough," Nelle said.

Bran claimed the glass, too, throwing it back. "I haven't."

Nelle reached for her water with a shaking hand. The ice shifted as she took a sip, splashing her face. She blotted at her lip with a starched cotton napkin. Bran's thigh pressed against hers under the table, and she didn't know how long she could sit there pretending. He'd said so much in the bathroom and she hadn't had any time to unpack it. She twisted the napkin in her lap.

Santino tried to catch her eye, but Nelle fixed her sight line on the script inked above his eyebrow. Up close it wasn't so bad. She leaned closer to examine the curls, discovering cursive letters embedded in the flames.

Bran's arm crossed in front of her, forcing her back, out of the way as he grabbed the edge of her plate and pulled it towards himself. "Face tattoos, huh? That's a choice."

"Yeah, man. It was." Santino's tone relaxed as he continued. "I worked at this logistics center before all this. That's a fancy way to say warehouse. It had so many rules. No hats. No phones. And we were supposed to keep our tattoos covered but I got hot one day—it was fucking July, no air—and I rolled up my sleeves. This one manager who always had it out for me dinged me on it. Made me go home early, and I needed those hours back then. Anyway, I got mad, and I figured fuck it. Went into my next shift like this. They told me to cover it up. I asked how, if I can't wear a hat. They fired me on the spot but then I was performing at this club and a producer said they liked my sound and 'my look.'"

"What does it say?" Nelle asked.

"'God is love.' I don't mind if it warps, or fades. I like seeing it every morning in the mirror."

In response to that Bran picked up the burger, taking a huge bite. He grabbed for the napkin in her lap.

"Really?" she snapped.

Bran shrugged, his blue eyes hard when they met hers. "Just taking my half."

Heat rushed through Nelle's body. He was really going to do this.

Across the table Benj pushed Arlo out of the booth. "Can you get him out of here?"

Arlo nodded and took his friend by the arm, heaving him up. "Time to go, B."

But Bran tore out of his grasp. Nelle braced herself for another outburst, something cruel and true. Something she couldn't hide from. Bran writing his own dark ending.

Bran dug in his cardigan pocket and leaned down to whisper in her ear. "You were wrong about the song. It wasn't about you. It was for you."

"You mean for your *label*," she hissed and thought she heard him growl back.

He forced something into her hand. Something soft and round and worn. She glanced down at the weathered coaster as he staggered upright. He waited for her to lift her head and held her wide-eyed gaze.

Arlo found the opening in the curtain and pulled Bran backwards through it, allowing him one last declaration before disappearing.

"You're it."

## Chapter Twenty-Nine

Bran woke sideways on his bed, partially clothed and fully aware he was too old to be drinking like he had last night. His head ached, his chest ached—but that was probably the emotional blow of Nelle announcing her intent to divorce him.

Someone knocked at his door.

"Leave me alone, A." Bran winced at his own voice.

The door opened and Arlo peered into the room. "How did you know it was me?"

"Aya and Cormac don't knock."

"She might not knock but she sent me up here to make sure you're alive." Arlo was at Bran's for his Thanksgiving break. He'd seen enough hotels, he'd said. They all had. But Bran was starting to think Arlo just worried he was lonely.

"I'm not."

"Then she'll want me to make a puppet out of your corpse because you're still performing on live television this afternoon."

Bran let out a self-pitying moan.

"Get up. We need to get you hydrated. Do you want me to call one of those fluid bag delivery nurses?"

"I just need water." Bran palmed blindly at his bedside table. His hand caught on a plastic tube of something. Lube? "What the hell is this?"

"It's from Nadine."

Bran sat up, his head throbbing. "You let me bring some woman home?"

Arlo grinned, which was a terrible sign. "Oh, it's way worse than that."

The room spun. Gravity pulled Bran back to the mattress, headfirst and sideways.

He remembered sitting at the bar, how strange it felt to be in public with Arlo and Cormac again. But good, too—it felt real. He remembered Nelle arriving on a breeze of whispers, and following her to the bathroom. She'd tasted sharp. Her short hair had slipped so quickly through his hands, like a warning for him not to fuck up again. That didn't stop him from being kind of an ass when she'd told him she'd been talking to Tomi behind his back. He hadn't been thinking. She'd caught him off guard. She'd said the universe responded to desire, and he couldn't want her any more than he did—so how had it gone wrong? Who was she if not his sun, his stars, all the lights in the dark? And her response had been dropping the *D* word. One way worse than *dickhead*. Bran had had to make sure she knew that he was still in it. He'd always been in it.

He'd wanted her to know he'd try for her. He'd do anything for her. Everything for her.

Bran rolled onto his back, kicking the blankets that tangled around his legs. "Do you have a pen?"

"You doing morning pages now?"

"No, I had an idea."

"Ah. Inspiration deserves ink."

Bran's head lifted off the pillow, his neck cracking and stiff. He squinted at Arlo. "Why do you know that?"

"You don't remember saying it to me last night?"

Bran rubbed at his aching chest, and pain burned across his skin. That's when Bran remembered the tattoo parlor. He lunged up again.

"There it is," Arlo said.

Bran staggered to his feet, stripping off his shirt to see the bandage taped over his left pec. He was modeling half naked next week. He couldn't show up with swollen, inflamed—did tattoos peel? He tried to remember everything Nadine had said, words about aftercare and inflammation and flaky, oozy skin. "Aya is going to kill me."

"Good thing you're already dead. Nadine said that bandage can stay on for forty-eight hours, then you need to clean up the seepage—"

"Seepage?"

"—let it breathe, apply the lotion, and rebandage it. And prepare for itching."

Bran shook his head. "I need a pen."

The tattoo was a problem, but the words piling up in Bran's brain for Nelle were more urgent. His phone wasn't on the side table, neither was his notebook. Bran stumbled over to the guitar case on the floor. There was a flash of red as he opened the plush-lined internal storage compartment and pulled out a folded piece of printer paper. Details of a Cartier transaction took up a fraction of the space, leaving the rest of the page blank.

"Do you have a pen?"

This song wasn't like the other dozen he'd toiled over for *sex&secrets* so far. He had finally managed enough for an album, but the set didn't feel finished. He didn't know how to end it. The album needed to be a complete package, dynamic and stirring, and he needed a song that wasn't like the others. A song that wasn't as dark. One that had less heat, that wasn't forged and hammered, sharp and hard. He needed something soft and airy and honest… Something easy. This one would be easy, like tugging down a balloon by its string—he just had to catch it first. Bran had stopped hoping he'd get to write a song like this again.

"A pen! Arlo!" The edges of Bran's vision dimmed.

Arlo tossed a pen onto the middle of the bed and Bran scrambled for it. "And a bottle of water, I'm begging you."

"I'll get you a glass. I know you don't want to add to the devastation of single-use plastic."

"Great, fine, whatever."

By the time Arlo returned with the water, Bran had a verse and a chorus scribbled on the page. There was a smudge of blue toothpaste in the top corner from when he'd tried to brush his teeth and then needed to scratch out a word. He downed the water, and wrestled himself into a clean shirt with the pen and paper clutched in one hand. Snapping his guitar case shut, Bran started for the stairs, calling over his shoulder, "I need you to drive me to the studio."

"The Besties red carpet starts—"

"Hours from now. Studio's on Sunset and—"

"I remember where the studio is. Ron, right? The only engineer you trust?"

"We have a rapport."

"How do you know he's even there right now?"

Bran was halfway down the steps into the garage, Arlo jogging behind him, when he stopped and turned.

"It's kismet, A. Can't stop the universe. This is happening." Bran held out the car key. "Can you drive me so I can write the next verse?"

"Aya is going to kill you if you miss the red carpet." Arlo took the key and pushed past Bran to the driver's side door.

Bran grinned over the Ferrari's red roof. "Good thing I'm already dead."

"What do you mean he's not here?" Bran fisted his paper and resisted the urge to bang on the utilitarian desk of the studio's cramped lobby. "Where's Ron?"

Arlo leaned against the beige wall. "Guess the universe forgot to book him."

"I could call Ron," the receptionist offered. "But it's Sunday morning and the Besties—"

"Since when are the Besties such a big deal?" Bran snapped. "I need to lay down a track."

The receptionist leveled solid brown eyes at him. "The studios are open. But I'm the only one here."

"Well, that doesn't—"

"I can lay it down for you."

Bran blinked at her. He hadn't worked with anyone but Ron since—oh, except for Charlie, and he'd done that for Nelle. *For Nelle.* That was the whole point of this. "Yes, thank you, let's do that."

Arlo muffled a sound of surprise behind him, but Bran ignored it. The receptionist was already on her feet, mug in hand, leading them to one of the low-light, soundproofed rooms down the hall.

"I'm Bran," he called after her. "That's Arlo."

She held the door for him, straight-faced. "Yeah. I know."

"And you're?"

"Fei."

Bran stumbled a step. "That was my gran's name." He tossed a look back at Arlo. "That sure is something, isn't it?"

*Coincidence*, implied Arlo's pulled-together brows. Bran faced forward again. The smell of fresh coffee wafted up from Fei's cup. It wasn't a coincidence to him. It was a sign. He'd felt the loss of his gran so deeply in London, right before everything had gone wrong with Nelle. He could feel Gran now, guiding him towards getting it right. *We Kellys may fight but we always unite.* Nelle was a Kelly whether the world knew or not. If she needed the con, he'd be anything from wingman to mark if it meant he had her.

Once in the booth, Bran clipped the paper to a stand and positioned a stool in front of the mesh-covered microphone. "Okay, Fei. I want it unfiltered. I don't need to be produced. I want it raw, but I also want it soft. Think Jackson Browne live, can you do that?"

"You want me to hit Record."

He slung the guitar strap over his shoulder and sat down. "Exactly. I'll tell you when I'm ready."

First, he had to work out the guitar part. Bran tucked the instrument closer to his body. He kept his head low as he worked through the song. It was a little like driving, muscle memory tied to mental signals, allowing him to disengage while remaining completely occupied, body and mind. This song was a Ferrari with the engine hot. It wanted to go. And Bran was thrilled to press the gas and take it for a spin. He played the song, fixed a line that was too long, played it again, rearranged the bridge, played it again. It cornered like a dream.

The speaker above him popped, and Cormac's voice echoed through the room. "Can we get this moving?"

Bran raised his head to see the drummer had joined the pair on the other side of the glass. "What are you doing here?"

"Aya thought A needed backup. Which he obviously does, because you are supposed to be—"

"I'm where I'm supposed to be." Bran motioned around the little booth. "Music comes first. Now shut up so I can get this right."

It was another half hour before Bran was satisfied with his rehearsal.

Cormac held up his phone, a live stream of the red carpet starting on the screen.

Fei finished adjusting the levels. "I'm guessing you want one take?"

Ignoring Cormac, Bran signaled her with a nod and then closed his eyes. He took a deep breath and pictured Nelle, what it would be like to sing this song directly to her. He wanted to capture the intimacy, the closeness they'd cultivated. The way it felt to confide in her. He wanted to end an album about secrets with honesty. With a confession.

Bran played the song all the way through, start to finish. He waited for the last guitar string to stop vibrating before he asked Fei, "You got it?"

She nodded and after a moment the song pumped back to him through the booth's speaker. Bran stood while his friends reacted. Cormac drummed his fingers on his knee and Arlo's head shook to the beat.

"It's good. It's really—You just wrote that? While I was driving?"

"Aren't you glad you gave me that pen?"

"I'd be more glad if you put me on the writing credits and got me royalties."

"Fei?"

The woman shrugged.

"What?"

"You don't need to be produced, right?"

Behind her Arlo laughed and Bran perched back on the stool. "Okay, I'll bite."

"I think it would be a better chorus higher up. And then when you come back to the repeat at the end, *everything new*—go up some more. Change the note that time, push it all up. It's a simple song, it should be nuanced. Capture the need. You're getting full 'These Days' on the guitar, but you need to go Van Morrison 'Crazy Love' on the vocals."

"We don't have time for this," Cormac said. "Aya's waiting and Aya does not like to wait."

"Song's good," Arlo said again.

Bran put his hand out to silence them. He didn't want a good song. He wanted a perfect song. He sang the chorus to himself, pitching his voice higher. It worked. The falsetto was better.

Fei nodded along. "See what I'm saying?"

"Who are you?" Cormac asked.

"Fei," Arlo answered.

Bran pulled his feet onto the stool's rest, ready to play. "She's the producer of Bran Kelly's next Notable Song. I'm doing it again, you recording?"

Fei's voice hummed through the speaker. "Go for it."

Bran sang the song a few more times, feeling it shift into a higher gear under Fei's direction. *Faster on that line*, *try slapping the beat there*, *higher—higher!*

"That's it," Fei said on the final take. "You hit everything." She grinned, leaning back and letting the swivel chair take her on a victory lap.

"That's it," Bran repeated. "Album's done." He put the guitar away and exhaled. On his way into the other room, he checked his watch—which wasn't there. He'd been planning to wear his custom Chopard for luck, but he'd been in such a hurry that morning his wrist was bare. "What time is it? I need to get to the Besties. I'm not making the red carpet, am I?" He checked his outfit, black jeans and a grey chambray shirt. "I can wear this onstage, right?" Nobody answered. "Right?" Arlo and Cormac traded looks. "It's not that bad."

"What about…" Cormac mouth *Nelle* over Fei's head. "She needs to hear what you just wrote, B."

"She will. In January, when the album comes out."

"And if that's too late? What if you have an opening now? A chance?"

"I don't. She's done. She told me last night."

Arlo bent his head towards the phone fisted in Cormac's hand. "Show him."

"You show him."

"Show me what?"

"The bling cam." Arlo jutted out his chin and Cormac held out the phone to Bran. Queued up on the screen was a clip of Nelle on the red carpet. Kara Robins admired Nelle's manicure—nails shellacked in a thick, glossy, unmistakable kelly green. The camera zoomed in for a close-up.

Arlo watched over Bran's shoulder, describing one of three stacked rings on Nelle's left hand. "Simple, silver, kind of—" He drew a V in the air.

Bran tried to swallow around the newly lodged lump in his throat. Last night he'd tagged Nelle in, but he wasn't sure if being an ass before he did it disqualified the move. Now she'd surprised him. Again. What did it mean? What did she want him to do?

He'd have to figure it out on the way there. He thanked Fei and headed for the car, confused when his former bandmates crammed themselves into the little speeder with him.

Arlo wedged himself next to the guitar case in the back, while Cormac hunched over his knees in the passenger seat. "We're coming with you."

"You guys don't have to——"

"Yes, we do. We missed you win two Cleffies, we're not going to miss you win back your girl."

Bran pulled the car onto the road as Arlo shifted uncomfortably in the rearview mirror. "I need to note that metaphors likening women to *prizes* aren't really——"

"Fuck that, Arlo. She's a catch. And he's a catch. They are equal—that's straight feminism." Cormac braced for a turn.

"I'm not winning her back," Bran clarified. "I'm going to debut my next single and hope Aya doesn't cut my balls off and use them for a PopSocket."

But the idea took root inside him, growing as he drove, pushing old hopes to the surface.

Aya was waiting for them outside the theater. She marched them through a side door and into a dressing room, pausing only to reassure a PA that Bran would be ready to go on as planned. When the door closed, she held out a hand to stop the outburst of explanations. "I don't care. You're here. You're ready to play?"

Bran nodded.

"I told them you didn't need to rehearse with the band because you're doing it acoustic. They weren't happy not to have a sound check but I said we couldn't have the song leak before tonight. So we're fine. You're doubling my Christmas bonus."

"Aya." Bran spoke her name with longing meant for someone else. His voice changed the energy of the room, charging it with his presence, his penchant for impulse. "What if I didn't sing 'Midnight'?"

"You're singing 'Midnight.'"

"Nelle's heard 'Midnight.'"

Aya swore at the track lighting. "I should have known this was about Nelle. You didn't get close enough to the fire last night? Yeah, I heard about that, Kelly. Is she worth—"

"Yes." Bran's absolute certainty left no room for argument and silence filled the small space. His gaze fixed on the guitar case.

Cormac spoke first. "It's just him and a guitar and a stool. What are they going to do, cut off the broadcast?"

"Aya?" Bran asked, needing to know if it was possible.

She pinched her chin. "What would you sing?"

Cormac was ready with a video of Bran in the studio performing the new song. Aya watched it all the way through, giving no reaction.

But Bran didn't need one. Nelle was a gesture person. He didn't know how to make her breakfast, couldn't inspire her to be better—she was already the best. The only thing he knew how to do, the only thing he could do for her was prove that he heard her. That he was working to reach her level, be someone she could trust. He wasn't blocked off, he was trying. The song said it all, and with Nelle in the audience, she'd have to hear it. She'd have to hear it, and then she could decide to say yes too.

Tonight was his chance to show no fear.

Aya shook her head and paced to the door.

"Aya!" Bran said. "I'm gonna do it."

She glanced back at him. "I know. I'm going to get ahead of it. And you just tripled my Christmas bonus." She left with her phone cradled to her ear.

A long hour passed as Bran waited for the show to wrap up. He was the final performance. Arlo disappeared and returned with minutes to spare, carrying three tumblers of amber alcohol. "They tried to give me plastic cups."

Bran sniffed his. "You think this is a good idea?"

"Thought it might help with the nerves."

"I've performed before, you are aware."

Arlo knocked glasses with Cormac and shot his back. "Yeah but. New song and all. Different stakes."

*New song.* Bran inhaled again, smoky flavor filling his nose. He knew what Arlo meant. He'd be singing alone. Nobody would be mouthing along with him. There'd be no rush of voices joining his. People would be listening. Not shouting at the top of their lungs, bolstering him.

But that didn't make him nervous. The singe of energy in his gut was excitement. He let the glass dangle from his fingers, his other hand wrapped around the guitar's neck.

A PA led him to the stage, and Bran settled himself on the top step facing the audience. He set the glass next to him and rested the guitar on his thigh. He scanned the front rows as stagehands set up a mike in front of him, racing the commercial break.

And there was Nelle. Straight ahead. Twelve o'clock. Staring at him as he stared at her.

It was just like he'd imagined in the booth before recording. The rest of the room faded away. Behind the camera, someone counted him off and Bran hitched the guitar up. Nelle was watching him. Nelle was listening. This was the moment he'd been waiting for, to tell her what he hadn't gotten to say. He wanted her. He wanted all of her. He wanted to be hers. A song was his until the first time he sang it. He wanted this one to be hers too. He played the song for Nelle.

*"You carry it all with just one finger, you make it look so easy.*

*In the flashing lights and the long, dark nights, you're the only one who sees me.*

*Licking your thumb, a taste of grease, a stain that bleeds through clear,*

*On the note I wrote then tucked into my coat, words I know you want to hear.*

*'This one's for you,' I'd say before I sing some—*

*There's no point now in making that distinction—*

*Cause they're all for you,*

*Every last one, everything new,*

*It's all for you."*

## Chapter Thirty

The door slammed shut behind Nelle. Bran's back was to her as she landed in his entryway in her full Besties look, crisp white palazzo pants and a matching crop top. He stood facing the wall at the end of the hall, between the openings for the kitchen and den, his guitar case open on the long table under a large blue painting. She hadn't taken the time to change, to explain, to do anything but get here.

There had been a moment, when the lights had blazed back on and applause for Bran had turned to general post-show chatter, that Nelle had doubted whether the performance had really happened. She'd seen Bran on the stairs, guitar in his arms, drink next to him, casual as iced tea. But she'd transposed him somewhere else: to a wooden porch, where a warm breeze rustled the tall leaves of a corn field and a slow sunset blushed across the sky. She'd imagined him home.

But it had happened. Everyone was talking about it. She'd needed a reason to keep her head down, not feeling ready to stand, so she'd slurped the last sip of wine from a straw in a red Solo cup and checked her phone.

Flawed man sings perfect song, Benj had texted, PUT IT IN MY VEINS.

And then: Score from the Greek judge?

10/10, Nelle had typed, would forgive again.

And then she'd frowned reading the dropdown message from Mina, Was that what I think it was?

And the one a second later from Santino, You okay?

She should never have started this again. Should never have put that ring back on. Should have known they couldn't go back to the way it was.

"I knocked," she announced when Bran didn't turn. "You didn't hear me?"

At the sound of her voice, he tensed. He rocked his head side to side to stretch his neck and turned. "You don't have to knock to enter your own house."

"It's not my house." She took a step towards him, her hand out, palm down. "We can't do this anymore."

Bran eased back, onto the credenza, listening but saying nothing.

"It has to stop." Her chest heaved with a frustrated breath. "Did you hear me?"

His eyes flashed. "Yeah. I heard you. What do you want me to say?"

Nelle pursed her lips. "Nothing." It was better when he kept his mouth shut. When he couldn't draft up images of a quiet life that lured her in, as seductive as they were impossible. "You've said enough. And I'm sure your album will say more."

"And yours won't? We both played the game. We both made it entertaining."

She moved deeper through the hall. "Which is why it's over. It has to be. People are watching us. They're catching on." Mina and Santino were just the beginning. Soon everyone would uncover the overlapping details in their albums, like landmarks on a treasure map. His song was more than the three audacious words of her hook. He pushed her, dared her, and she always stepped closer to the fire. It was why she'd said yes to this whole thing at the bar. Cut her hair. Replied to that tweet. Put the damn ring back on and pressed Repeat. When he'd shoved that coaster into her hand last night—felt the rush of realization and hope that curled around her heart as her fingers tightened over the warped totem—she'd wanted to do something big too. Now he'd countered and they'd keep on like that: gestures getting bigger and bigger until there was no stopping them. Until it was blazing out of their control.

Bran squinted through the hall. "So what if they know? Let's just do this. Quit the runaround."

Nelle froze.

"Quit the rules and diversions. Quit all the bullshit keeping us apart. In a year we've spent four nights together—" Bran held up his fingers. "*Four.* I want more. Why not tell them we're married?" He rested his hand against his abdomen. "You're it for me, Nella."

Her eyes squeezed shut. She couldn't see him like that, open and waiting, weapons down, and not surrender too. She wanted to bring her hands to her ears and block his voice carrying her name with such intimacy. If people knew about them, she would be the moon, her glow pale and reflective, characterized by her relation to him. How could she stomach a headline like Bran Kelly's Wife Nominated for Six Cleffies? That wasn't the story she wanted. How could she jeopardize the name she'd made for herself?

The sound of shattering glass rang out from the kitchen and her eyes popped open.

"What was that?"

"Broken ice machine." He reached behind him, into the guitar case.

"That wasn't an ice machine. That was a seismic event." Nelle started for the kitchen like she wanted to investigate. She had to put some space between herself and the conversation that had gotten away from her.

But Bran blocked her escape, standing in the door frame and holding out a little red box.

The warning passed her lips on a whispered breath. "Bran."

His blue eyes wide and unguarded, Bran pleaded, "Say yes."

Nelle's gaze shifted behind him, and she said more urgently, *"Bran."*

Fear gripped her, hurt winced across Bran's face, and a man with a bat stood in the shadows near the dining table, one of the glass doors off the kitchen shattered and open behind him. "Nobody move."

His hands choked up the neck of the bat as he waited to see how they'd react to his command.

Bran lunged for his phone on the credenza. And the man launched after him, swinging. Nelle screamed over the dull crack of impact to Bran's skull—the discord of hands slammed at the high and low end of a keyboard. She tried to catch his fall and folded to the floor under his weight.

The man loomed above her in a dark, frayed hoodie. He shook his head fast and the hood slipped, revealing a pale, gaunt face. He yanked it back up, one hand gripping the fabric atop his head, the other white-knuckling the bat. "The lights were off. No one was supposed to be here."

Nelle clutched Bran closer, his head against her

chest, a wet warmth leaking from him, seeping into her clothes. Her eyes went to the bat, the broken glass embedded in the wood, Bran's blood staining the shards. "He needs an ambulance."

"No—no—he got a safe?"

"He's bleeding!"

"I don't give a fuck." He prowled towards her and tugged at Bran's arm.

"Stop it." Nelle swatted at him, trying to keep pressure on the cut at Bran's neck.

The man tossed Bran's bare wrist down with a curse. "He got any cash?"

"He could be dying!"

"Then you better find me something quick—" A knock interrupted him.

Security Steve called through the door. "Mr. Kelly? The backdoor alarm pinged."

"Shit." The man pointed the bat at her. "Not a fucking word."

Nelle's pulse raced as the seconds ticked by. Help was on the other side of the door. And Bran was bleeding. Blood was spilling out of him. Too much and too fast. Every second she waited.

"Steve!" she screamed. "Help!"

"Bitch!" the man spat. He jerked a fistful of her hair. Pain shot through her scalp and she kicked, connecting with the red box Bran had dropped. It tumbled across the floor, drawing his attention, and he let go of her to grab it. Steve crashed through the front door as the intruder fled out the back.

"Let him go! Get me towels—something—anything! And call a fucking ambulance!" Nelle's raw voice surprised her. The voice she knew better than anything.

How it went up and down, to get what she needed from it. And now it sounded unrecognizable.

Nelle fought the desperate panic that swelled inside her as they waited for the ambulance. "Hold on, Bran. I got you. I got you." She smoothed the hair off his forehead and blinked at the crimson streaks she left behind.

The paramedics arrived, talking fast and asking questions. Nelle could only question them back. "He's going to be okay, right? He's going to be fine?"

"Ma'am, you have to let go. Let us work."

Bran's distinguished jaw disappeared under an oxygen mask and they hoisted his body onto a stretcher. Nelle pushed to her feet, her bloody hand slipping on the smooth floor. One of her shoes had come off under her and she kicked the other free. It didn't help her balance. She stumbled, following the paramedics down the dark hall.

She stopped in the open door, just out of reach of the porch's floodlight. Standing at the edge of their private world, she held back while Bran was carried down the steps towards the red flashing lights of the ambulance. People swarmed the drive and Nelle pressed herself against the wall like she could hide.

The dishcloths they'd pressed to Bran's neck littered the end of the hall, stained with his blood. She didn't know a person could bleed that much. The thought blared through her loud as the siren that kicked up outside, *What if there wasn't any Bran Kelly left?* He'd be gone before she ever had the chance to tell the world he'd been hers. Before she had the chance to tell him.

Nelle struggled off the wall using her wrist, trying not to leave more bloody handprints. This was going to be news. It wasn't something they could bury. Fear stalled her at the doorstep. If she walked out of the house now, there was no going back.

The cement was rough on Nelle's bare feet. One side of the ambulance doors slammed shut as she leapt from the bottom step. "Wait!"

The paramedics didn't turn, but an officer caught her around the waist, pulling her back. "He needs to get to hospital, ma'am," she said.

"I want to go with them!"

"Only immediate family—"

A paramedic reached for the other door. Emotion seized Nelle's chest.

"I'm his family! I'm his wife!"

The arm at her waist loosened and she broke free, catching the second door before it shut. She hauled herself into the ambulance and forced herself to Bran's side.

"I'm his wife," she told them. "I'm staying with him."

*PHOTO: Hours After the Besties Nelle Arrives at Hospital Covered in Bran Kelly's Blood (link in bio)*

## Chapter Thirty-One

Bran clicked it. Bran clicked it because he'd been in and out for two days and he hated feeling like a stranger to his own life. Things had happened to him: stitches, brain scans, transfusions. And through a haze of pain-killers and blunt force trauma, he was missing pieces. Connective tissue between conversations with doctors, an early morning tinted-window drive, and waking up in his own bed to find Nelle watching him, headphones in her ears.

He clicked it, simultaneously furious at the violation and eager to bring part of the last few days into focus. He had tried asking Nelle, but she'd been uncharacter-istically evasive. He was desperate for answers, ready for clarity, even if that meant lowering himself to ex-aggerated clickbait.

Only it wasn't exaggerated. The page showed two photos, side by side. The first was a professional shot of Nelle on the red carpet in clean, bright white. The other was a grainy image of her standing in the ambu-lance bay, the same outfit stained with his blood, an ab-solutely shell-shocked expression on her face.

Pale. Like he'd never seen her. Blank. Which she wasn't.

Nelle's feet sounded on the stairs and Bran pushed the phone deep into the couch cushion, where he'd hidden the painkiller she'd given him earlier.

She helped him out of his shirt and straddled his lap. He watched her face carefully as she peeled the old bandage off his chest. She didn't look anything like the Nelle who'd come out of that ambulance. Her amber eyes were focused, her lips resting slightly apart as she applied a thin layer of lotion to his left pec. She traced the top of the tattoo, spreading the ointment over the ring's crown, the heart below and the hands bracketing it. Following the loop down she swiped her thumb across the inside of the band, where her name was inscribed on his skin.

*Antonella.*

He hoped for some clue as to what she felt seeing her name inked above his heart. No reaction. Maybe she'd had one the first time she saw it, but he'd been unconscious or doped up and couldn't recall.

Bran had spilled himself open on Sunday night—and that was all before the psycho with the bat had interrupted them. And Nelle had gone blank, closed up, revealing nothing.

Nelle yawned, covering her mouth with the back of her hand.

"Did you sleep?"

She didn't answer, dedicating her focus to his tattoo, which was distractingly itchy.

"You were up early. What were you listening to?" He tried to suppress the discomfort and ended up shuddering.

She stopped. "Does that hurt?"

Bran ran his palms up her yoga pants, his calluses

zipping over the star-patterned spandex. Ordinarily he'd consider it a good sign that she slept in his bed, sat in his lap, took such care of him. But her sweetness made him ache, like he was already missing it. There was so much that needed to be said—that she was clearly avoiding—that made him doubt the motives behind her touch. Besides, the physical stuff had always been easy between them. It was the truth they had trouble with.

"It itches. Can't you just—" He scratched at her thighs.

"No." She smoothed her thumb over her name again. "I don't want to mess it up."

Did that mean she liked it? Bran angled his head, ignoring the flash of pain at his neck, the searing burn that accompanied the quick stretch of skin. They'd had to dig around in his shoulder to remove all the glass.

"You don't need an infection on top of the blood loss and head trauma."

They both winced at the sound of a pan lid falling in the kitchen.

"Remind me why they're here?" he asked.

"They wanted to see you home."

"Didn't they see me at the hospital? I seem to remember Arlo hitting on the doctor."

"That was you, actually."

"Was it?"

"You were very flirty after a liter of blood and some morphine."

Bran frowned. "I didn't say anything—"

"No. You kept it very charming, telling them all how impressed you were by their medical brilliance." She leaned in a bit to whisper, "Competence porn." And then sat back. "Anyway. Cormac has everyone helping with Thanksgiving prep."

"They'll be here tomorrow too?" He dropped his head against the cushions. His eyes closed against the glare of sunlight on the ceiling. When he opened them Nelle was watching his chest rise and fall. She skimmed her fingertips up the rounded muscles of his arms and curled them under at his neck so she could brush her knuckles up his jaw.

"But they won't be here tonight."

He fit the curves of his hands into the joints at her hips. "Or the next night?"

She considered that a moment. "Or the next night."

"Or the next night?" He couldn't help pushing it as he pulled her closer.

All the nights, he wanted her to agree. Not just one at a time. All of them, lined up and strung together. There were words lodged in his throat that the bat hadn't been able to knock out of him. Words he'd been harboring when he reached for the red box he'd kept in that guitar case since getting home from Chicago. Permanent, possessive, primal words. Words like *forever* and *mine.*

Nelle nodded. "Or the next night."

He surged up to capture her mouth and the little moan she made as he held her hips against his. He tilted his head to deepen the kiss, sliding his lips against hers and parting them with his tongue, but the strain on the stitches across his back brought another searing flash of pain, cutting him off with a gasp.

"Bran?"

He ignored the concern in her voice. His grip tightened and he tried again, only for her to lean out of reach. "Bran, stop." Her eyes narrowed as she studied

his face. "Maybe I shouldn't stay—if it hurts you to—"
She climbed off of him, shaking her head.

He was up after her, spinning around her so he stood
between her and the arch to the hall. "No, stay. Please
stay. We need to talk and—"

"Are you two going to help or what?"

How Bran would have liked to turn and glare at his
former drummer, but he couldn't take his eyes off Nelle.
There was a tension in her face he couldn't account for.
She was taking care of him. She was kissing him. But
she didn't want to talk. Or she didn't want to hear what
he had to say. And it was pretty clear what he wanted
to say.

"We're coming." Nelle brushed past Bran, leaving
him to follow her lead.

They entered the kitchen as Cormac returned to the
stove. Nelle's friend Benj chopped celery behind the island, while Arlo snagged a piece that dropped off the
cutting board.

Nelle inhaled. "Onions and butter—is there a better smell?"

"Crushed peonies, cinnamon, citrus," Bran listed.

"Sex," Cormac countered.

Bran's gaze stuck on a bowl in the center of the island, piled high with clementines. He put his hand in
his jogger pockets to reduce the noticeability of how
stirring he found them. "Like I said."

Nelle shot him a look over her shoulder as she distanced herself, taking over the celery prep from Benj,
who moved on to peeling apples.

Cormac caught it, chanting on beat and off key.
*"Peeling back my thick skin, give your flesh a healthy
squeeze. Sticky sweet orange juice have me beggin' yes*

*yes please."* He raised an eyebrow, waiting for someone to recognize how clever he was.

"What's that?" Benj asked, taking the bait.

"BK2. Track eight," Nelle answered. Her knife stuttered on the chopping block, revealing her misstep.

"That's what you were listening to last night? On my phone?" Bran couldn't keep the accusation out of his voice. She didn't want to hear what he had to say, but she'd listen to his album?

"*sex&secrets,* huh?" The words were as cutting as the knife she drove through the celery.

Cormac intervened after a moment of rough chopping, sweeping the contents of the board into the onions and returning it to the island. The pan hissed—or maybe it was Nelle. Benj passed her a skinned apple and the blade winked at Bran as she began chopping again.

Cormac glanced Bran's way. "I get you ripped and suddenly you don't own a shirt?"

"I'm in my house. Everyone is in my house. I'm convalescing." Bran threw a thumb over his shoulder to the bandage taped to his neck.

"Your homecoming aside, the rest of us are getting on track for tomorrow. I've got a turkey brining in the restaurant's walk-in. If we can get the stuffing, gratin, and carrot soup done today, we'll be able to do gravy, Brussels sprouts, and corn tomorrow."

"What about pie?" Arlo asked.

Cormac didn't meet Arlo's eyes as he answered. "Aya said she wanted to handle dessert."

Arlo hesitated. "But you're making a backup, right?"

"Am I risking pissing off Aya by implying I didn't trust her with pie? No, A. I am not."

Arlo crinkled his nose and popped a chunk of apple from the counter into his mouth.

Cormac knocked the spoon against the pan's rim. "Don't worry, I sanitized the whole island before we started because I didn't know if you two had a Cleffy night repeat—"

Bran huffed. "I've been in the hospital."

"What happened on Cleffy night?" Benj looked to Nelle. "Have you been holding out on me?"

A gleeful smile crossed Cormac's face. "You don't know about Cleffy night?"

"The onions are burning. You should add the sausage," Nelle told him.

"Is that what you'd do, Shower Girl?" Cormac shot back.

Bran tensed, but before his estranged wife could escalate things, a crash sounded from the ice machine. Nelle, standing closest to the fridge, jumped back. The knife dropped from her hand, clattering against the cement with a steel clang. It bounced to the floor, narrowly missing her bare feet. Her face paled and for an instant Bran recognized the Nelle from the photo. Not blank, but flat with loss.

Bran rounded the island in three strides. "It's just the stupid fucking ice. I should have fixed it," he whispered, smoothing down her hair and kissing the side of her head. Aya had already had someone in about replacing the broken door. He should have remembered the machine.

She gripped his elbows, her racing pulse beating through her fingertips. They stood like that until her breath settled and her color returned. Bran tuned back into the sounds of the kitchen. The sausage sizzled.

There was a rhythmic scrape of the peeler as Arlo took over the apples. And a pop from Benj opening a bottle of wine followed by the quiet tap of a glass set on the counter.

An urge spurred his gut, directing him to step away from Nelle. He wasn't supposed to touch her like this, not in front of people. But as long as she was holding on to him, he wasn't letting go.

The front door opened with a blast of noise, reporters shouting from behind the gate. Nelle immediately released his elbow. He still couldn't bring himself to step back.

"It just startled me." Nelle tucked her hair behind her ears. "I wasn't expecting it."

Determined steps marched down the hall and Aya appeared in the kitchen, Mina right behind her.

Returning to the island, Nelle lifted the wine to her lips. Cormac scooped up the knife and held it out to her. Bran leaned against the counter behind them as Nelle squared her shoulders, set down the wine, and took the peace offering from his friend.

"Ready for business?" Aya asked, appraising the room. Benj had begun tearing bread into chunks, Nelle was chopping again to keep up with Arlo's peeling, and Cormac manned the stove.

Bran kicked the fridge with his heel. "Yeah. The ice machine—"

"Freezer repairman will be here between 3 and 5 p.m. Until the melee outside clears, make sure you notify Steve ten minutes before you plan to have anyone come in or out of the gate."

"Albi is on standby," Mina added to Nelle.

While the others ripped, chopped, peeled, and stirred

Bran could only stare unproductively at Nelle. Right in front of him, close but just out of reach. She was wearing his old baseball shirt, tied at the back. He fixed on the knot as Aya kept going down her list.

"'All For You' is available on all platforms—Fei is a dream to work with, by the way. Let's keep her. And I'm not going to say getting stabbed and having Nelle papped covered in your blood was good marketing, but. The single is doing exceptionally well."

She waited for Bran to react. He should be excited. But all he could think about was Nelle, how she was so much twisted into one knot. The Nelle outside this house, outside a hotel room, or a car, she was so put together, so completely composed. And then there was this side of her, undone in his old loose clothes. She was fierce and soft and kind and wild and what would he do, if she was trying to let him down easy? Waiting for him to be better before she finished walking away?

Aya moved on. "Okay. Well. There's also the photo shoot. I told them we'd reschedule when the stitches come out but that was before I knew about the—" she glared at Bran's red chest "—other complication. I think it's best if we cancel."

"Couldn't they airbrush it?" Arlo asked.

"Airbrush the part of his body that's going to get the most attention for their product? They could. But they won't."

"Are you ready for that conversation?" Mina rapped her knuckles on the counter to get Nelle's attention. "People want to know why you were here on Sunday night."

Cormac scoffed. "Are people stupid? They heard the song, didn't they? Isn't it obvious?"

"The *media* want a comment," Aya clarified.

"We could say..." Mina glanced sideways at Aya like a lawyer hesitant to discuss her client's defense in front of the opposition. "We could say it isn't what it looks like. You two were just trying to bury the hatchet in private before the after-parties. But Nelle can't be seen coming in and out of here. We would need to go now."

*And not come back.*

The message was clear: they couldn't continue like they had, not under this scrutiny. Bran gripped the counter behind him. Nelle had been clear in her message too: they had to stop.

Everyone waited for Nelle to answer. Bran imagined her nodding, walking around the island to stand by Mina's side. He'd have to get used to seeing her from across the room.

"Tell Albi to stand down until Saturday," Nelle said, staying where she was. Integrity, that was her thing, and she'd agreed to three nights with him. "And don't tell them anything. Just don't comment."

Bran exhaled. His head had begun to throb while he held his breath. The cut on his back smarted. But he couldn't afford to take the pain pills and be fuzzy for this conversation. Not when it was his whole life they were discussing. His world he was trying to hold together.

The room settled back into motion. Rip, chop, peel, stir. From the outside it would have looked like a casual scene. A group of friends gathered around the kitchen island. But reality thrummed with tension.

Mina locked her jaw and Aya took the lead again. "Anything else?"

Benj slid Nelle a look. "Yeah, what happened on Cleffy night? And why am I out of the loop?"

Nelle brought the knife down hard, halving an apple clean. "Yes, Bran, why does everyone know about Cleffy night?"

"Nobody knows about Cleffy night—not really." Bran's point was undercut by Cormac whistling "Domino." "C, you are not helping."

Cormac motioned to the rest of them, working on tomorrow's dinner. "No, you're not helping."

Nelle raised the knife again. "If only you were as good at keeping secrets as you are at selling them."

A two-toned chime sounded before Bran could manage a response.

Trying to place the sound, Cormac's forehead wrinkled. "You have a doorbell?"

"Turns out," Bran replied.

Aya disappeared to the front hall. There was another burst of noise from outside, and when she returned to the kitchen, Moony trailed in after her.

Benj looked him up and down. "Lawyer?"

Arlo nodded. "He probably smelled the blood."

"You know I represent your interests, right?" The round metal feet of Moony's briefcase clicked against the island's polished counter. "And I'm here with some good news, at least. The police found a suspect matching the description from your man Steve and recovered the stolen item."

"How?" Arlo asked. "Steve said they lost him in the hills. They only found the bat."

"It's not as easy as you might think to fence a seventeen-carat Cartier ring."

Arlo swore. "Seventeen. Jesus, B."

Bran tore his gaze away from the back of Nelle's head. "It was symbolic."

"Of what? Two million dollars?" Cormac knocked the pan's rim again.

Nelle had run out of apples to chop, but she kept herself facing forward and Bran was sure it was to avoid his eyes.

"I owed it to her anyway."

"So they found it?" Aya said, trying to get them back on track.

"Yes. The police should be returning it to you shortly. You can do—" Moony flicked his gaze to Nelle and back to Bran "—whatever you want with it."

A heavy silence followed that statement as everyone quietly digested what Bran might have wanted to do when he held a seventeen-carat diamond engagement ring out to the woman whose name he'd also emblazoned on his chest and played a song for on live television.

"Now the bad news," Moony said after a moment. "You didn't get a look at the guy?"

"No. He hit me in the back."

Moony tapped his teeth together. "That's the thing. There were no prints on the bat. And Steve only got a look at his clothes, not his face."

"But they caught him?"

"And the guy they caught is probably the guy. But the description is generic and he's saying he found the box. There's nothing to tie that man here, unless you got a good look at him."

"I saw him." Everyone looked at Nelle when she spoke. "I talked to him."

With a sigh Moony agreed. "You did." He hit her

with a look he'd had on ice, one he'd been saving just for her. Bran's hands balled. "But you also lied to the police."

"Excuse me?"

She had been so still, but now Nelle's fingers drummed the counter in a move Bran knew all too well.

"You lied to the police. At best you were confused— and I can't use the testimony of an unreliable witness— at worst, you manipulated your way into an ambulance."

Hard nails pounded the smooth cement, pinky to forefinger and back. Bran narrowed in on the sound. A metronome that might as well have been pumped through his in-ears, cueing him in on Nelle's timing, her pitch, the moment she insisted, "I didn't lie."

"You didn't tell the police and the first responders that you're Bran Kelly's wife?"

The tapping stopped.

*Why?* he had asked her, and she'd never answered. *Why not tell them we're married?*

She hadn't needed to answer. The answer had been the same since the first night. Nelle had agreed to marry him on the condition that it stay their secret.

Nelle fisted her hand, green nails disappearing into her palm. She didn't want to let it go. She wouldn't compromise—she shouldn't have to. She was Nelle.

Bran cleared his throat. "Steve really didn't see him?"

"*I* saw him." Nelle's voice, sure and clear, commanded their attention.

Moony pressed his hands together. "But you lied."

"I didn't fucking lie!" Nelle turned to face Bran head-on, her back to the rest of them. "Bad things don't happen to me."

He'd been waiting for this. The moment when she stopped holding it in and got back to breaking them down, how it had to be done.

"I know. I'm sorry I dragged you down." She had been untouchable. And he had pushed.

"Bad things are signs that you need to rethink, check your bearings, fix your course. Realign. Bad things don't happen to me because I know where I'm going."

She'd always excelled at twisting the knife. Bran let out a bitter laugh. "Nobody can control everything, Nella. Not even you."

"I'm not talking about controlling everything, I'm talking about controlling me. I'm talking about *my* path." She paused. Her eyes went glassy and he wanted to look away from the hurt he'd caused. "I was going to say no. I was going to tell you it wasn't worth it, not if people knew. But you need to tell them, Bran."

"We don't have to." He released the counter. "It doesn't matter. Just go."

"A man broke into our home."

*Our* home.

Bran closed his eyes against a sudden sting and inhaled a sharp breath. Nelle's voice grew tender, closer, while maintaining its protective edge. "Do you feel safe knowing he's still out there? I don't. And I don't want to protect a secret over our lives. It's not worth it. Nothing is worth losing you. Bad things won't touch us if we're together. That's my path. Straight to you."

"They'll twist it." He opened his eyes and locked directly on to Nelle's amber irises. "They'll say I cheat. They'll make things up. They won't stop."

None of it would be true—he wasn't going to cheat,

he wasn't going to leave her. He wouldn't stop trying
to be worthy of her.

*Forever.*

*Mine.*

But they'd also reduce her, he understood finally.
They'd make her story about her connection to him,
pivot the conversation away from who she was to who
she was with.

"They'll call you Nelly Kelly."

"I can take it." She rested her hands on his hips.
"It's just noise. We'll make music that's louder. I know
you're good for it."

Bran brought his free arm around her shoulders and
pulled her into his body. The contact brought such relief, his knees almost buckled. Her hair slipped softly
over his elbow as she looked up at him, fitting herself
under his shoulder. Every tight muscle in his body relaxed as he stood united with Nelle, with his wife, in
their kitchen, in their home.

Where six people waited for answers with expres-
sions ranging from impatient to bewildered.

He raised his voice to address them. "Nelle didn't
lie. We're married."

"Says who?" Moony wanted to know.

"Michael Jordan."

Aya pointed her phone at Arlo. "No more pain pills
for him."

"Judge Michael Jordan married us in a private courtroom ceremony last December," Nelle explained.

Bran clocked the still-skeptical faces. "I've got the
paperwork in my firebox."

Moony's head shook with disbelief. "And where is
that?"

Arlo rubbed his temple. "Under the sink."

"Under the—*why?*" Benj asked.

"It's a firebox. Filled with things you don't want to burn." Bran tightened his hold on Nelle defensively. "There's water in the pipes. It's a redundancy—"

"I got it." Cormac retrieved the box from its questionable cabinet and set to work on the combination lock.

"It's two-two-three—" Bran started.

"He knows," Aya cut him off.

"Can't you keep anything private?" Nelle hugged his waist.

Bran inhaled the top of her head. "We're doing Christmas in Iowa."

"To get away from them?"

"Yeah. And basic marriage rules: split holidays between our families."

She hugged closer.

"Here it is." Cormac passed the marriage certificate to Moony and the prenup to Mina.

Aya read over her shoulder. Bran braced himself for impact. She stared, the silence ticking by. And then she threw her head back and laughed. She tried to straighten, but the momentum took her down to the counter, where she buried her head in her arms. A muffled *Braaaaaaan* escaped from the pile that used to be Aya.

"You broke her," Arlo said.

"This," she said, pulling herself upright, "this is why you have me. Look what you do on your own!" She left her phone on the island and joined Cormac by the stove, taking a long swig from his tumbler of red wine. Her eyes met his over the rim. "You'll drive me home?"

He nodded slow and sure, and she finished the glass.

"That's…a first," Moony said, glancing at the page when Mina handed it over. He secured both documents in his briefcase. "I think this is all I need. But I have to enter it into the public record. It's going to be news."

Bran shrugged. He and Nelle had just agreed to see it through. They'd face the consequences together, whatever came. "What isn't? Someone out there has an entire house filled with ways to make money off me—at least this is for us."

Nelle craned her neck to look up at him. "I bought your gran's house."

He balked. "You couldn't have—my dad told Cormac he wouldn't sell to someone who—someone who—"

"Loves you?"

Bran swallowed. "He saw our 'feud' in the news."

"He's like everybody else. They don't know about us." She rose up and rubbed her nose against his. "They don't know that I love you."

"They don't know that I love you," Bran repeated, lowering his mouth to hers.

"Everyone will know what you two do if you don't break it up," Cormac said. "We don't need another Cleffy night during Thanksgiving prep. It's the turkey that gets stuffed."

All at once, everyone was talking: Benj demanding to know exactly what happened on Cleffy night, Moony announcing his exit, and Mina trying to compose a text to her voice reader.

Bran sank back, taking it in, keeping Nelle close. He'd felt hunted, he'd felt caged and he'd shut down. He'd closed himself off from the possibility that there were people among the takers who could give him something. Give him everything.

Aya's voice broke through the chatter. "If you two are going public, can I tell Gordon McKane their campaign is still on?"

Bran raised his eyebrows at Nelle. Did she want everyone in the world to see her name over his heart?

"Yes," Nelle answered.

"Then I'm getting you more money."

"Aya—"

Cormac stopped him. "Bran, just let her. Lucrative contracts are her love language. She keeps you rich because she cares."

Bran wasn't listening. He'd given in to the desire to kiss Nelle. No matter who was watching, no matter who saw.

Circle of Trust

Today 4:13 pm

*Cormac Doyle*
after Nelle wins, tell us which party you're going to

*Arlo Bannon*
he means good luck

*Benjamina Wasik*
she doesn't need it

# Chapter Thirty-Two

Nelle had just hit Send on a text to the group chat, thirteen upside-down faces and a tongue-out-crazy-eyes, when Bran snatched the phone out of her hand. He cringed when the lock screen popped up.

"No phones. Aya did this for me last year." He slid the device into the inner pocket of a fitted plaid suit. "Be here. Take this in. No distractions." He wedged his fingers under hers and lifted the back of her hand to his lips. The pear-shaped diamond bauble nestled point-to-point against her wedding band caught the overhead lights, scattering them sideways. She didn't wear it every day, favoring the simple chevron ring she'd had first, but if she couldn't wear a seventeen-carat diamond to accept her Cleffies, when could she?

Bran squeezed her hand. "And I'd better hold this now. Your arms will be too full by the end of the night."

She twined their fingers. "I'm keeping a hold of you. Everyone in here is looking at you like they've got X-ray vision after that Gordon McKane shoot."

There were two photos that kept popping up on Nelle's feed: Bran wearing nothing but sunglasses and briefs, lying in a hammock with a guitar, and Bran dripping wet, hands slicking back his hair, standing in

front of a pool filled with inflatable pink flamingos. But
Nelle's favorite—the one she put on her phone's lock
screen—was her husband leaning against a deck rail.
In one hand he held a juicy rib, a smear of dark red bar-
becue sauce on his cheek. His blue eyes looked straight
into the camera as he sucked more sauce off his thumb.

That was her man. And she was keeping him close.

"I know what can happen at these things, someone
shiny and new trying to catch your eye from across
the room."

"I know what can happen after these things. And
you're very shiny."

She did shine, standing at the sound of her name in
a glittering teal bodysuit. A matching skirt of iridescent accordion-pleated chiffon fanned from the band
at her waist. ("Gem tones," Mina had said again, nodding with approval.) She would always shine, no matter how people tried to reduce her, to dim her power.
She didn't have to be afraid of playing with fire. Bran
had dubbed her the queen of light because Nelle was
the goddamn sun.

She glowed when she kissed Bran, lingering with her
forehead pressed to his, soaking up his shared joy, his
pride. She could have done it without him. She would
have. But to be able to look down and see him there, to
not have to look away, to kiss him and not care who saw
or knew or what they would say was an electric feeling.
No matter what happened, they would link hands and
step out of the building, out of the spotlight, through
the dark, through the quiet, together. That was happi-
ness in a way she'd never thought to wish for, but the
universe had provided big-time.

She'd said yes, and now she shimmered under the

manufactured lighting, looking up with genuine gratitude and wonder. This was abundance. And she lit up
the room when she expressed it.

"They say you should follow your dreams. But I don't
subscribe to that. Go where you want. Walk sure, walk
tall. Lead and your dreams will find you. Live for the
day they catch up to you and say, 'You're it.' They got
you. But that was the plan all along. So you can smile
back and say, 'I got you too.'"

\* \* \* \* \*

# Acknowledgments

Guys! It's time to thank you all for your love and support! Starting with Deborah Nemeth, Kerri Buckley, and Elaine Spencer, consummate industry professionals who made this manuscript into a real book. That you all thought it was worthy—still wow. Three wows, one for each of you.

Jeff and Steven, thanks for the infinite enthusiasm and the "ohoto." Giancarlo, what a bonus it's been to get to have your friendship and know your warmth all these years. And Sarah, my first reader, the staunchest of believers in this endeavor. As I say to G, couldn't have done it without you, wouldn't have wanted to.

Thanks to my local subterranean bookstore for introducing me to all my clubs. I've learned so much from each of them. Indie City, thank you for the writers' space, the critique, and encouragement. Especially Renee, who fixed Chapter 30, and anyone who had to watch me almost crack my head open before I implemented the two-chair system. Romance Book Club and Jen, I'm so thankful for this community, in all its iterations and corresponding group chats. LPWG, we need a better name, but the content remains of the highest quality. Kate, Julie, and Julia: you are rocks in the thrashing sea of my chaos. And Barely-Read-the-Book Club: I can't say anything about how important you are to me or my perfectly crafted air of mystery will be ruined.

And to my family, thank you for also being friends, for your excitement both across the kitchen island and the divides of this year. Mom, you'd like some of the puns in here, and definitely would appreciate the Van Morrison references, but if you skim to look for them, maybe don't read any more of Chapters 21–22. And finally, Alex, I may have dedicated this book to myself, because I am so proud of making it, but you made it possible. Let's be in love forever.

*About the Author*

A fan of topknots, fried Brussels sprouts, and other people doing the dishes, Hanna Earnest lives, laughs, and writes in Chicago, contributing to the world's supply of book boyfriends and girl crushes.

She wants to be friends on Twitter and Instagram @hannaearnest. Find out more at hannaearnest.com.

*Having conquered bullies, snobs, and boardrooms, self-made billionaire Roxanne has earned the right to mother a princess. She offers an impoverished prince a marriage of convenience in exchange for a settlement large enough to save his beloved kingdom. Mateo does not intend to marry and have a baby with a stranger just for money...until the successful beauty uses a weapon he hadn't counted on: his own desire.*

*Keep reading for an excerpt from* Lush Money *by Angelina M. Lopez!*

# *January: Night One*

Mateo Ferdinand Juan Carlos de Esperanza y Santos—
the "Golden Prince," the only son of King Felipe, and
heir to the tiny principality of Monte del Vino Real in
northwestern Spain—had dirt under his fingernails, a
twig of *Tempranillo FOS 02* in his back pocket, and a
burning desire to wipe the mud of his muck boots on
the white carpet where he waited. But he didn't. Under
the watchful gaze of the executive assistant, who stared
with disapproving eyes from his standing desk, Mateo
kept his boots tipped back on the well-worn heels and
his white-knuckled fists jammed into the pits of his UC
Davis t-shirt. Staying completely still and deep breathing while he sat on the white couch was the only way
he kept himself from storming away from this lunacy.

What the fuck had his father gotten him into?

A breathy *ding* sighed from the assistant's laptop.
He granted Mateo the tiniest of smiles. "You may go in
now," he said, hustling to the chrome-and-glass doors
and pulling one open with a flourish. The assistant
didn't seem to mind the dirt so much now as his eyes
traveled—lingeringly—over Mateo's dusty jeans and
t-shirt.

Mateo felt his *niñera* give him a mental smack upside the head when he kept his baseball cap on as he entered the office. But he was no more willing to take his cap off now than he'd been willing to change his clothes when the town car showed up at his lab, his ears ringing with his father's screams about why Mateo couldn't refuse.

The frosted-glass door closed behind him, enclosing him in a sky-high corner office as regal as any throne room. The floor-to-ceiling windows showed off Coit Tower to the west, the Bay Bridge to the east, and the darkening hills of San Francisco in between. The twinkling lights of the city flicked on like discovered jewels in the gathering night, adornment for this white office with its pale woods, faux fur pillows, and acrylic side tables. This office at the top of the fifty-five-floor Medina Building was opulent, self-assured. Feminine.

And empty.

He'd walked in the Rose Garden with the U.S. President, shaken the hand of Britain's queen, and kneeled in the dirt with the finest winemakers in Burgundy, but he stood in the middle of this empty palatial office like a jackass, not knowing where to sit or how to stand or who to yell at to make this *situación idiota* go away.

A door hidden in the pale wood wall opened. A woman walked out, drying her hands.

Dear God, no.

She nodded at him, her jowls wriggling as she tossed her paper towel back into the bathroom. "Take a seat, *Príncipe* Mateo. I'll prepare Roxanne to speak with you."

Of course. Of course Roxanne Medina, founder and CEO of Medina Now Enterprises, wasn't a sixty-year-old woman with a thick waist in medical scrubs. But "prepare" Roxanne to…

Ah.

The nurse leaned across the delicate, Japanese-style desk and opened a laptop perched on the edge. She pushed a button and a woman came into view on the screen. Or at least, the top of a woman's head came into view. The woman was staring down through black-framed glasses, writing something on a pad of paper. A sunny, tropical day loomed outside the balcony door behind her.

Inwardly laughing at the farce of this situation, Mateo took a seat in a leather chair facing the screen. Apparently, Roxanne Medina couldn't be bothered to meet the man she wanted to marry in person.

Two minutes later, he was no longer laughing. She hadn't looked at him. She just kept scribbling, giving him nothing to look at but the palm tree swaying behind her and the part in her dark, shiny hair.

He glanced at the nurse. She stared back, blank-eyed. He'd already cleared his throat twice.

Fuck this. "Excuse me," he began.

"Helen, it sounds like the prince may have a bit of a dry throat." Roxanne Medina spoke, finally, without raising her eyes from her document. "Could you get him a glass of water?"

"Of course, ma'am."

As the nurse headed to a decanter, Mateo said, "I don't need water. I'm trying to find out…"

Roxanne Medina raised one delicate finger to the screen. Without looking up. Continuing to write. Without a word or a sound, Roxanne Medina shushed him, and Mateo—top of his field, head of his lab, a god-damned *príncipe*—he let her, out of shock and awe that another human being would treat him this way.

He *never* treated people this way.

He moved to stand, to storm out, when a water glass appeared in front of his face and a hair was tugged from his head.

"Ow!" he yelled as he turned to glare at the granite-faced nurse holding a strand of his light brown hair.

"Fantastic, I see the tests have begun."

Mateo turned back to the screen and pushed the water glass out of his way so he could see the woman who finally deigned to speak to him.

"Tests?"

She was beautiful. Of course she was beautiful. When you have billions of dollars at your disposal, you can look any way you want. Roxanne Medina was sky-blue eyed, high-breasted and lush-lipped, with long and lustrous black hair. On the pixelated screen, he couldn't tell how much of her was real or fake. He doubted even her stylist could remember what was Botoxed, extended, and implanted.

Still, she was striking. Mateo closed his mouth with a snap.

Her slow, sensual smile let him know she'd seen him do it.

Mateo glowered as Roxanne Medina slipped her delicate black reading glasses up on her head and aimed those searing blue eyes at him. "These tests are just a formality. We've tested your father and sister and there were no genetic surprises."

"Great," he deadpanned. "Why are you testing me?"

Her sleek eyebrows quirked. "Didn't your father explain this already?" A tiny gold cross hung in the V of her ivory silk top. "We're testing for anything that might make the Golden Prince a less-than-ideal specimen to impregnate me."

*Madre de Dios.* His father hadn't been delusional. This woman really wanted to buy herself a prince and a royal baby. The king had introduced him to some morally deficient people in his life, but this woman… His shock was punctuated by a needle sliding into his bicep.

"*¡Joder!*" Mateo yelled, turning to see a needle sticking out of him, just under his t-shirt sleeve. "Stop doing that!"

"Hold still," the devil's handmaiden said emotionlessly, as if stealing someone's blood for unwanted tests was an everyday task for her.

Rather than risk a needle breaking off in his arm, he did stay still. But he glared at the screen. "I haven't agreed to any of this. The only reason I'm here is to tell you 'no.'"

"The king promised…"

"My father makes a lot of promises. Only one of us is fool enough to believe them."

She took the glasses off entirely, sending that hair swirling around her neck, and slowly settled back into her chair. The gold cross hid once again between blouse and pale skin. She stared at him the way he stared at the underside of grape leaves to determine their needs.

Finally, she said, "Forgive me. We've started on different pages. I thought you were on board." Her voice, Mateo noticed, was throaty with a touch of scratch to it. He wondered if that was jet lag from her tropical location. Or did she sound like that all the time? "I run a multinational corporation; sometimes I rush to the finish line and forget my 'pleases' and 'thank yous.' Helen, say you're sorry."

"I'm sorry," Helen said immediately. As she pulled the plunger and dragged Mateo's blood into the vial.

Gritting his teeth, he glared at the screen. "What self-respecting person would have a kid with a stranger for money?"

"A practical one with a kingdom on the line," Roxanne Medina said methodically. "My money can buy you time. That's what you need to right your sinking ship, correct? You need more time to develop the *Tempranillo Vino Real*?"

Mateo's blood turned cold; he wondered if Nurse Ratched could see it freezing as she pulled it out of him. He stayed quiet and raised his chin as the nurse put a Band-Aid on his arm.

"This deal can give you the time you need," the billionaire said, her voice beckoning. "My money can keep your people solvent until you get those vines planted."

She sat there, a stranger in a tropical villa, declaring herself the savior of the kingdom it was Mateo's responsibility to save.

For centuries, the people of Monte del Vino Real, a plateau hidden among the Picos de Europa in northernmost Spain, made their fortunes from the lush wines produced from their cool-climate Tempranillo vines. But in recent years, mismanagement, climate change, the world's focus on French and California wines, and his parents' devotion to their royal lifestyle instead of ruling had devalued their grapes. The world thought the Monte was "sleepy." What they didn't know was that his kingdom was nearly destitute.

Mateo was growing a new variety of Tempranillo

vine in his UC Davis greenhouse lab whose hardiness and impeccable flavor of the grapes it produced would save the fortunes of the Monte del Vino Real. His new-and-improved vine or "clone"—he'd called it the *Tempranillo Vino Real* for his people—just needed a couple more years of development. To buy that time, he'd cobbled together enough loans to keep credit flowing to his growers and business owners and his community teetering on the edge of financial ruin instead of free-falling over. He'd also instituted security measures in his lab so that the vine wouldn't be stolen by competitors.

But Roxanne Medina was telling him that all of his efforts—the favors he'd called in to keep the Monte's poverty a secret, the expensive security cameras, the pat downs of grad students he knew and trusted—were useless. This woman he'd never met had sniffed out his secrets and staked a claim.

"What does or doesn't happen to my kingdom has nothing to do with you," he said, angry at a computer screen.

She put down her glasses and clasped slender, delicate hands in front of her. "This doesn't have to be difficult," she insisted. "All I want is three nights a month from you."

He scoffed. "And my hand in marriage."

"Yes," she agreed. "The king has produced more than enough royal bastards for the Monte, don't you think?"

The king. His father. The man whose limitless desire to be seen as a wealthy international playboy emptied the kingdom's coffers. The ruler who weekly dreamt up get-rich-quick schemes that—without Mateo's constant monitoring and intervention—would have sacrificed the Monte's land, people, and thousand-year legacy to his greed.

It was Mateo's fault for being surprised that his father would sell his son and grandchild to the highest bidder.

"I'm just asking for three nights a month for a year," Roxanne Medina continued. "At the end of that year, I'll 'divorce' you—" her air quotes cast in stark relief what a mockery this "marriage" would be "—and provide you with the settlement I outlined with your father. Regardless of the success of your vine, your people will be taken care of and you will never have to consider turning your kingdom into an American amusement park."

That was another highly secretive deal that Roxanne Medina wasn't supposed to know about: An American resort company wanted to purchase half the Monte and develop it as a playland for rich Americans to live out their royal fantasies. But her source for that info was easy; his father daily threatened repercussions if Mateo didn't sign the papers for the deal.

In the three months since Mateo had stormed out of that meeting, leaving his father and the American resort group furious, his IT guy had noticed a sharp rise in hacking attempts against his lab's computers. And there'd been two attempted break-ins on his apartment, according to his security company.

Billionaire Roxanne Medina might be the preferable devil. At least she was upfront about her snooping and spying.

But have a kid with her? His heir? A child that, until an hour ago, had only been a distant, flat someday, like marriage and death? "So I'm supposed to make a kid with you and then—what—just hand him over?"

"Didn't the king tell you...? Of course, you'll get to

see her. A child needs two parents." The adamancy of her raspy voice had Mateo focusing on the screen. The billionaire clutched her fingers in front of the laptop, her blue eyes focused on him. "We'll have joint custody. We won't need to see each other again, but your daughter, you can have as much or as little access to her as you'd like."

She pushed her long black hair behind her shoulders as she leaned closer to the screen, and Mateo once again saw that tiny, gold cross against her skin.

"Your IQ is 152, mine is 138, and neither of us have chronic illnesses in our families. We can create an exceptional child and give her safety, security, and a fairy-tale life free of hardship. I wouldn't share this responsibility with just anyone; I've done my homework on you. I know you'll make a good father."

Mateo had been trained in manipulation his whole life. His mother cried and raged, and then hugged and petted him. His father bought him a Labrador puppy and then forced Mateo to lie about the man's whereabouts for a weekend. Looking a person in the eye and speaking a compliment from the heart were simple tricks in a master manipulator's bag.

And yet, there was something that beckoned about the child she described. He'd always wanted to be a better everything than his own father.

The nurse sat a contract and pen in front of Mateo. He stared at the rose gold Mont Blanc.

"I know this is unorthodox," she continued. "But it benefits us both. You get breathing room for your work and financial security for your people. I get a legitimate child who knows her father without...well, without the hassles of everything else." She paused. "You under-

stand the emotional toll of an unhappy marriage better than most."

Mateo wanted to bristle but he simply didn't have the
energy. His parents' affairs and blowups had been filling the pages of the tabloids since before he was born.
The billionaire hadn't needed to use her elite gang of
spies to gather that intel. But she did remind him of
his own few-and-far-between thoughts on matrimony.
Namely, that it was a state he didn't want to enter.

If he never married, then when would he have an
heir?

Mateo pulled back from his navel gazing to focus on
her. She was watching him. Mateo saw her eyes travel
slowly over the screen, taking him in, and he felt like a
voyeur and exhibitionist at the same time.

She bit her full bottom lip and then gave him a smile
of promise. "To put it frankly, *Príncipe*, your position
and poverty aren't the only reasons I selected you.
You're…a fascinating man. And we're both busy, dedicated to our work, and not getting as much sex as we'd
like. I'm looking forward to those three nights a month."

"Sex" coming out of her lush mouth in that velvety
voice had Mateo's libido sitting up and taking notice.
That's right. He'd be having sex with this tempting crea-
ture on the screen.

She tilted her head, sending all that thick black hair
to one side and exposing her pale neck. "I've had some
thoughts about those nights in bed."

The instant, searing image of her arched neck while
he buried his hand in her hair had Mateo tearing his
eyes away. He looked out on the city. *Jesus.* She was
right, it had been too long. And he didn't need his little
brain casting a vote right now.

She made it sound so simple.

Her money gave him more than the three years of financial ledge-clinging that he'd scraped together on his own, a timeline that had already caused sleepless nights. The only way Mateo could have the *Tempranillo Vino Real* planted and profitable in three years is if everything went perfectly—no problems with development, no bad growing seasons. Mother Nature could not give him that guarantee. Her deal also prevented his father from taking more drastic measures. The chance for a quiet phone and an inbox free of plans like the one to capture the Monte's principal irrigation source and bottle it into "Royal Water" with the king's face on the label was almost reason enough to sign the contract.

Mateo refused to list "regular sex with a gorgeous woman who looked at him like a lollipop" in the plus column. He wasn't led around by his cock like his father.

And that child; his far-off, mythical heir? The *príncipes y princesas* of the Monte del Vino Real had been marrying for profit long before Roxanne Medina invented it. He didn't know what kind of mother she would be, but he would learn in the course of the year together. And if they discovered in that year they weren't compatible…surely she would cancel the arrangement. After the initial shock, she'd seemed reasonable.

Gripping on to his higher ideals and shaky rationalizations, he picked up the pen and signed.

The nurse plunked an empty plastic cup with a lid down on the desk.

"What the…?" Mateo said with horror.

"Just the final test," Roxanne Medina said cheerily from the screen. "Don't worry. Helen left a couple of magazines in the bathroom. Just leave the cup in there when you're finished and she'll retrieve it."

Any hopes for a reasonable future swirled down the drain. Roxanne Medina expected him to get himself off in a cup while this gargoyle of a woman waited outside the door.

He stood and white-knuckled the cup, turned away from the desk. Fuck it. At least his people were safe. An hour earlier, his hands in the dirt, he'd thought he could save his kingdom with hard work and noble intentions. But he'd fall on his sword for them if he had to.

Or stroke it.

He had one last question for the woman who held his life in her slim-fingered hand. "Why?" he asked, his back to the screen, the question coming from the depths of his chest. "Really, why?"

"Why what?"

"Why me."

"Because you're perfect." He could hear the glee in her rich voice. "And I always demand perfection."

*Don't miss* Lush Money *by Angelina M. Lopez,*
*available now wherever ebooks are sold.*

www.CarinaPress.com